FAIR HAVEN

Published by Winterbourne Publishing, Western Australia.

ISBN: 978-0-9874511-6-3 (ebook) / 978-1-7637115-0-1 (print)

Fair Haven

Wendy Palmer

Winterbourne
Publishing

~O~NE~

THE PIE SMELLED ABOUT RIGHT NOW. It was early-season pears and late-season blueberries, mixed. The pears hadn't been quite ripe, and Albemarle would have things to say about that, and about the almond meal Hazel was trying in the crust.

Hazel didn't care today. Albemarle had been in an awkward mood for the whole of his watch. Being Stronghold Haven's Mancer gave zhem leeway, quite a bit. Hazel's forbearance gave zhem more. But Albemarle didn't quite deserve full consideration today, in the matter of the pie.

Checking on the progress of the crust, Hazel found it suitably golden. He folded cloth about the sides of the clay dish and slid it from the little oven. On the other side of the wide kitchen, the cooks and their helpers were chopping and stirring amid the first rising scents of dinner. They ignored Hazel at his floury end of the great scarred oaken worktable. They knew what pie meant.

Holly did, too, but here he came, wandering into the kitchen to prop a hip against the table where Hazel was setting the pie to cool. He stretched out long bare legs—Holly had truly lethal legs and didn't mind making sure everyone knew it—and flipped his beaded braids back over his shoulder with an irritated jangle.

Ring-decorated fingers flashing, he signed, ~Albemarle [pejorative].

Trade, the simple sign-based communication used by the Sbalosi river traders, didn't traditionally have a range of nasty words for people. It had a single sign that you could interpret how you wished. Holly meant: *Albemarle's being more of a shithead than usual today.*

He was using Trade to complain because Albemarle had never bothered learning it. Albemarle barely bothered with Mutual, the spoken language used in common by the mix of peoples here on the east coast of Eldemira.

'Doesn't smell right,' Albemarle said, clomping into the kitchen in Holly's wake like zheir boots had iron nailed to the soles. 'The pears weren't right.'

Saying aloud, 'I know, Albemarle,' Hazel signed to Holly, ~I know Albemarle is being a shithead today. Down here making a pie, aren't I? ~Help.

That with an emphatic jab of his right hand into his left palm that would have been a shout in Mutual and deeply scored capitals in writing.

Hazel plated the pie and put it on a tray with a teapot and a stack of crockery. He would take it up to the dining hall, to the rest of the Mancer Guard. Only Holly was officially on duty. He and Albemarle would take tea with the rest, before Albemarle tried to force Holly back to the atelier and Holly tried to herd Albemarle outside to the bailey as per the schedule. Afternoon tea would give Holly a breather from Albemarle and Albemarle a distraction from zheir own head. It might be enough to get Holly through the afternoon watch without breaking said head.

Holly took the tray. 'Hazel darling,' he murmured, in lieu of falling to his knees in gratitude. 'Evie's called for you.'

'Ass,' Hazel said, shorthand. 'Save me some pie.'

'Nah.'

Albemarle shifted zheir tall, broad bulk sideways, blocking Hazel's exit. 'I need rags.'

Holly said, on the edge of an explosion, 'Kitchen staff's right there, Albemarle, ask for it yourself.'

Albemarle turned pale, fathoms-deep eyes on zheir guard. Hazel directed a similarly blank look at Holly. His friend knew better than that. Albemarle didn't talk to anyone zhey didn't have to. Hazel was tasked with sourcing zheir monthly rags. It was no bother to him; it was a pleasure, because Hazel was a fixer by nature. He got them from the kitchenhands and returned them to the laundry in a soaking bucket, the same as he had done for his sister, back when well-meaning strongholders thought talking loudly counted as communicating with the profoundly deaf.

Haven's Mancer either had monthly courses or was skirting close to darker Mancy on a clockwork schedule. Neither would have greatly surprised Hazel, though the latter would have disturbed him somewhat.

He knocked when he got up to Evelyn's office and went in on her acknowledgement. She was, not unusually, frowning.

'Sorry,' he said. 'Holly didn't exactly hurry down to tell me you needed me.'

An old woman sat before the commander's desk, petite and beshawled, back to the door, grey head bowed over paper. She did not look around until Evelyn waved a hand to get her attention and nodded toward Hazel. This pantomime was so familiar from growing up with Maya that Hazel immediately understood he'd been summoned to act as a voice.

~Good afternoon, do you know Trade, he signed when she turned, and then stopped with both hands curling under his sternum, because this was not a little old lady.

The wary face under the fine, dead-straight hair was smooth, and androgynous, and dominated by large and elongate green-grey eyes, opaque as wet pebbles. Those depthless eyes, more than the cross-cues—hair too long for a Haven man but too short for a Haven woman, knotted shawl about the shoulders, lace at the sleeves of the masculine-cut coat—told Hazel their visitor was a Mancer.

But Mancers couldn't be deaf. They worked Mancy with their voices; they hummed or sang, and had to make the tune match the whisper in their heads. Hazel's sister Maya, deaf from birth, could speak, and sing, but she couldn't carry a tune, not to the precise extent that a Mancer must.

Someone born to be a Mancer, who couldn't hope to work a Mancy. It was pitiful; it was also an impossibility, given what the Mancy drive did to Mancers.

Working his way through to this conclusion in his slow way, Hazel noted the dust of travel in the slight creases at the corners of zheir eyes, the torn and dirty state of the lace on the coat.

From the other side of her impeccably neat desk, Evelyn rolled a finger. It wasn't Trade; it didn't need to be. *Get on with it.*

Hazel repeated his first signs, slower, making them distinct instead of the fast flow he and Maya had used. ~[greetings][query][understand].

The visitor had been staring at him while he stared at zhem. Now zhey slowly raised one hand and signed the affirmative, a nod with the fist, without looking away from Hazel's face.

Hazel waited but no more was forthcoming. He looked to Evelyn.

'Smile, Hazel,' she said. 'You're standing there scowling and—' She waved a hand. '—hulking. Zhey don't know you're a pussycat.'

She didn't say, *And the scar doesn't help you look less like a brute.*

Hazel smiled. The visitor did not look relieved. If anything, zheir eyes got wider and more wary.

'Ask zhem if zhey can read and write. This will go a lot faster if zhey can.'

He did not necessarily agree with that, but he obediently signed the question, keeping the shaping of his hands and fingers slow and clear.

Again, the reply came after a long pause. Their visitor made the negatory sign, gently closing zheir fist oriented so the knuckle of zheir thumb pointed at zheir own chest, the curl of the littlest finger toward Hazel. It literally meant [zero], but its meaning extended readily to no, and none, and nothing, and never, all the negatives of life.

Hazel saw that the notepaper in front of the visitor was mostly blank, but had *Good morning, I am Commander Evelyn Holyoake, who are you, where are you from?* written in Evelyn's looping script.

He signed that next, painstakingly, with the tedious fingerspelling. ~E-V-E-L-Y-N-H-O-L-Y-O-A-K-E. Commander Evelyn.

Evelyn's sign was a combination of [royalty] and [winter], her younger sibling's cheeky contribution.

He touched his chest. ~A-R-I-H-A-Z-L-E-M-E-R-E. [nickname] H-A-Z-E-L. Hazel.

His sign was a plain [nut][wood].

He pointed at their visitor, who, frowning over zheir fingers, gingerly spelled out, ~A-S-H.

Hazel raised his brows. ~[query][fire][past].

The stranger flashed an imperious look of offended pride, an expression which twinged on Hazel's memory. Before he could work out where he'd seen it before, zhey smoothed zheir face to blankness and answered, ~[silver][tree].

Zhey did the signs again, smoothly now, combining them. ~Ash.

Hazel finally looked back at his commander. He signed as he spoke, long habit. It hadn't been kind or fair to leave Maya out of conversations. '~Zheir name is Ash.'

'All that, and you got a name.' Evelyn's voice was flat.

'~And Ash knows who we are now.'

'You really think zhey can't read and write?' Evelyn was sounding sceptical, but that was her default stance. 'If zhey can spell?'

'Knowing how to fingerspell in Trade isn't the same as recognising the same word when it's written down in Mutual,' Hazel pointed out.

He'd stopped signing, but his fingers were itching. Ash's eyebrows, as fine and straight as zheir hair, and pure black like zheir hair must once have been, were slanting at the rudeness. Zhey really had very expressive eyebrows, especially for a Mancer.

And zhey were older than zhey'd seemed when zhey'd been keeping zheir face neutral. Every Mancer was driven to work Mancy; they sought covenant with a stronghold as soon as they could. Ash would not be any different. Given zheir age, then, Stronghold Haven could not be zheir first stronghold.

Maybe the deafness was very recent. That accounted for zheir somewhat clumsy Trade, but not zheir potential inability to speak or zheir expressive face, so unusual for a Mancer. Hazel's instincts, informed by his experiences with his sister, suggested that Ash, like Maya, had been deaf for a long time, if not since birth. But how—

Evelyn tsked and drummed her fingers on the desk. 'Find out where zhey're from and what zhey're doing here.'

It was quicker now. Ash was looking no less wary, but zhey were tracking the signs better, so Hazel could speed up. After a moment, he paused and looked at Evelyn again.

'~Zhey don't know where zhey're from,' he reported, without inflection. '~Zhey don't remember. Zhey didn't come up from the port. Zhey came overland.'

He waited.

Evelyn said, 'I'm sorry?', always a dangerous sign. 'You want me to report to Them Upstairs that a Mancer quietly knocked on our postern gate and we have no idea what stronghold zhey came from or what zhey want?'

'~We know what zhey want.'

~Sanctuary, Ash signed, even before Hazel looked to zhem to confirm.

'Well, that's clear, anyway.' Evelyn sat back, arms folded. She met Hazel's eyes and looked away.

~Price?

~None, Hazel replied without even glancing at his commander. When Ash's eyebrows quirked disbelievingly, he again made the loose fist of the negatory sign, lightly shaking it for emphasis. ~No price for sanctuary. We hold to the covenant. The atelier is yours.

In a slow slump like a collapsing snowbank, Ash lowered zheir head into zheir hands. Zheir whole body semaphored limp relief. Hazel exchanged another look with Evelyn.

~Welcome to Stronghold Fair Haven by the Sea, Ash, he signed, when zhey'd composed zhemself.

It did not escape him that the sign for the formal request for refuge and the sign for their stronghold were both stylised versions of [safe]. He smiled as gently as he could at the Mancer, who was looking bewildered and hopeful, zheir hands plucking nervously at the unravelling lace at zheir coat sleeves.

~Welcome, echoed Evelyn, and sighed. 'Take zhem away, pry the real story out of zhem, and be quick about it, Hazel. I have to make the formal report by tomorrow morning.'

~Two~

Hazel took Ash to the undercroft's dining hall, the refectory-like main room that took up most of the ground floor of the stronghold, on the assumption that their visitor was hungry and the hope that there would be pie left.

There was a single slice, and Holly, and Albemarle. Kito and Nightingale from the alt-watch were up the other end of the Mancer Guard's usual trestle table. Kito was still working through her slice of pie, chewing slowly. Second Jerome, of the night watch, blinked sleepily over his cup, having just woken up. He'd set his Mancy leg on the bench next to him. First Jerome, also from the night watch, and the other two alt-watch guards, Morano and Titus, were absent.

'Pears weren't right,' Albemarle greeted Hazel glumly.

'You still ate two slices,' Holly pointed out. He was looking more cheery, and eyed up Ash with open speculation. 'Good afternoon, I'm Holly.'

That smile and that tone of voice could be enough, for Holly, to start a path to bed. Hazel felt a prickle of something he might have called territorial, if he were that sort of person.

'~Deaf,' he said succinctly. '~Everyone, this is Ash Mancer.'

Albemarle rose. 'Shall I collect my belongings?'

~Good afternoon, Holly signed, ignoring their Mancer looming over him. ~R-O-W-A-N-H-O-L-Y-O-A-K-E. Called H-O-L-L-Y.

He gave the [winter][tree] sign Maya had gifted him, and added, ~Captain Holly.

~Captain? Ash repeated.

A flicker of doubt crossed zheir determinedly neutral expression as zhey took in Holly's decorated hair and copious jewellery and predatory smile and, well, general demeanour. Zhey couldn't even see his tooled leather skirt yet, or the buckles on his sandals. Ironically, those shoes were the most practical thing about Haven's Mancer Guard captain, not counting the bottle-green coat with its linen panels and secret pockets. Ash might just possibly truly not remember where zhey'd come from, but zhey remembered the cultural cues that had held sway there, apparently.

Hazel gave zhem an innocent look. ~Does he not look much like a Mancer Guard captain?

Ash, eyes narrowed, signed, ~I would not know what a Mancer Guard captain is meant to look like.

Hazel tapped his temple. ~Oh, yes. Silly me. You don't remember.

Ash took a little breath and then pointedly turned zheir attention back to the table. The other Mancer guards nodded to their visitor politely but mutedly. They all knew better than to ask questions of a Mancer. Second Jerome took his prosthetic leg off the bench to make room for the two of them to sit down.

As Hazel had expected, Ash's attention became riveted to the Mancy leg; zhey watched intently as Second Jerome strapped it into place over the stump of his knee. Mancers weren't much for people, including other Mancers, but they were fascinated by any sort of Mancy. It went through them like blood went through the heart, simultaneously their purpose for being and the essential ingredient *of* their being.

Hazel sat opposite Holly and patted the empty space beside him, looking over his shoulder at Ash. The Mancer hesitated. It seemed zhey had not been expecting to eat with zheir Mancer Guard.

That might have confirmed Evelyn's suspicion—and, to be fair, Hazel agreed with her—that zheir memory was perfectly intact, and this was not how the Mancer guards at zheir last stronghold had conducted themselves. Or it might merely point to some ingrained assumptions about how formal relations were meant to be. Or it might have just been sheer disappointment that Second Jerome wasn't going to stand up yet so zhey could see the Mancy leg in action.

Ash was awkward as zhey clambered over the bench, resting a hand briefly on Hazel's shoulder for ballast. Zhey squeezed up against Hazel's side so zhey had some distance from Second Jerome.

Zhey looked at Holly again, still trying to hide a little astonishment. ~Are you the commander's sibling?

Though Evelyn was older, short-haired and had frown lines instead of laugh lines, the family resemblance—very dark skin, high cheekbones, midnight eyes, lush eyelashes, boldness writ large—was too strong for zhem to suggest the marriage link that a common surname might indicate in some places.

~Don't hold it against me. Or do, however so you prefer.

Holly's cheerful reply was lost on Ash, Hazel saw. He gathered their visitor had a firm enough grasp of the core Trade signs, but wherever zhey were from, zhey'd not had the opportunity to layer meaning into traditional Trade signs or to develop zheir own cant, like he and Maya and Holly had.

He pushed the last slice of pie toward Ash and turned his full attention back to Albemarle, who was still standing, impassive as stone. '~Albemarle, what are you packing for?'

He spelled out Albemarle, and showed Ash the combination of the two signs that made up zheir signed name: [white][bird].

'You have a new Mancer.'

Hazel had been reflexively signing. He stopped at that, but Ash made the negatory sign to Albemarle. Zhey could lipread, then, to some extent.

'~Ash is deaf,' Hazel told Albemarle patiently. '~So zhey can't be a practising Mancer.'

Though how zhey weren't insane from zheir incapacity—

Ash made the negatory sign at Hazel too. ~Do not make assumptions about what I can and cannot do.

That was a very Maya-like rebuke. Hazel made [apology], a draw of the thumb across the heart with a bow of the head, before turning back to the other ruffled feathers. '~We're your stronghold, Albemarle. We're not throwing you out, no matter how many more Mancers we collect.'

'That's inefficient.' Zhey sat down and picked at the crumbs on zheir empty plate. 'Them Upstairs may disagree.'

The table full of Mancer guards fell silent. Second Jerome put his cup down.

'~The covenant holds,' Hazel said mildly. '~No one's leaving unless they want to leave, Albemarle.'

News of the visitor—the visitor who was plainly a Mancer—had begun to spread. The people of the lower stronghold, servants and junior retainers, laundry staff and kitchen staff, guards and gardeners, came by the table to lean over Hazel, sneaking glances at Ash as they asked for a favour.

Hazel was often asked for favours or to fix things. He practically had a queue this afternoon, their murmurs of 'Hazel darling, can you…' ringing in his ears louder and louder. He started to make a list with a Mancy pen.

Holly watched disapprovingly, tapping his fingers on the tabletop. He didn't understand this, Hazel knew. He didn't understand that when old Mahdi asked for help with a sticky door, she didn't want Hazel to send one of the artificer's carpenters to see to it. She wanted her grandson in the laundry to come and fix it and, by the way, make dumplings with her and coo over her flower sketches. Anyone could summon the carpenter. Not many would take the time to persuade a busy young man to visit more often. Not the whole list was like that, but much of it was.

Once his patience had run out, Holly said, '~Albemarle, time to go outside. No arguing, you have to take a dose of sunshine, sunshine.'

On Hazel's watch this morning, such a proclamation, as gently as Hazel might have tried to deliver it, would have sent Haven's Mancer into one of zheir frenzies. Even now, after pie and an enforced separation from spuddling in the atelier, Albemarle drew slowly tense, stiffening by degrees as zhey decided if zhey could tolerate being forced back onto zheir schedule.

'This crust,' Kito said. She waved her fork at Hazel. 'You put almond in it?'

'~Almond meal.'

She shook her head, her glossy black hair tickling her cheekbones. 'Not good, Hazel darling. What's wrong with the old recipe?'

'Too much butter. You are incorrect. The almond is good. The pear is wrong. Blueberries are acceptable. Apple is preferred.' Albemarle stood again, ponderously. 'I will go outside, Holly.'

After an appreciative nod to Kito, Holly flashed his smile and flicked two fingers at Hazel. 'Bring it, you fucker.'

Hazel had beaten Holly, last time, in the spar.

'~Look at me, I'm bringing it,' Hazel said ruefully as the Mancer Guard made shift. '~Come along, Ash. This is the Mancer's routine.'

Ash was too fixated on watching Second Jerome stand up, taking in how the prosthetic leg's flexible thin metal strips, reminiscent of the busk in corsetry, flexed as he put weight on it. If zhey'd had hearing, zhey'd have been listening hard to the hiss of Mancy through the cogs and springs of the interior workings. Albemarle had worked a wonder; Second Jerome only had to have zhem charge it full of Mancy twice a week or so, and he could run, spar and handle the stairs like he'd never lost the flesh leg.

He grinned. 'Should I do a spin for zhem?'

'Can't hurt,' Hazel said.

Second Jerome twirled himself in a circle, letting the Mancy leg do the work. Ash made the slice of the palm that meant [wonder]. A small smile had touched zheir face, transforming a rather severe aspect into something far warmer. Hazel felt a strange jolt go through him.

He coughed lightly. '~Come along, Ash,' he repeated. '~You can watch it help Second Jerome fight.'

This time, Ash followed. Zhey seemed only to be watching the motion of the leg, extending and compressing in perfect synchronicity. But in the stone corridor to the bailey, zhey touched Hazel's sleeve.

~Your name again?

Hazel nodded. He'd wondered if Ash was overwhelmed in Evelyn's office. He signed [Hazel] and started to spell it, but Ash stilled his hand with zheir own. Hazel looked down stupidly at the slender fingers laid over his.

Ash's nails were bitten to the quick, the back of zheir hand was covered with the little white scars that were the price of Mancy work—same as guard work—and zheir ring finger had once been broken and had healed crookedly. Zheir knuckles had the same sort of dirt as zheir face, ground in from an overland journey. He should have taken their visitor to wash first. He wondered if that was why Ash hadn't touched the pie, or if perhaps the Mancer came from a culture that did not routinely share food with strangers.

Having efficiently snared his attention, Ash removed zheir hand. ~I know your name is Hazel. But I lipread, a little, and everyone calls you Hazel what? I can't catch it.

Hazel stuttered with his hands, the Trade equivalent of saying, 'Um, oh, well, ah…'

Holly, who was strutting along backward so he could watch the conversation, laughed in delight. He waved for Ash's attention. ~Hazel [endearment].

Like [pejorative] and [expletive], unembroidered Trade only had a single sign to indicate [endearment], left hand slapped over the heart, garnished with a circle of the right hand's forefinger. Hazel rather suspected it was traditionally used in a gritted-teeth sarcastic way, something like *Dearest, stop telling the customers about weevils while I am convincing them of the quality of our flour.*

Ash looked blank. Zhey didn't know the sign, the one single simple sign to communicate casual fondness. That was as sad as someone born to Mancy being deaf. Hazel shook his head. Ash had as good as told him zhey could still do Mancy and he could see with his own eyes the old nicks on zheir hands to confirm it, if the fact that zhey weren't insane wasn't enough. By the same token, zhey almost certainly had people zhey used endearments with, too, and they had together made up their own signs for it.

Holly spelled D-A-R-L-I-N-G, then put it together. ~Hazel darling.

Ash's clear gaze flicked back to Hazel and Hazel watched as the Mancer measured him, his solid breadth, his calloused fighter's hands and gnarled fingers, his shaggy dark hair with the streak of white where the scar started, the seam it made down the side of his face from his scalp to his jawline, his scruffy beard marked with the same telltale white slash. He knew he looked like the worst excesses of soldierly thuggery. He didn't look like anyone's darling. No wonder Ash's lipreading had failed zhem.

He turned aside and tapped the sconce on the wall, where a patterned copper tube glowed, casting warm light over the wall and flagstones through graceful cut-outs that resembled sprigs and tendrils of ivy. Similar tubes decorated all the sconces along the windowless hallway, which was really more of a tunnel through the thick walls of the stronghold.

~This is another of Albemarle's projects. No flame. Fa'avae, our artificer, makes the tubes for zhem to zheir design, and zhey fill them. We'd be in the pitch dark right now without them.

Ash, burnished in the buttery light, reached up to touch the tube, zheir lacy sleeve pulling back over zheir wrist. Zhey were wiry; Hazel could see the hollow flex along zheir wrist as zhey stretched zheir arm. Zhey sported a tattoo there, curlicued in greens and blues.

There was no need to warn zhem off, even as zhey picked the tube out of the sconce to examine it closely. The copperlits did not shed heat unless set to. The light picked out glints of true silver threaded through zheir pale grey hair.

The copperlits were not only one of Albemarle's earliest Mancies, and one of zheir best, but also the one that had doomed zheir future efforts. Haven's sensitive Mancer was a notoriously slow worker. Zhey spent long enough filling the tubes every morning that it further delayed zheir work on new Mancies, and Fa'avae and the stronghold staff just kept coming up with more uses.

Hazel had seen Albemarle's notebooks, thick with scribbles, broken-spined, crammed with extraneous papers. Zhey had sketches and proto-types planned out that would take zhem years to complete. Zhey were both one of the best theoretical Mancers of zheir generation, and the greatest practical disappointment that could be imagined.

Ash slotted the tube back into the sconce. ~Elegant.

Holly shouted, 'Ash said your copperlit is beautiful, Albemarle.'

'Don't care,' came floating back from where Albemarle stomped along. 'Already know.'

'~Did you have anything like this at the stronghold you came from?' Hazel asked.

Ash raised zheir hands, dropped them into clenched fists, then quickly answered, ~I don't remember where I came from.

Zhey lowered zheir hands to zheir sides and stood unnaturally still, opaque eyes staring past Hazel, face blank, but eyebrows tilted into worry.

Hazel smiled. '~Yes. I forgot that again. Silly me.'

The casual Haven slang didn't quite meet the level of the Trade pejorative and its variations; it was signed by making rabbit ears with the index and little fingers.

Ash lifted zheir chin, proud defiance written all over zhem and repeated it back at him. ~Silly you.

Hazel fought a bigger smile and walked on, and heard Ash start after him.

The sunlight spilling over the bailey was blinding after the muted golden glow of the passageway. The yard was longer than it was wide. The grey wall of the stronghold behind them made one long boundary, and was lined with benches. The matching curve of the looming outer wall, the curtain wall, was kept clear. The east end was stopped by the old wall of the kitchen gardens, which stretched around the rear of the stronghold's grounds, holding beehives and fruit trees and vegetable plots and beds of herbs, both culinary and medicinal. The western end bookended at the taller, thicker wall that separated the practical working areas from the central courtyard where the stronghold's lords, called the purple for the colour only they wore, came and went.

Albemarle clomped to zheir usual seat in the deepest wall shade and sat, hunched over and sulking. Zheir guards had determined, with much trial and error, that one of the things their stronghold's Mancer needed to tolerate zhemself was to get fresh air for one hour every day. Zhey did not recognise that, so it was written on the iron schedule, stamped by Commander Holyoake. Albemarle obeyed Evelyn, or at least her stamp of authority, but zhey didn't have to be gracious about it.

Other benches were already filling with off-duty Haven staff. Not much better daily entertainment existed in the undercroft than watching the brutal few minutes it took for Holly to hand his Mancer Guard its collective arse before training started in earnest.

A palanquin of sorts had been carried through the small gate from the central courtyard and set in the sunshine. A couple of lordlings lounged in their private box with cushions behind their backs and under their arses, blankets on their laps, and rugs at their expensively-shod feet.

Hazel eloquently muttered, 'Shit,' while absently signing [expletive].

He should have expected it. Not only that a few baby purple who followed stronghold gossip might want to see the first spar since Hazel had miraculously disarmed Holly, but also that the news that a Mancer had knocked at the postern would already be spreading upstairs. Curiosity had dragged a couple of cats down the stairs. One was their patron's son.

He turned, but Ash had already slunk away from Albemarle and into a cluster of kitchen staff. Zhey had tossed zheir knotted shawl around zheir head and over zheir face in such a way that zheir features were obscured except for a few locks of that silky-looking silvery hair. Zhey slumped among the kitchenhands, suddenly looking harmless and old and on the feminine side of neutral.

Hazel gave an uneasy sign of approval—that had been a little too practiced—and moved to the centre of the yard, stripping off his coat, switching his true steel for a blunted practice blade, and pulling on gloves. The dirt was hardpacked underfoot, frozen after the recent run of clear frosty nights, winter's last visitation before spring pried loose its icy hold.

He wondered if Ash had slept somewhere undercover or out in the cold while zhey'd crossed overland. He wondered how often zhey'd had to hide like that, huddled in zheir shawl, desperate to be overlooked.

Titus, Morano and First Jerome were already there, in the padded jerkins they wore for practice. They had probably been waiting for some time; Ash's arrival had put the schedule out. That would not be helping Albemarle stay calm. Second Jerome, Kito and Nightingale joined them. They drew their practice swords.

Hazel, sighing, drew his sword.

Holly drew his.

~THREE~

THE GROUND MUST FEEL VERY HARD today. Both Jeromes were down and groaning. Nightingale was down. Kito was a cannonball, quick despite being built like a tiny solid rectangle, but nowhere near as viper-fast as Holly; she got a hit in and went down. Titus flung herself out of the way as Holly danced like a lightning storm after her. Hazel bought their youngest guard another few moments on her feet before Holly, all speed and control and fluid grace, pirouetted around him, sent her sword flying and knocked her down. Morano flurried and went over, swearing and clutching his knee.

'Ari Hazlemere,' Holly said, levelling his sword at Hazel and sighting down its length with one fierce, dark eye. 'My old nemesis. We meet again.'

'You're ridiculous, we are *friends*,' Hazel said, beginning to smile.

'Not in the spar, we're not.' Holly went for him like a striking snake, so fast Hazel barely had time to counter him.

Holly had kicked off his sandals and shrugged off his coat and jerkin before they'd gotten started. He was darting about the small arena of the practice yard in his leather skirt and a thin shirt that stuck to his chest. His dark skin was glistening and his lean muscles were flexing. The lordlings loudly whistled their approval and cheered him on as he beat Hazel back step by step, crowding him into the outer wall.

Yesterday, Hazel had, by some improbability of technique, timing and strength, knocked Holly's sword out of his hand and was paying for it today—he'd eaten fire, as the saying began. He might as well just drop the sword and himself to get it over with. He ducked and Holly's sword scraped across the stone by his ear.

'Head in the game, Hazel darling,' Holly ordered softly.

Hazel parried hard and leapt away from the trap of the wall. 'May I surrender?' he panted.

Something about the way Ash, polished to beauty by the copperlit glow, had appraised him in the hallway made him reluctant to be the brute the Mancer thought he was.

Holly paused long enough to etch a graceful arch with one eyebrow. 'You're the last guard standing between Haven's Mancer and an invading Mancer Guard. May you surrender?'

'A-yah, fuck you too, Holyoake,' Hazel said, amiably enough, and stepped into the fight.

Holly had clearly been having too easy a run of it. Hazel pressed him and won ground, both of them having to dodge their fallen comrades, who had mostly rolled onto their backs with their hands under their heads to watch the fun wherever they had landed. Morano was still bitching about his knee.

'Better,' crowed Holly as their swords locked and Hazel shoved him backward. He was grinning savagely.

Holly had unearthly speed and a surfeit of talent; Hazel had strength and practice, and his own goodly surplus of patience. He also had a weak left side, still recovering from the injury that had left the scar down his face and more scars on his torso, and Holly was just a wee bit merciless. He slammed into Hazel on the left, unbalancing him long enough to flatten him, only not breaking his nose in the process because Hazel managed to keep his sword up to block the blow.

'Hah!' Holly said, and wiggled his hips and shoulders in a merry victory dance just before Evelyn tripped him over and put the point of her sword to his throat. 'Fuck.'

Evelyn produced one of her rare smiles, blasting it at her downed sibling, a not unprecedented position for them. She was Commander of the Mancer Guard for good reason, after all, and it wasn't because she possessed the uncanny ability to make reports to Them Upstairs without punching any of them in the face.

Thinking of which—there could not be many causes to bring her to find her captain in the sparring yard.

'Zhey can lipread,' Hazel warned her from the ground. Ash must have been hiding that facility in her office, to delay having to answer questions.

Evelyn looked peeved—she'd jumped to the same conclusion as Hazel—but she nodded. Sheathing her sword, she sidestepped briskly until she was turned away from both Ash and the box where the two young lords were laughing and talking loudly as they finished their wine.

'The rumours are flying faster than I expected.' A subtle tip of her head at the velvety palanquin. 'Lady Fairhaven is already querying and I can't lie to her. I'm going to need to make an informal report to Lord Valerian. He'll decide about any formal report to the lady. Can you tell me anything yet?'

'No,' Hazel admitted. 'I think—' *I think zhey must have been isolated and lonely.* '—you're right that zhey remember more than zhey're admitting to. Can you put Valerian off till later tonight?'

'I can,' Holly said brightly. He leapt to his feet. 'The one on the left's his son, right? Lorian? He's been eye-fucking me at the feast night for months.'

'Holly, you're not whoring yourself out to make my job easier,' his sister said. She helped Hazel haul himself to his feet, bracing herself solidly against his weight.

'Do you have eyes, Evie? I'm whoring myself out because that boy is pretty with a capital-F for fuck-me-stupid.'

'So you're going to engage in predatory behaviour toward our patron's adolescent son just to truly infuriate him before I have to tell him we agreed to sanctuary for a rogue Mancer without consulting him?'

Holly spread his arms wide. 'Evie baby, do I look like a predator to you?'

'You absolutely do, you shit.'

'We had no choice,' Hazel said quietly, dusting himself down. 'That's the covenant. A Mancer asked for sanctuary. There is no consultation about it.'

'There are ways and ways to let the purple know they're not allowed to refuse an inconvenience at best, a threat at worst.'

Hazel left the siblings arguing delaying strategies and collected his coat and sword. He eyed Ash, making zhemself inconspicuous among the kitchenhands. *A threat*, he thought. *A-yah*. Ash hunched further under Hazel's sidelong scrutiny.

The rest of the guard had gathered to warily watch Holly.

'One of you got a hit on me,' he said, turning from Evie and flourishing his sword. 'Who was it?'

'Kito,' the other chorused with infinite relief. Kito groaned.

'You know what that means.' Holly, half an eye on the palanquin, stripped off his shirt and rolled his shoulders to show off the play of lean and gleaming muscles. 'Come do it again, lover.'

While Holly badgered Kito into attacking him and then ripped her technique apart with a magnificent lack of tact, Evelyn caught Hazel's elbow.

'Valerian's here,' she murmured. 'Get Ash out.'

Hazel flirted a glance and saw the Mancer Guard patron stalking through the gate and over to where his son and friend lounged in their private box, avidly watching Holly strut about near-naked. They'd been quite loudly discussing tying him to a bed. That'd put Holly in a certain kind of mood; he only liked pretending to cede control, not actually doing so. The other guards were in for it. Everyone in his vicinity was in for it.

The lord's attention swung between his young heir and the focus of his young heir's rapt gaze. Holly twirled his sword, well aware of the dissection and smirking at it.

'Don't think you can skip out on the run, Hazel darling,' he purred. 'You'll catch up later.'

Sparring usually ended with a run from the bottom of the subterrane steps to the very top of the stronghold and down again, repeated at Holly's whim. They did it in two groups, so they didn't leave Albemarle alone. Titus had thrown up the first few times—she wasn't the only new Mancer guard so afflicted—and wailed, 'When are we ever going to have to do this in a fight?' She wasn't the only Mancer guard to make that complaint either.

Hazel said, 'But, Holly, how am I supposed to stay motivated without your metronome of an arse ticktocking up the stairs in front of me?'

Holly slapped his metronome of an arse in acknowledgement and jabbed a finger at his guards. 'Who just laughed at poor Kito on the ground here?'

'Second Jerome,' everyone said.

'I didn't!'

'Come at me, fuckster,' Holly said, smoothly shifting so all eyes followed him in the direction that was not Ash.

Hazel took his cue and snagged Ash's sleeve as he went past. The Mancer obediently rose and followed him back to the dining hall. Zhey drew zheir shawl back to zheir shoulders in an anxious, fidgety sort of way. Hazel thought about how to make zhem more comfortable, comfortable enough to let something slip.

~Do you want to eat? Do you need the infirmary, the doctor? How about coming down to the baths with me?

Ash had been giving him a firm shake of the head to each suggestion, but at this last, zhey huddled smaller. ~Is that the price?

~Price?

~The price for sanctuary?

Hazel looked at his hands. Was he not being clear? He and Maya had been very fast and had used a lot of slang specific to Haven; he was probably running the signs too much together. He slowed it down and spoke aloud; he guessed Ash was better at lipreading than Maya had been, and might welcome the extra context for zheir comparatively poorer Trade. He'd have to trim his beard around his lips to make it easier.

'~Not price. Baths. More of Albemarle's Mancy. Hot running water. Communal, but also private spaces for whoever wants them. And a banya. Glorious if you're cold or sore. Do you want it?'

~I want. Ash seemed to realise how much zhey were hunching and straightened. Zhey were wearing zheir frown again, two short straight vertical lines between the two long straight horizontal lines of zheir eyebrows. ~I want sleep.

Hazel read that as *I want to be left alone.* Evelyn had ordered accommodation prepared just along from Albemarle's room so the tiny contingent of Mancer guards could watch over both. Beckoning Ash, he led zhem to the broad and shallow stairs to the subterrane, pausing only to snag some chalk from the corner of the hall where the undercroft children played after meals.

The base of the stairway opened into a wide lobby where the spokes of the subterrane hallways conjoined, cast by copperlits into a receding succession of warm pools of light amid grey shadows. Utilising the chalk on the grey stone, Hazel drew a bed and an arrow for the way to the Mancers' chambers. He didn't think zhey'd care where the guard quarters were, so didn't mark that hallway. He skipped the Mancy atelier as well. That would take some careful introduction; he did not want Ash finding zheir own way there.

After some thought, he added a chicken drumstick to the hallway to the kitchens, and a stylised tub for the hallway to the baths, though their baths were large mosaiced pools without a metal tub in sight; that was the laundry, further down the same hallway. Below that, he attempted a snake-entwined rod for the infirmary, then stepped back to assess his handiwork. The chicken drumstick could have used work; the medical rod wasn't shabby, though the snake looked more insouciant than mystical.

Ash was examining the pictographs, head on one side. Hazel tapped each drawing and coupled them with their signs, finishing with, '~You'll have a guard with you anyway, but it might help you find your bearings.'

Down the Mancer hallway, Ash's chamber glowed gold. Though the room was borderline cold—Albemarle's Mancy venting system constantly cycled fresh air through the subterrane—the stronghold staff had done their best to make it welcoming for the unexpected guest. It had been swept and scrubbed, pale linens layered thickly over the feathered mattress, pillows piled high, a freshly-beaten woven rug covering the flagstones, a washcloth, bowl and ewer on the side table, and a vase of flowers.

It was still small and windowless, and exactly what it was: a white-washed dungeon cell. When Albemarle had insisted on chambers near the atelier, Lady Fairhaven had had all the disused cells renovated so zheir wish could be granted and zheir guards could be quartered to hand. The Mancer Guard wasn't large enough to spill over into Albemarle's hallway anymore, so it was unoccupied aside from zheir room, and now this one.

Copperlits were everywhere. Hazel absently collected an armful, turning each to darkness with a press of his finger. The stronghold staff did, technically, know what it cost Albemarle to charge these useful little tubes, and did, generally, try not to be profligate, but it seemed they'd also wanted to impress Ash and make the room cosy.

Ash looked about, hands clasped, left over right.

Hazel put most of the copperlits down again and held up a single tube. '~Shake it.'

He matched sign to action, shaking the tube to rapidly cycle through its levels of brightness, from a mild dimness to relieve absolute darkness to a bright noontime summer. Flinching, Ash shielded zheir eyes.

Hazel hastily brought the brightness down, and waited for Ash to emerge. '~Sorry. Press once here to darken it. Press along here three times for heat. Don't touch any of them you set to heating, they'll burn you, leave them in the corner until they run out.'

Ash nodded once. Zhey'd locked zheir hands together again, knuckles going white. Hazel suspected zhey were trying to stop zhemself from snapping at him to just get the fuck out.

Very aware that he had not yet discovered any further information to help Evelyn in her meeting with Valerian, Hazel dropped the copperlit on the pile he'd collected and tried again. '~We gave Albemarle a suite up with the purple when zhey first arrived, but zhey wanted to be down here. I know it'd not be what you're used to.'

Somehow conveying put-upon politeness by the very shift of zheir hands, Ash told him, ~It's fine.

And then, with a small smile that put brackets at the end of zheir long straight mouth, ~I don't remember what I'm used to, Hazel.

'~Of course you don't. Silly me. If you hate it, we'll organise a suite.'

~It's fine. I'd like to be near the atelier too.

Hazel remembered the tattoo he'd glimpsed on Ash's wrist, the peacock shades of blue and green. Some strongholds marked their Mancers. They weren't allowed to; nonetheless, some did. He doubted Ash would let him push zheir sleeve back up and openly ogle it.

'~Do you have fresh clothing? Shall I take yours? They'll be returned clean by morning.'

The Mancer was looking more and more bewildered by Hazel's unrelenting helpfulness. Zhey shook zheir head emphatically.

Inured to heels digging in by Albemarle's longstanding stubbornness, and needing a better look at that tattoo, Hazel pressed. '~Just the shawl and coat, then.'

He'd been part of Albemarle's Mancer Guard for coming up on two decades, first as an initiate, he and Holly trotting about after Evelyn and the other guards as they and Albemarle slowly worked each other out. The two of them had been the last of the initiates sent by Stronghold Haven to train at the prestigious Glelissi Mancer Academy; their patron didn't go to the expense anymore. And then they were the youngest of the junior guards, until the numbers dwindled through attrition and promotion and transfer and they became the oldest of the senior guards.

Through all that time, he had become used to Albemarle and zheir eccentricities. He'd helped work out the schedule that kept zhem on the even keel that made everyone's life easier. He'd learnt the precise shorelines of the gentle pressure and firm command needed to keep zhem sailing true past zheir many reefs. And he'd helped feed and wash and dress zhem, when they'd spiralled off zheir course and sunk, dragged down by zheir own anchor, into stricken catatonia.

So it was without thought that Hazel, wearing his most blandly cheerful expression, stepped over to Ash and undid the knot of the shawl. He whisked it off, draped it over his shoulder, and started on the buttons of the dusty coat underneath, absently humming a tune Albemarle liked, or at least appeared to find soothing.

Ash had gone still again, like zhey had in the hallway back from the spar. The stiffly silent compliance did not help remind Hazel that other Mancers weren't Albemarle. He slid the coat from zheir shoulders. He intended to examine the tattoo under the pretence of helping Ash's hands free of the coat, the tangle of torn lace at the sleeves a viable excuse.

But Ash wore a wide-necked tunic under the coat, and Hazel was arrested by the sight of zheir collarbones, another long straight line. The eyebrows, the twin grooves between them, the nose, the mouth, and now the flare of the collarbones, catching and pooling the warm light of the copperlits in their hollows. The Mancer was all strong lines in an entrancing horizontal and vertical pattern.

Hazel, not much given to feeling desire, admired the aesthetics of it, a detached appreciation in the same vein as his appreciation for Holly's sculpture-worthy legs, the angles of Kito's dramatic cheekbones and razor-sharp bob, and the perfect circle formed by Morano's round face and scrupulously shaven and waxed dome of a head.

He was staring. He made himself raise his transfixed gaze, and was again hooked, this time by Ash's throat. Nothing so pleasant here: the Mancer wore livid welts and scabbing abrasions all around the column of zheir neck. Zhey'd been cruelly collared, in the not-far-distant past.

Even in the mindless routine of dressing and undressing Albemarle, Hazel never touched bare skin. He'd put his fingers over Ash's throat before he'd known he was going to, feeling smooth warmth under his calloused fingertips, and the cursed defilement of wounds like those borne by escaped slaves finding refuge in Eldemira from over the wild oceans.

'~I'll escort you to the infirmary.'

He was taken aback then by the sheer force of Ash's glare, all the long straight lines of zheir face drawn tight. Zhey were signing something between zheir own chest and Hazel's sternum, unable to raise zheir hands higher because of the half-off coat.

~No infirmary. Just take your fucking price.

Didn't know the [endearment] sign, did know the [expletive] sign. A-yah.

Hazel felt unaccountably weary as he stepped back and signed again, '~There is no price. You are our guest. G-U-E-S-T. We are Fair Haven. We hold to the covenant. The stronghold asks no price of the atelier.'

Haven didn't even hint that Albemarle should produce saleable projects. Not even their practical artificer had suggested anything of the sort. Profit was a possible benefit of hosting an atelier, but never a requirement.

Ash's face had gone utterly blank, but zhey moved with tense resolve, putting zhemself back under his hands. Zhey looked up at him, and zheir gaze was full of defiance and resignation all at once, and something else Hazel couldn't identify.

Zhey signed, very deliberately, ~Take your price, Hazel.

Interpreting that as somewhat awkward permission, Hazel eased the coat the rest of the way free, letting the left sleeve catch on Ash's fingers. Ash dropped zheir arm as soon as zhey could, so Hazel's view of the tattoo was almost as brief as the original glimpse, but he was closer, and ready for it, and had a decent memory. He'd be able to draw it for Evelyn.

He tossed the coat over his shoulder with the shawl, watching Ash track the movement anxiously. '~I promise we'll have them back by morning, clean and dry.'

Albemarle's mother had been a laundress. Many of zheir first Mancies had benefited the laundry, much to the eternal gratitude of the washer staff and the polite acceptance of Lady Fairhaven, who had probably been hoping for a different focus. If the laundry staff wouldn't extend the shine of their gratitude over the new Mancer, Hazel had been a fixer of problems for enough of them to make the promise with confidence anyway.

'~And the rest?'

He waved his hand over Ash's travel-stained tunic, zheir dusty woollen trousers, the worn boots. Ash looked down at zhemself, and then stared at Hazel, hands limp at zheir sides.

Ash needed the same patience Albemarle needed. That was fine. Hazel said, '~I'll assume that's a no. I'll have someone send over a spare set. Good evening to you, Mancer.'

He'd half-turned away and only caught part of Ash's reply from the corner of his eye. He blinked, then scissored his fingers for zhem to repeat zhemself.

Ash obliged, the lines between zheir eyebrows pronounced, a slight flush in zheir cheeks. ~Why are you trying to get my clothes off if there really is no price?

Frowning, Hazel set his hands to his nape, pressing his elbows back to stretch his shoulders. He was pleasantly sore from the fight with Holly, and slightly frustrated—just slightly, partly because he wasn't by disposition given to temper, but also partly because he'd had plenty of practice, thanks to Albemarle, at not getting *very* frustrated.

The move pulled him taller and broader and emphasised that he was big, muscular, and armed. And, never forget, brutishly scarred. He saw

Ash's eyes widen and abruptly understood that the Mancer was more than merely apprehensive of him.

Their whole interaction, here in the private space Ash had specifically requested, with Hazel blithely ignoring zheir refusals and stripping zheir clothes off, turned about and took on an entirely different and extremely unflattering cast.

He was horrified, both at himself and at the implication, and made the [shocked] sign accordingly, springing both fists open for emphasis. '~Do you think I'm forcing sex on you?'

The Mancer made an abortive move to reply, and stilled. Zhey did not know how to answer, apparently.

'~I'm *Mancer Guard*. I *protect*. I would *never*—'

Hazel contained himself—it was hardly Ash's fault that Hazel had been overbearing and scared zhem, and signing in zheir face with frantic jerks of his big hands was hardly going to reassure zhem.

He shook his hands out, held them palms-up to Ash, and then signed in a far more restrained way. '~I'm sorry, Ash. I forgot how I look to strangers. No one will do that here. You are safe.'

He practically backed out of the room, hands held up. He was angry at himself, and outraged in a more generalised way: what the fuck kind of stronghold had Ash come from? Who the fuck had zheir Mancer Guard been, to make zhem think zhey couldn't trust the covenant?

He would have preferred to entirely remove himself from Ash's vicinity, but he couldn't just leave. It was too early for First Jerome to come on watch, and Holly would be with Albemarle, guiding him through bathing and dinner, or he'd have turned the duty over to Morano or Kito so he could help Evelyn wrangle Lord Valerian.

It'd be difficult, with two Mancers, unless they kept the pair together at all times, and wouldn't Albemarle love that. They'd have to recruit more bodies into the Mancer Guard, after running at a minimum for so many years. They'd have to be very quiet about it, too, if they didn't want to signal to other strongholds that they had a new Mancer.

Hazel took the chalk out of his pocket and began to draw on the wall opposite Ash's chamber, one icon per large grey stone, calming as he worked. He drew the same symbols he'd used in the lobby, for the kitchen, baths, and infirmary. He hoped Ash would see zheir way to using the lattermost sooner rather than later, but he wouldn't press it, not after that shameful performance in there.

Hand on hip, he thought about what else Ash might want to request while the Jeromes were on duty overnight. He drew a rough outline of a tunic, in case zhey decided zhey wanted clean clothes once the intimidating fucker who'd been threatening zhem was gone. He drew a wine bottle. A book, which he rubbed out. An open book with pictures on its pages, then. An ewer, for fresh water. Another one, with steam coming out, for hot water.

A scraping scuffle came from behind, boot on stone. Ash must have followed him to the door. Zhey probably thought zhey were being quiet, but of course zhey couldn't hear zhemself make noise. Maya had been the same.

Hazel closed his eyes and allowed himself to miss his sister dreadfully for the space of two breaths.

Then he turned to look at Ash's hands, to see if he was needed. Ash signed an apology, and Hazel brushed it away; it was not owed to him.

He pointed at the wall. '~What else might you need?'

Ash stood close beside him to examine the icons. Hazel had the distinct impression zhey were forcing zhemself to do it, to show him zhey weren't afraid. He shifted away, giving Ash the same space Albemarle needed.

'~Tea?' Zhey hadn't taken any in the dining hall that afternoon. Hadn't eaten the pie either, but Hazel wouldn't hold it against zhem. '~Coffee?'

Ash watched him carefully and Hazel realised, with a touch of amusement, that zhey were trying to reason out if a real amnesiac would be able to remember their preferences. He threw zhem a bone and drew both, a cup for the tea, a taller mug for the coffee. He drew a slice of pie as well, just in case.

Ash traced a finger over the little ideograph. Zhey smiled at him, rueful.

Didn't know [endearment]. Did know [expletive] and [sex]. Sported the crimson marks of a metal collar, abraded into the skin about zheir neck.

Oh, a-yah, and fuck this, truly.

'~Ash. I don't need to know where you came from. But I do need to know the threat it poses. We have to be ready to fight for you, if your previous stronghold tries to take you back. I know we must look weak to you, only eight in the Mancer Guard. We had the full contingent once, but Albemarle goes nowhere except zheir room, the atelier and the dining hall, never travels, doesn't do field tests, doesn't sell projects that need regular charging. We'll talk to our patron about recruiting more now we have two Mancers.'

By now, Ash was leaning forward, intently flicking zheir gaze between Hazel's flashing hands and his mouth, those two horizontal lines etched deep between zheir eyes as zhey tried to keep up with the signing, which went well beyond standard Trade.

Hazel kept on with the barrage regardless. '~But Haven can and will defend you. We can hide you, we can get you away if that's what you prefer, or, if it comes to it, we have a strong militia, and we keep the covenant.'

Ash gave a somewhat wan nod of understanding, hands knotted together.

'~But we need forewarning, on what to expect.'

~No one will come for me.

That might have been the most unconvincing lie so far. '~I don't believe you. Anyone who dares put a collar on a Mancer will chase zhem down if they think they can.'

The Mancer stared at him, biting zheir lip.

'~Ash, we need to know. Please.'

Ash stuttered the start of an answer before switching smoothly. ~I do not remember.

Huffing out a breath, Hazel looked at his growing grid of drawings, brushing at the chalk dust on his fingers. Beside him, Ash hunched into zhemself, perhaps expecting another assault on zheir story.

'Good evening, sir.' That was First Jerome, early, coming quietly up the hallway, always light on her feet under her heavy robe. 'Oh, it's you who's been scribbling on the walls, is it? What's this one supposed to be?' She tapped the chicken drumstick, which he hadn't drawn any better the second time around.

'~What'd you call me?'

'Oh.' She might have blushed, under her veil. 'I suppose I thought we better start doing things properly, with the new Mancer and all.'

'~You try a "sir" out on Holly?'

'Lapped it up.'

'~Bet he did.' He waved at the wall. '~I know you don't know so much Trade yet, so this is in aid of helping Ash communicate with you, if zhey need something tonight.'

First Jerome looked over the wall of iconography, and at Ash. 'Zhey can't read?'

'~Zhey can lipread. Make sure the light is good, and face zhem straight on. No need to shout or talk slowly. Try not to move your hands, it'll be distracting unless you're actually signing Trade.'

'A-yah,' she said easily. 'We'll manage, Hazel darling, stop fretting.'

Her warm dark eyes crinkled at the corners and her veil shifted over her cheeks as she smiled at Ash. She had lovely thick eyelashes, almost as pretty as Holly's. The little brackets at the corner of Ash's mouth appeared as zhey smiled shyly back.

Hazel showed Ash First Jerome's sign and spelled it out for zhem.

'~This is A-Y-A-L-A-J-E-R-O-M-E but we call her First Jerome because she always does the first night watch and Second Jerome, J-E-R-O-M-E-L-A-T-T, with the leg, does the second. You'll see him in the morning unless you're a late sleeper. Morano, M-O-R-A-N-O, is on first day watch tomorrow, he knows some Trade. He'll bring you up to breakfast and attend you for the morning.'

Ash frowned. Zhey took the chalk from Hazel's unresisting fingers and drew a face on the wall, with a stormy cloud of hair and a wide smile. Like most Mancers, Ash was good at pictorial representation, capturing essence in a few strokes—the smile was a simple dash of pale chalk on grey stone, and yet still somehow conveyed sweetness.

Zhey tapped zheir effort with the chalk, and waved at Hazel with zheir other hand. Hazel looked at it with his head on one side. He could only think Ash was requesting a companion for zheir bed, which seemed unlikely but also might explain zheir reluctance to sign it.

Ash added some spots to the face, on each side of the nose. It didn't help. The Mancer looked thwarted, in a foot-tapping way that Hazel had to resist smiling at.

~Fingerspell?

First Jerome snorted at his confusion. 'Hazel, zhey're wanting to be able to ask for you if zhey need you.'

That also seemed unlikely. First Jerome took the chalk in her gloved fingers and drew a line down the side of the face, murmuring, 'No point being shy about it.'

She looked back to Ash and the Mancer nodded. Satisfied, she dotted in extra freckles too, which made Ash suddenly produce a mischievous little smile aimed entirely at Hazel. Feeling uncomfortably warm, he began to show zhem his sign again, but First Jerome tapped his fingers.

'Zhey haven't forgotten your name-sign,' she said. 'Zhey wanted you to recognise yourself in this rather adorable picture.'

Hazel, highly sceptical and moderately embarrassed, reclaimed the chalk and drew a representation of Holly's face, with a cascade of a dozen snaky lines from a topknot to represent his multitude of braids.

'~Holly'd be better.' He added, without saying it aloud, ~He's not scary.

Holly could be, of course, but Ash didn't need to know that right now.

~You're not scary.

He smiled, pained to feel grateful for that small politeness. '~Good evening, Ash. Good evening, Ayala.'

He went to make his report to Evelyn.

~Four~

Holly is summoned to Lord Valerian as soon as practice is over; the same message tells Evie her own meeting is delayed. Evie refuses to reward Holly with a palm slap. He nods to Kito and Morano to walk with Albemarle back to the undercroft, and goes through the small gate into the central courtyard, dressed but still sweating, carrying his sword and coat, shaking his braids back into order.

The lord commanded his son out of the bailey earlier, much to the lad's sulky displeasure. The palanquin is tucked away near the wall but there is no sign of either of the two lordlings who'd been watching Holly so avidly.

The central court, unlike the bailey Holly has just slipped in from, is designed to impress visitors, mostly the castellans of other strongholds, as well as the lesser nobility who hold estates outside the cities without the privilege and responsibility of the Mancer covenant, and also wealthy merchants, clergy of all the various stripes, scholars from Glelissi, even specialists from the Mancer Academy, come to try to interview Albemarle for their theories.

Mancers, too, should visit, but Albemarle's reputation and actual behaviour strongly discourage that. Only Asquith, Albemarle's friend in the loosest sense of the word, has made the trip south along the coast from zheir own stronghold.

The huge gates, iron-faced oak, stand open, as they always do in daylight hours at friendly Stronghold Haven. That surely must've tempted Ash when zhey'd walked up the winding road from the port to reach the stronghold's perch on the towering white cliffs. Or perhaps zhey'd come through the parklands and fields that stretched southward and westward, or even up through the southern band of forest.

Either way, their new Mancer had not walked through those encouragingly open double gates, across the even paving, around the great fountain with its smiling statue pouring water from two jars, and up the grandiose flight of steps to the ornate main doors of Haven. Instead, zhey'd circled the outer wall until zhey found the postern overlooking the seaside cliffs, and knocked until it opened, and somehow made it clear to the guards on duty that zhey were to be brought directly to the Mancer Guard, not its lord upstairs.

While the curtain wall and lower stronghold, the undercroft and subterrane, are built of local grey granite, the walls of the stronghold proper, the upper floors where the lords and ladies in purple live and work and welcome guests, are salmon-pink sandstone, imported from the southwest by Lady Fairhaven's parents, when they'd upgraded their clifftop chateau with an eye to becoming a stronghold.

It'd seemed eccentric at the time, driven by a lord who'd also ordered the estate's cows stencilled with Haven's ivy pattern for the aesthetics of it, but Lady Fairhaven reaped what her parents had sown only a few years after inheriting the lordship. And, to be fair, the stencilling stopped rustling in its tracks.

The sandstone glows rosy in the late afternoon sun as Holly skips up the sweep of steps to the main doors. He exchanges a friendly enough nod with the pair of stronghold guards on duty there. On the one hand, he, like any one of the Mancer guards, outranks them. On the other hand, undercroft staff are not supposed to use the grand entrance steps. There is, instead, a set of stairs from the dining hall that corkscrews to a back hallway on the working side of the upper stronghold. That way, the purple and their senior retainers, collectively Them Upstairs, don't have to see the mechanics behind their smooth ride.

But which guardian of the doors, in their right mind, would try explaining that to Captain Rowan Holyoake?

Inside, in the public area of the upper stronghold, he puts his coat back on, unfastened, and slots his sword in place. Pushing his braids back, he's directed by a stiffly smiling upper staffer, an equerry of some sort—the undercrofters do not much interact with the most senior of the purple's staff, except at the monthly feasts—toward Lord Valerian's office.

It's on the far side from the great hall. Holly should've realised the lord would have taken his father's office.

He knocks briskly on the closed door and enters without pausing. 'You wanted to see me?'

Lord Valerian has been standing by one of the west-facing mullion windows of the large and lushly furnished corner chamber. He's in formal clothes, coat and slashed-sleeve doublet and knee breeches with silk stockings. He has a view over the courtyard and gateway from there; he might have been craning to follow Holly's progress from bailey wall to main door. Holly wishes he'd put a bit more swish into it, in that case.

The south-facing window, famously, overlooks the broad swath of lawn leading to the landscaped wilderness of the pleasure gardens.

'Captain Holyoake,' the lord says, turning and giving Holly a rather contemptuous once-over.

Holly is surprised he wasn't marched in under guard by Valerian's people.

For all that Holly's sister regularly reports to the Mancer Guard patron, and for all that Holly was once the personal protégé of Valerian's father, Lord Florian, Holly barely knows the man. He can count their exchanges on the fingers of one and a half hands, which averages out to a short and stilted conversation once every few years. Lord Valerian does seem to spend a good portion of the feast nights judgmentally staring at Holly with narrowed eyes, though.

He's receiving the same look now.

Valerian, whose ancestors are of northern stock, is as fair-skinned as Albemarle, but actually appears to enjoy the outdoors when not attending his duties, so sports a healthy tan instead of sickly fish-belly shades. He has richly chestnut hair in a widow's peak—indeed, he is a widow now—and pale grey eyes that Holly assumes aren't always glaring coldly at people. Only a few years younger than Holly, he has the well-set body of a sturdy middling-aged man whose easy and somewhat sedentary lifestyle is beginning to make itself known.

He moves with drilled-in grace to sit behind his desk, pointing a finger at Holly and jerking it at the chair set before the polished surface. Holly bites back a smile and obeys the exact shape of the order, lounging on the hard-backed chair to the best of his ability, long limbs sprawling in all directions, sword hilt poking him for his trouble.

The lord stares at him in a silence long enough for Holly to become restless, before softly saying, 'I must admit to surprise that Commander Holyoake indulged in nepotism in appointing you as captain.'

Holly raises his eyebrows. 'Evie lobbied for Hazel, but your father's intentions were clear.'

The man left *instructions*; Valerian, the dutiful patronship heir, knows that better than anyone.

Also, Hazel pitched the only fit Holly has ever seen him pitch and threatened to quit if they appointed him. Holly hopes he's reconciled himself; they'll eventually have to expand the Mancer Guard now they have two Mancers, and Ash's set will need its own captain. Kito deserves it, fair, but the atelier will not be well served by not one but two rash and impetuous captains, even with Evie holding the reins tight.

Valerian doesn't appear to be listening. 'I remember you, when you first arrived at Haven. I was, oh, fourteen, perhaps. You were, what, seventeen?' He doesn't wait for Holly's nod. 'You were so fast. My father said he'd never seen the like.'

'Still fast,' murmurs Holly. Middle age hasn't caught up with him yet; the flagrant speed of youth has been replaced by the economic precision of experience.

'You wouldn't have noticed me, of course. I was too quiet in my studies and you were too…busy…in yours.'

'That's a delicate way of accusing me of fucking around, my lord,' Holly says, genuinely amused.

Lifting his cool eyes to meet Holly's, Valerian says, 'And now you're just as fast as you ever were and you think you're going to fuck around with my son, is it? He's only fifteen, for fuck's sake.'

Holly looks steadily back. He'd blatantly encouraged Lorian with body language and sidelong glances during the spar, specifically to annoy Valerian and engineer this disciplinary meeting, bumping Evelyn's meeting back until Hazel can, in his sweetly unassuming way, worm more information out of their cagey guest.

Therefore, he doesn't explain that he doesn't fuck children. He says, 'Wasn't your wife only fifteen when you married her? Did you show the same scruples on the wedding night?'

Valerian surges to his feet and storms around the desk. Holly tips his head back, smiling, as the lord sets his hands onto the carved armrests of the chair and leans over him.

This is an imposing display of lordly spleen, but then, it was a low blow. Valerian had not been much older than his bride when he'd entered the arranged marriage, only sixteen, the age of consent here, older than in many other places. According to gossip, what began as an awkward union between two children blossomed into a true love match over time.

Valerian no doubt *did* show the appropriate scruples, on the wedding night and every night of the marriage.

He was reportedly devastated by his wife's death some three years ago. Lorian is their only child and his treasure. Holly's fucking with the two people Valerian cares about most.

But he's here to delay Evelyn's meeting as long as he can. That isn't going to be achieved by bowing and meekly m'lording Valerian with a tug of a metaphorical forelock.

Impressively, the lord's voice is still quiet and measured as he informs Holly, 'If you lay a finger on my boy, I will personally flay the skin from your flesh, grind your bones to dust, feed the remnants to the pigs, and spread their shit on unsanctified ground.'

'Noted,' says Holly.

It's almost endearing, how specific Valerian made the threat. The Holyoakes come from an ancestor-worshipping culture; they prize relics of the bony sort. He and Evie left everything behind when they fled the war. They darkly joke about which of them will be first to provide bones to build a new reliquary for the other. The consensus is it will be Holly, which will do Evie no good at all. He's the younger sibling, and so, not her ancestor. But it will help her children, should she get around to making some.

Holly waits for Valerian to relax and ease back before adding, 'But have you considered that he is sixteen very soon? I couldn't help overhearing he and his friend discussing the celebration plans for the next feast. I believe he's planning his own little birthday surprise.'

Just to be entirely clear, he waves a lazy hand up and down his own sprawled body.

Then he says, 'And once he's sixteen, you have no grounds to stop him.'

Valerian hauls Holly up by his shirt. He's shorter than Holly, and stockier than Holly, but he might very well be stronger than him, and again Holly feels a reluctant admiration. He always thought Valerian awkward, aloof, a touch dull; he's liking the coldly controlled temper. He'd like to see the control fracture. He thinks he's going to.

'Now, now, my lord,' he chides. 'It's not my fault the lad talks louder than he thinks he does while he's undressing me with his eyes.'

He watches in fascination as Valerian takes a breath, and then another, and packs away his rage. The lord still has spots of colour burning high in his cheeks, but he releases Holly's shirt where the cloth has been bunched in both fists.

He puts the desk between them again, saying coolly, 'Not a long or difficult process, I imagine, since you fight half-naked.'

Holly gives a little bow of his head in acknowledgement, letting some of his braids swing forward. He does strip off as far as he can in the training. He likes the sun on his skin and hates the cling of sweaty clothes. He likes discombobulating Second Jerome and making shy Nightingale blush. He likes it when Kito flicks his nipples and says, 'Put those weapons away, boy'.

He likes, also, that Lord Valerian noticed.

'So Lorian intends to accost you at the next feast night, is it?'

'If I heard him correctly. He has *quite* the scenario going on in his head, my lord. Bondage and domination.'

'Of course he does,' Valerian mutters, sounding less like a lord now and more like the beleaguered father of a determined adolescent.

'Of course he does,' Holly echoes, holding wide his arms and dipping his head to direct Valerian's attention along the length of his sinuously muscled body.

Valerian stands stiffly behind the desk. His wintery grey eyes, stormy a moment ago, are cold and remote again. 'Understand me, captain. Your sister's position depends on my good will. Legal or no, you allow Lorian to—' It is his turn to wave a hand in the direction of Holly's languid slouch, dismissive. '—play out his fantasies upon you, and she will no longer be Commander of the Mancer Guard.'

Holly tsks, outwardly unmoved. 'Oh no, my lord, that kite won't fly. Haven's Mancer only follows zheir schedule on Commander Holyoake's authority. If zhey don't have a schedule, zhey don't function. You won't like that.'

Albemarle might not be performing to the expectations that had grown about zhem because of zheir youthful promise, but Holly can see at least three Mancy inventions in this room alone, not even counting the copperlits—the endless-ink pen on the desk, the clock on the mantle, the failed far-scry mirror—and the purple have private bathrooms powered by Mancy, among endless other little luxuries.

To his surprise, Valerian laughs, a soft sound in the quiet space. 'Albemarle doesn't care who the commander is. Zhey obey the office, not the person occupying it.'

This is an annoyingly good point. Holly was counting on Valerian not knowing overly much about the unsociable Mancer lurking in the sub-terrane. He's obviously interacted with zhem more often than with zheir guard captain in the years since he took on the patronage. More likely, he dutifully reads every one of Evie's reports.

Holly does not express his opinion that Lady Fairhaven would have a great deal to say should she get wind of a Haven authority making threats against anyone, let alone Evelyn. Instead, he slowly smooths out the wrinkles Valerian left in his shirt, trying not to smile.

'Pour me a drink, my lord,' he says, 'and let's work this out like the gentlemen neither of us are.'

Valerian makes a self-satisfied noise. Holly suppresses an impulse to snatch up the Mancy pen from the desk and stab the back of the lord's hand. It's time for him to grovel, and he riled Valerian up enough that the abasement is going to take some time. That is, he reminds himself, the whole goal of this meeting, to earn Evie time to do her job right.

He sits and accepts a cut-glass tumbler of smoky peat whiskey. Lord Valerian's father brought that taste with him when he moved his family south to live with his noble cousins at Haven, safe from the incessant ice-storms and pirate raids plaguing the northwest coast back then. The rest of the stronghold drinks wine, fermented from rice, or clear pear cider, or cold herbal tea.

Lord Valerian sits too, leaning back, stretching his legs out comfortably. He thinks he has the upper hand, holding Evie over Holly in a way decidedly not worthy of Fair Haven by the Sea. Holly is still working out how to get that particular knife off his throat, so he supposes that the lord does have the upper hand.

For now.

Holly sips the whiskey, savouring the warmth in his throat, eyeing Valerian over the rim of the glass. 'I am not interested in bedding children, age of consent notwithstanding. Your son will get nowhere with me.'

'Forgive me if I am not convinced by a sudden attack of conscience upon facing consequences,' Valerian says icily.

'You will not have to ask around for long to discover that my taste in men is well-known and does not include skinny virgin boys with silly floppy hair and no arse to speak of.'

Holly, taking another sip, bigger, is greatly tickled to see that Valerian has to fight off an expression of indignation on behalf of his son. And perhaps himself. He also has silly floppy hair. His arse is magnificent, however.

He drinks again and quickly goes on, 'But have you considered, my lord, that *his* taste in men is reckless, and when I turn him down he may very well turn his greedy eyes and tender arse toward even less savoury prospects?'

Valerian, looking appalled, tries a few responses out before saying weakly, 'Cannot literally turn both eyes and arse…'

Holly swallows the rest of his drink in one gulp and thumps the glass down on a little side table by a spectacularly ugly vase. Forgetting he's not teasing Hazel, he says, 'Can if you're playing coy.'

He may have drunk his whiskey too fast. That's the only explanation for why he stands up, smoothly turns his back to the lord and patron of the Mancer Guard, then cocks a snaky hip and shoots him a look over his shoulder that is wide-eyed and eager and wet-mouthed and so very willing.

Valerian is duly horrified, and something else, too, if Holly is not mistaken, and he very rarely is. 'Stop that at once!'

Holly's not given much to remorse or guilt, but he does feel now that he has gone a touch too far. If he'd been with Evie, or Hazel, or a lover he's fond of, he would've admitted exactly that and soothed the hackles away with words and touch.

But here, he's Holly to the hilt, and he does what Holly always does in a fight: he doubles down.

'Imagine that bent over a bed down at the port and a couple of sailors—'

Valerian's ice is thoroughly cracked; he launches himself past his desk and crashes into Holly. Holly, his reactions as fast as his swordplay, has already moved when Valerian reaches him, so he dances clear without more than a glancing blow of Valerian's big chest to his back and a scrabble of strong arms that fail to hold him.

Spinning away across the room, he puts his hand on the pommel of his wicked blade out of very long habit. Just as quickly, he's jerked his itching fingers away again, but Valerian has noticed the gesture. The lord stands breathing heavily, his whole face flushed.

'Not Evelyn,' Holly says quickly, with a sinking sense of his own impetuous mistake. 'Take away my captaincy, but don't punish Evie for my misdoing.'

He's still in fight stance, he realises. He forces himself to shift his weight, to stand like he's not the killer he's trained to be. His breathing catches. Not a warrior, this lord. He manages the Fairhaven estates for his father's cousin, the yields and rents and budgets. He supports the

Mancer Guard only as an inheritance from Lord Florian, a gesture of filial respect.

He's a quiet and dutiful man, playing at being a hard-hearted villain to try to protect Lorian, and Holly in return waved the despoilment of his only son under his nose and threatened him with that hand laid on his hilt.

Valerian closes his eyes. 'Get out,' he says tiredly. 'Send Commander Holyoake to me.'

Holly steps cautiously nearer. 'I was trying to point out you might want to keep a watch on him, that's all,' he says, as meekly as he can.

'That's all,' Valerian repeats. He opens his eyes. They are storm clouds. 'Thank you for your concern, captain. Get the fuck out of my office.'

Holly tries. He really tries. But at the door, he turns back. 'I'll take the demotion without a word, but tell me Evelyn is safe from reprisal.'

Valerian engages in petty vengeance by refusing to answer, raking him with those stormy eyes and turning a stiff shoulder on him. He stalks back behind the safety of his desk. Holly follows, swift and silent, and judges that Valerian is entirely taken by surprise when he turns and finds Holly standing right there.

'I said—'

Holly takes his wrist, firmly. The other man starts and tries to pull free. Valerian's frowning, but he's more puzzled than angry or alarmed. Despite Holly's slip, Haven is a safe place. People don't deliberately harm each other here; it makes the threats flashing like lightning between them—his fingers on his pommel, Valerian's thumb on Evie's position— beyond empty, mere posturing of the most ridiculous sort.

Holly isn't threatening Valerian now. Holly thinks he didn't imagine the slightly wistful tone of the lord's reminiscence of their youth, the heat that flared in his pale eyes even amid his horror at Holly's demon-stration of coy invitation. Holly can feel Valerian's pulse, thrumming under his fingers.

'Tell me,' he says again, very softly, 'that Evelyn is safe from reprisal. And then you can tell me what quiet young Val wanted busy, busy Holly to do to him all those years ago.'

Valerian shoves Holly backward, a compulsive, hard motion. Holly's shoulders hit the wall. He slouches back and waits, lit by the refracted rays of the dying sun falling through the window beside him.

The lord has streaks of high colour across his cheekbones. He says, strangled, 'She's safe.'

Holly smiles. He wasn't concerned beyond the initial instinctive flash of alarm—Valerian is simply not the vindictive type he's been pretending to be, even if that sort of thing was allowed to pass in Haven—but it is nice to hear, regardless, and it's giving him a game to play.

A truly lovely game.

'And?' he purrs. 'Tell me.'

Valerian shakes his head. Holly reaches out lazily and catches the broad lapel of the lord's elegantly fashionable coat. He tugs, just once, and Valerian comes to him like he's in chains.

Holly puts his mouth to his lord's ear and murmurs, 'Tell me, Valerian. What do you want?'

His lips part, but words are trapped in his throat. It's in a rush, when he finally says it. 'I want you on your knees.'

Pushing his sword back so it won't impede the oiled slickness of the motion, Holly slides to his knees. 'And?' he says again. 'Say it.'

Valerian stares down at him, mesmerised. He looks desperate. 'I want to fuck your mouth,' he says hoarsely.

Lowering his lashes in a display of demure compliance, Holly undoes the loops and buttons of Valerian's breeches and opens his drawers. Valerian's already hard and Holly tongues his thick and rigid length, revelling in the resulting soft curse and clutch of hands over his braids. Valerian is pleasantly clean—thank you, Albemarle, for the fresh water so abundantly piped into the stronghold and heated via Mancy—and surprisingly gentle as Holly grips his hips and takes him in his mouth.

In fact, after a moment or two in which Valerian does not respond to the strong hint of Holly's hands insistently pulling his hips forward, Holly has to sit back and say, 'Move your hips, my lord.' He glances up and meets Lord Valerian's startled gaze. 'You said you wanted to fuck my mouth, so don't stand there and make me do quite all the work.'

Valerian makes a sound halfway between a snort of laughter and a groan of agony as Holly slides his lips over his hard cock again. This time, the lord isn't so shy. He lets Holly's braids slide rhythmically through his fingers and thrusts into his mouth, shallowly at first, and then deeper, fraught gasps escaping him as he loses control. Holly can feel the flex and clench of the muscles of Valerian's arse under his grasping fingers and he once again is both surprised and pleased by the unexpected strength of the man. Valerian abruptly makes a choked noise and fills Holly's mouth and throat in a stuttering rush, Holly swallowing about his cock as his convulsions ebb.

The lord sags. He seems stunned. Holly quietly tucks him away and rises. That had been fast, faster even than the first time Holly had gone to his knees for Hazel, behind a tree in the pleasure gardens. He thinks he's just fulfilled a long-standing fantasy. He also thinks he's bought enough stalling time for Evie, and possibly a reprieve for himself too, depending on how generous Lord Valerian intends to be now he's feeling like he's thoroughly conquered Holly.

But Valerian isn't looking like he's feeling like anyone's conqueror. He's collapsed back onto his chair, and has his head in his hands.

'All right?' Holly asks, pausing in his stride for the door. He can't imagine he's left the man worse off, but the whole aspect speaks of despair.

'I can't believe I did that,' Valerian mutters into his hands. 'I'm so sorry, Captain Holyoake.'

That is surprisingly formal, given what they've just been doing.

'I've greatly abused my position as your patron,' the lord goes on, and might have continued in that vein if Holly hadn't outright laughed.

Valerian lowers his hands and another stormy indignant look displaces his somewhat dazed expression.

'Lord Valerian,' Holly says, throwing his formality back at him. 'It's sweet you think you were the one in control of that little situation.'

That unseats the shuttlecock on the loom where Valerian was industriously weaving himself a broadcloth of guilt. 'Oh, you are outrageous!'

Holly answers him with dainty little curtsy, crossing his ankles and holding up the hem of his leather skirt in a delicate pinch.

Valerian rubs at a spot between his eyes. 'Well. Do not let it be said I do not pay my debts. Come back over here and I will, ah, see to you.' Holly arches a brow, and Valerian blushes. 'With my hand.'

Holly has an unpleasant realisation in the wake of the telling spill of red across Valerian's cheeks and the uncertain offer. The man married very young and was famously besotted with his wife, and heavy with grief since her passing. Holly now suspects he's accidentally hit an awful trifecta: Valerian's adolescent crush, his first man, and his first lover in widowhood.

No wonder there was so much pent-up neediness in the clutch of his hands, the sounds he made. No wonder he hadn't taken it for a game. Holly knows the soft look Valerian is unknowingly wearing. He's seen Hazel wear that soft look.

Here is a ship sailing straight for sharp reefs, and Holly immediately looks to turn the rudder so the poor man won't founder.

'Nah,' he says. 'Despite the skirt and the hair, I am a man, I have a cock, and I like to spill buried deep inside my lovers. I can do better than a bit of incompetent fumbling.'

The lord is back on his feet now. '*Incompetent fumbling*!'

'At worst, I suppose I can get myself off handily by remembering the sheer look of desperation on your face just then. My lord.'

'You utter dick,' says Valerian.

Holly laughs, though there's an edge to it. 'At least you're uniquely placed to warn your son of the disappointment of fulfilling a fantasy now, aren't you, Val?'

He winks and skips merrily on his way, satisfied that Evie has her delay and Valerian is safe. He's not worried about himself.

~FIVE~

HOLLY FLUNG HIMSELF ONTO THE BENCH beside Hazel at their table in the dining hall. He snatched up flowers from the vase in the centre—the undercroft staff were expecting the new Mancer at the table for breakfast and were still trying to make a good impression, it seemed—and started to braid the stems into Hazel's hair, tugging on the tangled locks until Hazel shifted sideways to give him easier access.

Kito glanced up and went back to reading. The other tables were full of people, plates and chatter, but none of the other Mancer guards were at breakfast yet. Morano was coming on watch and Second Jerome would be handing over to him before heading off to bed. First Jerome would still be sleeping, and the alt-watch juniors, Titus and Nightingale, might be too, preparing for their own upcoming overnight watch.

'What is this strip of material you are wearing?' Hazel asked Holly. It was an even shorter skirt than yesterday, and high-heeled ankle boots with a lot of buttons.

'I'm just feeling very Holly today.'

'You certainly are,' Hazel said, since Holly had wrapped one leanly muscular leg round his waist to hook himself in close as he worked. Softer, he asked, 'Was it a bad night?'

He'd half-hoped Holly would turn up in his bed for a cuddle last night, as he was wont to do, a habit from their homesick time at the academy together. But that might have meant Holly had had a truly awful night, so he was, overall, glad he hadn't.

'Not bad. Eventful. I'll tell you about it in excruciatingly inappropriate detail over breakfast.'

'A-yah.' Luxuriating in the feel of Holly's quick fingers moving through his hair, Hazel returned his attention to the map he'd spread before him.

His mug was holding down one top corner, the vase the other, his forearms the bottom.

'What are we doing, Hazel darling?'

Hazel absently hummed to the question as his eyes tracked over the principalities within a few days' cart ride of Haven. Ash hadn't said zhey'd come by cart, nor by foot; zhey'd been vague, most likely on purpose, but zhey had at least admitted to coming overland, and the dust ground into zheir skin confirmed it. That made it somewhat easier, especially since the condition of the scrapes about zheir neck gave Hazel a timeline.

The other clue was zheir original home, before zhey'd made covenant with a stronghold. He assessed the varied hues and features of the occupants of the dining hall. Many were on their way to or from the port, working at Haven for a season while they saved the coin to move onward. Others, like Hazel and the Holyoakes, were lifers, or planned to be. The former turned into the latter quite regularly. Haven was safe, and deliberately, stubbornly, kind when the rest of the world was often not.

Mountain folk, Hazel decided. Ash's light bronze skin and uncompromising features, even with the androgynous Mancer topography, suggested an ancestral link with the proud and secretive people—though really, which peoples weren't one or both?—who tended the coffee groves in the highest foothills of the Wildewynne mountain range, to the mid-northwest.

Hazel was from mid-north, too, but further east. He and Maya had come out of the foothills and straight south along the coast to reach Haven, after their mother died and their father failed to protect his deaf daughter from the superstitions of their neighbours. Hazel had gotten her away when the crops failed for the third consecutive year and the mutters about appeasing the spirits became a poised tension every time Maya walked across the square to the market.

He was an accepting sort of person—things were what they were and generally there was naught to do *but* accept them—but some lines could not be crossed, and a superstition solid enough to merit a scapegoat was one of them.

He'd heard the rumours of Haven's kindness, but he'd also just witnessed his kindly neighbours turn on a little girl; mere rumours did not factor into his choice at all. They'd come to Haven because, of all the jurisdictions within reasonable reach of children travelling alone, it was one of the few that would not define Maya as legally incapacitated just for being deaf, trapped under the guardianship of a father or brother or husband forever. They both, their whole lives, worked to make sure Maya was not limited by how others saw her.

He could not know if Ash had fallen afoul of similar prejudices. Even as a deaf child or youth, zhey'd have had zheir obvious Mancer vocation written all over zhem, which might have staved off the worst of it. Regardless, zheir family would've had to renounce their blood ties and any right to guardianship as soon as Ash's Mancy rose. Zhey'd have been irresistibly driven to facilitate the release of the burgeoning Mancy—which meant, without exception, an atelier, safe within a stronghold. Zhey would have left zheir family and gone straight to the nearest one. Most Mancers did.

Albemarle hadn't. Albemarle had fought off the overwhelming Mancy drive, gone to the academy library and researched every stronghold, and chosen Fair Haven by the Sea and its new atelier. It was, in fact, still a point of pride for Lady Fairhaven, no matter how it had worked out.

The couple of strongholds marked on the map near the Wildewynnes were more than two weeks' travel from Haven. The ring of abrasions about Ash's throat was healing, but fresher than that. Zhey'd come from somewhere closer. Probably not along the coast, given the dust, and given the open relations between the coastal strongholds. They'd have heard if a Mancer was being treated like that. Hazel touched his own throat.

Holly coughed pointedly and pulled Hazel's hair. Hazel stirred from his contemplation. 'I'm trying to work out which stronghold Ash came from.'

'Hold on there, my love, you told Evie last night to advise Lord Vee not to make any formal announcement to Lady Fairhaven because secrecy has to be the play against the threat of Ash's old stronghold.'

'Zhey didn't tell me. I just…'

He'd seen the way Ash's hands had stumbled, when he'd outright asked zhem. And it'd seemed to him that Ash had been about to sign *Don't*. Don't tell? Don't fight? Don't make promises you can't keep?

Either way, they needed more time, and a few more signposts in the landscape of their ignorance, before they let Ash formally emerge into the notice of the purple. 'Kito, come here, please.'

She obligingly moved over to sit opposite them, and Hazel drew the tattoo for her and Holly on the back of the notepaper he'd been trying to order his speculations on. He'd given a rendition of the tattoo over to Evelyn already, but she'd been left none the wiser. As he drew it again, the layers of what he had glimpsed became even clearer.

It was a feather, glossy with blue and green and even a daring glimmer of purple. But adamant black lines overlaid the feather, slashes across the vivid colours. The lines both transformed the vane into the blade of a knife, and were some sort of symbol in their own right. Hazel suspected it was a highly stylised Mancer rune.

Neither of them recognised any part of the tattoo, the feather, the knife or the rune. Hazel asked Kito to show it around. 'But don't tell anyone it's from the Mancer.'

'Not an idiot, Hazel darling,' Kito said scathingly, before hopping over to another trestle. 'Hoi, you lot, I saw this design in a book and I want it tattooed somewhere the sun don't shine. Am I writing "goatfucker" on myself in someone's language or cursing myself or insulting someone's gods, or what?'

No one recognised it at the first table. Kito kept making her rounds as Hazel looked back at the map. A stronghold near enough for Ash to have reached them in perhaps less than a week, on foot in the worst case, but far enough that Haven didn't have a relationship with it. It had to be inland. There were some large and unfriendly strongholds in that direction.

Evelyn had probably already worked that out. No wonder she was frowning more than usual. Lord Valerian would be wearing the same expression by now.

Hazel deliberately turned his thoughts to the shape of his day. He'd trimmed the beard hair around his mouth this morning, for lipreading, but should take the time to visit the barber, clean himself up a bit more. He'd have to see Miriam in the infirmary; he'd run out of salve and his scars were itching. The one on his face had been a livid puce in the mirror this morning. He might have been rubbing at it in his sleep. He'd draped a wet washcloth over it, but the salve was better for soothing it. He wondered if the barber could cut his hair so as to disguise it, and shook the idle notion off. There was no disguising it.

Then he had the Hazel-darling-will-you list from yesterday to work through. The stronghold's undercroft staff had mostly been getting a look at the new Mancer, but the requests and complaints had been real enough, and fixing people's problems was almost as good as baking a pie for easing Hazel's mind.

He'd make Albemarle an apple pie, zheir favourite, to atone for yesterday's experiment with the pears.

Holly finished his braiding and patted Hazel one last time on the head.

Hazel went cross-eyed trying to glimpse the handiwork. 'Is this your way of reminding me I need to visit the barber? I know I do.' *A-yah, I really do.*

'No,' Holly said, drawing the word out expressively. 'Making you extra pretty today, love, the new Mancer can't take zheir eyes off you.'

'Hols, no.' Hazel was mortified. 'Zhey're staring because zhey're terrified of me.'

'What? No. Are you sure?' Holly moved with his preternatural speed, shifting from draped against Hazel's broad back to kneeling on the bench in front of him so that Hazel could better appreciate his righteous wrath. 'How very fucking dare zhey. Where is the little shit?'

'Come on, Holyoake, don't make the poor fucker scared of *both* the only Mancer guards fluent in Trade.'

'I just want a polite word or two,' Holly said, ignoring his own history, reputation and personality entirely. 'Or maybe three.'

Kito arrived back at the table, and tossed down the tattoo sketch. 'No takers. What's twisted your knickers, boy?'

'Hear this utter fuckery, Kay. That cheeky little Mancer shit—'

'Holly, stop—'

'*Hazel*!' His name was a rising wail, coming from the stairs to the sub-terrane: Second Jerome, coming up in haste, on the verge of hysteria.

'Albemarle,' Hazel and Holly said together, and bolted, Kito behind them.

Second Jerome led them at a run down the atelier hallway, his Mancy leg hissing as its springs took the strain. It gave the general direction of the problem even before he panted, 'Morano thought he'd show Ash the atelier, we weren't thinking.'

'My fucking relics, you weren't.' Holly sounded unimpressed.

Hazel spun Second Jerome around one-handed and shoved him back the way they'd come. 'Fetch Albemarle's blanket.'

He could already hear the noise up ahead, echoing around the atelier's antechamber. It was both startling—it had been some months since Albemarle had truly kicked up—and eminently familiar. The three of them burst into the antechamber.

Morano had at least had the minimal good sense to hold his ground between Albemarle and Ash, though he looked at a loss. Ash had zheir back to the hallway, and of course did not turn as Hazel and the others ran in, too engrossed with the threat to notice Morano's grateful glance their way.

Albemarle was screaming and beating zheir fists against the wall by the doorway to the atelier, which had been solely zheirs for all the long years of zheir tenure. Zhey could be forgiven, perhaps, for presuming it was, therefore, solely zheirs in truth. Zhey certainly had not reacted well to the idea of another Mancer crossing the threshold.

Even as Hazel sprinted across the antechamber, zhey abruptly flung zhemself at Ash, slamming stolid Morano aside.

Hazel, shedding petals, tackled zhem to the ground with ruthless efficiency.

Behind him, Holly would be grabbing Ash to hustle zhem to safety. He heard a series of sounds—a wordless yelp, a surprised curse, a clang—that he could only sort out when, holding the thrashing Albemarle to the floor with his full weight, he looked back over his shoulder.

He saw Holly, casually holding a struggling Ash in a headlock, examining a long, deep cut in his other forearm with blithe disregard for the blood already sheeting down his skin and dripping on the floor. Kito kicked a dagger aside and moved in, pulling off her scarf to wrap the gash.

Ash, meanwhile, pulled a second dagger, very well placed for stabbing Holly in the thigh.

'Knife!' Hazel shouted, but his friend had already twisted it out of Ash's hand and flung it across the antechamber, where it hit the wall and fell to the ground with another of those ringing clangs.

'Calm,' Hazel told Albemarle, and then lifted a hand and signed the same at Ash.

Ash flipped from looking as panicked and desperate as a trapped animal to as highly offended as a dowager handed the wrong fork at dinner. Zhey made a gesture which had nothing of Trade to it and yet clearly conveyed, *This fucker has me in a headlock, you dick, don't tell* me *to calm down.*

'~Set zhem down, Hols,' Hazel said, swallowing a smile.

'Nah,' said Holly. He gave Ash a shake. 'That's my sword arm, lover, you better hope I recover.'

Hazel didn't relay that.

'Stand still and let me bind this,' Kito snapped at Holly.

Second Jerome arrived and threw Albemarle's blanket over zhem and Hazel. They had worked out a long time ago that Haven's Mancer didn't sleep well unless zhey had a lot of weight holding zhem down, but also didn't sleep well if zhey were too hot from burrowing under piles of blankets. It was Miriam Vo, the stronghold doctor, who had thought up the idea of taking a thin blanket and filling it with the small metal links that usually made up chainmail. A great deal of trial and error had gone into balancing the need for weight verses the strength of the seams verses the noise of the filling, but the sewing staffers had it down to a fine art now.

Hazel felt Albemarle soften under the extra weight, zheir outraged shrieks trailing into whimpers. Zheir paroxysm was on its downward course. He squirmed out from the blanket and peeled Ash from Holly's hold. Ash immediately pulled away from them both, and then lost zheir scowl to give Hazel an odd look. Hazel remembered he had flowers braided into his hair.

Kito's scarf was already soaked. '~Walk Holly to the infirmary, SJ,' Hazel said. '~Kito, will you take Ash, please?'

Kito hesitated. 'To zheir room?'

'~To the infirmary.'

But when Kito tried to collect Ash's elbow, zhey shoved her away. ~I've as much right to the Mancer atelier as zhey do. Tell zhem.

Hazel didn't relay that either. Albemarle was not in a state to accept facts. '~Not the time to insist on it, Ash.'

~It has to be the time. Or zhey will never let me in, and you will allow it, because zhey're your Mancer, and I'm the interloper.

Hazel hesitated. Ash had both a point and the right to equal access to the atelier. And zhey had to work; zheir days of travel would have screwed tight the ravaging need to release Mancy. Zhey hid it better than Albemarle did, but that didn't mean zhey weren't hurting just as much as Albemarle would be if zhey were away from zheir atelier too long.

Hazel waved Kito to go after Holly and Second Jerome. To Ash, he tapped his index and middle fingers on his other palm, the [wait] sign. It evoked someone drumming their fingers in a cliché of impatience, and indeed, Ash flashed a suitably impatient look his way and paced about the antechamber, collecting zheir daggers with sharp jerks, radiating zheir displeasure.

Morano, shoulders slumped, had taken up guard position just by the antechamber entrance. Holly would have sharp words for him later. It didn't matter how long they'd kept Albemarle steady; an intrusion into the atelier was an obvious trigger and should have been recognised as such, especially by an experienced day watch guard. Hazel laid currency in his own head that First Jerome was about to be elevated off nights.

Rubbing a hand over his smooth scalp, Morano watched Ash hide the blades about zheir person. 'Should we be letting someone wound this tight have weapons?'

Hazel, smiling, held out his palm in invitation. '*You* take them off zhem, then.'

'Your sense of humour surfaces at the most inopportune times, Hazel.'

'Zhey'll let them go once zhey feel safe,' Hazel said.

At least, he assumed zhey would. He'd never heard of Mancers habitually going armed; that was, after all, what a Mancer Guard was for. He wondered if it had been zheir time in the outside world or in zheir previous stronghold that made Ash so grimly determined to carry those twin blades. Ah, well. Hazel had taken time to trust Haven himself; after the villagers he'd grown up among had shattered his faith in the kindness of neighbours, he'd had to make a conscious choice to trust the kindness of strangers. Ash would come to the same decision eventually.

He checked on Haven's Mancer. Albemarle had the blanket pulled up to zheir nose. Zhey sounded drowsy as zhey said, 'At least I never made any of you bleed.'

Albemarle had broken noses, ripped out chunks of hair, and torn skin in deep scratches, all of which had bled copiously. Zhey did not have much memory of how zhey behaved in zheir deepest paroxysms. And there was, of course, the accident six months ago. It was true, though, that zhey'd never drawn a weapon. Zhey wouldn't even countenance the idea of a weapon, let alone design or create one.

~Tell me what zhey're saying, Ash demanded.

Hazel shook his head.

~*Tell me*. Zhey slashed zheir right palm across zheir left so furiously that it made a clapping sound.

~Wait.

He got a very dramatic [expletive] in return, and bodily checked zhem from approaching the prone Albemarle. Ash pushed at him, and flounced off into another pacing circuit. Hazel had time now to note that zhey had zheir coat back, clean, with the lace at the cuffs sponged back to pure white, repaired, and starched.

~Trust me, please. It will not work to confront zhem directly.

Ash was employing the effective technique of refusing to look at him. Maya had done the same, when in a snit. ~Tell zhem I have the right to access.

'What're zhey saying?' Albemarle asked, muffled under the blanket.

Wincing, Hazel said, 'Nothing.' He'd hoped Albemarle would fall asleep. Zhey were usually left exhausted after one of zheir outbursts.

'What do zhey want to talk to me about?'

Hazel, scattering flowers from his hair, snorted. Looking down at Albemarle, he said, 'Albemarle, what do you think? Zhey want to negotiate access to the atelier.'

~Interpret, you shit!

Hazel added [pejorative] to the list of signs Ash knew, that [endearment] was not on.

'What if zhey're a spy?' Albemarle announced.

Hazel definitely wasn't interpreting that outlandish accusation. He didn't even know a sign for spying.

A stronghold might conceivably steal Albemarle's legendary journals, but they would do it no good. Mancy didn't work that way. Mancers only created projects using their own designs, and no Mancer borrowed ideas from others. Most Mancers struggled to hold back the tide of their own ideas long enough to design and sing one into being.

No, kidnapping was the primary threat to a successful Mancer. For Albemarle, with zheir brilliant theoretical mind but terrible practical performance, that tactic carried high risk for low return. And anyway, sending another Mancer to carry out a kidnapping would be beyond ridiculous, verging on obscene. Albemarle was being irrational.

That boded ill. Hazel had to force zhem back into the daily routine, let zhem sink into the security of the familiar.

He adopted his sunniest smile and the bright, almost singsong tone he used on Albemarle's worst days. '~What's on the schedule, Mancers?'

Ash looked at him like he'd gone insane, while Albemarle said, 'Breakfast.'

'~Breakfast!' He clapped his hands like the nursery teacher. '~Are we ready to go to breakfast?'

~*Fuck off*, signed Ash, while Albemarle sighed and said, 'I'm not actually three years old, you know.'

'~Oh, we're going to have *such* a lovely day together.'

~SIX~

Breakfast could have gone better, and could have gone worse. Hazel felt obliged to keep behind Ash as they walked up from the subterrane, in case the infuriated Mancer made a break for the atelier while Albemarle wasn't in residence. He left Morano at the top of the stairs, just in case, and sat next to Ash, ready to clamp a hand on zheir knee if zhey tried to decamp. Kito returned from dumping Holly in the infirmary, bringing Nightingale and First Jerome with her. Those three lined up on Albemarle's side of the table. Young Titus showed up and sat on Ash's other side, looking nervy. Second Jerome had disappeared to sleep off his night watch and morning disgrace.

Ash seethed zheir way through some congee, looking like zhey despised every scant mouthful. Albemarle placidly ate the same breakfast zhey always ate: toasted bread with plum compote and no butter, oat porridge with one swirl of honey and a generous spoon of cinnamon, a single salty poached egg with absolutely no chance of runny yolk, and three cups of pale green tea.

The guards ate what they could in between watching the two Mancers, alert in case Ash lunged for Albemarle's throat or Albemarle descended into another paroxysm from the way Ash was glaring at zhem.

The latter, at least, was unlikely. They were back on schedule, and Albemarle's feelings about the new Mancer's arrival, not properly acknowledged or expressed the day before, had now been relieved. Hazel had high hopes that access to the atelier could be successfully arranged—

—right up until they returned to the antechamber.

'I'm telling you, zhey are a spy and zhey are not to come into my atelier. Zhey're not even a Mancer, anyway.'

Now that Albemarle was standing, arms crossed, in front of the atelier door rather than snugged up under a blanket, Ash could read zheir lips well enough. Hazel assumed the go-between role anyway. Ash's frown deepened throughout Albemarle's flat statement, glancing between Albemarle's face and Hazel's hands, expression flickering from alarm to dismay to annoyance.

Zheir eyebrows went up at the last claim. ~I am so.

'Yesterday I said they have a new Mancer, and you said no.'

~I meant I'm not trying to replace you. They have *another* Mancer, not a new one.

'But you're deaf.'

Ash pointed to the atelier door. ~I'll show you how I work.

'No.'

Albemarle slapped zheir hands over zheir ears, and then shut zheir eyes for good measure when Ash tried to sign at zhem. Ash tapped zheir foot, producing a dramatic roll of zheir own eyes in accompaniment. The other guards shifted uncomfortably, ready to intervene if the altercation went beyond words.

Hazel pushed fingers through his hair, dislodging a last scatter of petals. '~Albemarle, time to share your toys.'

'No.'

A rising note elongated the strident single syllable and warned Hazel he couldn't push any further. He'd been about to invoke the covenant, as Ash was now demanding he do, but he changed tack, stroking his chest at Ash to ask for patience. Ash glared daggers but at least did not resort to zheir real ones.

Hazel made his tone cajoling. '~You know how to share, Albemarle. You share with Juniper and Asquith all the time.'

Albemarle had never shown any signs of desire for others. Zhey were much like Hazel in that regard. Unlike Hazel, zhey also showed no particular interest in romance, companionship, or sex for the sake of occasional physical pleasure. Zhey never interacted with anyone at all unless zhey absolutely had to.

But zhey did carry on a correspondence, or possibly an argument, with two other Mancers, Juniper and Asquith, and had for years, adding to long, detailed letters every evening, interleaving painstakingly labelled schematics, and then, once a week, slitting, folding and tucking the papers until they were sealed safely in what Albemarle called a letterlock. Zhey received the same in return.

Albemarle had had to suffer through a meeting with Lady Fairhaven about it: *You're not sharing weapons, are you, dear?* she'd asked doubtfully, and Albemarle had said, *I don't design weapons and Mancers don't sing one another's designs anyway,* and that had been that.

It didn't quite count as friendship. Hazel supposed that just as he registered some people as veritable works of art—Holly being the prime example—but felt no urge to fuck a work of art, Albemarle saw some people as books of wisdom, to be taken off the shelf when required, and reshelved out of the way as soon as zhey were done.

Still, zhey shared zheir work with those two Mancers, who shared in return. Asquith, a skinny and talkative Mancer with pale clear eyes that shone like topaz, had even visited once or twice, though never for long. Now that Hazel thought about it, Albemarle hadn't let Asquith into the atelier either. No wonder the visits were short. Asquith would have needed to go home, when the ever-present Mancy drive grew over-powering.

Albemarle said, 'Holly lets people into his room all the time, does that mean he has to let in who you tell him to?'

'Score one to the Mancer, a-yah,' Kito said, delighted.

'Don't encourage zhem,' Hazel said. 'Most of you lot can bugger off, we're all going to be doing double duty for a while, there's no point tiring yourselves out.'

'Says the boy who's supposed to be off-watch. Stop fretting, Hazel darling, and bugger off yourself. Me and Morano've got this.'

~Don't go.

Ash caught Hazel's sleeve, brushing fingers over the back of his hand, shaking zheir head and looking up at him with a hint of a plea hiding behind zheir frown. ~Please, Hazel. None of them know how to voice for me.

'~They'll learn.' Hazel caught Kito's eye. '~In fact, that's what you all should be doing this morning—taking lessons from Morano, he knows the basics and a little beyond.'

He wiped at his forehead. He was feeling odd, strangely warm. He wondered if he was coming down with something. Kito, hands on hips, looked like she wanted to keep arguing, but she gathered the other guards with a twitch of a finger, silently delegating Nightingale into position in the hallway as she led them out.

'Zhey can have the atelier when I'm not in there,' Albemarle announced abruptly, once it was just the two Mancers and Hazel in the antechamber.

~When is that?

Hazel drew Ash to the wall where one of the copies outlining Albemarle's daily routine was tacked. He tapped the mealtimes, the mid-afternoon training time when Albemarle was forced to sit outside, and the bathing time, signing the equivalents as he went. It was perhaps three hours' worth of the day. He tapped the blank space past the last items on the list—correspondence, warm herbal tea, sleep—to indicate that Ash could consider a nocturnal schedule should zhey so desire.

Ash bristled. Hazel laid both his hands over zheirs before zhey could launch another storm of signing.

Holly was very much in the habit of bitching about Albemarle in Trade to bolster his patience on zheir bad days, and zhey never reacted. But Albemarle had spent an awful lot of time near Hazel and Holly and Maya, and patterns interested zhem. Hazel would be greatly unsurprised to find out Albemarle knew more Trade than zhey bothered to let on.

Therefore, Hazel turned his back to Albemarle and stood too close to Ash, so his broad bulk would block Albemarle from seeing the flash of their hands. Body strung tense, Ash tilted zheir face up to him, irritable and anxious and touchingly hopeful.

He was feeling the unfamiliar warmth again as he lifted his hands. ~Take it. Take it for now. Let's get you past the threshold. Trust me, this is best.

Ash snapped, ~I decide what is best for me.

~It's best for Albemarle. You're correct when you say zhey're Haven's Mancer. You're our guest, yes, but that makes you just a visitor for now.

The Mancer stiffened further. Zhey looked, for a moment, genuinely hurt before schooling zheir features into proud offence. Once again, the haughty expression struck Hazel as familiar, brushing against long-distant memories.

He hardened his heart and added, ~Until you trust us, that's all you are.

Ash stepped back. ~But you keep the covenant, Hazel darling.

Not even Maya at her adolescent worst had managed such sarcastic signing. Hazel supposed it was those sternly eloquent eyebrows in conjunction with a certain angle to the swoop of the hands.

'~Yes, and that's why Albemarle is letting you into the atelier, aren't you, Albemarle?'

'Zhey can come in so I can show zhem what zhey're not allowed to touch when I'm not here.'

'Fine,' Hazel said.

He put both hands on Ash's shoulders to steer zhem, both so zhey would not rush in and startle Albemarle, and so that Hazel could easily yank zhem from harm's way if Albemarle happened to have failed to recognise zheir true feelings about zheir sacrifice.

Ash's slender shoulders felt rigid under his hands, and he soothingly stroked them before remembering, once again, that Ash did not know him, was frightened of him, and could not realise that his touch would never be anything but dispassionate.

He whisked his hands off and stepped in front of Ash instead, to lead the way slowly and, not incidentally, stay between the Mancers.

The atelier took up as much space on this side of the subterrane as the kitchen and baths together did on the other. It was illuminated by copperlits, larger than those supplied to the rest of the stronghold. The cavernous room contained five long and broad stone workbenches, looking like they'd sprouted from the flags of the floor. Each held one of Albemarle's half-completed projects, components and schematics scattered across its surface. A row of large wooden crates of copperlits sat just inside the door, waiting to be filled with Mancy. Uninterrupted by any windows or other doors, the walls held storage cupboards, cabinets and shelves, full of esoteric equipment, materials and abandoned projects.

Albemarle must have had, somewhere deep inside, some minor compassion for the plight of a fellow Mancer. Zhey cleared off the bench nearest the door, kicking a crate of copperlits aside and dumping the armful of contents onto another workbench.

'Zhey can have this. Zhey can't go anywhere else. And I'm locking up my work.'

Indeed, zhey scooped up a collection of what looked like at least five sketchpads, the latest stuffed amatl paper notebook, a tidy set of the leather-bound journals that recorded finalised designs, and a whole bunch of loose papers with rough scribbles all over them, and tossed the lot into a cabinet, already stuffed with more of the journals. Albemarle had quite the backlog of projects. Zhey slammed the cabinet door, locked it, put the key in zheir pocket and stood with arms folded.

Ash touched the bare workbench. Hazel had been ready for another bout of outrage, but instead he could see from zheir breathing that zhey were relaxing, pleased. He even received a shy but genuine smile, enough to light up zheir face like when zhey'd watched Second Jerome spin on his Mancy leg.

It was warm in the atelier today. Hazel wondered if Albemarle had accidentally set one of zheir copperlits to heat.

Albemarle edged closer, smacked down a blank notebook and one of zheir Mancy pens, and then stomped off to the workbench furthest away. That was about as magnanimous as zhey got.

'Zhey can take that and go away. It's my turn right now.'

Ash blatantly ignored Hazel's dutiful relay. Zhey picked a copperlit out of the crate Albemarle had so dismissively kicked. ~Broken?

'I have to charge them,' Albemarle said dolefully.

Ash, turning the copperlit over and over, watched Albemarle with zheir head on one side. Zhey couldn't have heard the misery in zheir voice, but Albemarle was visibly drooping at the very thought of the daily travail. Zhey readily complained about all sorts of petty-seeming injuries, but when it came to anything touching on Mancy and the atelier, zhey either refused or endured; this one, zhey endured.

~I can help. If you show me. And if I touch you.

Hazel stopped halfway through voicing. ~Albemarle can't let you touch zhem.

~It's the only way I can help.

~Then you can't help.

Tension crept back along zheir shoulders. ~It's the only way I can perform Mancy.

Hazel was flummoxed. He couldn't see a way to fix this. Albemarle would not tolerate touch, not unless it was very firm, very deep touch, a difficult mark for a newcomer to hit.

He had to sign, ~Then you can't perform Mancy here, Ash. We'll have to move you to one of the other strongholds in the coastal alliance.

Ash twitched, a compulsive shake of the head. Zhey looked, for a moment, horror-struck, as if all zheir plans had come asunder, which, really, they had. Just as quickly, zhey composed zhemself. Drumming the fingers of one hand on the bare workbench and trundling the copperlit back and forth like a rolling pin with the palm of the other, zhey looked between Hazel and Albemarle.

~Hazel, can you hold a tune?'

Hazel made [affirmative] with one hand and [query] with the other.

~Will you let me touch you?

There seemed no better option than to repeat the same two signs.

~I will show you. It might suffice. Please. Tell Albemarle to start work.

Hazel turned to Albemarle. '~Start filling up the copperlits, Albemarle.'

'Why are zhey still here?' Albemarle grumped as zhey clomped over to the crate.

The iron embrace of the schedule was cradling zhem, however, and zhey set to work, mood easing as the routine took over. Kneeling, zhey plunged zheir hand into the crate to grip a copperlit, and began the Mancy song for infusing it with the power that made it glow.

Zhey'd move zheir hand haphazardly from tube to tube during the song. It would take zhem most of the morning. Despite how absorbed zhey seemed, eyes shining and abstracted, zhey'd charge some copperlits twice and miss more completely. Zhey loved the song, but had so much disdain for the task itself that zhey could not be other than shambolic at it.

Haven's Mancer was, technically, very strong. Zhey were one of the few whose songs bore words, though Albemarle sung them in a sort of mumble, the way people sang when they only half-knew the words of a familiar ditty whose tempo was too fast to keep up with anyway.

That was the disconnect between zheir theory and zheir practice. It drove zhem wild, almost daily. Zhey loved it nonetheless.

Once Albemarle's body had softened and zheir eyes had closed, the pleasure of the song sweeping zhem deep, Ash turned to Hazel. ~Will you hum the tune? I will touch your throat.

'~Vibrations,' Hazel realised.

~Not just vibrations. It…feels different. Ash brushed a hand down zheir body, dragging Hazel's gaze with it. ~Here.

'~But Mancy can't come through me, even if I copy the tune exactly.'

~Let me try.

Zhey set zheir hand over Hazel's throat, zheir middle fingers spreading warm on his skin over the beat of his jugular, the thumb and smallest finger pressing against his collarbones.

Hazel swallowed heavily. He started to hum Albemarle's copperlit song.

Ash made zheir own humming noise, inharmonious, no melody or rhythm to it. Zhey frowned. Zheir grip tightened, inexorably, enough for Hazel's eyes to widen before he understood and allowed Ash to push him to his knees. His hand settled to zheir hip for balance as he went down. He made himself relax, and lifted his chin to further bare his neck to zheir hold.

Trust was everything between a Mancer and zheir Mancer Guard. He did his level best to radiate it.

Ash's gaze went to Albemarle, back to Hazel. Zheir lips parted. Zhey knelt too, and reached zheir left hand into the crate, mirroring Albemarle but still watching Hazel with those unfathomable heathland eyes.

There were, so ran the wisdom of the academy, two types of Mancer stares. One was the blank look Albemarle wore whenever zhey'd been diverted from the atelier, and that Ash wore when zhey were trying to hide zheir emotions; zhey were not as adept at it as Albemarle, perhaps because Trade relied too heavily on body language and facial expression for zhem to be able to completely take refuge in blankness.

The other was the intent, intense focus of a Mancer working Mancy.

It was this look that Ash had now as zhey stared at Hazel. He assumed it was because he, or the vibrations Ash was reading through his skin, had become part of the Mancy project. He felt flayed open, sliced through to his spine.

Kisane save him, it was hot in this atelier today. Perhaps he was falling ill. Perhaps he had a fever. He hummed louder, concentrating on precisely matching Albemarle.

Careful not to touch Albemarle's own questing hand, Ash managed to take hold of the opposite end of the copperlit tube the other Mancer was currently crooning zheir song at. Almost immediately, Ash's atonal droning transformed into a melodious warble, in the same pitch as Albemarle's song.

Their hand spasmed against Hazel's throat. He'd hardly ever been this close when Albemarle was performing Mancy, and never since the accident. The air smelled like a storm.

Ash's warble became, completely, the melody behind Albemarle's song.

Then Albemarle began to sing actual words for the copperlit song, clear and bright, unintelligible to all but zhem.

And then the whole crate of copperlits flashed like lightning, the copperlits along the walls momentarily flaring bright in sympathy.

Both Mancers toppled backward.

'Oh!' said Hazel.

'Oh,' moaned Albemarle.

Ash lay flat on zheir back and signed [expletive], which about covered it.

~Seven~

Hazel loitered to watch Ash and Albemarle working together on one of Albemarle's panels, guarded by Nightingale, who had literally dropped to her knees and praised her personal deity for the miracle she was witnessing.

The panels had been Albemarle's major project for six months. Zhey'd painstakingly created a prototype, which had shattered. Zhey'd adjusted zheir design and made a second prototype, and had it delivered to the stronghold's artificer, Malika Fa'avae, whereupon zhey'd received the unpleasant news that she couldn't reproduce it. Unlike the copperlits, which were ordinary, if pretty, metal tubes filled up with Mancy, the panels had Mancy woven right into them during the process of creation. Albemarle had to create every single one. Since the panels were intended to be installed in a continuous line along the inner side of the curtain wall, Haven's Mancer had rather invented a very heavy rod for zheir own back.

Between charging copperlits every morning, and meticulously transforming bronze sheets into the intricate ivy patterns of the rectangular wall panels, Albemarle's Mancy and its wild beauty had been caged to drudgery for months.

But now Ash was here, and Ash had found a way to amplify other Mancers' works to sate zheir own need. Together, the two Mancers had charged all the copperlits in the space of a few heartbeats, and now Hazel watched them produce two panels before Albemarle dropped the words —words!—of zheir Mancy song, staggered over to him, and put zheir arms around him.

It was stiff and awkward, but undeniably a hug.

'Thank you, Hazel darling,' zhey muttered, and went back to work.

The Mancers didn't need Hazel as an intermediary for this. The copperlits were of ordinary metal, but the panels weren't. Albemarle began at one end of the plain bronze sheet, bending over it with cutting and etching tools and muttering zheir Mancy song. As soon as a few inches, now transformed into the whorls and curls of the vegetative pattern, passed under zheir tools, Ash could touch the panel without touching Albemarle.

Hands laid on, feeling out the Mancy vibrations through the metal, Ash began zheir tuneless droning, which rapidly took on the melody of Albemarle's song. It looped back to Albemarle, whose mumble transformed into clear words in the strange language of Mancy, issued from a mouth that was wide with joy and a face that was beatific.

And a third panel slid from the workbench.

Hazel could have watched it all day.

'It's called mensuration,' Nightingale told Hazel. Then she blushed. 'At least, that's what my people call it. What does the academy call it?'

He silently contemplated this question. He supposed the Mancy researchers at the academy would indeed know about this and have their own word for it. They had all sorts of words.

But Mancer guards didn't go to the academy to learn Mancy theories couched in academic terminology. Holly and Hazel had never even entered the famously extensive library where Albemarle had done zheir research and chosen untried Fair Haven by the Sea for zheir stronghold. Forcing someone like Holly to sit still in a classroom was an exercise in frustration, and guards like Hazel were frustrating the other way, not too quick but too slow.

They'd endured a few lectures in between the more practical training, a vigorous course in disarming, disabling and dispatching with swords and other weapons, makeshift or otherwise. None of the experts at these sparse lectures had mentioned that Mancers could sing along with another's song, and all of them had undermined themselves by reminding the initiates that every Mancer was different so there was no point getting attached to any theories anyway.

When Hazel shook his head, Nightingale shyly explained, 'It's using the same melody, together, with secondary Mancers playing off the tune of the primary Mancer. It augments the Mancy.' She ducked her head, blushing again, and quickly added, 'Obviously.'

'Not all of them can do it?' Hazel asked, thinking that if that was true, Ash was lucky that zhey could.

Nightingale pondered this before saying, 'I can't see why they couldn't. But the Mancers have to work together, so none of them really want to do it, especially if they have to take the secondary role on someone else's design. They all hate that, you know. So mensuration is rare, but that doesn't necessarily mean the ability to do it is.'

Hazel, musing on this in his usual slow way, delegated Nightingale into position inside the atelier and took himself off to the infirmary to check on Holly.

The air outside the infirmary smelled disconcertingly of bitter herbs and astringent alcohol, wafting out through the open door of Miriam's extremely well-ordered domain. Holly lay on the high and narrow infirmary bed, drugged into compliance while Miriam strapped his heavily bandaged arm to his torso, because they all knew that incapacitating the limb was the only way to force Holly to rest it. Hazel was too late to mutter a traditional healing incantation over the stitches, a superstitious habit from the mountains that he'd never broken but which Miriam fondly tolerated.

It was always odd, to have the two people who'd broken his heart confined to the same small room. Only a tiny bit odd, because the twin devastations were such a long time ago now, but still, he paused in the doorway and ruefully smiled.

Holly had been predictable. They'd arrived at the same time, fleeing their separate cataclysms—the curse of the Hazlemeres' village to the north, the vicious civil war ripping apart the Holyoakes' province to the south. Hazel was an older brother, responsible and protective. Holly was a younger sibling, irresponsible and cozened. Evelyn, strong and well-trained, had been recruited straight into the stronghold guard. Maya, tearful and overwhelmed, had been relegated to the schoolroom, where the teacher made do with vague gestures and raised voice to try to teach her to read and write.

Hazel and Holly, just a touch too young for the stronghold guard, were sent to the stronghold's ornamental gardens to weed and rake and prune. Already bonded from their serendipitous meeting on the road up from the port, they'd become fast friends.

Holly—Rowan, then—had been contained at first, almost quiet, long enough for Hazel to learn to enjoy his cheerful company and to admire his rangy strength and speed. But his natural zest gradually reasserted itself as the warzone receded from the front of his mind. His flippant liveliness was the perfect antidote to Hazel's tendency for solemnity and solitude.

And his cheerful company and rangy strength and speed were more than merely enjoyed and admired by the more discerning of the younger stronghold inhabitants. He discovered, with some enthusiasm, sex, and that being Holly was far more fun than being Rowan.

Hazel supposed Holly just hadn't wanted his closest friend to feel left out. 'I've had enough of this unresolved tension between us, Hazlemere,' he'd announced one day, dropping his rake. 'Ravish me, darling.'

Hazel had been thinking about the brand-new Mancer Guard, hastily cobbled together in the wake of Albemarle's abrupt arrival at Haven but which Holly was still too young to apply for. He'd been thinking about the initiates Lord Florian was currently recruiting,

He said, absently, 'Thanks, Holly, but I don't think I'm attracted to men.'

He hadn't yet worked out he wasn't attracted to women either. Holly probably had.

'But have you considered that I can get us both off within three minutes behind this tree here?'

'That's fine, but have you considered that if we engage in mock sword-fighting with the rake handles on the lawn over there, Lord Florian can see us from his window and he'll probably insist on you joining the initiates when he sees how fast you are?'

'Your ideas are almost as wonderful as mine. Hazel, my love—it can wait three minutes.'

Hazel had hesitated, but only for a moment. He was sixteen; he didn't feel desire for any particular person, but he liked sex—the to-date solo practice of it—well enough. 'A-yah, suppose it can.'

Holly took him by the hand, smiling, and took him behind the tree, and took him in his mouth.

Holly had taught Hazel that he could still have perfectly pleasant sex even if he felt merely friendly toward his partner. Inadvertently but inevitably, Holly had also taught Hazel that he was capable of tumbling head over heels into love without ever feeling a speck of sexual attraction. And Holly had taught Hazel the grace of letting go of someone who was not, and possibly never would be, ready to fall in that kind of love with any one person.

Past the haze of adolescence, after the years at the academy, Hazel had loved Miriam with less intensity than he'd loved Holly, but perhaps more depth. Their relationship had lasted much longer, over five years. With the detached precision she exhibited in her infirmary, she'd seemed a good match for him. They'd settled in together. Miriam began to talk of children, though not for long.

She'd sat him down and explained, in her cool and measured way, that yes, she loved him, and that yes, at first she hadn't minded his lack of attraction to her, in light of his steady admiration and his readiness to bed her to her exact preference; Hazel took instruction well.

But she'd started to mind it, and she'd been trying for a very long time to not mind it, and now she could not go through one more day without having the person she loved look at her with passion in their eyes and kiss her like they wanted to.

He'd experienced the bone-deep pain of feeling completely accepted for who he was and yet understanding that acceptance did not translate, in the end, to anything more than tolerance. It was made bitter by that calm *trying for a very long time to not mind it*. How honest she had been.

That had been years ago; he and Miriam had made their peace, quicker than Holly had with her. Holly's reaction to the pain she'd caused Hazel was in direct proportion to the pain he knew *he'd* caused Hazel over their own affair of the heart.

For some time now, Miriam and Kito had been circling each other in a long and lively courtship that neither of them was taking overly seriously. Miriam was considering children again; he knew, from periodic assessing looks, that she was working her way up to asking either him or Evelyn for the obvious contribution. Only the tiny bit of tact she possessed was stopping her so far.

Hazel mustered a broader, realer smile for his past loves. Holly, long limbs sprawled, smiled dopily back, utterly stoned on Miriam's favourite poppy infusion. Miriam greeted him with twin kisses, delivered, as always, to the miniature constellations of freckles that decorated the apples of his cheeks. Her soft lips brushed the scar on the left side. He idly rubbed the spot after, while she plucked a few more blossoms from his hair.

'How's he doing?' he asked, resting his hip against the bed and smiling down at Holly.

Miriam opened her mouth to give one of her coolly precise diagnoses, but Holly snagged his coat and dragged him closer. 'What happened to your throat, my love?'

Hazel rested his fingers there in semi-conscious imitation of Ash. The Mancer must have left bruises. 'Show you later.'

'Oh, yes, please,' Holly murmured breathily and Miriam snorted with dry amusement.

'Settle down, Holyoake,' Hazel said, gently lifting Holly's hand from where he'd started tangling fingers into the hair at Hazel's nape and straightening out of reach.

'It looked worse than it was,' Miriam told Hazel crisply. 'Only twelve stitches. Rest for *at least* three weeks. No training at all until after the feast night. And see me daily to have it cleaned and dressed and salved.'

As she spoke, she was cataloguing Hazel, examining his throat before shifting her assessing gaze to the side of his face. 'Do you need more salve, Ari?'

Hazel touched the scar, tracing its length. 'It's not sore but it's been itching,' he admitted. 'And I might have a fever.'

Miriam looked surprised. She touched the back of her hand to his forehead. 'You feel cool enough. Last night, was it?'

He said, 'Maybe. Mostly this morning, in the atelier. Warm in the chest.' He pressed two fingers to his sternum. 'Radiating. A bit tight, maybe.'

Holly made a noise, something between a whimper and a giggle, and Miriam turned to him. 'Ask him,' he said, 'ask him who he's looking at when his skin feels hot and tight, Miriam.'

Miriam's immaculately arched eyebrows shot up. Hazel looked between her and Holly blankly.

'The new Mancer,' Holly supplied. He waved his free arm lazily. 'Ash.'

'I'm spending a great deal of time with zhem,' Hazel said, adopting Miriam's own detached tone, 'so it makes sense that occasionally these symptoms would overlap with zheir presence.'

'Have you felt any symptoms when zhey're not there?' Miriam asked thoughtfully, tucking a jar of her vervain and honey salve into his hand.

'No.' Hazel transferred the jar to a pocket. 'Why?'

She and Holly exchanged another look. Holly said, 'He's wearing my exact expression when Evie starts going on about the Mancer Guard budget.'

Hazel shook his head. They had an irritating air of amused conspiracy about them. 'We done? Can I walk him back to his room?'

Holly hummed approval. He wound his fingers under Hazel's coat. Hazel caught his wrist and helped him sit up.

'Go ahead,' Miriam said. '*Rest*, Rowan.'

'Holly,' Holly said. He half-hopped, half-slid off the high bed, his usual grace gone too languid to hold him upright. Hazel caught him around the waist and Holly slackened against him.

'I cannot be having with the nicknames, you know that,' she said sternly.

'A-yah, Merry,' Holly said, and earned a tsk and a flick of her finger on his shoulder.

Hazel guided Holly along the hallway, arm still about his waist. Holly took a few breaths. 'I can walk,' he said. 'I'm perfectly lucid.'

Hazel obediently let him go and he almost fell over. 'By the bones,' he said, falling into Hazel's arms. 'Lucid, yet out of control. Oh, Hazel darling, that's the best kind of intoxicated.'

'Aren't you always lucid and out of control?'

'How long since we've fucked?' Holly asked him, draping his whole length over Hazel, crowding him into giving way.

Hazel noted, with a mix of wry amusement and mild resentment, that Holly was targeting his weaker left side, using the intermittent feebleness there to bodily force him against the wall where the infirmary hallway opened into the lobby.

His friend slung his good arm around Hazel's neck. 'Since before the accident, right? Months.'

It'd been some considerable time before the accident. 'Oh, Hols, love,' Hazel said, gently chiding. 'You know what happens when we fuck.'

'We have a bang-up good time, my love.' Holly turned his face into Hazel's neck, nuzzling.

He didn't try to kiss him. He knew Hazel was indifferent to being kissed on the mouth; he could be downright repulsed by the very thought of it, on some occasions and with some people.

But Holly also knew Hazel liked the feel of teeth. He nipped and Hazel shivered.

He managed to say, 'And then I follow you about making puppy eyes—'

'Big melty gorgeous puppy dog eyes.'

'—till I get over it again.'

'I can always use a little mindless worship,' Holly murmured into the stubbled skin under his jaw, tickling, nibbling. 'And you could use a little distraction.'

Helplessly, Hazel tilted his head, letting Holly have his way, as he always did. He slid his hand under Holly's braids, around the nape of his neck, rubbing his thumb over the tender skin there. He knew what Holly liked too.

Absently, he asked, 'Could I?'

Holly laughed. 'This is going to be so much fun to watch, I can't tell you.'

'Watch *what*?' said Hazel, bewildered.

Holly made an amused noise and pressed harder, hand at Hazel's waist now, under his coat, then under his shirt, tracing spirals over his lower back. Hazel relaxed under his expert fingers, thoughts drifting.

People casually touched him, all the time, because he was safe and kind and helpful and the residents of Haven appeared to think that meant he deserved plentiful hugs despite it being a rather low bar for decency. He occasionally garnered real interest, from people whose objective beauty or intelligence or kindness sparked the aloof admiration of aesthetics that Miriam had grown to despise, but it never occurred to him to make an approach himself.

Sex itself was only ever a somewhat aloof act of physical release, an occasional need most easily dealt with alone. Hazel got himself in tangles trying to explain that without making his potential bedmate feel angry or unattractive or disappointed or used or teased or led on. Or, sometimes, the opposite, that he was suffering through sex for their sake, because they could not understand how he could enjoy the physical act without feeling desire. Pretending to feel desire never crossed his mind with any seriousness; he'd be awful at that.

The option existed, of course, for anonymity with strangers at the port, paid or otherwise, but Hazel found that truly dismal, at least partly because the look of him, big and brutish even before the scar, drew those with specific tastes that he only rarely felt able or willing to oblige. It all just made him feel tired. No aesthetics to any of it.

So it had been some time since he'd had a less casual touch, a more intimate touch, spirals drawn on his lower back by someone who wanted to fuck him.

Hazel could not physically desire Holly and Holly wanted to be desired, wildly; Holly could not romantically love Hazel and Hazel wanted to be loved, deeply. They were better, far better, as friends than as mismatched lovers pretending not to want what the other couldn't give them. Every now and then, Holly forgot the inevitable outcome, and Hazel was a little too addicted to gratifying other people's desires to ever turn him down.

Besides, making beautiful, responsive Rowan Holyoake moan and claw and gasp lovely filthy words against his skin was one of his great aesthetic pleasures. In his turn, Holly knew him and his foibles and how to make his physical release feel as good as it was ever going to.

Hazel was, therefore, well on the path to allowing Holly to take him to his room, strip him bare, and do as he liked—except…

'The offer's not poppy-induced,' Holly reassured him in his throaty murmur. 'It's Hazel-induced.'

That both made Hazel laugh and feel ridiculously flattered, which was, of course, Holly's intention. Holly was smiling down at him with full knowledge of his victory when Kito's voice rang out loud.

'Hoi, boys! Not in the hallways.'

She was leading the two Mancers out of the atelier hallway across the lobby, Nightingale behind them. The junior guards, Nightingale and Titus, had trouble making Albemarle keep to the schedule. It took someone like Kito to forcibly pry zhem from the atelier for rest and sustenance.

Holly gasped theatrically. '~Thank goodness,' he said, still draped all over Hazel, his one-handed signing awkward. '~This bastard was taking merciless advantage of me while I'm high as fuck on the poppy.'

Even Albemarle laughed at that one.

'~Fuck off, Holyoake,' Hazel said amiably.

He was, however, bothered to see that Ash looked anxious rather than amused. He abashedly removed his palm from Holly's nape; it must have looked quite domineering, a big hand clamped around a slender neck.

Holly signed, ~Just a joke, Ash. My arm's fine, thanks for your concern.

~You did grab me from behind, Ash pointed out. ~What did you expect me to do?

~Take it with a smile like everyone else.

~Joke, Hazel signed, very firmly. 'Holly, not with Ash, all right? Zhey're…nervy about that kind of thing.'

Ash had been watching his mouth intently, zheir tactic when Hazel stopped signing. Zhey looked irate at whatever zhey had gathered from lipreading, and from his face more generally; zhey seemed adept at reading minute changes of expression, as Maya had been.

At zheir glare, Hazel obligingly corrected himself. '~Never mind. Just nervy with me, actually.'

Ash's hands went to zheir hips before zhey flashed, ~I *did not* say that.

'But Hazel's the safest person in the stronghold,' Kito said. She signed [safe] and [Hazel] at Ash. 'Oh my stars, everyone knows he'll never misconstrue a touch for an invitation.'

'~Lunch,' Hazel said brightly. 'Sleep or food, Captain Holly?'

'I better eat, I suppose,' Holly said. 'And since I can't eat your—'

Hazel shushed him and Holly laughed and wrapped his good arm about him for another kiss at the juncture of earlobe and neck. They all walked over to the stairs to the undercroft, but Hazel quietly drew Holly back from the rest.

'I didn't realise the whole stronghold knows I'm a freak.'

He didn't usually think like that. He was quite sure most stronghold residents categorised him along the lines of an older brother, knowingly or intuitively, and it suited him perfectly well. It seemed that seeing Holly and Miriam together, those memories and the accompanying echo of emotion, had disconcerted him after all.

'So many things to unpack from such a short sentence.' Holly squeezed his fingers. 'Kito was exaggerating when she said everyone, you're not a freak, and Hazel, my love, it's not even slightly a bad thing to be recognised as safe.'

Hazel realised Ash had turned back and was watching them. Their heads had been turned toward each other, so lipreading would have been difficult. Still, he shifted uncomfortably.

'~Excuse me, this is a private fucking conversation,' Holly told zhem.

~Excuse me, I'm fucking deaf.

'~Spiky little fucker!' Holly said cheerily.

Ash gave a twitch that suggested zhey had not literally understood Holly's signing, which was lazy Haven slang, but got the message all the same. Zhey caught Hazel's eye. Hazel shoved Holly between the shoulder blades and sent him up to lunch. He waited.

Mouth set, Ash touched zheir throat, then touched zheir thumbnail to zheir heart and dipped zheir head. Hazel involuntarily skated his fingers over the bruises zhey'd left on him, but he waved off the apology.

~I should only need to do that when I can't hear a new song any other way, and I will be more careful next time.

'~Any time, Ash. It's no trouble to me. You're one of Haven's Mancers now.'

Ash hesitated. ~You didn't hurt Albemarle, when you knocked zhem to the ground this morning.

Zhey hadn't used [query]. It wasn't a question, or at least not a literal question, but there was still something puzzled about Ash's expression.

Hazel shook his head. '~Of course not. I know the Havens are informal, but we're trained to act for the good of Haven's Mancer.' Aware Ash was frowning fiercely now, patently unconvinced, he added, '~And both Albemarle and I are well-padded. We bounce.'

He gave his flank a comfortable pat to corroborate. Ash, following the motion of his hand, stared blankly at his thighs as if verifying the evidence. Finally, zhey started to sign something, but then tightened zheir hands into fists and shook zheir head.

Zhey gave him a smile instead, small but genuine. Hazel returned it, gratified for no reason he could identify, and led the way up the stairs.

At the table, all the other guards, under Morano's instigation and in rough unison, signed, ~Greetings, Ash, how are you, welcome to Stronghold Fair Haven.

Ash put knuckles to zheir mouth and looked so shyly pleased that fully half the Mancer Guard blushed in reciprocal pleasure.

Lunch was thus a far cry from the tension at breakfast. First Jerome and Kito even felt relaxed enough to start one of their long-running but low-drama arguments about the injunctions of First Jerome's religion.

'But *everyone* must be covered head to toe, no one's being singled out,' First Jerome said, as she had said before. She added, 'Mancers can do as they like, of course.'

'How does the sex go, then?' demanded Kito.

'It goes in the *dark*, after we're *married*.'

'How's that working out for you?'

'As a matter of fact, extremely well,' said First Jerome, whose wedding they'd all been invited to the previous month.

'Ooh,' Kito sang.

'Details, this instant,' said Holly. 'I never spare any of you poor fuckers.'

The discussion gave Hazel an idea. Eldemira, while technically ruled—more accurately, administered—from Glelissi, was a large continent made up of independent states, territories and provinces, all with an awful lot of idiosyncratic and highly localised traditions and beliefs. Hazel's village had been big on guardian spirits, godlings like foxy Kisane, to take care of the oddments that high pantheons overlooked. Holly's people turned their reverences toward their own ancestors. First Jerome had a single deity, Morano had at least five. Titus had none but followed the teachings of a prophet who said the deity was still to come. Second Jerome's sect whispered that that same deity had already been born, stillborn. Those two definitely didn't discuss religion at the table. Kito said she followed a celestial worship which involved nudity under the moon, but she was a bigger fuckster than Holly, so who knew?

Nightingale, meanwhile, came from a southwestern part of the continent that openly revered Mancers. Hazel couldn't tell if she was tongue-tied around Albemarle due to respect, shock, or disappointment, or if she really was just that naturally shy.

He signed at Ash, '~Are there any observances or rites you would like to have performed here, Ash? Meals or special days or clothing?'

The answer would give him a clue as to Ash's origins, and perhaps even the habits and inclinations at the stronghold zhey'd come from.

Ash paused in evident thought, raised zheir hands as if to reply, and then, straight-faced, signed, ~I don't remember.

Hazel made a show of slapping his forehead before bouncing the rabbit ears. ~Silly me.

~Silly you, Ash agreed, smiling.

Zheir silver hair had fallen over zheir face. Hazel would've liked to brush it back, feel if it was as silky as it looked, cup zheir chin and catch that mischievous smile properly.

'~How's that fever of yours coming along there, Hazel?' Holly asked.

He was looking highly amused about something. Kito mouthed, *Oh my actual stars*, and nudged Morano, who was gaping.

'~Fine,' Hazel said, nonplussed. '~I'm going to go make pie. Apple, Albemarle?'

Albemarle grunted zheir agreement.

'~Preference, Ash? Oh, wait, you don't remember.'

He gifted Ash zheir own impish smile. Ash's shoulders hitched and zhey let loose a single, sharp bark that startled everyone; Hazel had made zhem laugh. He paused to savour that.

He was feeling a touch unsettled again, that warmth glowing right at his core. Baking should help. He stood up to head to the kitchen.

Kito said, out loud this time, 'Oh my holy *stars*. *Holly*. Holly! Are you *seeing* this?'

'Run along, Hazel darling,' Holly said, waving with his unencumbered hand. 'See you at training.'

'My actual fucking stars,' Kito exclaimed yet again, sitting bolt upright. 'Holly can't train.' The remaining Mancer Guard turned their gaze to Hazel as they made the same realisation Kito had. 'We've got a chance at beating Hazel instead!'

'You've got a tiny little chance,' Holly said, 'but only because Hazel will be fighting lefthanded.'

'Ah,' Hazel said.

'You have to strengthen that side, my love, you know you do. You're all healed up, so stop putting it off.'

'~I'm nice,' Hazel told his comrades, walking backward away from the table. '~When we're in the spar, everybody has to remember I'm the nice one.'

'We're going to kick your arse, Hazlemere,' Kito shouted after him.

'No mercy, no surrender,' shouted the other guards as dramatically as possible.

'~S'not even our motto,' Hazel muttered.

~Eight~

The stronghold settled back into its routine and its new Mancer settled with it. Zhey started to eat proper meals, and to go to the baths, though not the infirmary, and to accept clothes and other comforts, and zhey didn't ask the price. Zhey helped Albemarle charge the copperlits every morning—Hazel was no longer needed there, now Ash had the tune—and worked with zhem on zheir panels for most of the day.

Holly said, 'You know zhey must have had a Mancer partner who is no doubt missing zhem *tremendously*,' and Hazel said, 'Hmm,' because he did know that.

After the mid-afternoon break, the two Mancers would come out to the bailey, and Albemarle would sulk and fidget while Ash quietly watched as Hazel at first barely held his own against, and then started beating, the other guards with his left hand.

Ash was more relaxed with Hazel now, at least when the other guards were around. He still tried to avoid being alone with zhem; his solitary attendance put zhem on edge. He tried once to teach zhem the Haven Mancer knock code on the atelier door, but Ash would not focus on his hands long enough to memorise the pattern, flitting glances at his face instead as if alert for any trace of threat. He was standing too close, it seemed.

He gave the task to Nightingale, and even considered switching with Second Jerome's shift, before deciding Ash would like the thought of him loitering outside zheir chamber door in the dead of night even less than zhey liked the early mornings when he was the only guard around.

On the day before the monthly feast, when Ash had been with them for three weeks, the two Mancers finished the last panel. It was the mirrored twin of the first successful one Albemarle had made, months ago. That one was designed to fit onto the lefthand side of the great double entrance gates. The last one fit onto the righthand side. Between the two was a tiny latch, which the gate guards would have to flick to link them. All the panels in between formed a continuous ring around the inner curtain wall, including more special panels for the small sally port beside the main gates and for the rear postern gate, with similar simple latches to maintain the link. It would have taken Albemarle months to finish it by zhemself.

'What does it do?' Morano asked Albemarle.

'Lady Fairhaven said she wanted a moat,' Albemarle said. 'We're too high and close to the sea cliff for an actual moat.'

Their lady probably had, in passing, at some point in the last decade or so, mentioned she liked some other stronghold's moat.

There was to be an unveiling ceremony at the feast, the monthly affair where most of the undercroft staff had the privilege and reward of a welcome up into the purple to enjoy an evening of music, drinking, and a lot of food.

'Bad news,' Holly said, slinking into the atelier antechamber on the morning of the feast. Miriam had finally given him leave to shed his sling, much to his own relief and the relief everyone who had to put up with him at his restless worst. 'Evie says Ash absolutely cannot come up to the great hall, not even disguised as a little old lady. We've got a lord from another stronghold visiting.' He pulled a face. 'I have to go as Rowan. The Captain of the Mancer Guard has to make a good impression.' A sour twist on the last two words; he was quoting Evelyn.

'At least trousers make your arse look fantastic,' Hazel said. 'That'll make a cursed good impression.'

'True,' Holly said, brightening. 'So Ash stays behind and a guard stays with zhem.'

'I'd volunteer,' Hazel said slowly, 'but zhey're still nervous of me when I'm alone with zhem.'

'Oh? Ash is nervous when you're alone together? I wonder why that could be.'

Hazel touched his sword hilt, and then the scar, and then his hair, which he hadn't yet had tidied, and then waved his hand to indicate the general breadth of his presence. 'Yes, I wonder.'

Holly did the same swoop of his hand, but with an appreciative expression. 'Yes, all that, my love, all that. Agreed. Why are you standing out here in the antechamber?'

'Oh,' Hazel said, uncomfortably. 'Aesthetics.'

Holly got the ridiculous smile that he, and frankly, the rest of the Mancer Guard, had been wearing lately. 'Aesthetics,' he echoed.

Taking Hazel's hand, he pulled him into the atelier. Ash was still where zhey had been when Hazel had walked in and turned about and walked straight back out again, tugging at the neck of his shirt because he was unaccountably warm again.

Zhey were propped on zheir elbows on the workbench Albemarle had so reluctantly given zhem, one of Albemarle's thick journals laid open in front of zhem, a copperlit sitting beside zhem.

Zhey were wearing an entire outfit provided by the stronghold seamsters. They'd carefully produced clothes that were similar to those Ash had arrived in, in that the outfit provided no strong gender indicators of the sort Holly toyed with so cheerfully. Close-fitting trousers, thin linen undershirt with silver embroidery lovingly adorning the length of each sleeve, a simple woollen vest dyed to Haven's green, closed with neat tabs. Lace-decorated coat set aside, boots and stockings discarded to bare narrow feet, undershirt sleeves partly pushed back to display well-shaped forearms, the muscle at the wrist flexing desultorily as zhey turned a page, intent. Zhey had the thin scars of Mancy work crawling over the skin there, too, like zheir hands. The tattoo Hazel had scared zhem getting a look at less than a month ago was on blasé show, its bright colours glistening in the warm light of the copperlit.

Zheir pale silvery hair had rivers of gold rippling through it from the glow. Zheir skin was made gilt. Also on full display, if under zheir light clothes, were the strong lines of zheir shoulders and back and arse and legs, thanks to the expert tailoring of the seamsters. Hazel wanted to stroke zhem from the top of zheir silver head, down the supple curve of zheir back, over the sweet mound of zheir arse, along the defined length of their thighs, up zheir shapely calves to zheir neat ankles and long feet. The soles were paler than the rest of zheir skin. Hazel wanted to clasp them in his hands, see if the Mancer squirmed.

'Oh, aesthetics,' Holly said, enlightened in an annoyingly ostentatious way. 'Yes, I see. Makes you want to bite it like an apple, really, doesn't it?'

'Can I ask you a question?' Hazel said, quite abruptly.

'Please do. Truly, Hazel, please ask me the question.'

'Could I possibly be—'

'Yes!' shouted Holly. 'Yes, you are attracted to Ash, you great idiot. By the bones of my *fucking* ancestors, love, you are stubborn sometimes.'

Hazel folded his arms. He was indeed being stubborn when he argued, 'But I don't do that, Holly. And if I was suddenly going to start…'

He wiggled his fingers at his friend, long-limbed and lean, a sculptor's dream, and especially beautiful right now, after he'd prettied up his braids the day before—not even Rowan Holyoake was audacious enough to monopolise the barber, or the helpful volunteers with nimble fingers, on the day of the feast itself for the hours his hair took. He sometimes set his hair into cascading twists for the feast, or had his helpers make what seemed like hundreds of exquisitely thin braids. This time he'd kept his usual style but dipped the lower halves of the braids into something that had turned them a coppery brown, and threaded in small beads of bright lapis lazuli. It was strikingly gorgeous, like Holly himself, and Hazel openly admired it.

Holly's face transformed from fondly amused to just plain fond. He ran his thumb over Hazel's cheek. 'Smooth talk, my love. You can't help who you want. Have you considered that you might not be attracted to men or women, but you are attracted to Mancers?'

'I never have been before.'

He looked across the atelier, over Ash's supine form to where Albemarle was pulling equipment out of one of the cupboards. Albemarle never turned the intense Mancer gaze on anything but zheir Mancy. It would have felt like taking advantage to look that way at someone who would never look back.

'Certainly not,' he added, repulsed at the very idea of such a gross invasion.

Even as he spoke, however, he had a barely conscious memory of meeting Asquith on one of zheir rare visits, bony and bespectacled, inky hair in a casual topknot, stark cheekbones, ready smile, intent topaz gaze. Some Mancers did look back.

'Not met many,' Holly said, merrily skipping to the end of Hazel's more meandering thought process. 'I'm not attracted to every man I meet, either. Or maybe, lightning struck and it's just Ash, and that's fine, too, Hazel darling. Zhey are delectable.'

Huffing out all his air, Hazel shifted his weight, trying to keep his attention off Ash. 'Is this really what it feels like?'

'Like what? Aesthetics that go straight to your groin instead of just being mildly pleasing for your eyes? A-yah. That's exactly what it feels like.'

'I hate it,' Hazel said. 'I don't know how any of you live like this, and I'm just going to ignore it until it goes away.'

'Yes? That will definitely work.' Holly wasn't even trying to hide his laughter. 'Or, you know, ask zhem if zhey'd like a fuck.'

Hazel had not considered a course of action that involved actually trying to bed Ash, who was made edgy by his mere presence. He hedged, 'I'm sure the Mancer handbook forbids relations with their guards.'

He thought the academy, at least, would have explicitly forbidden it, but their trainers had mentioned nothing of the sort. Having experienced the generic obsessive magic engineers known as Mancers in theory, and the specific obsessive magic engineer known as Albemarle in practice, Hazel had not seen this as an oversight until now. There might be an implicit taboo of the sort that went straight over his head, but Holly would have caught that and Holly—

Holly snorted. 'What handbook? If Mancers followed a handbook, our lives would be a shitload easier. Except it would be a single page with "we do as we please" scrawled on it in runes, and in this case, what would please Ash is—'

'Stop talking!' Albemarle shouted. They'd exhausted zheir patience. 'Quiet in the atelier, you know the rules.'

'The rules in the handbook,' Holly shouted back before adding seriously, 'Hazel darling, do *something* about it, because you're so distracted by that eminently snackable arse that you've overlooked that zhey're reading after zhey told Evie zhey're illiterate.'

While Holly, smiling his wicked smile, watched Hazel make this sinking realisation, Albemarle came stomping over, holding a round copper basin, hammer marks imprinted all over it.

'What handbook?' zhey demanded.

Holly nudged Hazel. 'Exactly my point, dear Albemarle.'

Albemarle's movement had caught Ash's attention and zhey looked over zheir shoulder to see who zheir fellow Mancer was talking to. Sitting up quickly, Ash tapped the journal, looking sheepish.

~Art, zhey signed, by which zhey meant schematics. ~I can read Mancer runes.

Hazel gave zhem a friendly and not at all sceptical nod.

~Albemarle said I could pick the next project.

This, Hazel felt even more sceptical about, but Albemarle said, slowly, 'I thought…that since zhey helped…it would be polite? Was that right, Hazel?'

When Hazel concurred that it was, Albemarle, again slowly and awkwardly, presented Ash with a single solid pat on the shoulder and retreated back to the far side of the atelier, shaking zheir hand like zhey'd burnt zheir fingertips.

'Aww,' Holly said. '~Zhey like you, Ash.'

Ash rubbed zheir shoulder with a sceptical expression of zheir own. After all, apart from just smacking zhem quite hard, Albemarle had only given Ash access to one journal out of the several dozens zhey were keeping locked up.

'~Sorry, Ash, you can't go to the feast,' Hazel told zhem. '~Which guard would you like to stay with you?'

Ash gave him one of zheir careful looks but then zheir gaze darted behind him, where Holly was leaning against another bench.

Holly, aloud, said, 'Don't choose me, I had my braids re-done for tonight,' but when Hazel glanced back, he was finishing off signing something that Hazel did not quite catch but which did not appear to match the verbal message.

Hazel signed, emphatically, ~Ignore Holly.

Ash signed, ~You, please.

'A-yah, Holly, you fuckster,' Hazel muttered. '~Very well.'

His hands were twitching with the need to ask if Ash was sure in light of the unease he inspired; Holly reached around in a loose hug to enclose his hands in his, quietening him.

'Take it, love,' he murmured, before wandering over to help Albemarle, who had started to pull equipment out of a cupboard.

Ash turned a page in the journal and looked dubious about what zhey found there. Zhey looked so adorable with zheir nose wrinkled that Hazel openly stared at zhem, mind blank. Apparently presuming curiosity, Ash nudged the book so he could see the page. Hazel obligingly peered closer. He probably had to get spectacles ground at some point.

'~Oh, that, yes.'

~This is a weapon of some sort? It's the only weapon I've seen Albemarle design so far.

Keeping his voice at a rumbling whisper, Hazel explained, '~It's the only thing remotely like a weapon you'll ever see zhem design. Zhey don't like weapons. But zhey really, really don't like wasps.'

Ash glanced at the schematic again and zheir signing went staccato. ~This is a…gun…for shooting…wasps…one at a time?

'~Don't laugh at zhem, Ash, it upsets zhem.'

Ash, looking at the design, did not appear to be paying attention to his hands, but zhey sobered nonetheless, schooling zheir features into the neutral expression zhey'd determinedly tried to wear zheir first few days here, before zhey'd relaxed into the care of Haven. Hazel was sorry to see it again, but it was his job to protect Haven's Mancers, and Albemarle needed protecting in a way Ash didn't seem to.

Lying back down, twitching one ankle in the air, Ash continued flipping through Albemarle's neat journal. Albemarle transferred designs from zheir working notebooks into the journals as soon as zhey felt they were complete. Zhey came up with far more designs than zhey had time to bring to fruition as projects, and Ash was taking obvious pleasure in browsing the menagerie of choices in just one of the journals. Zhey zhemself could not complete any of the projects independently, of course, because no Mancer could sing another's song. But Ash could sing another's song *with* zhem.

Hazel wondered if Ash would ever find a way to create zheir own designs. Zhey would surely hear incipient tunes in zheir own head, insistent, compelling zhem to seek out the resources and safety of an atelier. The sheer raw need of the Mancy, burning in zheir veins, insects under the skin, must have driven zhem to despair and impotent fury before zhey'd discovered how to satisfy it by amplifying, augmenting, other Mancers.

The Mancer zhey had left behind must truly be missing zhem.

He could see that Albemarle was restless, fretfully reorganising zheir equipment cupboards again. The stronghold went off-schedule on feast days, the kitchen staff overwhelmed with preparations, everyone else wrangling their shifts so they could visit the baths and harass the laundry staff and the seamsters and find time with the barber for a tidy-up. And Haven's Mancers had no project right now.

'~Come for a walk, Mancers,' Hazel said.

With the gentle push and firm pull combination he and Holly had perfected, they got Albemarle out through the dining hall's south door, by the alcove that led to Evie's office and the staff quarters. Ash obediently trailed along behind. The day was bright after an early drizzly squall, common at this time of year. The stronghold children were playing among the trees at the edge of the southern lawn, the blades of grass still damp.

The lawn was the setting for the legendary story—Lord Florian glancing out his office window one morning to see young Rowan Holyoake playing at swords with his friend, using their rakes. The sheer speed of the boy, the phenomenal natural talent.

The story was that Florian had run out the main doors and across the central courtyard to the gardens in his indoor slippers, frantic to ensure that the gifts of the gardener boy wouldn't be wasted for one more moment. Actually, Holly had been summoned up to the lord's office, blisters on his hands from the rake handle, the taste of Hazel still on his tongue. He'd not so much been offered a place with the initiates as informed he'd be joining them immediately. Lord Florian would have granted him anything. He'd asked for Hazel.

Hazel had never said it aloud, but he did think he might have been just as perfectly happy left among the gardening staff as he was in the Mancer Guard. Holly was needier than anyone would ever guess. He'd needed Hazel to come with him, and so Hazel had come.

They passed into the pleasure garden, the path leading them among shrubs that released drops of caught rain and fragrant oils as they brushed the leaves, and into the shade of the first grove.

'There's our tree, Hazel darling,' Holly said silkily, bodily bumping him. He went for the left side; Hazel didn't give an inch, and Holly smiled with lazy pleasure.

Hazel nudged Albemarle along the path, and they wended further into the carefully constructed and maintained wilderness. Here a glade, there a copse, there the natural-looking gush of a spring, its sound and scent filling the air.

Here a man chopping wood.

'Ah,' Hazel said, and took Ash's arm, turning to guide their little party away. Lord Valerian deserved privacy and Hazel wasn't sure he should be meeting Ash yet.

Holly, however, had not correspondingly collected Albemarle. He stood light on his toes, battle-ready, watching as Valerian, bared to the waist, rolled his broad shoulders and bent to set another log on the stump that was his makeshift chopping block. The muscles in his bare back and his tightly-clad thighs flexed hard as he lifted the axe and brought it down with a single precise blow, splitting the wood cleanly.

Holly watched. Holly liked strength and competence.

'It's like me with the pies,' Hazel murmured to him. 'He's done it off and on since his wife died. Less, lately.'

'Explains something,' Holly said, but nothing else.

Valerian must have heard the cadences of their voices amid the birdsong, or otherwise sensed their eyes on him. He turned and started to see them there. He set the axe down and pulled his discarded shirt on over his head.

'Good morning, Captain Holyoake,' he said as he shrugged into his coat as well. 'How are you?'

He was speaking stiffly; he was always awkward with Holly, if he couldn't avoid him. Holly took some people like that.

'Oh, you know,' Holly said. 'Busy.'

Hazel knew Holly; he knew that despite the disinterestedly polite tone, this innocuous reply was meant to fuck with Lord Valerian, and fuck with him it did.

He turned to Hazel and bluntly asked, 'Why are you not the Mancer Guard captain, Lieutenant Hazlemere?'

Hazel was horrified, both that Holly was deliberately antagonising their patron and at the very notion of taking the command; Evelyn, worried about the perception of nepotism, had already tried that one, before Lord Florian's written bequest served its purpose.

He managed a neutral, 'Not bossy enough.'

'This is our secret Mancer Commander Holyoake wants the bigger budget for?' Valerian waved to Ash exaggeratedly. 'Tell zhem—'

'Speak to zhem directly,' Hazel interrupted.

'Sounding bossy enough to me,' the lord muttered. 'You're welcome here, Ash Mancer. But any information you can provide that will prepare us for your previous stronghold's reaction will be greatly appreciated.'

Ash's eyes flickered between Valerian's face and Hazel's hands as he introduced him and relayed his words. When Hazel's hands stopped moving, he and Ash exchanged a long look, the Mancer's mouth quirking into its parenthesis as zhey couldn't quite resist one of zheir impish little smiles.

Lord Valerian looked between them, frowning, and Hazel realised he was smiling dopily back at the Mancer. He cleared his throat. '~Zhey don't remember.'

The lord curtly nodded as if he'd expected no better. Evelyn must have briefed him well. He did give Ash and Hazel another lingering look, before turning to Holly, eyes icy.

'Captain, I'll have a word.'

Holly folded his arms, immediately slouching, offering a curt nod of his own. Hazel caught his eye but he gave nothing back, so Hazel led the two Mancers away.

~Nine~

Back in the atelier, Ash tried to pick a project. Just as zhey were handing the journal, open to the chosen page, across to Albemarle, Hazel got a glimpse of the design.

He precipitously seized the journal and snapped it shut. Holding the journal closed between his flat palms, he was treated to a blank Mancer stare from the pair of them. He tucked the journal under his arm to free his hands.

~A moment of your time, please, Ash.

Ash followed Hazel out to the antechamber. Hazel shut the atelier door firmly. He wasn't prepared to risk Albemarle eavesdropping.

'~Albemarle already tried to create that design,' he told Ash. '~It didn't work. Zhey're a little sensitive about it.'

Zhey'd been catatonic for a week, was the translation of that polite fiction.

Albemarle had had a few projects turn out functional but not as intended, and a few unsuccessful prototypes that had needed edits to the design, the moat panels the most notable example.

But this, a far-scry mirror, was zheir only flat-out failure, a design zhey couldn't fix. The useless prototype had sat in Valerian's office since his father's tenure. Hazel believed the patrons kept it as a memento mori of sorts. On the very rare occasions Albemarle entered zheir patron's office, one of the Mancer guards went first and made sure it was covered.

'~I know it'd be handy, but you'll have to choose a different project. This one's a dead thing on Lord Valerian's shelf.'

Ash took the journal back from him, and opened it back to the far-scry design. Zhey traced over the schematic with a fingertip, eyes intent, vertical frown lines set deep. Hazel watched this with confusion. It seemed like Ash was trying to find the flaw in the design, but there was no point to that. The design's schematic could only ever approximate the Mancy singing in Albemarle's head. No other Mancer could fix the wrong notes in that song by staring at a drawing of it.

Handing the journal back, Ash signed, ~Mancers have created versions of this sort of thing before. Didn't Albemarle ask zheir associates for help refining the design?

Hazel raised his brows. The question was surprising on many levels—the assumption that the reclusive Albemarle must have associates despite every indication to the contrary; the subsequent implication that more Mancers than just Albemarle regularly wrote to each other; and then this notion that they could and would actively help each other hone their designs.

That Albemarle might have been collaborating rather than merely consulting with Asquith and Juniper was shocking. That Mancers could actually do that—could, in fact, help fix wrong notes by looking at a drawing of a song—was world-shaking.

'~Could they have helped Albemarle?' he eventually asked.

Ash must have seen something like alarm in his face. Zhey rushed to assure him, ~We can't create a project just from another Mancer's design. We can't hear another's song unless zhey sing it for us. But we can—

Ash rolled zheir hands in the air, before sighing, and producing a sign Hazel didn't recognise, along with a helpless little smile.

Hazel repeated [unknown] back to zhem, shaking his head to show he didn't understand it. He could usually pick out bits of known Trade in new signs, and make a guess at the meaning, but he couldn't make this one out at all.

~I know. I can't think of any way to explain it to you that doesn't use Mancer runes.

'~It's not—' What had Nightingale's word been? 'M-E-N-S-U-R—'

Ash caught his meaning and demonstrated a complicated sign that had elements of [song] and [together] and [speed] all mixed up in it. Hazel had to copy it a couple of times before he thought he'd remember it.

~No, it's not mensuration. [unknown] is different. Call it…tinkering.

'~Is ["tinkering"] a sign you and your Mancer partner made up?'

Ash was halfway through the affirmative nod of the fist before zhey remembered zheir amnesia and snatched zheir hand down. Hazel smiled at zheir guiltily accusing glare. He hadn't meant to trick Ash into giving anything away—he'd long since stopped bothering with that game—but that didn't mean the prickly Mancer wasn't fun to gently tease.

After a tense moment in which Ash understood that Hazel did not intend to chase after zheir lapse, zhey gifted him a rueful smile, self-consciously tucking zheir hair behind zheir ear.

'Oh,' Hazel said.

He lightly touched Ash's ear, always hidden under the fall of zheir hair before. The delicate lobe was scarred and notched, as if an earring had once been brutally ripped free, the tear healing badly. Hazel stroked the old damage with his thumb, fingers curled against Ash's warm cheek. He could feel where the ear had been pierced through the scar tissue, as if Ash had worn earrings after the injury too.

He stopped. Ash had assumed a careful stillness, accepting his touch in much the same way that prey might accept the slithering of a predator close by, because to move would be too dangerous. Zhey were looking up at him with wide eyes and parted lips.

Hazel snatched his hand back, muttering a heartfelt, 'Fuck,' under his breath. He was once again appalled at himself. He touched plenty of people casually, habitually, and plenty of people touched him in the same comfortable way. But Ash was not those people.

'~Sorry. Surprised. What happened there?'

Zhey pressed a hand to the ear, squeezed the lobe and felt the edges of the notch. Zhey flicked him a glance, then, shrugging, untucked zheir hair to hide the ear again. Zhey held out one hand until Hazel understood and returned the journal to zhem. Zhey riffled through the pages and held up an alternative design for Hazel's nod.

As soon as zhey received his nod, zhey went back into the atelier to show it to Albemarle, who had just finished zheir reorganisation. Stepping back, the senior Mancer showed no sign of approval nor disapproval, but together, they set to work laying out their materials and tools.

Hazel kept a close eye on this, but Ash mildly followed Albemarle's impatient instructions, reading lips and gestures and body language. Zhey must have been very familiar at following the lead of another Mancer; if zhey felt any resentment over it, it did not show.

The other guards came and went, showing off outfits for the feast. Kito wore her brightest colours. She'd dyed her hair in blue streaks, as glossy as the peacock hues on Ash's wrist, and had it trimmed to the precise line of her slashing cheekbones, razor-sharp.

Hazel smiled at this and Kito patted his cheek fondly and said, 'Aww, do I meet your aesthetics, Hazel darling?'

He said, 'You know you do.'

First Jerome was in her usual mantle, but she'd put on a perfumed veil of a shimmery material and blackened her eyelashes. Her partner worked in the bakehouse off the kitchen and would meet her upstairs, also in mantle and veil. Morano was playing it safe in his dress uniform; he'd freshly shaved his head and looked like he might have polished the scalp, and he smelled nicely of bergamot and rosemary. Second Jerome wore a traditional ensemble of his people, long tunic and loose trousers, lots of gold bangles on both wrists, heavier on the eyeliner than usual. His outfit was plain cream, but since the Haven seamsters never saw an expanse of material they didn't want to embroider, it was covered in bottle-green and gold stitching in elaborate swirling patterns of wild ivy.

The juniors had gone to some trouble with hair and clothes and cosmetics and jewellery and perfume. Titus, local to Haven, was in an elaborately elegant collared dress with a long green overrobe. Nightingale had likewise fallen back on tradition; in her case, her silken pink and yellow robes were suspiciously akin to the formal Mancer robes, except with much more material left to drape at the sleeves and a wide sash, green, wrapped around her waist to show off her figure. She'd put her long black hair up in a topknot and decorated it with a comb inset with glinting topaz.

Both looked nervously excited to receive an approving smile from Hazel. All the guards knew about his aesthetics, if not, perhaps, precisely the reason for them.

Titus lingered after Nightingale had gone to finish her last preparations. 'Are you certain you wouldn't like me to take the watch tonight, Hazel?' she asked. 'I'm not sure I deserve…' Hazel waited. 'Well, I'm not really…'

She had been recruited to the Mancer Guard under such trying circumstances. It must have been difficult for her, over the last six months. He recalled she'd volunteered to stay behind, the couple of times Albemarle had refused to go to the feast, and the other guards had let her. He should have been paying more attention.

'Yes, you do deserve to go,' he told her gently. 'Yes, you really are Mancer Guard, Titus. New doesn't mean unworthy. Don't cry, you'll smear your eyes.'

She sniffed and laughed. 'Thanks, Hazel darling.'

She wrapped her arms around him for a hug and he kissed her forehead. He was aware of Ash watching quietly.

Holly came to chivvy Albemarle into washing zheir face and dressing for the feast. The traditional robes were an impossibility; Albemarle hated them no matter what material the seamsters tried. Something about the way they sat on zheir body bothered zhem immensely.

Eventually, the ever-optimistic and inventive seamsters had presented zhem with a version of the Haven Mancer Guard coat, loose and voluminous and without the linen armour layers or leather rein-forcement patches, and none of the hidden pockets and seams designed to squirrel away secret weapons and tools. More cloak than coat, it was what zhey wore whenever zhey had to appear at formal occasions, a rare inconvenience.

With a visiting lord, zheir presence would have been very politely required by Lady Fairhaven tonight even if zhey weren't inaugurally lighting up zheir moat. Nonetheless, it was perennially difficult to drag zhem away from a new project, and there was no resorting to the schedule when Albemarle very well knew there had not been a schedule today and that Ash had been excused from going.

'~*Banned* from going,' Holly corrected.

Eventually he promised plenty of crispy, spicy fishcakes at the feast, indigestion be damned, and Hazel promised to bake an apple pie with the amount of cinnamon that annoyed the quartermaster and made everyone else gag, and Albemarle was jollied into leaving the atelier.

Hazel stood in the antechamber, half-hearing and half-sensing the tide of lower staff streaming up from the subterrane working areas and out of the undercroft living areas, making for the corkscrew stairs up to the purple for their evening with Them Upstairs. He could hear the distant babble of excited talk, the susurration of cloth brushing against cloth, the soft ticktock of high-heeled shoes clicking against the flags, the murmuring river sound of a happy crowd on the move.

Holly delivered two covered plates from the kitchen. He laid them out on a workbench in the atelier, with wine, and a small copperlit, and some flowers in a vase, all arrayed on a snowy linen tablecloth.

He poured the wine for them, saying, 'Let's find out if Ash can hold zheir liquor, shall we?'

Hazel suspected Ash was one of those unlikely sorts who'd be able drink even Kito under the table. 'A-yah, that's quite enough, fuckster,' he said. '~Have a lovely evening, Holly. Do all the things I wouldn't do.'

His friend was decked out in a tight butterfly-bright coat, shimmery with silken blue and silver, and a whole lot of extra jewellery, silver and lapis lazuli, to make up for the trousers Evelyn had made him wear. His copper-dyed braids, threaded with the matching lapis lazuli, set off his ensemble to perfection.

'~Plan to,' Holly sang, casting a hand over himself, because he knew he was a vision.

He caught Hazel's hands, set them on his own snaky hips and nudged him into giving him a whirl about the atelier, their bodies moving in the accord of long and easy familiarity. Ash watched solemnly.

'Ah, you're gorgeous, you know it,' Hazel said, releasing him with a pat on his leanly toned arse.

'~Can you dance, Ash?'

While Hazel gave Holly a somewhat harder flick on the arse—the absolute *fuckster*—Ash shook zheir head.

Holly, by no means dissuaded, smiled. '~No? Hazel will show you how. Put your head on his chest and he'll sing you a song too. He's got a lovely voice.' He patted his chest with a flat palm, simulating vibrations. '~You can tell that, can't you?'

'I will murder you,' Hazel said, arms akimbo. 'Don't think I'm not capable of it, Holyoake.'

'~Dessert awaits in the kitchen. If not already here, yes?' Holly winked and danced out.

And then Hazel was alone, truly alone in the subterrane, with Ash, who looked at him with zheir depthless sage-green eyes. Zhey were, Hazel thought, already nervous, and why wouldn't zhey be, with him randomly groping zheir earlobes at the slightest provocation?

He ran a hand through his hair. '~I'll eat out in the antechamber, if you're not done with your set-up and want to keep working.' He collected his plate to make good on his offer, then put it down to add, '~We don't expect you to keep working.'

He picked up his plate again. Ash took it from him and plonked it back on the table. ~Take off your coat and eat with me.

After a moment of silence, zhey added, ~Please, though with an imperious look that made it clear the courtesy was only offered under the duress of Hazel's bemused look.

Smiling, he found a couple of stools tucked under the back work-bench—Albemarle preferred to work standing, and hadn't offered Ash a seat—and brought them over to their makeshift dinner table. He obediently hung up his coat, and they sat across the workbench from each other and uncovered their plates, full of samples from the array destined for the refreshment tables in the great hall: slices of tender meat on dark chewy bread, tiny soup-filled mushroom dumplings, grilled vegetables, spicy seafood titbits.

They ate in companionable quiet until Hazel set his spoon down to sign, '~What did Holly tell you, to make you pick me for tonight?'

~He didn't make me. He said everyone else would be disappointed to not go to the feast, but you wouldn't mind. He didn't make me, though, Hazel.

Hazel nodded. He could have guessed Holly would spool out that manipulation. It hadn't even been wrong.

~Have you known Holly long?

'~Almost twenty years. We walked up from the port together, me and Maya, him and Evelyn. Us from the north by the coast road, them from the south by ship. Happy coincidence.'

Ash nodded, zheir smile rueful. ~Who is Maya?

Zhey repeated Maya's sign with care. It started the same as Hazel's sign but then twisted. She was [nut] and [rabbit] together.

~M-A-Y-A, Hazel fingerspelled. '~My sister. Deaf from birth.'

Hazel finished signing [sister][deaf][always] and Ash waited, very still, watching his hands. Zhey looked searchingly up at his face. It took him a moment, and then he understood.

Trade had developed, or was developing, from the simple signs used by the Sbalosi traders. One of its current idiosyncrasies was that it indicated past tense at the very end of a sequence. Ash was expecting to see [past], or perhaps even a blunter sign.

'~Ah. Maya's not dead. She's just not here in Haven. She moved away, a long way away. She's perfectly happy and healthy. I've got three niblings. More by now, maybe.'

She'd married while Hazel was at the academy. Then her new husband had inherited a bakery in a town in the southwest, Trifold, from a great-uncle. It had been sudden. It had been a stroke of extraordinary fortune. They'd have been fools not to go and claim a solid livelihood like that. But it made the wedding practically an elopement. Hazel hadn't had time to get back to Haven for goodbyes.

Now they were busy, running the bakery and raising their children. They were busy. There never seemed a good time to take the weeks it needed to go visit, to impose, to leave the others with Albemarle, to deny them their rostered time off.

Maya had her own life. He had his own life. He got a letter, every now and again.

~I'm sorry, Ash signed.

'~Why?'

~You're sad.

'~It is what it is,' Hazel said with a shrug that felt a little big for his body. '~It was my job to make sure she's safe and happy. I'd be a complete arsehole if I was sad that she's safe and happy somewhere else, right?'

Ash was giving him a studiously blank look. He shifted uncomfortably and looked down, watching his blunt fingers make the signs. '~Maya is why Holly and I are fluent with Trade when the others aren't. Why our Trade is a bit…quirky.'

And why Hazel continued to speak aloud, even though they were alone, to give Ash the context of lipreading for his signs, or vice versa.

The quick movement of Ash's own hands, always a pleasure to watch in their fluid elegance, drew his attention up again. ~Hazel darling. You can be sad, and proud, and brave enough to let her go, all at the same time. I wish—

But Ash decided not to share what zhey wished. Zhey pushed zheir plate aside and leaned across the narrow bench to run a tentative finger down the scar on Hazel's face, a strange echo of Hazel's stroke of the gnarled scar tissue of zheir earlobe earlier.

~When did this happen, then?

The touch of Ash's fingertip on his skin rendered Hazel speechless, motionless. He wanted to turn his face into Ash's hand, to ask for more. He reminded himself that people touched him because he was safe to touch, and therefore he had to *be* safe. He *was* safe. Actually feeling attraction didn't change that.

Ash was waiting for an answer. He was aware that he had repeatedly asked Ash about their past, and was signally failing to share the same.

Giving a soft cough to clear his throat, he said, '~This was a Mancy accident, about six months ago. Albemarle's first panel, the prototype, shattered. I was struck by shards.'

He indicated the left side of his body, from his face all the way down his torso to his hip, hidden behind the table.

Ash made a gesture of acknowledgement, an absent movement of zheir hands. Zhey had the vertical lines of zheir frown between zheir eyes.

Hazel rushed to reassure zhem. '~I knew I couldn't be injured too badly, because Albemarle went straight back to work.'

Afterwards, Schulze had quit. He'd been the Mancer guard due to relieve Hazel, and came running in upon hearing the explosion just as he'd entered the antechamber. He'd found Hazel, dazed with pain on the floor, gushing blood, and Albemarle placidly adjusting zheir design to better match the Mancy song in zheir head.

'I can't devote my life to someone who doesn't care if we live or die,' Schulze had said. 'I can't even look at zhem, Hazel.'

He'd moved his whole family down to the port, and was working guarding trade caravans now. Titus, then a stronghold guard, had been chosen as the first new initiate since Nightingale two years before, when Obenga retired.

Ash was still frowning. Again, zhey signed, ~I'm sorry.

Hazel shrugged. '~That's the nature of a Mancer, yes?'

Ash started to sign, stopped, started again, then pressed zheir hands to the benchtop, tense enough that the tendons stood out. Zhey couldn't, Hazel guessed, bring zhemself to admit that the only answer was the nod of the fist that was [affirmative/truth].

He'd been watching Ash's hands for three weeks. They were usually in motion, talking or performing Mancy. When stilled, Ash tended to hold zheir left hand cupped over zheir right.

He had to wonder now if zhey did that habitually to hide the full extent of the damage: the ring finger on zheir right hand had been broken and not properly splinted, an exact match to the injury he had previously noted on zheir left hand.

He realised he was touching the long scar on his face. He lowered his hand, ventured a smile. '~Mancy accident yourself?'

Ash followed the jerk of his chin to those crooked fingers. Zhey shook their head, made the fist. Again, the tense hesitation, before zhey signed, ~But the hair was.

Hazel almost reached across the table to touch the silky-looking strands, let them run through his fingers like water. He tugged a lock of his own mess of a mane. '~Mancy turned your hair silver?'

Ash smiled zheir small yet immensely mischievous smile. ~Grey. Instantly. We went awry.

He didn't miss the reference to a past Ash claimed not to remember. He didn't miss the reference to a 'we'. He also did not miss that Ash had deliberately chosen to share these details with him. He didn't want to pay back the tentative trust by stomping all over it, so he elected not to point it out at all.

He said instead, '~At least it was a pretty accident,' and then winced, because what had sounded like gallantry in his head sounded cursed stupid aloud.

Ash gave a soft puff, laughing. ~Flattery, Hazel darling?

'~Poorly done. Sorry. I'm not the most eloquent of people.'

The Mancer's smile faded as zhey stared at Hazel. ~You've been at Haven twenty years?

It felt like a change of subject, and not. '~Except a few years at the academy. We'd— *I'd* found where I belong and I didn't want to go anywhere else. The same stronghold and the same job for twenty years.'

It probably sounded deathly dull to Ash, though it wasn't unusual; most people stayed within a few miles of where they were born. A few travelled willingly across the continent and even over the seas, seeking work or on pilgrimage or through simple wanderlust. But the great plague of a few generations ago had made remnant populations static and travel rare, expensive and dangerous.

People tended not to do it, unless they had to, and then they fled to a place like Haven.

Hazel cleared his throat. '~We… My village wanted to sacrifice Maya to appease the local harvest spirits after a few failed harvests. We had to leave. Haven… Haven was a good place to come to. It still is.' When Ash responded with a look he could only read as appalled, Hazel added, '~It sounds awful, I know. That's why I don't tell it so often. They were just normal people who got frightened and were steeling themselves to do what they thought they had to do, that's all.'

Ash's unblinking look faltered. Zheir expressive eyebrows angled. ~You seem like you forgive them for a terrible choice?

'~I do. That's not to say I was thrilled about it all, not then and not now. Our father's likely passed by now, but we'll never know. We're never going back. I won't forget. But I do forgive. It's no way to live, otherwise.'

Ash nodded, very slowly. Face abstracted, zhey vanished into zheir thoughts.

'~I suppose I'm just trying to tell you Haven is safe, no matter where you've been before,' Hazel said diffidently.

Zhey nodded again, and looked at him, intently. Then zhey signed, in a flurry, ~I was born in a stronghold. I was in the same stronghold for thirty years. I'd never left before now.

Zhey dropped zheir hands to zheir lap and hunched zheir shoulders, but kept zheir gaze steady on him, waiting.

Mancers were uncommon enough as it was. For a stronghold to be lucky enough to acquire one from birth… They should have heard of it. He hadn't, and surely it would have been spoken of at the academy. But he didn't think Ash was lying or even exaggerating. *Oh, I was actually born in a village right near a stronghold.* No. If zhey said zhey were born in a stronghold, that's what zhey meant.

Hazel was feeling his way forward, like a man crossing a stream of unknown depth, carefully probing the slippery stones underfoot. '~Rare,' he said. '~For a Mancer to be born where zhey need to be.'

~Not where zhey *want* to be, Ash signed, a certain defiant set to zheir mouth practically begging Hazel to argue.

Holly might have, but Hazel didn't. The official line at the academy was that Mancers did not care which stronghold took them in; thus, it was tactical for a stronghold to use a Mancer Guard to abduct one. Since there only about fifty or sixty Mancers at any given time scattered across Eldemira, but already some eighty registered strongholds—and ever more ambitious purple looking for promotion from lord of a manor to castellan of a stronghold via building an atelier, guaranteeing a patron, and signing the covenant—supply and demand made conflict inevitable. And a successfully abducted Mancer would never complain of a covenant violation if the new atelier was well stocked.

The bitter truth was that Mancers were so driven to turn idea-songs into designs and designs into projects that there was almost no mistreatment they would complain of, if the atelier and its materials and equipment were good enough.

It was what it was, and there was little to be done about it except to mitigate it as much as possible: the Mancer Guard, the academy taught, protected its Mancer, not merely from external threats, but from the stronghold hierarchy if necessary.

It mostly worked, *if* the Mancer made a good choice of stronghold when the acidic obsession first crawled under zheir skin.

And that was the fantasy on which the academy tripped, decades if not generations of tradition accreted over that one assumption. Mancers almost never had the willpower to pause long enough to choose a stronghold. They just went to the most convenient one.

Albemarle was rare, in deliberately choosing Haven. And here was another rare one, choosing Fair Haven by the Sea.

Ash had been where zhey didn't want to be. So zhey'd left and established covenant with Haven. Zhey didn't think zheir original stronghold would be greatly happy about it, or zhey wouldn't have hidden which one it was, wouldn't still be hiding that one salient fact despite finally trusting Hazel with most of the truth.

With great reluctance and a corresponding lack of hope, Hazel silently signed, ~Which stronghold, Ash?

Ash shook zheir head.

~Please, Ash. We need to know so we can be ready to protect you.

~If they find me, you cannot protect me. Knowing won't help you. You must be able to say you did not know. That's how *I* protect *you.*

~It's a big stronghold, then.

Ash's face went stubbornly blank; zhey clenched zheir hands together.

Hazel tapped the benchtop, two quick beats with his open palm. Smiling, he said, '~I'll fetch dessert, shall I? Before one of the mousers skulk in.'

He was on his way back out of the kitchen carrying two bowls of sweetened baked yam—indeed, he'd shooed off a scrawny kitchen cat just in time—when every copperlit went out, leaving him in pitch blackness.

~TEN~

THE DARKNESS WAS ABSOLUTE. Hazel could not see his own hand, even after he'd dropped the bowls to crack on the flags and raised his fingers to right in front of his eyes. No natural light reached into the subterrane, and there were no candles or lamps, not with the copperlits so convenient.

The venting, also Mancy-driven, must have shut off, too. The airless dark felt like a physical force wrapping about him and squeezing, like ropes and a blindfold and an unknown captor. He could hear his own heavy breath, and that was all, as if the velvety darkness had muffled all other sounds.

This recalled Hazel to his responsibilities; no matter how startled he was, Ash, who didn't even have the benefit of hearing zhemself breathe, would be worse off. He should never have left his Mancer alone. The complacency of years of mostly uneventful service had lulled him shamefully.

He groped till he found the wall to his left and used it as his guide, moving at a rapid march. He sensed the reprieve from the close weight of stone as he came out into a larger space, the lobby where the radiating hallways of the subterrane converged. The hallway to the laundry and baths and infirmary would be to his right, then the curve of wall to the broad stairs to the dining hall. He kept his hand on the wall and followed the curve the other way, to the first gap, the archway leading to the guards' quarters. He crossed it and went on. The next gap marked the hallway holding the Mancer chambers. He crossed it. The next was the way to the atelier.

He briskly followed its wall down, crossed the empty antechamber, bounced off the wall on the far side, and fumbled along till he found the atelier door.

Inside, he immediately heard Ash's breathing, loud and harsh and low, further to the rear of the atelier than their dinner setting. The Mancer was panicked, and on the floor, either fallen there in zheir blind attempt to flee, or crouching in hiding. Hazel forayed into the dark in as direct a line as he could manage, crashed into a bench, tripped over a crate, and fell onto a warm body that he just had to hope was Ash.

Ash let out what could only be called a squeal, and flailed an arm about.

I, thought Hazel, very distinctly, *am about to get stabbed.*

He whipped his hand up Ash's arm in time to grab zheir wrist and press it to the floor. It flexed under his hand; Ash's whole body tried to thrash and Hazel held zhem down with the brute force of his own torso and legs, sword hilt tangling between them. He squeezed the wrist until he felt the muscles release, and then tore the dagger from zheir lax hand and tossed it away.

He was saying, ridiculously, 'It's me, it's me, it's Hazel.'

He caught zheir other hand when it thumped into his ear, and did the only thing he could think of: he forced it to his face, forced fingertips that were trying to form claws to rasp over his beard and press against the scar.

The Mancer went limp under him. Zheir fingers moved slowly, tracing the shape of his face. He brought the hand he'd captured to his mouth, said, 'Hazel. Safe,' in the vague hope zhey could lipread with zheir fingers, and set it back against the scar. He slid his other hand under Ash's vest and shirt and formed the signs, awkwardly, against the smooth skin of zheir stomach, again hoping touch could replace sight.

Ash shuddered all over, and turned zheir face into Hazel's neck, breathing him in, taking in his scent. Hazel wondered what he smelled like to zhem. The same soap everyone else used, with its lemon tang. Cinnamon, from the pies. Sweat and leather. The mix made for a haphazard sort of perfume.

Zhey were using zheir remaining senses to ground zhemself and quell panic. He thought, on the edge of a mild hysteria, *I'd let zhem taste me, too.*

Ash clutched zheir free hand into his hair, pulled his face down, and brushed zheir lips over his, soft and open-mouthed, tasting.

A-yah, there we go, Hazel thought, and then, as Ash did it again, more confidently, and a mistimed wave of heat surged from his head to his toes and back again, *Oh, this is why people like kissing.*

The copperlits came back on, as smoothly as they'd extinguished a few moments before.

Hazel looked down at Ash, supine under him, one hand locked in his hair, the other against his rough cheek. His own hands were, respectively, at Ash's waist and laid over the hand that rested against his scar. Neither moved. Hazel didn't know what Ash was thinking. He was fighting off the strong urge to follow the revelation of that soft kiss wherever it would lead. He wondered how much it showed in his face. He wasn't good at hiding his feelings in general, and had no practice whatsoever hiding desire in the specific.

Ash, biting zheir lip, slowly eased zheir hand out of the knots of Hazel's hair. Zhey drew a thumb across zheir heart, and lowered zheir gaze in lieu of a slight bow.

An apology. That effectively murdered any desire that might have remained once Hazel remembered his duty. He waved off the apology and got to his feet, helping Ash up with one hand.

'~Stay here,' he ordered.

He was at the atelier door, scanning the antechamber, listening for telltale sounds beyond, when he felt Ash's hand brushing against his waist. The Mancer was standing so close to his back that zhey were jostling him. Zhey'd retrieved zheir dagger, and were carrying both of the matched pair in one hand, other hand tucking against his back.

~Stay here, he started to sign again, and then realised he couldn't follow the standard procedure, which would see the Mancer locked into the atelier with the only key until the source of the disturbance was uncovered and dealt with.

That was fine for Albemarle, who would merely go back to work, heedless of danger and fleshly needs. Engrossed, zhey might not attend the guards' all-clear code knocked on the door, but zhey at least could hear it. Ash wouldn't be able to, and the door was too thick for vibrations to come through. Zhey would never know when it was safe to unlock the door.

He couldn't lock zhem in and take the key with him, in case it was taken off his dead body. The precedent existed; it was exactly why the secured Mancer held the key when a stronghold was under threat.

He should, in fact, lock himself in with zhem, and wait for rescue. But Albemarle was out there, and Holly, and the rest, and he couldn't bring himself to wait in safety. Guards weren't meant to, anyway. They usually had family in the stronghold who could be used as a lever to get the door opened. Hazel didn't, but he had ties as strong as family.

Albemarle didn't. Mancers never did.

'~I'll slide the [safe] rune under the door when we're in all-clear,' he told Ash.

That could be worse. If he was killed without time to tell the other guards, that would be worse. Ash would be waiting for an all-clear message that couldn't come, and if the other guards tried sliding their own notes under the door, zhey would ignore them and be right to.

He'd just have to not die, then.

Ash shook zheir head, and locked zheir free hand around his wrist, and shook zheir head again, face set in stubborn determination, eyes wide and fearful. Zhey only let go to sign, ~Take me with you.

Zhey smacked zheir hand over Hazel's, physically pushing his refusal aside, and repeated zhemself stridently, before making the argument pointless by sliding past him and out into the antechamber, turning to be sure he followed.

'~Come with me, then,' Hazel said, a touch puzzled—zhey were frightened, plainly, and truly safer in the atelier—and added, '~But you must get out of my way if I have to use my sword.'

Ash nodded anxiously. Zhey looked pathetically relieved to not have to stay behind, and, putting the daggers away, clasped both zheir hands around Hazel's left hand; his right was on his sheathed sword.

Hazel wriggled his fingers until he had linked his hand with Ash's properly. This was poor form for a trained killer seeking a fight, but he could feel the strain in the Mancer, the fear. If holding zheir guard's hand helped zhem more than hiding in the atelier would, Hazel would not deny zhem.

They walked, holding hands but with Ash behind Hazel's bulk, across the antechamber. Hazel drew his sword and they started along the hallway. Hazel could feel Ash's other hand against his lower back again, zheir body brushing against his as zhey stayed as close as zhey could to him. Big and brutish could be reassuring sometimes.

Hazel stalked along, alert for any out-of-place sound while he mentally counted off the entrances into the undercroft. Through the main gates, locked now, up the grand entrance stairs to the purple, and down again via the interior corkscrew stairs while the great hall buzzed with warmth and light and people. The north door from the bailey, closed in by walls all around, with the single gate between bailey and central court locked and bolted. The northeast kitchen door, with rough steps down to the subterrane from the kitchen gardens and laundry yard, closed in by walls all around. The south door, from the lawns and the pleasure gardens, the only side door not cut off from the postern gate by extra walls.

The postern gate would be locked and guarded, and there was Albemarle's new moat, which, whatever it did, was designed to protect the walls and should have been turned on—

He stopped dead, and started laughing. He sheathed his sword, and turned to Ash, squeezing zheir hand where their fingers were interleaved, before letting go to sign, '~It was just Albemarle turning on zheir moat. The Mancy needed for that must have made the copperlits go dark briefly.'

He had not been afraid of a fight, but felt the pleasure of deliverance nonetheless, and saw the same reprieve mirrored in Ash's face. If it had been anyone else, he would have taken their face and kissed their forehead in the sheer relief of knowing the others were safe.

But it was Ash, who had been convinced that Hazel never misinterpreted a touch or made his own touch suggestive of anything other than friendship. And Hazel was alarmingly attracted to Ash, and did not trust himself to not give that away if he touched zhem now.

So he kept his hands by his side, even when Ash swayed to rest zheir head against his chest, just briefly, before lifting up on tiptoes to press zheir face into his neck, breathing him in again.

Even when Ash pushed at him, leaning zheir weight solidly against him so that he gave way until his back was at the wall.

Even when Ash stayed on zheir toes to kiss him, both hands in his hair to tilt his head down to zheir mouth.

The heat roared through him, uncontrolled and uncontained. He abruptly had both arms wrapped around Ash, pulling the Mancer off zheir feet and tight against his body, every part of him sounding out response like bells to a fire. Ash didn't seem to mind; zhey squirmed and wrapped zheir legs about his, pulling hard on his hair as zhey tried to climb him. He obliged by skating his hands under zheir round arse, hoisting zhem higher and even closer.

Amid the kisses, his breath was coming hard. He would be coming hard in too short a time, just from the hungry slide of Ash's mouth on his, the taste of zheir tongue, the friction of zheir body taut against his, if he didn't get himself under control. He wasn't used to feeling this.

It took every inch of discipline he possessed to let Ash down, to lift his mouth out of reach, to gently disengage zheir fingers from his hair.

Ash was panting, too, and very flushed. ~Sorry, zhey signed. ~Sorry. I was overtaxed.

The Trade sign there was to do with complaints of the tariff and toll variety. Hazel mentally adjusted his reading to 'overwrought'. He himself wasn't sorry, or only that his self-control was equal only to stopping now or not at all.

He was, however, dismayed that Ash was apologising, same as zhey had in the atelier. He hadn't meant to give Ash something zhey didn't want.

He thought again of the tense, quiet Ash who had come to Haven only three weeks ago, who had assumed every kindness had a price, and who, it turned out, sought touch when frightened.

He thought about who, in zheir previous stronghold, might have seen that, taken that, used that.

He thought about the mistake he had just made, in doing the same.

Hazel tried to fix it. '~It's fine. Touch is comfort, I know. No harm done, no need to say sorry.' What had Kito's word been? '~I won't misconstrue.'

There was no sign for that, not even in Haven slang; he used [negatory] [understand].

~You refuse apology very often, Ash told him, looking even more severe than usual. ~In this case it is very much warranted, Hazel.

'~But why?'

Ash looked puzzled. ~Because of Holly.

For the first time in some twenty years of friendship, Hazel thought, *Oh,* fuck *Holly,* savage with it. Jealousy was another unfamiliar feeling, and it burnt almost as hot as desire did. He had to beat it back with a stick before he could manage a smile.

'~Of course, a-yah, Holly often takes people that way. That's fine. He'll oblige.'

Well. Hazel assumed he would. Holly, to the appreciation of many people in the stronghold for opposite but equal reasons, didn't dally with women, but Ash wasn't a woman. Wasn't a man, either, of course, but that wouldn't bother Holly any more than it bothered Hazel.

Ash's frown, those twin vertical lines, became more pronounced. Zhey raised zheir hands to answer, shaping [query] before Hazel heard, above or below the thudding in his ears, quiet, careful footsteps behind them.

He started to turn, expecting Holly, or one of the others, even as the sensible part of his brain told him, *They wouldn't be quiet, careful footsteps if it were one of yours.*

He drew his sword, pushing Ash behind him. He'd never come close to being as fast as the Holyoake siblings, but he was fast enough. With a clang that rang through the narrow stone hallway, he blocked a blow that would have taken his head half off his shoulders if his instincts hadn't been as sharp as his sword.

His assailant fell back under Hazel's immediate hard press, retreating out of reach. Hazel paused, poised, eyeing off the green coat of a Mancer Guard—a different shade to theirs, paler than their bottle-green—and grasped the implications, where the visiting lord must have come from, who this lone guard had crept away from the feast and into the subterrane to find.

He put his free hand behind his back. He shaped the signs as clearly as he could with only one hand in entirely the wrong position relative to his body. ~Atelier. Lock. Wait for [safe].

There. Now he definitely couldn't lose this fight. Not that he would, not against a single swordsman who wasn't Holly.

He heard Ash's soft retreat. The stranger, dark curly hair, dark cold eyes, leaned to watch zhem go, and Hazel tapped his sword against the wall, the ring of it snapping his opponent's attention back to him.

But only for a moment.

The stranger's eyes had widened, and he was backing away. Fear. Hazel was seeing fear. 'Fuck you, Silverthorne,' he shouted, and started to run.

Hazel turned. Ash hadn't retreated. Zhey'd taken one of Albemarle's copperlits down from the wall. Perhaps zhey meant to strike the guard with it if he got too close, or hurl it at him.

Ash raised it to zheir lips. Zhey hummed into it, a soft tune that sounded very close to Albemarle's copperlit song, but that, crucially, *wasn't*.

Then zhey pointed it at the running man and pressed the spot which should turn the warm light off. Instead, something like a red-hot coal flashed out of the copperlit and struck the intruder in the back. He dropped and lay a very particular type of still.

Hazel silently went up and half-turned the body for the unnecessary confirmation. Dead. Ash had shot a fleeing man in the back. Ash had turned one of Albemarle's Mancy projects into some sort of projectile weapon, and shot a man dead.

He let it drop back onto its face and looked back at the Mancer. Ash was blank-faced, impassive, watching him with zheir fathomless eyes, unblinking.

'~You shot one of your Mancer guards,' he said weakly.

Mancers didn't go around attacking their own guards. It was an impossible thought, as impossible as a Mancer singing another's designs, as impossible as Albemarle producing anything at all that could become a weapon.

Ash let the copperlit drop. It clanked loud on the flags. Its warm glow was completely drained. ~They were never guarding me. They were imprisoning me.

When Hazel, still quietly shocked, merely nodded slowly to this, Ash added, ~I had to, Hazel. He would have told them I was here.

'~A-yah, I suppose he would have.'

And with that, Hazel snapped into his function. He was Haven Mancer Guard, and he protected Haven's Mancers.

He turned his head, wondering if he could hear sounds at the convergence of hallways. If he couldn't, he surely would soon, as soon as someone decided to look for a visiting Mancer guard whose absence would be highly visible.

'~You need to get out of sight,' he signed to Ash. '~I'm going to move the body closer to the atelier and…' This would be a distasteful task. '…*disguise* the wound. We're justified in killing intruders to the atelier.'

~If only he had run in the other direction, then, you wouldn't be looking at me like that.

Hazel shook his head. He pointed at Ash's feet. '~And turn that cursed thing back to harmless.'

Ash looked down at the copperlit. ~I can't. Albemarle has to, with zheir song.

'~Then get rid of it before zhey see it. Zhey *cannot* find out about this, Ash.'

He did hear noises then, rapid footsteps and edged voices. He scooped up the copperlit, shoved it into Ash's arms, and gave zhem a shove, too. ~Out of sight, now.

Ash, with one last frown his way, obeyed, scurrying back toward the atelier.

Which left Hazel standing over a suspiciously-marked dead body when Holly and Lord Valerian, the other guards and Albemarle behind them, led another captain of another Mancer Guard into the hallway.

~Eleven~

'Lord Valerian is being a miserable sod right now. What the fuck did you do to him?'

'That's exactly what I did to him,' Holly says slyly to his sister.

They're halfway through the feast. Evie is looking well in a long flowing gown with a split up one side, teasing with glimpses of legs as lean and muscular as Holly's. She's not often out of trousers. He's *in* trousers, just as rare, but he promised her he would be.

When Evie, because of the visitors, insisted he wear trousers, and put herself in a dress, she was falling into line with the cultural norms of Stronghold Fair Haven, though Haven is notoriously relaxed even on a continent where Mancers make a two-gender classification system laughable. Their own people's customary dress was simultaneously stricter and simpler—everyone wore a sarong-style ankle-length wrap, colour and pattern prescribed by kinship. The dictates were strict enough that the Holyoakes would have suffered minor persecution if they'd stayed, given both have a style all their own, and who knew if the shortness of the skirt or the bifurcation of the trousers would have been seen as worse.

Holly looks about the Havens revelling in the feast in every imaginable style and colour and expression; some match their people's customs, and some don't. Having lost his, Holly is all for the comfort of tradition, but not when it comes to forcing Evie, or anyone, into unwanted roles.

The rear tables have been pushed back and the dancing has started, Finnegan on his fiddle and Olowa on her drums providing the music, fast and upbeat, and Evie is giving Holly a filthy look.

'Please tell me you didn't.'

Holly runs his beringed fingers across the tabletop like he's playing on keys. 'A-yah, then I didn't.'

'You're saying that because I told you to say it.'

'A-yah,' Holly says again, agreeably. He's had some wine, but isn't drunk, just younger-sibling annoying.

'You are a plague and a scourge,' she informs him.

Holly smiles beatifically. There was a long and acrimonious stretch of time when the Holyoake siblings—once just two among many, and among many cousins, of the wealthy Aumona family—wouldn't dare tease each other like this, where everything between them was bitter and fraught.

That was years ago, but Holly still feels deep gratitude for moments like this.

He chucks her under her chin. 'Go dance with someone, Evie. Dance with Miriam, she secretly loves it when Kito gets jealous.'

The visiting lord is from Stronghold Cristati. He may or may not actually be Lord Cristati; Holly missed that. His fine doublet is plum-purple, a loud signal of the status that gave his sort their nickname. He's got smooth black hair, olive skin, dark eyes that glint with gold flecks in the copperlits. He's attractively plump but looks stern, imperious, a typical purple of the supercilious ilk that Holly and Hazel met during their academy years.

He has brought along a Mancer Guard, but no Mancer. There is a not especially delicate message in that.

They are all being very careful, the Haven Mancer Guard, Evie, and probably Lord Valerian, who is seated beside Lord Maybe-Cristati, and looks unhappy about it, or about the adolescent who is currently making his way through the tables, or about Holly in general.

Albemarle was supposed to be up there at the honour table too, for Lady Fairhaven to acknowledge the brilliance of zheir moat, but as soon as they'd seen the foreign Mancer Guard, Albemarle's guards had instinctively sat zhem close, and Morano, whose wife works at the port and couldn't come tonight, is babysitting. The boyishly charming Second Jerome is making nice with the visitors.

Albemarle is not good at diverting from what zhey see as truth. If asked, zhey would absolutely and in detail explain that zhey'd had help making that moat. It wouldn't be fair to Ash to deny zhem zheir credit. Second Jerome will make sure no one thinks to ask and Morano will make sure no one gets to ask.

The rest of them are trying to act as usual, sipping wine, dancing, teasing each other, laughing, watching those other Mancer guards.

Lord Valerian's son arrives in front of Holly, who has sat on the bench with his back to the table so he can observe the visiting Mancer Guard more easily. Holly is expecting coy. The boy climbs straight into his lap.

Lorian wraps his arms about Holly's neck. He's a pretty boy, with his mother's looks, pale brown skin and long eyelashes, but his father's mouth and that floppy chestnut hair. His breath smells strongly of wine, and he is exactly as big-eyed and wet-mouthed as Holly thought he'd be.

'It's m'birthday,' he mutters against Holly's cheek.

Holly has had to turn his face aside to avoid a mouthful of too-young boy. This lets him make eye contact with the father of said too-young boy. Holly smiles. Valerian most certainly does not.

'Is it really your birthday?' Holly says, so bland in his sarcasm that he knows Lorian doesn't have a hope of catching it. 'You must have been keeping very quiet about that, I had no idea— ah, that's more assertive than it needs to be, Lorian.'

He pulls Lorian's hands from where they had been delving straight between his legs.

'You're m'birthday present,' the lordling tells him owlishly. 'Want to unwrap my present.'

'Oh? And who, exactly, gave you said birthday present?'

'Giving it to myself.'

When Holly once again dodges Lorian's attempt to kiss him, the boy diverts and sucks on the side of his neck instead. Holly pushes his head away.

When Lord Valerian asked for a word in the garden earlier in the day, Holly half-expected a proposition and was surprised to find himself disappointed when Lord Valerian merely told him to pass a message to Commander Holyoake. They wouldn't be getting any extra budget for the new Mancer. Recruiting more guards would be far too visible a move while Ash has to be hidden.

Then Valerian stood silently, as awkwardly stiff and cold as he ever was, as if Holly hadn't gone on his knees for him a few weeks before and wasn't a heartbeat from suggesting the same thing right now. He could still picture the man, bare-backed, wielding that axe, all hidden muscle and lightly furred skin. Holly wanted his mouth all over that.

The lord cleared his throat. 'You'll be kind, won't you? You'll be kind to my boy, when you turn him down tonight?'

'Do you think I wouldn't be?'

Valerian looked away for a single telling beat before meeting Holly's gaze coolly. 'You weren't, to me.'

'I was,' Holly said. 'I was, lover, you just haven't realised it yet.'

Valerian shook his head, irritated.

'Tell you what,' Holly said, smiling. 'I'll be less rude than you wanting to demote me just because you don't like me.'

The lord tapped his fingers on his magnificent thigh but refrained from reminding Holly that he'd been vicious about his son and almost drawn a blade on him. That didn't fly as an excuse for petty vengeance in a place like Haven, not once they'd got past the fraught emotions of those few moments.

Instead he said, 'Is that less rude than believing I'd punish your sister for your behaviour?'

'You wouldn't?' Holly said, smile widening. 'You might have reassured me of that before you made me get on my knees.'

'I didn't—' Valerian started, before cutting himself off. His pale skin readily showed his flush.

A pedant might very well have pointed out that he had indeed done so, if Holly had truly believed that Evelyn was under threat and there was only one way to save her. If Holly had not been acting exactly as he wanted, not an unusual situation for Holly.

'Oh, Val,' he said. 'You're going to lose every argument we ever have because you let me do that, and it's not even *my* morality that was offended by it.'

Valerian threw up his hands in guilty frustration. 'Just be gentle with Lorian, Holyoake,' he muttered as he collected his axe again.

Now, at the feast, Holly is obediently gentle, when he usually would not be if someone were attempting to assault him. Gently, he pushes the boy's mouth from his neck. Gently, he disentangles the boy's fingers where they are playing with the beads in his braids. Gently, he slides the boy from his lap.

Lorian refuses to catch himself and ends up at Holly's feet, smiling languidly up at him, rubbing a possessive hand over his ankle and up his calf, snaking under the trouser leg. This boy is quite, quite determined to get himself fucked.

Kito pulls a face at Holly, amused. Holly does not need to look back at the high table to know that Lord Valerian is glaring at him, unamused.

He pulls the boy back up and makes him sit demurely beside him. He puts an arm around him, hugging him close while barring him from resuming his incursion onto the nearest available lap.

He says, 'Lorian, have you considered putting in a good word with your father for the Haven Mancer Guard? Let me tell you *all* about budgets and how they work.'

About ten minutes of unremitting financial talk later—Holly patchworking together the highlights from some of Evie's denser lectures—Lorian staggers away from him, looking confused and disappointed, but, and here is the salient point, not emotionally devastated by rejection.

Holly offers Valerian a smug little bow from where he's lounging against the Mancer Guard table. Valerian rolls his eyes but he does look relieved and grateful.

Holly is idly wondering if relieved and grateful for rejecting his son will translate to relieved and grateful for less high-minded services—he *cannot* get the sight of the man chopping wood out of his head—when the Mancer guards from Cristati make their way over to the Havens' table.

They've shaken off Second Jerome and are here to socialise with their professional colleagues, setting down drinks, introducing themselves. There's eight of them. The other eight would be back at their stronghold. And probably a second set of sixteen, for the other Mancer, who Ash had to work with at Cristati.

If Ash came from Cristati.

Ash came from Cristati.

They're all men. They all look a bit like the Cristati lord, olive-skinned with dark hair and eyes, so they're probably local to that stronghold's surrounds. It looks like there's also a height requirement. Tiny Kito, even if male, would not have made it into this guard despite her outsized talent; Second Jerome wouldn't have either, even if he still had both legs. Holly's not sure any of the Havens would have qualified, except himself.

The captain, Tassone, is new to the job, swaggering with it. He's big, competent, contemptuous. His second, Hazel's equivalent, is watchful, with cold, clever eyes. That one, Dimitriou, is the best-looking of the lot of them, and eyes off the men appraisingly. He notices Lorian, staring mournfully, and yet also sullenly, at Holly.

The rest are indistinguishable, loud, a bit pushy, a bit drunk. And then they start to target the Havens.

One of them tells Kito and Miriam it's such a waste that two pretty ladies are dancing with each other rather than him, and tries, persistently, to cut in. One makes a loud comment about Morano. Another starts touching Titus's short and crinkly hair without permission.

Another one tells Nightingale she's pretty, and then, when she blushes in shy pleasure, says, 'But you'll look prettier on my cock.' His friends howl with laughter at her horrified expression.

Holly isn't stupid. He knows the Cristati Mancer Guard is deliberately provoking its Haven counterpart. He's impulsive and fast to react, but he knows when he's being played and, as much as it cuts his soul, he won't respond, except to tuck Nightingale under his arm and pull Titus to sit on his other side.

Kito would make the same decision, he is sure, since she's also not stupid, but she's had a few more wines than Holly and now a couple of the Cristatis are tugging on First Jerome's veil, and that of her partner, cooing about sneaking a peek.

First Jerome bats a hand away and looks up the table at her seniors, silently appealing not for help but for permission.

None of them have their swords. Kito has her trishul knives. Kito might question the need for First Jerome's strict modesty, but she'll defend her right to keep it. Her fingers are tracing circles on the pommels.

If Hazel were here, with his guileless eyes and disarming spray of freckles over his broad nose and cheeks, it would be different. He'd calm the situation, send the Cristati Mancer guards back to their own side of the great hall without them noticing, until later, that they'd been spanked like unruly toddlers.

Hazel isn't here. Kito is here, with her knives. Holly is here, and Holly has no option but to go bigger than Kito and try to be less lethal than she and his own inclination would be.

Holly springs up onto the table. He strolls along, kicking off empty plates and full cups of wine, which spray pale liquid over the Cristatis. Swearing, they push back their bench en masse and knock it flying. Their hands are reaching for the swords they should not have had.

Holly stops his traverse in front of Tassone. He looks down at him, hands on hips.

'Haven hospitality,' jeers the Cristati captain.

'Tell your guards to get their hands off my guards or my second lieutenant here will cut them off and feed them to them fist-first up their collective arses.'

'Sounds like your kink, not mine, honey.'

Holly gives a savage smile.

'I remember you, Holyoake,' Tassone says. 'We overlapped at the academy for a year or so. I think you might have sucked my cock.'

'Lover, if I'd sucked your cock, you'd certainly remember. Now you back right off.'

'You were always so fast, back then. The trainers loved you, didn't they?'

'What's not to love?'

'They thought you were amazing.' Tassone stretches the syllables, making of the word a soft taffy. 'And yet here you are, guarding the most useless Mancer you could find. Nice and safe. All your lauded potential. Why don't we step outside and we'll see how well complacent reliance on speed stacks up against someone who's actually worked for their skills?'

It does sting, a little. He'd been the best of his cohort, guarding the best of the emerging crop of Mancers. If Albemarle has fizzled, hasn't he?

But he smiles. 'Why step outside when we can start right now?'

Holly makes to kick the fucker in the face and someone yanks him off the table by his ankle. Holly bangs a knee on the bench on the way down but lands cat-like on his feet. He fronts up to the interfering fucker who's ruining his fun. He's expecting Evie, but it's Lord Valerian, who has somehow made it across the great hall to their table in a flash.

He hears Tassone and his men laughing sneeringly behind him.

'Swallow it,' Valerian hisses.

'We already played that game, lover,' Holly says, and answers his patron's glare with a scowl of his own. 'We can't afford to look weak to these people.'

'They know that, captain. They're deliberately trying to cause an incident. It might be provocation so they can openly declare hostilities on us without breaking the covenant. Or it might be a diversion to get at Albemarle. They'll come at us in secret if they can confirm Ash is here.'

Bloody Valerian and his annoyingly good points. Holly shakes off Valerian's firm hand and seeks out Albemarle. He sees the handsome Cristati lieutenant, Dimitriou, talking to Lorian but looking over at the oblivious *and always honest* Albemarle. That's too close for comfort.

Valerian thinks so too. He claps his hands. 'The moat!'

Albemarle rises. Zhey want to sing zheir Mancy right there, but Holly and Valerian guide zhem to Lady Fairhaven at the high table. She's more subtle with her purple shade than the Cristati lord is, lilac and iris under-skirts peeking from under a silky cream robe. Valerian is, too, with amethyst showing through the slashed sleeves of his overshirt, picked up by subtle threads in his rich doublet.

Albemarle throatily sings the almost-words, calling zheir moat into being. It triggers something, and Holly still doesn't quite know how the so-called moat will operate, but the Mancy surge causes all the copperlits to go dark.

He can hear the murmur of voices, startled but not frightened, under Albemarle's husky song, the hoarse drone of it eerie in the dark. He feels a hand in his. It's Valerian, he thinks. Valerian probably assumes Holly intends to use the darkness to commit violence against the Cristati Mancer Guard. Holly wishes he'd thought of it before Valerian did.

He is wondering if he should light a candle, if he could find one, and go down to check on Hazel and Ash, or maybe he shouldn't, because in the dark, hands find one another. He squeezes Valerian's fingers. He wishes he could have taken Valerian up on his awkward offer. Those strong fingers, slightly calloused, would have felt bloody good, fumbling or not.

Holly has the thought, Holly acts on the thought. He sways over and presses his body against Valerian's sturdy one, full contact from thigh to hip to shoulder. He's warm and solid and he presses back against Holly.

The copperlits flick on again as quietly and as suddenly as they turned off. Holly sways upright again, not looking at Valerian. Everyone claps, with great faith, since they can't see the outer walls from here, and there'd probably be no visible difference if they could. Valerian lets Holly's hand go to join in the applause. Lady Fairhaven pats Albemarle, just once, on the shoulder, before letting Kito and Morano guide zhem back to their table. Lady Fairhaven knows what zhey can tolerate.

The Cristati lord says, 'It must have taken an extraordinarily long time, to make these panels of yours.'

Lady Fairhaven, Haven's canny matriarch, knows of their new Mancer, of course, and also knows zhey must remain resolutely unacknowledged by the stronghold hierarchy. She smiles vaguely, not biting.

'The time it took was indeed extraordinary,' Valerian says with such smoothness that Holly feels quite proud of him.

Albemarle is working zheir way through a huge bowl of chilli fishcakes now, happy and ignored, with the senior guards on either side to make sure it stays that way. Holly moves closer, attention on his stronghold's Mancer.

Valerian finishes his polite and soothing conversation with the visiting lord. He comes over and puts an arm about Holly's waist, casual, friendly, unremarkable to watching eyes. Because the Cristatis *are* watching now. Holly is standing in Haven, surrounded by friends, and they have enemies circling. He's tense, shifting in and out of fighting stance, and Valerian squeezes his waist, settling him.

The lord says into Holly's ear, 'Where is my son?' and Holly looks about and says, 'Where's the Cristati lieutenant?' and together they say, '*Shit*.'

Holly crosses through the dancing toward the door to the back hallway and the corkscrew stairs to the undercroft. The sturdy door at the top of the stairs between the ground and first floors is locked at night, but not on feast nights. It's guarded, but not from Lord Valerian's son. All Lieutenant Dimitriou needs to do is get a confirmatory look at Ash and get back upstairs to his people before Hazel can catch him.

And Hazel—Holly loves Hazel; he would and does trust him with his life. Hazel darling may be the most experienced and competent one of all of them, except Evie. But he's never unnecessarily ruthless. Holly very much fears he'll let Dimitriou get away before he has a chance to think it through and accept what must be done.

A couple of the Cristati Mancer guards are lingering by the back door of the hall, blocking the way out into the hallway. Holly's own people are pinned down guarding Albemarle and can't run interference.

Holly has a moment of hot indignation—Cristatis guarding a Haven door against him, how very dare they?—but Valerian whispers, 'They *want* the excuse, Holly. Provocation.'

It's the first time he's used Holly's nickname. His breath is hot in his ear. Holly pivots and whispers a kiss over his hair, murmurs, 'You want me alone, lover.'

In unspoken accord, Valerian gets his hands on Holly's hips. Holly lets him walk him backward with disrespect for the surrounding dancers, mouths hovering close together, hands exploring more than is decent. They are temporarily enamoured lovers, intent on each other and finding any whit of privacy.

They certainly are not moving to foil a Cristati plot and rescue a wayward son without giving an aggressive stronghold any worldly cause to act against Haven.

'He won't have gone upstairs with him, will he?' Valerian mutters. He kisses Holly, makes a small appreciative noise. He's a decent actor. 'He was very determined. They might just be in his room.'

'Some hope. The Cristati will have persuaded him down by whatever means.'

'The little idiot,' Valerian says.

Holly buries both hands into Val's soft hair, plants his mouth over his, and kisses him obscenely, all tongue and teeth. He pulls the lord close with his ropey strength, closer, grinds against him, bangs him into the wall beside the door—so narrowly avoiding the two Cristati guards that he brushes against one—and slides about until he finds the doorway. He whisks them through it and up against the wall on the far side of the hallway, interposing his leg between Valerian's thighs and applying merciless friction. Valerian should be bloody well moaning by now but he's still and silent under Holly's ministrations, pressing his face hard into Holly's shoulder.

Holly sucks on Valerian's earlobe to cover a cross whisper. 'Help a fellow out, would you? Make a noise.'

'You try giving it up to someone who openly dislikes you,' Valerian hisses back.

'I fucking *am*, right now.' He makes a show of glaring back over his shoulder. 'Do you mind? We're engaging in fuckation here and we didn't invite an audience.'

The Cristati guards are peering around the door at them, trying to reconcile their orders with whatever manners they'd retrieved from the depths of the swamp they crawled out of.

'Or is that what you're waiting for, an invitation?' Holly continues. 'I don't do orgies with the likes of you. Move along, boys.' When they still don't make shift to retreat, he shouts, 'For fuck's sake, I'm trying to get my cock sucked here and he's shy, you fuckers!'

The Cristatis finally duck back out of sight. Valerian is spluttering. Holly purrs, 'Just an average feast night for me, my lord,' and tows him to the stairs down to the lower stronghold.

There's no guard stationed at the stairwell, and the door is unlocked. Holly's indignation winds up tighter.

They find the body at the bottom of the narrow corkscrew. It's one of the stronghold guards, one of the handful who drew the short straw for guard duty on feast night, on the gates and doors that never go unwatched.

She's young. She'd have been taken by surprise. Haven was too safe, sometimes, so stubbornly kind that the outside world could feel like an ambush.

The Cristati lieutenant made no effort to hide the body. Perhaps he assumes it'll seem like an accident. It's grotesque; her blank eyes stare up at Holly though her body lies ventrally, on its stomach, crooked and limbs askew where it tumbled from the staircase.

Holly thinks her name is Shao.

He's running the scene though his head: he decides Lieutenant Dimitriou talked Lorian into bringing him downstairs. Shao resisted, as she should have. Lorian insisted, as a lord's son would have. The guard let them pass.

Maybe Shao said, 'I'm telling your father, Lorian.' Maybe she didn't, but she took a half-step toward the great hall. Either way, Dimitriou turned around, snagged her coat, and threw her down the stairs, like tossing away a piece of rubbish.

At that point, Lorian went from lustful adolescent to hostage. Valerian is breathing rapidly beside Holly as they stand over the smashed body with its smooth innocent face and its wide startled eyes.

Holly understands that there are several circumstances under which Cristati will have at Haven; he didn't really need Lord Valerian to spell it out for him.

The first won't happen. If Cristati openly attacks Haven to take Ash back, Haven will flash out its distress signal, and the other coastal strongholds will respond, in defence not of their friendly neighbour, but of the Mancer covenant and its sacrosanct sanctuary clause. Even the crown would commit soldiers, marching them down the coast from Glelissi.

The second can happen. If Cristati engineers some sort of confront-ation, ostensibly not about the Mancer at all, then they can move against Haven on those legitimate grounds and the covenant will not apply. Allied strongholds might defend Haven. They might not. Cristati is strong and the alliance is loose, informal. If a Mancer were to die or vanish in the ensuing chaos, that is nought to do with Cristati. This was their method at the feast and may indeed be their strategy going forward.

The third almost certainly will happen, with or without the umbrella of the second. It is the least risky for Cristati. Once they know for sure that Ash is in Haven, they can send a small force to infiltrate and take zhem. It's exactly what a Mancer Guard is for—both in the offensive and the defensive. Albemarle has never been a good target. Ash, amplifier for other Mancers, is the living epitome of a good target.

It is what Ash was trying to protect zhemself and Haven from, by refusing to name zheir origin. The tactic was exquisitely effective: it stopped Them Upstairs from boasting widely of Haven's new acquisition and giving away zheir location, while warning zheir new Mancer Guard to be wary. It also hid the full extent of the challenge Haven was going to face, in case Haven proved unwilling to face it.

Ash didn't know Stronghold Fair Haven. Zhey couldn't know it would keep the covenant no matter what, the moment zhey asked for sanctuary.

But this murder is more aggressive than Holly anticipated. He realises Dimitriou's incursion is not a simple reconnoitre to confirm Ash's presence. The lieutenant is acting very much as if he knows Ash will be in the subterrane, and he's going to retrieve zhem.

They are already inside the third scenario.

It's bold, but Holly admires the boldness. The opportunity must have literally crawled into the man's lap and told him it wanted to unwrap him for its birthday. Until then, Cristati may have been planning a sortie overnight, or they may have just been visiting to show off their peacock feathers, an implicit threat: *we know*.

Right this instant, however, the subterrane is empty, the undercroft is empty, almost all of Haven is in the great hall, and Lorian is a shiny key fitting neatly in Dimitriou's hand. If he can get past Hazel, and that is a rather large and capable *if*, he'll use the lord's son to take Ash out the gates.

It won't even matter that he's leaving behind his lord, his lord's retainers and his colleagues. If Haven were to retaliate against them, there is the excuse Cristati needs to openly attack, no Mancer to muddy the waters and trigger the alliance. Haven is strong, but it is small. Cristati is stronger, and it is big. Lady Fairhaven would have to swallow it and let her guests go unharmed to avoid the provocation.

But for the audacious venture to work, the Cristati lieutenant *must* get Ash out of the stronghold, fast.

Holly, missing his sword, orders, 'Go get the Mancer Guard.'

Valerian shakes his head. 'I'm going to find Lorian.'

'I'll make sure he's safe.'

'No, you won't,' Valerian says. 'You're Mancer Guard. You can only work for the Mancers' safety.'

And there Lord Valerian goes again, rolling out yet another of his annoyingly good points. Luckily, Holly has one of his own. 'The Cristati has to keep him alive and he's got a better chance of rescue with all of us than with just me. *Go get Kito*. Now, Val.'

Valerian hisses through his teeth but the cold logic wins him over; he turns back toward the stairs—where the Haven Mancer Guard is already on its way down, Albemarle in its midst.

'Albemarle wanted to go to bed,' Kito says loudly. With a silencing hand gesture, she adds, almost shouting, 'Captain Tassone is looking for his lieutenant.'

Indeed, Holly catches a glimpse of the light green coat behind his guards, a dark head which isn't one of his. He appreciates the warning.

Kito reaches the bottom, and stops, looking at the body of the stronghold guard. Her gaze flashes to Holly and down again. The others come to a ragged stop too. First Jerome, carefully hovering her hand by Albemarle without touching zhem, uses her body to first block zheir sight and then as a repulsive force to nudge zhem away. Albemarle keeps zheir head down.

The Cristati captain toes the body of the young Haven guard, cool contempt in his eyes. 'Slipped, did she? Careless.'

Holly smiles. *I don't know this ends for Ash*, he thinks. *But I know how it ends for you now, lover.*

It's Valerian who takes his arm, squeezes, murmurs something inaudible but inferable in his ear. Holly makes himself relax.

And then, from across the empty undercroft dining hall, coming up the stairs from the subterrane, they hear a muffled clash or two, a shout, a strange pulse that's more a tap inside the ear than a sound, and a thud.

Holly runs.

~Twelve~

The others had only just stepped into the atelier hallway when a sound like a baby animal in distress came from somewhere behind them. The guards, on high alert, swung that way in concert, like a ravening pack of dogs tracking prey, and then Valerian rushed through them.

'Lorian!' Hazel heard him say. 'Holy Mother, are you harmed, my poor boy?'

'He— He— He made me come downstairs,' Lorian wailed.

The Havens and, more importantly, the foreign captain, were turned toward the new disturbance in the lobby. Hazel, not without a wince of visceral disgust, plunged his sword into the dead man, aiming for the neat hole Ash's weapon had left in the centre of his back. It didn't bleed much, of course, but enough red welled to obscure the edges of the damage to skin and clothes, hiding what looked like singe marks.

The visiting captain dismissed the fuss about the sobbing lordling, now collapsed securely into his father's arms, and came to face Hazel over the body.

'You stabbed my lieutenant in the back.'

'He tried to access Haven's atelier uninvited. I was within my rights to deal with him.'

As Holly joined the stand-off, the man made a show of looking about. 'I don't see a fucking atelier.'

'A-yah.' Hazel could tell Holly was utterly furious behind his devilish smile, so he said, 'That's because he ran away when he saw me guarding it.'

The captain's face darkened. 'My men don't run.'

He ran from his own fucking Mancer, Hazel thought, which, actually, should be a rather terrifying notion.

But he merely gestured downward with an insolent shrug to indicate that perhaps the captain could draw his own fucking conclusions from the evidence in front of his own fucking eyes.

Holly pressed his lips together, no doubt to swallow a laugh, and signed, ~I love you, Hazel darling.

The captain sneered at him and pivoted to address Lord Valerian, who kept his arm protectively around the shoulder of his whey-faced son. The side of the boy's face was puffy and beginning to bruise.

'This is a grievous insult to a peacefully visiting party,' the man snapped.

'He was where he should not have been, Captain Tassone,' Holly countered.

Jerking his chin at Lorian, Tassone said insinuatingly, 'He was *invited.*'

Lorian burst into fresh tears. 'He made me. He pushed Shao. He made me go with him. He hit me.'

First Jerome and Titus had already guided Albemarle away from a conflict that was sure to upset zhem, even if zhey didn't understand all of it or tried to block it out. Now, Lord Valerian pushed his son at the remaining Mancer guards.

'Please take him upstairs,' he murmured.

The handful of Haven purple were generally polite to other Haven residents, their vassals and retainers and servants. But Valerian's deference in this case was because he knew he had no right to ask the Mancer Guard to tend anyone other than the Mancer.

Still, Nightingale accepted the charge, walking the shaking lordling back out into the lobby.

Valerian then turned back to Tassone, the concerned solicitousness of the father immediately displaced by the brisk diplomacy of the lord. 'It seems to me we have one dead guard on each side and can let the matter rest there.'

'*Valerian,*' Holly hissed. Their patron calmly ignored his fury, hand pressed to his chest when he tried to push closer.

'Cristati lost a lieutenant,' Tassone said. 'Haven lost a chit of a girl who can't keep her balance on the stairs. Hardly equal insults.'

'Seems to me I lost a witness to an abduction,' Valerian said, and now there was steel in his tone. He'd wrapped his fingers around the seething Holly's upper arm and held him firmly in place, still looking only at the Cristati captain. 'I do wonder what Lord Lorian will have to say, in the matter of insults to his person? I wonder what the lords and ladies of other strongholds would have to say about such a scandal, should it become widely known?'

Tassone paused. Hazel could see his mind working, trying to turn the death of his lieutenant into a clean first strike, worthy of openly assaulting the walls of Haven without inciting defence from its allies. If Lorian hadn't been quite so recriminatory in his distress, and a lord, and, especially, if the Cristati guard had been killed anywhere else but just close enough to the atelier, Hazel guessed he would have risked it.

Instead Tassone reluctantly bowed to the inevitable, and to Lord Valerian, and excused himself upstairs. 'Prepare the body,' he called over his shoulder. 'I'll report to my lord. Pray he is as reasonable as I.'

As soon as he was gone, Holly snarled, 'You sold out your people, Valerian. His man murdered Shao, you know he did, and you're letting them get away with it.'

Hazel looked down at the body at his feet and tried not to change expression.

Valerian's cool calm did not flicker. 'You will not fail to note that I also threw my own son's perfectly valid grievance in as a bargaining chip, captain. We cannot afford open conflict with Cristati. I did what I had to do.'

'That's shit and you *know* it's shit,' Holly shouted at him. 'Would you have done the same if it was one of us?'

'Yes,' Valerian said, sounding surprised to be asked, which was when Hazel felt it was a good idea to gently interpose himself.

'Can anyone write Mancer runes?' he asked, standing next to Holly and linking arms with him. He could feel his friend practically vibrating in outrage where their bodies met. 'Or do I need to disturb Albemarle?'

He already knew, of course, that no one knew Mancer runes, or if they had managed to pick some up over the years like he had, they were hardly going to admit it in front of one of Them Upstairs. But it did break Holly's wrath and the blank annoyance of Kito and Morano, who felt the insult as keenly as their captain did. Second Jerome just looked awkward, hunching to rub the join between stump and Mancy leg.

'Let's go do that,' Hazel said, starting off without letting Holly go.

'I'll just see to the bodies, then,' Lord Valerian said with enough sarcasm that Hazel had to wonder if the man had a death wish.

'With me!' he said brightly as Holly tried to wrench out of his hold to turn on the lord. 'Everyone, please.'

The other three Mancer guards fell in behind them. They were radiating tension as they crossed the lobby and headed down the hallway that housed Albemarle's chamber, but they had it under control by the time they reached zheir door.

Hazel exchanged a look with First Jerome, where she and Titus stood quietly to attention. Then, sighing, he knocked.

'No,' Albemarle shouted from inside.

'Ash's locked in the atelier,' Hazel called. 'I need to slide the rune for "safe" under the door.' Silence. 'Please, Albemarle.' Silence. 'Zhey could be reading all your journals.' Silence.

Hazel hesitated. Albemarle could be perfectly fine, and sulking, or zhey could be upset and on the verge of either a paroxysm or swinging the other way into dread catatonia. Holly, when Hazel looked to him for assistance, just produced the complicated shrug that meant he also couldn't tell.

'All right,' Hazel said sadly to the resolutely shut door. 'I'll write it myself.'

The door opened. Albemarle loomed in the doorway. Behind zhem, Hazel caught a glimpse of zheir forest of ferns in shades of green. Ferns thrived under the copperlit light and Albemarle grew them in rigid rows and columns of pots affixed to two of the four walls of zheir chamber, obsessively tending them when zhey weren't obsessively working Mancy. Hazel didn't know if it was a Mancer trait or an Albemarle trait. He wondered if Ash, too, would expand zheir intent focus on the Mancer projects into an evening hobby. Perhaps zhey had left behind an aquarium of tropical fish or a meticulous catalogue of rare buttons at Stronghold Cristati.

'I was *writing* it,' Albemarle groused, thrusting a folded scrap of amatl at him. 'Have some patience.'

Hazel, smiling, drew his thumb over his heart.

'Oh, shut up,' Albemarle said, and slammed the door.

Upset, then, but not catastrophically so.

Leaving First Jerome and Titus at Albemarle's door, and Second Jerome at the mouth of the hallway, Hazel took Holly, Kito and Morano back around to the atelier. A couple of grim stronghold guards were already moving the Cristati lieutenant's body. A fine ending to the feast night for them, but slightly better than for the guards delegated to move Shao's body.

Hazel knelt at the door to the atelier and slid the paper underneath. It seemed an age before he heard the grating of the bolts drawing back and the scrape of the large bronze key in the lock.

Some Mancers put Mancy into their atelier locks. Lucky for Ash that that had been beneath Albemarle's concern. Or perhaps zhey could have hummed that zheir own way too.

The door swung open, but the doorway stayed empty. Hazel entered cautiously, and found Ash behind the first workbench where the remains of their convivial dinner sat. Zhey were not quite brandishing a glowing copperlit. It was either a newly converted one, or Ash had refilled the original with zheir altered Mancy song.

~I told you to get rid of that.

Ash tucked it away under zheir arm as the others came in. ~I will. I can't hide it inside the atelier, Albemarle would find it. Ash tapped zheir ear. ~Zhey'd hear it.

Zhey added a sign that meant [echo] but Hazel read as 'resonance'.

'~What is it you have to hide?' Holly asked, catching the signs as he followed Hazel in. '~Apart from the fact that Stronghold Cristati wants you back?' He fingerspelled the name. '~What's your sign for them? Don't be coy, lover.'

Ash looked at Holly, frowning, lightly biting zheir bottom lip. Slowly, zhey first signed [Cristati], a disconcerting meld of [glory] and [pride], before continuing, ~I meant to protect you. I don't know how they found me so fast. But we stopped the guard before he could report back.

'~They knew you were here already.'

Zhey twitched, a shake of zheir head like trying to dislodge a biting insect. ~No.

'~The lieutenant took a hostage and murdered a guard on his way downstairs. He knew you were here already, or he wouldn't have risked it. Retrieval, not reconnaissance.'

Ash folded zheir hands together. Zheir face had taken on the Mancer blankness, except the distinct twin grooves of zheir frown and the thin, firm line of zheir long mouth, slightly downturned.

Hazel gently pried the copperlit from under zheir arm and, shrugging back into his coat, tucked it into an interior pocket. '~I think things may best be served now by a pause. Ash should go to zheir chamber. We'll all need to rotate shifts through the night. We can talk this through in the morning, Holly, once we've waved Cristati out the gate.'

~I'm going, Ash signed.

Hazel could find it difficult to convey tone when interpreting Trade, especially when Ash was being Mancer blank. So although he voiced, 'I'm going,' when Ash formed [go]—which the others would've understood easily enough anyway—his reflexive interpretation did not properly capture the intent of the unusually slow and broad sweep of Ash's palm away from zheir chest.

The other guards thought Ash meant zhey were following Hazel's suggestion and going to zheir chamber for the night. Ash meant zhey were going a lot further than that.

Hazel stepped in front of zhem, fist held in the negatory sign. He shook his head in slow emphasis.

Ash flashed, ~Am I a prisoner? No? Then I am going, Hazel.

Now the other guards were awakening to what Ash meant. '~Hold on, Ash,' Morano said.

'~Have you considered the Cristatis are still here?' Holly asked. '~You walk outside our walls, you're fair game, and they're *right here*.'

'We'll protect you,' Kito said. 'Hazel darling, tell zhem we'll protect zhem!' She clumsily formed [protect].

'~I've told zhem.' Hazel turned away from Ash so zhey couldn't see his mouth. 'Let me walk with zhem, I'll talk zhem out of it. You all—'

Ash dragged on his sleeve, made him look at zheir hands. *~Stop that. It's fucking rude, you overbearing arsehole.*

Hazel drew his thumb across his heart and received in return the silently furious equivalent of Albemarle's, 'Oh, shut up,' from earlier.

Much as he had done for Holly, Hazel tucked his arm through Ash's. He still had the modified copperlit jabbing him in the ribs. He'd meant to show the other senior guards its new function, but had decided against it while emotions were flowing fast. Time enough tomorrow, once they'd seen Cristati on its way, to reveal Ash's peculiar talent. Time enough tomorrow to gently find out more about it. If he raised it now, Holly would turn it into an interrogation and prickly Ash would certainly leave the stronghold rather than take it.

He walked Ash toward zheir chamber, trailing the other guards. Evelyn, herself trailing Nightingale, met them on the way. She'd assigned herself to watching the Cristati Mancer Guard, and reported they and their lord had left the feast and gone, to all appearances, to their guest lodgings on the upper floor. Stronghold guards were now stationed at the end of the guest accommodation hallway and the top and bottom of every set of stairs between there and the Mancers.

The lord had taken the news of one of his people's death with apparent equanimity, thanks in no part to Lord Valerian's tactful handling and Lady Fairhaven's serene influence. It turned out she had gone to school with the lord's mother, Lady Cristati, and Lady Cristati's favourite cousin, too. She'd promised to write a letter, smoothing it over.

The Holyoake siblings walked together, talking quietly, the captain and the commander conferring.

'All right, yes, in the morning,' Evelyn agreed eventually, though Hazel knew she'd be itching to tackle the threat. 'As soon as we've safely seen Cristati off.'

'I think,' Hazel said over his shoulder, 'we need an interview with Lorian too. The Cristatis *might* all have known Ash was here already, Holly—or maybe only the lieutenant knew.'

Holly paused, before saying, 'Oh, because of something the little idiot gave away while his Cristati was leading him by his cock.'

'Yes, but let's not call him a little idiot when we're asking him.'

'But have you considered that he *is* a little idiot, Hazel darling? That's what happens when cousins marry cousins.'

'Lord Valerian did not marry his cousin,' Evelyn snapped. 'Lady Margarite was Lady Fairhaven's niece. Lord Valerian's a second cousin via her grandfather.'

They reached Ash's door. The other Mancer guards and Evelyn, low voiced, quickly began to arrange the roster that would see them balance adequate security overnight with the need for sleep. Hazel followed Ash into zheir room, leaving the door open.

The Mancer, ignoring him, took from a hook the coat zhey'd arrived in.

Hazel signed zheir name, but not with any great hope. Ash wasn't looking at him, such an effective tactic. He slid his hand onto the Mancer's slender shoulder, felt the tension there, and the warmth. Regretfully, gently, but inexorably, he turned Ash to make zhem face him.

Ash insisted, ~I'm going.

'~If that's what you truly want…' He stood aside and gestured at the door.

Ash, deprived of the argument, looked flummoxed. Then zhey smoothed zheir features to blankness and twirled zheir coat onto zheir shoulders with dramatic defiance. Zhey tossed zheir shawl on and started for the door.

Hazel fell into step a regulation pace behind and to zheir left. If Ash had been in a stronghold for the years zhey'd claimed—

~What are you doing? Ash demanded, turning on him sharply.

—zhey'd recognise the academy-trained positioning *immediately*.

Hazel suppressed a smile. Ash was looking *riled*. '~Accompanying my stronghold's Mancer on zheir rash and ill-advised venture beyond zheir stronghold walls.'

He put his hands behind his back, standing tall and straight, soldier-fashion, to exact academy specifications; the effect was slightly ruined by his open coat, which he had left unbuttoned to accommodate the poke of the copperlit from the inner pocket.

Ash gave him a filthy, narrow-eyed look and Hazel had to fight very hard to keep a straight face. Albemarle was not at all fun to poke at; Ash was a delight.

~I revoke sanctuary.

Hazel sobered. He hadn't expected that expedient solution. '~Don't do that.'

Zhey shouted, ~I've fucking already done it.

Not if Hazel didn't voice it to Evelyn, zhey hadn't. '~Haven keeps the covenant.'

'~The covenant does not apply.'

'~Of course it does.' Ash shook zheir head. Hazel stepped in closer, diverting a reach for zheir face into a single stroke over zheir rigid shoulders with both hands. He was gratified to feel zhem settle in its wake just a little. '~Ash, you called for sanctuary and Haven has given it. We have given it. So what if it's Cristati? So what if they found you sooner than you expected? We always knew they would eventually. But we said yes to you. We didn't say "yes, but…", or "no, if…". We said *yes*.'

Throughout this speech he leaned closer and closer to Ash, wishing he had his hands available to touch even as he was grateful, on behalf of his professionalism and Ash's personal space, that he didn't.

But Ash had slowly slipped zheir own hands against his chest, under the coat lapels, not pushing him away, just resting zheir warm palms there as zhey attended, staring at his mouth.

'~*Yes*, Ash. Have faith and let us do for you what we promised we would do.'

Ash's gaze dropped. Hazel fought a powerful urge to close the last distance between them. He allowed himself only to lay his hands over Ash's where the Mancer still rested them on his chest. Ash's head dipped down as if zhey would set zheir forehead there next.

Holly came to the doorway, and smiled. Hazel shook his head at him, which Holly duly ignored. 'Ah, don't be shy, Hazel darling. I think that's your cue zhey'd like a cuddle. If not a kiss.'

He pecked his fingertips together in the appropriate Trade sign.

Tried it. Zhey apologised and said zhey wanted you. Funny, that.

Mindful that Ash had already called him rude once tonight for deliberately excluding zhem from a conversation, Hazel turned zhem around so zhey could see Holly.

Ash started. Looking over zheir shoulder, Hazel watched zhem sign, ~Sorry, Captain Holly. I do like the way his voice feels.

Ah. Zheir hands on his chest, absorbing the vibrations of his voice as zhey watched his hands and mouth, while he strung together enough words to persuade zhem to trust Haven and stay.

'~I do, too,' Holly said. '~Low and rumbly, like a bearhug. It sounds like the taste of honey and ginger tea, Ash. Try it sometime. I like it when he says yes, too, don't you?'

'Stop arsing about, Holyoake,' Hazel said, though he was reluctantly amused by Holly's cheery hyperbole. 'Honey and ginger, fuck off.'

'~And he takes instruction so very well. Maybe you'll try that sometime, too.'

'No, *really*, Hols.'

Hazel could feel the heat of his embarrassment travelling down his cheeks and throat and he thought Ash was abashed as well; zhey took a few steps from him, averting zheir face.

A minor miracle occurred when Holly seemed to realise he'd gone far enough. Less insinuatingly, he asked, '~Has our friend talked you into staying yet?'

Ash hesitated. Zhey glanced back at Hazel, and slowly nodded zheir fist.

'~And he thinks he doesn't have a way with words.' Holly flashed his brilliant smile. '~Shall I leave you here, Hazel?'

'~What for?' Hazel said. '~Zhey're persuaded.'

Holly looked between the two of them—he seemed to be expecting some sort of signal from Ash and shook his head when he didn't get it. 'Come along, then, let's leave the Mancer to get some rest.'

He drew Hazel out with a last wave, and said, once Ash couldn't see his face, 'The night watch is on orders to wake us if zhey try to leave.' Hazel must have looked doubtful. 'If nothing else, Hazel, Ash is a shocking liar if zhey think zhey're protecting you.'

'Us,' Hazel corrected.

'Yes, us, or, you know, you.' Holly hesitated. 'Can I come to your room tonight, love? Not for sex, unless you want it. Just—I'd like some company.'

'Me too,' Hazel said, giving his hand a squeeze. They headed toward their own quarters with fingers entwined, Holly leaning lightly so their shoulders brushed.

Behind them, Ash's door quietly closed.

~Thirteen~

The morning meeting began poorly.

Lord Valerian had shadows under his eyes and looked wan. He'd slept badly, it seemed, and then been awake early to keep Cristati satisfied and, most importantly, ready to depart on schedule. By the time he'd made his last bow and retreated to his office, the lack of sleep and the stress made him impatient and irritable with the awaiting senior Mancer guards.

'No,' he said to Evelyn's polite request. 'My son has been through enough without having to be interrogated about it.'

Hazel watched Evelyn do her scant best to hold on to her own scant patience. 'My lord, Hazel has raised a judicious point about why the Cristati lieutenant was so certain he'd find Ash.'

'What you're saying,' said the lord, 'is that you think my boy is a damned idiot.'

'You said he was, yourself,' Holly sang under his breath, not actually quietly.

Hazel put a hand on his friend's jiggling thigh, warning, soothing. Holly laid his own hand over Hazel's and, winking at him, pulled it higher till Hazel's fingers were indecently tangling with the hem of Holly's already indecent skirt.

Hazel frowned repressively, for all the good it would do. Holly had offered to take the edge off, in bed last night, and Hazel had said, 'Thanks, Hols, but I think I'm quite liking the edge for now.' This little performance was just in aid of fucking with Lord Valerian again, and Lord Valerian was distinctly not in the mood.

'It's also possible Shao's death was actually an accident,' Hazel pointed out pacifyingly, sliding his hand away and very much aware that

Valerian was watching him do it. 'Lorian could tell us if it looked like a deliberate push or a scuffle that went wrong. If it was an accident, then the foray downstairs was probably just a reconnaissance gone too far. But if the Cristati blatantly risked shoving her, it was retrieval from the start.'

'Has the Mancer given you any indication how Cristati even came here looking?'

'I would go so far as to say Ash was shocked to find out Cristati had already come sniffing about,' Hazel said. 'Zhey tried to leave.'

Lord Valerian's better nature at least fought him before he said, 'Should we let zhem?'

'That's not how the covenant works.' He saw Holly and Evelyn nodding from the corner of his eye.

'Fucking academy indoctrination,' Valerian muttered and went quickly on when Holly straightened, raising a hand in a lordly shushing motion that made Holly's midnight eyes narrow further. 'We've been very quiet, so why did they visit Haven in particular?'

'We kept it from the purple, as Ash intended us to do,' Evelyn said. 'But the staff go to and fro from the port, and the port's a busy place with lots of people coming and going. It's not a stretch to think that at the very least the rumour of it reached Cristati ears that quickly. But for all we know, they're merely visiting every stronghold within a certain radius, looking for the exact sort of hint they got from us. We'd hoped for more time, but—' She shrugged. 'The horses of hope gallop, and we are afoot.'

'So they came visiting on the strength of a rumour,' Lord Valerian murmured, 'or just drew a circle on a map…'

'…and then your son verified it to their man,' Holly said in the same musing tone.

'Rowan,' Evelyn snapped, which meant she was fumingly angry. 'My lord, Cristati wants Ash back, desperately; that much is obvious. We must work out if our visitors knew zhey were here, or none of them knew for sure, or one of them found out, and if he told anyone else before he went to the subterrane. If we can know this, we can anticipate their next move.'

Lord Valerian's pale gaze roamed over their faces; even Holly sat quietly to let the man think it over. At last he rang a small bell by his desk, and sent the responding retainer, a bespectacled little clerk, for his son.

Hazel cleared his throat into the ensuing awkward silence. He lifted the copperlit from his lap. 'There's also this.'

He aimed it at the side of the room and pressed it the way Ash had. The light bolt shot out of its end, fast and noiseless but with a painless spike of pressure in the ears that Hazel hadn't had the capacity to notice the first time. Most of it dissipated harmlessly over the plastered stone wall. That was lucky; Hazel hadn't accounted for the damage if it had turned out the weapon pierced stone as readily as flesh.

When the bolt sliced through the air, it'd clipped a garish ornamental vase on a side table. As Holly leapt to his feet with an oath and even Evelyn jolted, the vase wobbled ominously. It seemed about to tip off the table, before it, eerily silently, splintered and crumbled into a neat pile of tiny ceramic shards.

'What fuckery is this?' Holly exclaimed.

Hazel had meant to tell him about the weapon last night, but he'd only gotten as far as reporting on the conversation he'd had with Ash in the atelier before Holly had interrupted with his own impressions of Cristati from the feast, and then they'd gotten distracted and fallen asleep in each other's arms. It was nice to occasionally surprise him, though.

Lord Valerian had stayed motionless when the bolt arrowed across the room. Coolly, he said, 'I liked that vase.'

Holly snorted. 'Did you, though?'

'It was a gift!' Valerian snapped. 'Be careful with your aim next time, Hazlemere.'

'And that's all you're saying?' Holly cast him a scathingly disbelieving look.

'It's obviously a weapon, captain,' Valerian said, 'and it's obviously of no further danger. No need to overreact.'

Holly's hands went to his hips. Hazel hastily got in, 'Ash sang Mancy to this copperlit and converted it into a weapon.'

Diverted, Holly said, 'Ash? Strangely, that makes much more sense than the idea that Albemarle might have made it.'

Evelyn took the copperlit from Hazel and examined it. 'Dead now?'

'Zhey can recharge it, I think. But only Albemarle can turn it back into a light.'

'I was of the understanding that Mancers can't change other Mancers' designs,' Valerian said slowly, 'let alone an actual created project.'

'So was I,' Hazel agreed. 'So's everyone. But maybe "can't" is more accurately said as "aren't sufficiently motivated to".'

'Or maybe it's just Ash,' Evelyn said. 'A hearing Mancer would never voluntarily amplify another Mancer like zhey do. Too much of zheir own work

to get on with. Perhaps the fact Ash is forced to work on other Mancers'
designs makes zhem learn the song well enough to alter the notes.'

'That makes a lot of sense, commander,' Hazel said. 'The Mancy song
zhey hummed was the copperlit song, but with just enough changed
notes to make it a new tune. Like a reprise.'

Holly, meanwhile, had stalked over to the wall, tracing his fingers over
the plaster where the light had spread like a drop of ink in water before
rippling away. 'Hoi, Hazel, did you kill the Cristati man, then?'

'I did not. Ash shot him with this. I made it look like a sword wound.'

Lord Valerian raised an eyebrow. 'They took the body with them. Will
your camouflage hold up to closer scrutiny?'

'Perhaps not, but they've no way of knowing it wasn't Albemarle's
design. We don't widely circulate that zhey don't make weapons, after all.'

'They may suspect, given you bothered disguising the wound at all,'
Valerian said sharply, and Hazel winced.

'There's another of those annoying good points of his,' Holly said,
stalking back across the room to lounge against Valerian's desk in his
short skirt. 'You might have fucked it, Hazel darling.'

Hazel pushed both hands through his hair, silently acknowledging the
likelihood of this.

'It was always going to happen,' Evelyn told him.

Lord Valerian turned his cool-eyed assessment from Holly's invasion
of his desktop back to Hazel. 'And Ash can do this to any Mancy creation?'

'I'm guessing,' Hazel said, 'that, if zhey know enough of its song, zhey
can do it to any Mancy that it *can* be done to.'

He had not yet questioned Ash; his guess, that Ash's talent was specific
to weapons but broad in application, was based purely on the Cristati
lieutenant's reaction, the fear and the hatred and sheer unsurprise when
he'd seen Ash take up the copperlit. The man had known *exactly* what
was about to happen to him to end his rash adventure.

He added, quietly, 'Not everything can be turned into a weapon.'

'Find out for sure,' Valerian commanded. 'And if there's a design in
Albemarle's arsenal that better suits this ability of Ash's, make the
Mancers get on it.'

Hazel nodded, but said, 'Albemarle won't like it.'

'Any of it,' said Evelyn grimly. 'Weapons, my sacred relics, how zhey'll
react...'

'We shouldn't tell zhem,' Holly said. His face was set. 'Zhey don't need
to know.'

Impassively, Valerian asked, 'Anything else?'

Hazel hesitated, then said, 'Ash was born in Stronghold Cristati. Zhey'd been there zheir whole life. If you want a measure of just how much they'd want zhem back.'

In the chilled pall that fell over them with that statement, a stuttering knock sounded at the door, and Lorian came in. The promise of the bruising on the side of the boy's face had blossomed magnificently. He stopped when he saw the senior guards arrayed before his father, Hazel sitting quietly, Evelyn as straight and controlled as a horseback rider, Holly loafing with his hip on the desk, magnificent legs on display.

He seemed about to turn on his heel, before, fretfully entwining his fingers together, he stood his ground. 'You summoned me, Father?'

Valerian nodded. 'They have questions. You will answer.'

Holly immediately launched off with, 'Did you tell the Cristati we had a new Mancer?'

Lorian gaped at him. 'No!'

Evelyn stood so that she was between Holly and Lorian. 'Lorian, no need to be alarmed.' It wasn't in her nature to soothe, but he responded to her briskly neutral tone, visibly settling. 'We'd like you to run through what happened last night, from the moment Lieutenant Dimitriou approached you.'

Gaze nervously switching between Evelyn and his father, Lorian slowly flushed until it was obvious what he would say. 'I approached him.'

'And then?' Evelyn prompted.

'Well, you were so *boring*,' Lorian said indignantly, leaning slightly to address Holly past the commander. 'I was so disappointed.'

Evelyn shifted to once again block Holly's sight of the lordling. Hazel leaned forward and put his hand on Holly's bare knee.

'Yes, all right, my love,' Holly jerked his knee, shaking Hazel's hand off. 'I'm not going to lose my shit at the child for not meeting his silly fantasy.'

'I'm not a child,' Lorian shouted at him. 'And Dimi recognised that even if you couldn't.'

'Please do keep lauding the man who used you as a hostage and murdered a Haven guard,' Lord Valerian said without inflection. 'I'm already exceedingly impressed by your recent behaviour.'

'You're both so boring! I can't believe I was crushing on him and he's as bad as you!'

'Do you remember a Haven is dead and our stronghold is at risk?'

Sulky and chastened, the boy folded his arms and looked at the ground. 'He wanted to go to the baths,' he muttered. 'He'd heard about our Mancy baths and he wanted to take me there. He said—'

He flushed again, much faster, a tide of red washing across his face, warming the pale brown so it almost matched his hair.

'A-yah, we all know the sorts of delights he promised to enact in the steamy warmth,' Holly said. 'Move along.'

Lord Valerian wore, for a moment, a look like he did not know and would like to, before returning his icy look on his son.

'But then Shao said we weren't allowed unless a Mancer guard was with us. I said she had to let me because I was a lord and she was just a servant.'

'Oh, Lorian,' Valerian said, for the first time with some emotion—deep disappointment—in his voice. 'I surely raised you better than that. Purple is not a privilege, it is a *responsibility*. Especially for you, of all people.'

'I know, Father.' Lorian's face lost its sulky mien. His shoulders bowed. The petulance of the adolescent was gone; the nascent man spoke. 'I shouldn't have. I tried to push past her. She wouldn't move, I was pushing her a bit.' Hazel exchanged a fast look with Holly, but Lorian went on before the suspicion could fully form. 'And then…' He was ashen now, distress rising. 'Dimi grabbed me.' His hand rubbed over bruises imprinted on his wrist. 'He said she was to be quiet. He pushed her out the way. She— She—'

'Lorian, this is very important,' Evelyn said softly. 'When the Cristati lieutenant pushed Shao out of the way, and she fell. Did he deliberately push her down, or did it just happen while they were struggling? Maybe he lost his temper?'

'He deliberately did it.' He sounded very sure. 'It wasn't temper. He— He laughed about it, while he was dragging me across the undercroft to the subterrane stairs. He said if a woman's place wasn't the kitchen, the bottom of the stairs with a broken neck would do. I— I didn't under-stand. I was—crying. He laughed at me. I tried to hit him, bite him.' Lorian looked at his father pleadingly. 'I did fight him. I couldn't get loose. He punched me. I fell. Then I heard some noises and shouting, and then you were there.' His gaze dropped. 'Thank you.'

Evelyn sighed. She glanced at Valerian. 'It sounds very much as if Dimitriou knew what he was going down there for, doesn't it? He had Lorian in hand as a hostage, so he didn't care what kind of trail he left behind him.'

But had he known before he met Lorian? Hazel shifted, drawing the boy's eye. 'When he asked to see the baths, did you agree straight away, or did he need to persuade you with big promises?'

He was working on one of his deep hunches, the same as for his guess about Ash's talent. He gathered Lorian had been quite drunk, and drunk people got fixated. In Lorian's case, it had been his birthday fantasy. From what Hazel had overheard in the bailey, that pleasant imagining had not involved the baths, it had been all about Lorian's bed and the potential of the bedposts and silken scarfs. The lieutenant wouldn't have needed to resort to dirty talk with Lorian unless Lorian had been resisting the idea of the baths.

'I didn't want to go at first,' Lorian confirmed. 'I wanted to go to my room. He kept saying he really wanted to see them. I said—' His face changed. 'Oh, no. Oh, shit.'

'You said we'd be recruiting for more Mancer guards soon, so he could join up and see the baths then,' Holly said.

He glanced over at Lord Valerian, pleased with himself. Valerian sighed.

'I wasn't that stupid,' Lorian protested, in a tone of voice that acknowledged he knew he hadn't been far off that stupid. He slumped again. 'I may have mentioned employment opportunities. I didn't say why.'

'Wouldn't have needed to,' Evelyn said. She was, Hazel saw, struggling to keep her face neutral. She probably wanted to throttle the boy, and only years of practice not throttling Holly was keeping her in check. 'Here's another important question. Did he have the chance to talk to any of his people before he took you downstairs?'

'Very important, Lorian,' Valerian said. 'Think.'

Lorian closed his eyes. Eventually he said, 'No, no, he didn't. We went straight out the back door of the great hall, just after the copperlits came back on.'

Hazel breathed a sigh of relief. Valerian and Evelyn had relaxed too. The air was suddenly easier to breathe, in a way that made it clear how stifling and thick the cloud of worry had been. Cristati still did not know for sure Ash was here. They strongly suspected it, that was plain, and their suspicions would only be stronger now, especially if they followed the same chain of logic Lord Valerian had, regarding if and why Hazel might have disguised the death wound. But for now—

Holly was still poised, tense. He flicked his hair back, making the beads in his braids clack like a knock-code. 'Are you certain?' he asked. 'The captain knew enough to post guards to keep an eye on anyone leaving the great hall for the undercroft.'

'Wait,' Lorian said. 'He did say something to one of the others as we left.'

'Oh, for fuck's sake, Lorian,' said Holly and Valerian in explosive unison.

~Fourteen~

Preparations were complete in the atelier, copper sheets, wires, springs, screws and stiff oilcloth all laid out in a precise array beside knives, saws, scissors, sewing needles, and pliers. The design, re-drawn enlarged onto a big amatl sheet, was pinned down at the start of the production line. It looked like a lever of some sort, with no real connection apparent between the schematic and the prepared materials.

Albemarle was knocking a fist on the benchtop, a slow beat communicating increasing frustration. Ash had insisted on waiting for Hazel. Both Mancers were on edge; the ravening need for Mancy was on them, made worse by the general tension in the stronghold today.

'I did tell Ash more than one of us can hold a tune,' Kito told Hazel. 'But zhey only want you, Hazel darling.'

'Stop reading into things.' Hazel ran a hand through his hair. Ash was watching him with the intense Mancer gaze. '~You want me on my knees?'

Holly wrapped his arms around his neck, pressing his lean length against him with a dramatic, 'Well, fuck, Hazel darling, since you mention it.'

'Sort yourself out, Holyoake.' He lowered himself before Ash, trying very hard not to blush because Holly, wearing his worst smirk, was pointedly fanning himself. '~It's just Mancy work.'

'~Is it, though? Is it, Ash?'

Ash blinked, the intense look wiping away into a determinedly neutral expression. Zhey ducked zheir head, nodding zheir fist, before spreading zheir hand across Hazel's throat. He swallowed, feeling the beat of his pulse hard against zheir palm. With zheir other hand, Ash held the far end of the cloth Albemarle had stretched out.

Albemarle began to sing the Mancy, slurring the words in a surprisingly jaunty tune. Hazel hummed along, and Ash closed zheir eyes, zheir fingertips digging in as zhey read the vibrations in his throat into zheir own skin. Zhey began to match the pitch and rhythm of Albemarle's melody. As before, zheir delicate harmony flowed back to Albemarle, and Albemarle's muttered words sought, found, and held clarity.

Ash, still singing, let go of Hazel to seize tight hold of the cloth with both hands. He rubbed his throat absently and caught Ash's frown, zheir gaze once again measuring him like he was part of the project, cutting through to his bones. The Mancer had seemed lost in the Mancy, was still lost in the Mancy if that intent stare was any indication, but the frown was anxious, apologetic.

Hazel waved away zheir concern. He didn't think Ash had left bruises this time and he wouldn't have minded if zhey had. But he retreated to the antechamber so he wouldn't distract the Mancer further. He hadn't known Mancers could be distracted once a project got underway.

Kito, accompanied by Holly, came back close to lunchtime to take the watch. She tapped Hazel lightly. 'I meant to say, that tattoo of Ash's? Bit late to be useful, but I saw a version of it on the Cristati lord's wrist.' She traced an outline on her own wrist. 'Just the feather with the colours. Ash must have added the knife lines zhemself, later.'

'To hide it?'

'Have you considered zhey just might not like having to wear the sign of a stronghold zhey wanted to escape?' Holly said. 'Zhey put a Mancer rune over it and turned it into a knife. Who knows what it says. It could say "Fuck you, Cristati".'

'It says "transformation". Like in music. Maybe you'd say "metamorphosis".'

They turned around. Albemarle was standing in the doorway of the atelier. 'It's lunch,' zhey said to zheir guards' surprised looks, which merely intensified them, because Albemarle had never yet kept zheir own self to the schedule. Zhey signed [meal]. 'Ash said so.'

Then zhey surprised them all again. 'Cristati, is it? Hmm. Yes. They steal Mancers.'

Hazel realised the Mancer Guard had been so determined to protect Albemarle's sensitivities that they'd successful kept the identity of the stronghold threatening Haven a secret from zhem. That may have been an error of judgment. Albemarle did not appear in any way upset or alarmed, merely dryly informative.

'What do you mean, dearest?' Kito asked zhem.

Kito was Albemarle's favourite, in so far that zhey cared enough to have a favourite. She didn't have to be quite as careful as the rest of the Mancer guards when asking things of Albemarle.

'Sometimes Juniper or Asquith write things in their letters which are not relevant,' Albemarle explained. 'Gossip. Juniper said Cristati stole a Mancer named Inigo. Asquith says they stole a Mancer named Mithra.'

Zhey lost all interest in the conversation, and plodded across the ante-chamber. Ash came out behind zhem. Respecting that zhey couldn't touch zheir atelier partner, zhey'd been waiting patiently for Albemarle to clear the doorway. Zhey paused when zhey saw Hazel, Holly and Kito looking at zhem, before, almost guiltily, hurrying after Albemarle. Kito briskly accompanied the pair.

'You better go have that talk with Ash, Hazel,' Holly said lazily, as they followed them out to the lobby. 'Zhey've had a dose of Mancy now, zhey're as calm as zhey're going to get.'

There was nowhere in the undercroft to have a private conversation that wasn't a bedchamber or Evelyn's office. Neither would be conducive to persuading their cagey Mancer to talk.

'Take zhem for a stroll around the garden, love. Weasel it out of zhem with that sweet smile of yours.'

Hazel demurred. 'It probably needs your ruthless touch, Hols.'

Holly stroked his fingers along Hazel's chest, put one finger to the hollow of his throat, and gave a single meaningful tap. 'You're the one zhey trust, Hazel darling.'

'Zhey don't—' Hazel stopped, thinking of how Ash's whole body had relaxed under his when zhey'd stroked his face and understood it was him in the dark.

He saw Holly's eyes sharpen, his interest quicken. 'And I think there might be a story here you've failed to share.'

'I'll just take zhem for a walk, shall I?' Hazel said, sidling away like a coward.

'I'm going to harass you till you spill it, my love,' Holly shouted. 'Spill it all over me, darling.' He winked at a couple of laundry staff coming down the stairs, who obliged him by giggling.

Ash sighed when Hazel made the invitation during lunch; zhey knew what was coming. But zhey pushed zheir soup away with one hand and set down the tiny spring zhey'd been repetitively compressing with the other.

It was Albemarle who said, 'No,' in zheir flat way. 'You cannot take zhem, I am using zhem. Have zhem this evening.'

'I just need to borrow zhem for twenty minutes. We'll be back before you've finished eating. Ten minutes, Albemarle. An entire pie all to yourself, Albemarle.'

He managed to extricate Ash with that promise, and took zhem out to the garden through the south door and across the lawn into the trees. He led zhem around a meandering path, away from Holly's tree. He didn't need to add that association to the memory of Ash's lithe body in his arms last night.

They came to the moon gate, a perfect upright circle of unmortared granite, overgrown by ivy and moss, small ferns softening its bottom curve. Practically speaking, it both marked and disguised Albemarle's air vent project. Aesthetically speaking, it was a lovely artwork of unabashed whimsy. Ash, like most visitors, was promptly charmed, stepping within the circle and touching the weathered stone arching overhead.

Maya had gone through a phase of asking which things made sound—she'd been both astonished and disappointed to discover that the sun and moon rode silently through the sky, at least to human ears, and that similarly the twinkling of the stars in the night sky was not an indication that they delicately crooned messages to those below.

When she'd seen the newly-erected moon gate, she'd exclaimed, ~Oh, but this must make a noise!

Hazel had been reluctant to disappoint his little sister again. '~What sort of noise would it make?' he'd asked in lieu.

~It would sing. She'd laid her hand on it. ~It sings! Ari, it sings!

He didn't tell her it was just the vibrations from Albemarle's air vents, invisibly set into the ground under and around the moon gate, as they exchanged fresh air into the subterrane. It was too rare to see her smile like that, in those first months after reaching Haven.

Now Ash touched the stone curving over zheir head and lit up in a way that made Hazel absently touch his heart. He had no doubt zhey were perceiving a song vibrating into zheir fingers just like Maya had. Zhey tilted back to follow the arc with a delighted smile, all the stern lines of zheir face and taut lines of zheir body relaxed into enchantment amid spears of golden light falling through the limbs of the trees overhead.

Hazel was a stoic man, given to neither dramatics nor exaggeration, but it was safe to say the aesthetics were fucking *killing* him.

He beckoned zhem onward. Beyond was a secluded glade with the sound of running water nearby. Hazel could almost taste the fresh scent of the rivulet, or it could have been Ash, that smell of rain and lightning that lingered when zhey'd been performing Mancy.

A rough bench was set under the dappled shade of an oak, fresh in leaf with the warming weather. The sunlight danced through the greenery and over Ash when zhey sat neatly on the bench, painting zheir silver hair so it glinted like the ripple of water through a rocky mountain rill.

Hazel realised he had missed the opportunity to run his fingers through the silky locks the previous night, and would never get another. He had to stop himself from swearing out loud.

~What did Kito say, again?

Ash had noticed him staring and jumped to the entirely correct assumption. Hazel rubbed his beard, rueful. 'I won't misconstrue. Sorry. I'm really not misconstruing. I just…' *really want to misconstrue.*

~You like my hair. You said it's pretty. And you like Kito's hair. And she said?

Oh. 'Aesthetics.' Disarraying his own hair further, he thought for some time how to convey this, and eventually signed a combination of [art] and [make], by which he implied artistry. '~She said she meets my aesthetics.'

~And what does she mean?

Again, Hazel didn't answer immediately. It was an opportune moment to explain that he didn't feel attraction—from the question, Ash suspected something along those lines already. It felt misleading to say that to the one person he did feel attraction for, but that couldn't be helped, not if he didn't want to make Ash scared of him again.

He sighed. '~It mostly means I find people pleasant to look at, without wanting to take them to bed.'

Ash nodded slowly. A flicker of some emotion crossed zheir face, too swift to read. ~And that's me? I meet your aesthetics like Kito does?

'~Not quite like Kito does,' Hazel admitted, looking at the ground.

Fuck, this was awkward. *Guess what, Ash? You won the fucking Glelissi public lottery and you didn't even know you held a ticket.* There was a significant difference between looking at someone with dispassionate, uncovetous admiration, and looking at someone because you wanted to bear zhem down to the soft moss and use your mouth on zhem until zhey clawed zheir fingernails into your back.

And he was not helping himself.

He now well and truly saw the justice of Holly openly laughing at him when he'd insisted he would just ignore his attraction to the Mancer until it went away. He'd had no practice hiding inappropriate desire: he was just going to have to get much better at it, very fast.

In the meantime, a change of subject was in order.

He cleared his throat. '~So. Couple of very small things to talk about. Do you want to start with Cristati, or what you did to Albemarle's copperlit?'

But Ash was looking down at zheir lap, hair a curtain about zheir face, sitting stiffly still.

Hazel carefully knelt at zheir feet, and inserted his hands above zheir lap, where zhey couldn't help but see them. '~Ash? What is it?'

~Embarrassed, zhey signed, head still bowed.

~Why?

~Last night.

Hazel rested his hands flat on zheir knees, indicating that he wasn't talking until zhey'd elaborated.

~I kissed you when I shouldn't have, and you didn't even want it. I'm so sorry.

Hazel kept his hands flat, because they had treacherously tried to leap into signing, *I wanted it. I want it now. I want it all the time.*

His thumbs had begun to stroke over Ash's knees of zheir own accord. Hazel removed his hands hastily. By Kisane's eyes, he could not let himself touch the Mancer anymore. It didn't matter that he casually touched other people as often as they touched him. Ash wasn't other people. He didn't feel brotherly toward Ash. Ash was burning him up.

Sitting back on his haunches, he waited till Ash dared look at him. '~I already said you don't need to fret about it, Ash. I understand. It wasn't— I found it— Fuck. How do I explain I liked it without making you think I'm going to ravish you?'

Ash gave zheir sharp laugh. Zheir shoulders hunched and then zhey straightened, smiling. ~I know you're not going to ravish me, Hazel darling.

Zheir unfathomable gaze met Hazel's, those grey-green eyes huge and serious.

A small part of Hazel wailed that it wasn't fair, that Holly already had so many willing men—he even had Lord Valerian on a string even if the lord didn't know it yet—he didn't need a Mancer as well. Hazel crammed that whiny little voice away and got himself back to business. He shook his head, shook his whole body, shaking away the desire and the lingering envy.

Sitting again beside zhem, he said, '~Ash, am I right to assume you can turn any suitable Mancy project into a weapon?'

Ash looked away. Hazel knew that tactic. Ash did not want to have this conversation. Ash was, as Holly had so succinctly put it, a spiky little fucker at times like this. Perhaps zheir curiosity about Hazel's aesthetics had purely been distraction.

Notwithstanding, Hazel put his hand on zheir upper arm. Zhey weren't wearing zheir coat, just one of the elegant vests the seamsters had designed for zhem. He felt the warmth of zheir skin through the thin linen of the embroidered undershirt. He had to resist letting his hand move, letting his thumb caress across the lithe muscle he felt under his palm.

He'd literally just told himself he wouldn't touch Ash anymore.

Appalled, he yanked his hand back. He'd brought Ash's attention with him. Ash slowly told him, ~Not any project, no. Though, Albemarle's designs are particularly suited to it. They…they're amenable, and predictable, and…consistent…in a way other designs often are not.

Hazel nodded. He'd wondered. Albemarle did beautiful work. He thought about the way Ash had looked at the wasp gun design, amused— and then tense. '~Will you tell me more?'

~It is best if I begin at the beginning.

'~All right. You said you were born in a stronghold. That was Cristati?'

~My name is A-S-H-L-I-N-S-I-L-V-E-R-T-H-O-R-N-E, after my father. I was born to Cristati. It was obvious from birth that I was a Mancer.'

Ash's face tightened as zhey waited for Hazel to acknowledge what this meant.

Anyone might have striking eyes and an androgynous face and show no affiliation for their particular culture's social gender cues without being a Mancer. The Holyoakes were a case in point. A latent Mancer nature might only come to the fore when the Mancy actually began to rise, which was often early adolescence, but could be years later.

Or a baby was born and the midwives would wash zhem and swaddle zhem and hand zhem to zheir parents with a meaningful sort of congratulations using a highly regulated pronoun.

Hazel was not sure how Ash expected him to react. He signed, ~Go on.

~My mother was disappointed at first. She had two sons, she wanted a daughter, she hadn't thought ahead. But Cristati had an empty atelier and now they had their very own Mancer, one they could train to their exact specifications. Her father, my grandfather, took me from her. He knew how valuable I would be to Cristati. It didn't matter that he'd have to wait years for the Mancy to rise. Cristati had already waited years.

Hazel nodded. Haven had had to wait, too, before Albemarle had chosen them. The only way to not have to patiently wait for your dice to roll up Mancer was to steal another stronghold's magic engineer. He thought of the two stolen Mancers Albemarle had named, but the thought was fleeting, because he was mostly thinking about training a Mancer to one's exact specifications. Ash's expression was carefully giving nothing away, making the signs harder to interpret.

'~Your family…'

Hazel could not think how to finish the question. Families had to formally renounce their Mancer child when the Mancy came on, so that the covenant would outweigh the web of myriad ancient laws preferencing bloodright claims.

And families did it, because the Mancy drive to create was stronger than any familial bond could ever be. They might even be relieved their exquisitely vulnerable yet absurdly valuable child was under a stronghold's protection and within an atelier's resources. It didn't mean they truly wanted to. It didn't mean they had to like it.

Ash ducked zheir head. ~Fully committed to the plans concocted by Cristati.

A-yah. And sometimes family could turn around and kick you in the teeth, too.

~Cristati expanded the atelier and recruited its Mancer Guard in readiness. But when I was a toddler, I succumbed to an illness, days of fever and rashes. I recovered, but it soon became apparent that my hearing was gone. My grandfather returned me unceremoniously to my mother's care and died of the disappointment.

Hazel had to raise an eyebrow at this straight-faced facetiousness. Ash's impish little smile flashed. ~Or so I was repeatedly told.

Hazel couldn't help it. He took Ash's hand and squeezed. Ash was being flippant, but a certain level of pain was peeking out from behind zheir meticulous neutrality. Ash patted his hand and took zheir own back to keep talking.

~My mother is…very determined, and her father had taught her the value of ambition. She had something to prove to him, I think, or to his shade, or to the rest of the family perhaps. I believe that in the years until my Mancy rose, Cristati conducted a great deal of research into Mancers, both privately and through the academy. My mother set me to learn

Mancer runes and to learn to read both lips and vibrations. She tried to teach me to speak as well, but it didn't take.

Ash put something decidedly satisfied and stubborn into zheir signs there; Hazel mentally adjusted his interpretation to more along the lines of, 'I refused to let it take.'

'~And Trade?' He was puzzled; if Ash had spent such a long time learning to sign, zhey should have been more fluent when zhey first arrived. Haven's slang expanded on but did not so dramatically diverge from traditional Trade. '~Or is a different sign language more common inland?'

Ash's hands went to fists. Zhey sat still for a long moment, before signing, ~I was not permitted to learn any sign language.

Hazel struggled with himself before he announced, '~That is absolute *bullshit—*'

~I know, I know. My mother saw it as a crutch, Hazel, one that would weaken Stronghold Cristati. They wanted me to pass as able in front of visitors, and Trade gives the game away.

'~You *are* fucking able—'

~Please, signed Ash. ~Please, Hazel, it's not the important thing right now. I know you're upset to think of Maya being treated like that, but—

'~I'm upset to think of *you* being treated like that, thanks.'

Ash abruptly folded zheir hands into zheir lap, left clutched tight over right, and stared straight ahead, wearing zheir little furrow of a frown. Hazel made himself wait patiently, aware his heart was overstepping its proper bounds.

Eventually, Ash stirred. ~Thank you, Hazel darling. You are very kind to your Mancers.

'A-yah,' Hazel murmured. 'Haven's Mancers.'

~Especially considering one of them has brought chaos down on Haven's head.

'~If we're not prepared to defend our atelier, we don't deserve to proclaim ourselves a stronghold, do we?' When Ash did not look overly comforted, he added, '~You were lucky, you know, landing in Haven, with the Holyoakes in charge of the Mancer Guard. No one gets past the Holyoakes.'

And, to be fair, Ari Hazlemere was no slouch with a sword, either.

Ash's hands absently formed [luck]. Zhey summoned a smile. ~If you are finished with your outrage…

Hazel raised mock-offended eyebrows and won a real smile. '~How did you learn Trade then?'

Ash grimaced. ~A nursemaid, for a little while. And one of my half-brothers was somewhat sympathetic to me, when no one was looking. And— Anyway, I learned enough to get by.

Zhey made a clean cut through the air to indicate a change of subject. ~Obviously when my Mancy rose at last, I was in some strife.

Ash paused and considered him. Hazel practically saw the mental shrug when zhey continued. ~That myth about Mancers peeling their own skin off if they can't do Mancy? Not quite a myth, after all.

Rolling back zheir sleeves over zheir graceful forearms and past the elbows, zhey showed Hazel the mass of white scars in the crooks of zheir arms.

Zhey held still for a beat, letting him look, and then signed, ~I now give you permission to indulge yourself in a very small amount of pity and concern.

Zhey held zheir arms out again. Hazel was both experiencing a genuine fond response to Ash's wry humour, and struggling to disguise the actual pity and concern Ash was being so lightly scathing about. He put his hands together so he wouldn't touch, and then couldn't help it. With one careful finger, he stroked over the ridged scar tissue, first on one arm, then the other. It looked like an animal had tried to flay zhem, starting at the elbow and ripping downward.

He could imagine a young Ash, clawing frantically, futilely, into zheir own skin in a fever to release the Mancy. Zheir people would have known to take away sharp objects. They hadn't known to cut zheir nails, however, and nothing could be done about teeth. They hadn't quite understood just how desolated a Mancer who couldn't do Mancy would become on the inevitable slide into madness.

He thought of how bitten down Ash's nails had been, on the day zhey had arrived. How long had zhey been without an atelier? How frantic had zhey been, when zhey had faced down Albemarle's obstinacy and insisted on zheir right to access the Haven Mancy workshop?

Ash had closed zheir eyes. Hazel supposed zhey were barely tolerating the touch, the pity zhey assumed came along with it. He took his hand away, and smiled sheepishly at Ash when zhey opened zheir eyes again.

'~Consider me indulged, then. Please continue.'

~It was desperation that made them steal a Mancer from another stronghold.

'~Inigo?'

Hazel'd had to fingerspell it; Ash answered with an unknown sign Hazel assumed was Inigo's. Zhey didn't look surprised, and Hazel remembered again that there was a hitherto unsuspected and yet well-established Mancer communication network hidden beneath the schematics they openly sent each other. Ash would know Albemarle had told him.

~No, zhey came later. First, Cristati stole M-I-T-H-R-A, Mithra. They thought a very experienced Mancer could help me, and, actually, they were right.

Zhey looked at Hazel and signed [mensuration]. ~Mithra taught me how to hear zheir melody through vibrations and harmonise with it, augment it. It released enough of my Mancy to bring me back to sanity.

~But I was impatient working with another Mancer. Mithra was a good teacher. I understand how patient zhey were now, but then zhey seemed old and slow and cautious to me. Zhey told me how Mancers do things, and I'm sure zhey're right but it felt old-fashioned, superstitious. I wanted to work on my own. I knew zheir songs so well, so I thought I could sing it alone. I didn't know any better. So I tried one day.

Ash paused here and heaved a great breath.

'~And this is when you found you could make weapons?'

Zhey nodded. ~We had been singing calids, small Mancy orbs that needed charging frequently, like Albemarle's copperlits. The stronghold sits on an island in the middle of a shallow lake. It's cold, damp. They used them for warmth, and drying laundry, and heating water and… Well, you know. The same as the copperlits, really, but we never did put lights into them. I don't know if it occurred to Mithra.

Zheir hands stuttered over Mithra's name a few times. Hazel laid his fingers across zheirs, stroked along the damaged ring fingers, just the once before making himself retreat.

Ash seemed fortified by the touch, however, and went on. ~I thought it would be a nice surprise for Mithra to come into the atelier and find most of the routine work already done. I think I started well. I remembered exactly how zheir song went. It felt like my song, too. But it wasn't. It couldn't ever be. I was listening to it through the vibrations where my fingers were touching the metal of the calids, and that's fine if the creator Mancer is there to keep it true. But alone, my own Mancy twisted the song. It turned the calid into something like you saw last night.

Again, the conspicuous pause for breath. Hazel restrained himself.

~Mithra was furious. When zhey saw what I had done, zhey attacked me. The Mancer Guard had to pull zhem off me. It was terrifying. Zhey'd always been so…accepting, in a vague sort of way. But I believe zhey would have killed me. Zhey were frenzied, maddened as a rabid dog. Zhey bit me.

Zhey touched zheir ear, the scarred lobe.

~The Cristati, on the other hand, were delighted. Even when Mithra died of the injuries zhey'd received when the Mancer Guard pulled zhem off me.

It was Hazel's turn to take one of those sudden, shuddering breaths. Any Mancer guard should know how to bring their stronghold's Mancer down without harming zhem. It was part of academy training; Albemarle was by no means the only Mancer with the potential to lash out destructively, toward the self or otherwise. That was the nature of Mancy.

~Yes. Quite. But it didn't matter, you see, because they had discovered what I could do. And I had to do it. I had no other way to satisfy my Mancy. I had to turn every one of those calids into neat and deadly little weapons while Cristati went out and got me another Mancer. Inigo.

Ash smiled, faintly. ~Inigo was not my friend. I suppose zhey'd somehow heard what happened to Mithra, or zhey were unhappy about being taken from zheir stronghold, or that Cristati wouldn't let zhem write to zheir colleagues anymore—I was a tightly kept secret—or that zhey had to share the atelier. Zhey certainly didn't like working with another Mancer no matter how well I could augment zheir work. But still, Inigo and I worked together for…it might have been the best part of a decade, I think. We don't really track time well, when we're working.

'~And all that time, zhey were never your friend?' Hazel asked, quietly astonished. He couldn't imagine anyone not liking Ash. Biased, he supposed, pressing a hand over his heart.

~I do not believe zhey ever much warmed to me. Like Mithra, zhey despised me when I changed zheir songs. But we were on good enough terms that zhey agreed to escape with me. That was my first attempt.

This was when the story truly got hard for Ash. Zhey rested zheir head in zheir hands, elbows propped on knees, whole body curling up defensively. If it had been anyone else, Hazel wouldn't have hesitated to move in for a hug.

Oh, fuck it, he thought, and engulfed his Mancer with '~May I?' as a bit of an afterthought.

Ash turned into his shoulder and let zhemself be held. Hazel could feel the heave of zheir back under his hands, the rapid breathing.

Gradually, zhey settled and sat up away again, pushing zheir hair back. ~Thank you, Hazel darling. I can continue. For a long time, I did not make useful weapons. I made things like the copperlit, with its single shot. It's Mancy but it's not even as practical as a longbow. Let alone even the cheapest musket. All my transformations were like that, small or too dangerous, or both. I have very little control over it; I believe the design has more influence than me.

~Inigo would create projects from zheir designs, and I would help, long enough to learn the song. And then I would work my Mancy on it alone. It always turned into something that could be used for lethal purposes, but it was never on the scale that Cristati had in mind.

~Eventually, Cristati gave Inigo specific instructions. Zhey were to only create designs that seemed like they would work better as weapons. Inigo resisted, of course, no Mancer likes to be told which designs to sing into projects. But… Well, Cristati had a firsthand lesson in what inability to release zheir Mancy does to a Mancer. They tortured Inigo, Hazel, by locking zhem out of the atelier until zhey came up with something that looked like a proper weapon.

'~I'm so sorry.'

Ash shook zheir head. Zheir hands were speeding through the story now, silent except for the whisper of skin on skin as zheir fingers brushed, the fluid grace at odds with the grimness of the tale. ~I had asked to leave, previously. And before you say it, Hazel, Cristati do not care about the covenant. I'd asked to leave, and been denied, on grounds of my own safety. But I knew what they intended to use me for and I saw what they were doing to Inigo, and so I decided to leave anyway and take zhem with me.

~I started by sneaking zhem into the atelier so we could create our escape. The Cristati atelier is on the upper floor of the stronghold, opposite the purple residences. We climbed out the atelier window and lowered ourselves down the side of the stronghold with the Mancy ladder we'd just crafted. It was not so far down as it would be here.

~Stronghold Cristati is right in the middle of the lake. We were caught crossing the causeway to shore; we should have Mancied ourselves a boat and struck out in the other direction. Our own Mancer Guard delivered us back to our prison. Lady Cristati had Inigo executed.

Hazel made [expletive] with a compulsive jerk of his hands. He had not been expecting anything of the sort. No one, *no one*, killed Mancers. The covenant forbade it as a mere formality. Ethics aside, it was just too wasteful of a rare jewel.

~Oh, Hazel, Ash signed, with a despairing sort of smile. ~You are too kind, and Haven is too kind of a place. Yes, of course they executed Inigo. Zhey gave me too much hope. Worse, zhey defied Cristati, and Cristati does not swallow insult.

Hazel thought of the Cristati lieutenant, Dimitriou, so bold and confident in coming down alone into the subterrane, and of the man's captain, Tassone, who had not bothered to disguise his contemptuous anger even surrounded by a foreign Mancer Guard. Yes, these were not people used to being humbled.

~Then they acquired their next Mancer, and this one they did not steal. This one came right across the causeway to the main gates, to ask for sanctuary under the covenant. Zhey were so young, and zhey had no idea zhey were walking into a prison with bars on the atelier windows. Zhey just arrived at zheir nearest stronghold, ravenous with the Mancy need. It was an immense stroke of luck for Cristati, and then they had another, because this new Mancer happens to also have a gift for [call it tinkering].

Hazel shook his head. It was that sign Ash had used when trying to explain how a Mancer might work on another's design. Ash sighed again. ~For…for editing another's designs. Zhey make zheir own, of course, but, while zhey cannot sing any of Mithra's and Inigo's original designs, zhey can alter them just by looking at zheir notebooks. Zhey can change them enough that zheir Mancy sings its own song, especially working with me in mensuration. That gives zhem almost a dozen years' worth of ideas that zhey can tinker with.

~Then, simply put, I sing zheir song wrong, and turn the project into a weapon. It took a few years, but suddenly my perverse creations were not looking so useless anymore. We were closing in on a truly effective weapon.

~I knew what Cristati would do once they had workable weapons on a large scale. I had no way of refusing. So I escaped. I did not try to bring my partner this time. I can only hope they did not punish zhem in my stead. I trust not, because they must assume they'll get me back, and [unknown name] is too useful if they get me back. We both agreed to risk it.

Hazel cocked his head. The unknown name sign looked like a rippling combination of parts of [baby], [night], [wise], and [bird], which under any other circumstances, he would have interpreted as Trade's work-around for 'owlet'.

He almost asked, and didn't, instead asking, '~How did you escape, given the first try went so badly?'

Ash clenched zheir fists again, tightly. Zhey looked away. ~I am ashamed to tell you.

Hazel guessed that Ash had used one of zheir uselessly small-scale and yet eminently lethal weapons. He knew zhey could be ruthless. And zhey would have had to be, to escape a properly trained Mancer Guard intent on holding zhem inside a stronghold.

'~You never need feel ashamed for doing what needed doing, Ash. No matter what it was.'

Ash tilted zheir head back, staring up at the sky through the dance of leaves over their heads. ~Tell me that again one day, Hazel, zhey signed, with very small movements of zheir hands. ~I might believe you.

Hazel let it drop. Ash was near the end of zheir endurance, he could tell. '~Just one more thing, then. Can this new project with Albemarle be a weapon? Is that why you chose it?'

The Mancer gave a tiny nod, and then another one when Hazel asked, ~Will it help Haven?

Hazel couldn't help himself then. He took Ash's chin and lifted zheir face so their eyes met. '~Thank you, Ash.'

Ash shook zheir head, zheir silver hair fallen forward over one eye. ~I'm why Haven is at risk.

Hazel shrugged. '~That's the covenant.' It was taking everything he had not to tuck that lock of hair back behind Ash's ear.

~Will you tell Albemarle?

Hazel had been contemplating this. He was a slow thinker, but a deep one. He'd eventually come to same conclusion that Holly had instinct-ively leapt to, but with a great deal more guilt than Holly evinced. To tell Albemarle not only that zheir new partner had a knack for weapons, but that Haven intended to use that knack in its defence—zhey would be stunned into catalepsy for sure.

He'd been Albemarle's guard, in one capacity or another, for near enough to twenty years; it hurt not to be honest with zhem. It would hurt zhem more to know what zhey were working toward right now.

And Haven couldn't afford for zhem to stop working. Ash couldn't do it on zheir own, not until Albemarle had given zhem the song and they'd finished the project together.

At the very foundation of the covenant lay the trust between a Mancer and zheir Mancer Guard. Haven was upholding the covenant for Ash. Hazel couldn't help but feel, at a fundamental level, that Haven was breaking its covenant with Albemarle. *He* was breaking the covenant with Albemarle.

A-yah, he was carrying some guilt. He made the negatory sign.

Ash wiped at zheir eyes. Zhey might have been carrying some guilt, too.

~FIFTEEN~

Hazel stays with the Mancers in the atelier. Holly takes the other guards running, up and down the stairs, to tell them about what Ash did to the copperlit well away from Albemarle. Holly, because he's just an all-round nice person, makes a point of serving Ash ginger and honey tea before they all head off for the run. When he closes the atelier door behind them, Ash is savouring the warm, sweet, spicy taste with zheir eyes closed, while Hazel is shaking his head at Holly, his warm brown skin warming further, its undertones almost rosy with his adorable embarrassment.

There comes the usual pause while those of the Haven Mancer Guard possessing breasts take a private moment to strap them or more firmly bind them or otherwise quell those suckers, as Kito puts it, which leaves Holly and Second Jerome, already stripped of their coats and swords, twiddling thumbs at the base of the corkscrew stairs.

'Maybe you should practice running the stairs without the Mancy leg, SJ,' Holly says.

'I used to have to go up and down the stairs all the time before Albemarle made the Mancy leg.'

'I mean without a crutch, fast. Like in a battle.'

'Well, I mean, that would be an awful lot of hopping,' Second Jerome says dubiously. 'I've got a strong calf on the other side but I'm not sure it's that strong. We haven't practiced escape techniques for a while, can't we do that?'

'Escape?' Holly says. 'There is no escape, there's only glory or death.'

'You shouldn't say stuff like that,' Second Jerome scolds. 'The juniors actually listen to you, you know.'

He obliges Holly by unstrapping the leg and hopping up and then back down the corkscrew stairs. He's fairly fast on the way back down, but that's more a matter of balancing while he half-slides. The way up looks strenuous.

'Prefer practising fighting without it,' he says as he reattaches the leg, sitting on the bottom step. He's looking a little flushed and sweaty; his kohl eyeliner has smudged a bit and his dark hair is mussed out of its usual smooth waves.

Holly wraps his braids in a silk cloth, bright blue and adorned with large pink hibiscus. It's his version of one of the vaguely-remembered ceremonial outfits of his southern homeland, obliterated by civil war. He prefers his hair wrapped up and out of the way when he runs, unlike when he spars—he loves the way his braids swing around his head as he pivots and parries and leaps about, knowing not even Kito would dare use them as a tether, but they just get annoying and disarrayed in the run.

Once the others reassemble, Holly leads them off at a sprightly pace. Just to show off, he turns and bounces up the stairs backward at speed as he outlines Hazel's adventures the night before, the demonstration of the weaponised copperlit in Valerian's office, and the information Hazel gleaned from Ash by the moon gate.

'But Mancers don't sing each other's designs,' Nightingale says quietly as they run along the hallway toward the backstairs.

She's looking down as she jogs, shy at interrupting, at arguing in the teeth of eyewitness testimony that Ash did exactly that, but she couldn't hold back the comment. Well might she be confused; outside of the academy, her people, who worship Mancers, are some of the most knowledgeable in Eldemira.

Holly makes the sign Hazel showed him, [call it tinkering], the sign Ash used to talk of the talents of zheir Mancer partner.

'Apparently,' he says, 'some can, in some sort of way.'

'Oh!' Nightingale is staring off into space, eyes wide, shocked. 'Oh, no...'

She stumbles and stops, and almost makes Titus trip over her. The remaining Mancer guards halt, too, some more glad of the rest than others. Titus leans on the wall, panting. First Jerome flaps her robe a little; the runs are hardest on her because her traditional garb is not meant to be run in and the inventive seamsters have yet to come up with an alternative that meets her people's stringent requirements.

'I'm really not good for any more surprises today, Nightingale,' Holly says.

'It's just...it's a *sin*.'

'That covers a wide range of activity, darling,' Kito tells her, giving her a warning nudge.

Nightingale straightens and assumes a wooden tone Holly knows means she's trying to give a detached report like a soldier. 'I think Ash must have been talking about bricolage. You know, when a Mancer'—her whole face screws up in disgust—'*fiddles* with another's design until zhey change the song enough to sing it zhemself. It's a really bad thing to do. And then to do it to an existing *project*, fill it up with *wrong* Mancy. It's—it's so *shameful*.'

'So, they can all do this, but it's just not the done thing? And you never thought to mention it?'

'Don't they teach this at the academy?' Nightingale whispers, eyes filling with tears at Holly's tone, sharper than he meant it to be.

'No, darling, they don't,' Kito says, before the academy-trained guard has to.

Holly has the sense he's made a bad mistake, forgetting how shy Nightingale is around her seniors, too shy to volunteer information she's assumed they already knew, especially information she obviously finds filthy.

Forgetting that the academy can only know and teach what Mancers admit to that venerable establishment.

Forgetting that people confess sins to their priests or other religious authorities that they might never reveal to an academic researcher.

'Sorry,' she says, her voice barely audible. 'I thought…'

Titus takes her hand and squeezes. 'Just breathe, Ruby, it's all right. Keep telling us.'

'They can't all do it, surely,' Nightingale goes on, still shaky. 'If it was a normal thing to do, it wouldn't disgust most Mancers, would it? It takes a certain sort of perverted mind.'

'Sounding a little intolerant now there, birdie,' Holly says, but softens it with a teasing smile.

Nightingale shakes her head stubbornly. 'It's like. It's like…' There are terrible things in this world, but young Nightingale is struggling to think of one, having lived in Haven for long enough that such things are distant. 'Not using the Mancer pronoun.'

'Truly shocking,' Holly says, and he's only being mildly sarcastic, because, actually, it is.

They have all seen Ash work with Albemarle in mensuration. And, according to Hazel, Ash strongly implied that Mancers engage in a mild level of bricolage when they write to each other and help fix each other's designs. But Nightingale's revulsion is directed at those who tinker with another's design without permission or, worse, outright mangle another's song.

It sounds to Holly very much like mensuration is a more acceptable version of bricolage, that in fact, the whole gamut of Ash's behaviour is all on one single line, from mensuration at one far end to singing the wrong Mancy into another Mancer's project at the other far end.

Nightingale and her people wouldn't see it that way. It seems Mancers didn't see it that way either. From what Hazel relayed earlier, and what Nightingale is saying now, Holly makes an educated guess that when Ash tried to work on zheir first partner's project alone, zhey unknowingly crossed the line from tolerated mensuration to taboo bricolage. No wonder Mithra reacted as zhey did, if it is truly as perverse to Mancers as Nightingale thinks it is.

The run's not over—they usually go all the way up and all the way down several times—but Holly dismisses the others and fronts up at Evelyn's small office to report both Hazel's gleaned information and Nightingale's inadvertently withheld intelligence. His sister's not there, and it's a flip of a coin as to whether she's with Valerian or Lady Fairhaven. Holly chooses the former, since the latter might amount to an interruption he doesn't quite have the fortitude to make.

But when he knocks and parades into Valerian's office, the lord is alone, working at his desk. He gives Holly a flat look. After their mutual outburst at Lorian, he turned on Holly and snarled, 'Don't talk to my son like that,' and it took Evelyn's forceful intervention to remove Holly without bloodshed, verbal or otherwise. The siblings then had a stiff discussion on what a father was allowed to say to his son verses what an unrequited and very former crush was allowed to say. Valerian, it seems, has not yet let the insult go.

Holly says, 'I was hoping to find Evie.' At the lord's pointed stare, he sighs dramatically and corrects himself. 'Commander Holyoake. She's not here, so I will also not be here. My lord.'

He dips a curtsy, deliberately invoking the last time he did that, and starts to turn away.

'You may make your report to me,' Valerian says, wintery eyes fixed at a point over Holly's shoulder.

So Holly strolls further into the office, and leans on Val's desk, displaying his long, lean legs, bare and gleaming in the copperlit light. He crosses one ankle over the other and the lord tracks the movement like his gaze is welded to it. Holly lifts his arms, defined with lines of muscle where he's rolled his sleeves back for the run, and begins to unwind the silk from around his braids.

Valerian, tapping a Mancy pen in a staccato rhythm, says, 'Watch my paperwork, Captain Holyoake, it's a desk, not a chair,' but he sounds a little strangled and he doesn't look away from the languid movement of Holly's fingers, except to glance back at Holly's legs.

Holly's smiling as he gives his report.

Valerian looks moderately horrified when Holly's finished. 'We've been letting Albemarle send zheir designs out into the world for years. And now you're telling me other Mancers can use them?'

'Apparently it's a rare talent,' Holly says mildly.

He doesn't believe this; he thinks it's taboo keeping it reined in, not rarity. Otherwise, Ash is phenomenally lucky, to be able to do it, and to snag at random another Mancer who can do it too.

'Why did Nightingale not tell us any of this?' Valerian snaps.

'She thought we knew.' Notwithstanding that he was sharp with Nightingale himself on this exact point, he adds, 'You can back off my guard, lover.'

'But she fail—'

'She's shy. Quiet little Val knows how it is to be shy, doesn't he?'

Holly deliberately switches which ankle is crossed over which with rather more movement of his legs than this minor adjustment truly requires, and leans back further on the desk, consigning the paperwork to the oblivion in which it belongs.

Val doesn't quite lick his lips but Holly would wager a goodly amount that it's not for lack of wanting to.

The lord straightens abruptly and glares at him. When Holly keeps right on smiling, running the silk cloth between his fingers, he clears his throat and tries to briskly return to business. 'Do you think this story of Cristati murdering their Mancers is true?'

Holly is fair enough to give this due consideration. 'Seems wasteful,' he says in deliberate understatement. 'I don't see a reason for Ash to lie, though.'

'To garner Hazlemere's sympathy?'

'Oh, zhey have that already and more,' Holly says.

And, in return, all Hazel would have to do is crook a finger; it infuriates Holly, for the principle of the thing, that he hasn't yet done so. He'll probably have to be prodded and nudged and outright shoved into action.

'Indeed.' Valerian pushes his chair back and briefly presses his fingers to his closed eyes. He looks tired. He'll be dealing with Lady Fairhaven and Them Upstairs, shielding Evelyn and the Mancer Guard. 'They are somewhat…enamoured…of each other?'

He's speaking carefully, and Holly knows why. Here's a bone he absolutely will not throw unless the lord grows a spine and directly asks for it.

Again, Valerian is careful, looking at Holly closely for reaction, as he adds, 'It's allowed, is it?'

Holly narrows his eyes. 'If you want to ask if *I* allow it, then go ahead and ask if I allow it, my lord.'

Val does not ask if Hazel is Holly's lover and if so, does he permit fucking about. Instead he says, 'Captain Holyoake, do you allow your guards to engage in relations with the Mancer?'

'I don't have a *policy*, you fucking bureaucrat,' Holly says, unexpectedly exasperated. 'It hasn't come up before now. We only had Albemarle.'

The lord will not be dissuaded. 'Didn't they have something to say about it at your lauded academy?'

They said absolutely nothing about it at the academy, not openly. There had been an undercurrent, though, and that undercurrent had a distinct direction to it: Mancers probably wouldn't want it, being generally too obsessed with Mancy for recreation, but if they did want it, they got it. Whether a Mancer guard procured a suitably willing and discreet party or *were* the suitably willing and discreet party, the Mancer got what the Mancer wanted.

So Holly says, 'Nah,' and smirks at Valerian's irritated huff.

He does take a moment, a very small and fleeting moment, to appreciate that Valerian has raised this with him rather than Commander Holyoake; he recognises that Val doesn't want to get Hazel into trouble, if it were to turn out that having a wild crush on the stronghold's Mancer is forbidden.

Val isn't to know that Hazel has no plans to act on it, being both too used to merely obliging other people's desires if approached, and too inexperienced with his own newly awakened desire to recognise Ash's reciprocal crush. Holly assumes Ash must be too inexperienced to push zheir suit as well.

By the lost relics of his ancestors, some people really need to learn to talk to each other.

Shaking his head, the lord persists. 'Does it not put a vulnerable person in an even more vulnerable position?'

It takes a moment before Holly realises Val means the Mancer. 'Ash isn't the vulnerable one here. If anyone's going to get hurt, it'll be Hazel.'

Valerian pauses, and his tone is delicate when he asks, 'And that doesn't bother you?'

It does bother Holly, but not for the reason Valerian assumes. He folds his arms, defensive. 'Hazel's a grown man, he can take care of himself.'

Heaving another sigh, Valerian touches his mouth. 'The Mancer is alone. If one of zheir guards demands— Generally speaking. I don't mean Hazlemere.' He has to add that, in haste, because Holly has shot upright, turning on him with a hand on his hip and a fierce scowl. 'A Mancer has no allies, if zheir Mancer Guard doesn't do right by zhem. It is not a fair relationship. One side has all the power.'

'The Mancer,' Holly says, settling back onto the desk with a slight show of sulkiness.

'Holly.' His name is the embodiment of pure exasperation. 'The Mancer Guard.'

'The Mancers have the power,' Holly insists. 'I don't know if you were paying attention when Albemarle first arrived, but zhey had at least seven Mancer guards dismissed before zhey accepted the final sixteen and me and Hazel as initiates. Zhey have the power.'

'I was, in fact, paying attention when Albemarle first arrived,' Valerian says, the unspoken *you dick* very much plain under his usual coolly measured tones. 'And if my father had chosen not to respect zheir wishes, there would not have been a damned thing zhey could have done about it. No family, no personal wealth, no recourse to a different atelier lest the Mancy drive destroy zhem before zhey reached it. Zhey would've had to accept it. That's not power.'

For all of Holly's sterling qualities, he is not good at seeing greys. He knows Hazel turns his deep thoughts in this direction in idle moments. He's seen him frowning at Ash as he muses on the gaps the legal covenant has failed to pave over, and the sort of stronghold Haven's new Mancer must have fled.

That's not Stronghold Fair Haven, of course, and Hazel eventually developed the same deep trust in Haven as Holly holds. But Hazel came from a village whose traditions turned superstitious neighbours into an incipient mob ready to hunt his baby sister as sacrifice to a harvest spirit; it would've been terrifying and Holly can respect why Hazel questions some of the academy's august traditions, without really knowing what to do with that questioning, who to take it to, how to make it better. He understands why Hazel hesitates to completely trust the traditions of a venerable but flawed institution.

Holly, however, watched his own people's traditions not so much toppled as ripped to shreds by savage and sudden civil conflict. The ground under his feet turned to quicksand; ever since, he's needed it to feel as solid as iron. Therefore, for all his insolence and irreverence, he cleaves to any palatable tradition and any institution strong enough to hold him up—Haven, of course, and the Mancer Guard, yes, and the covenant, and the academy.

He knows the Mancer has the power, because that is what the academy taught him, and he has iron faith in that establishment.

'And have we considered what Evie and the other Mancer guards were trained to do if Albemarle's wishes had been overridden?' he asks.

'The Mancer Guard turning against its own stronghold, is it? Is that ideal?'

'That's all for the patron to balance, Val,' Holly says cheerfully. 'You stand between the atelier and the stronghold. That's your job.'

'And you despise me for it. You made that perfectly clear last night.'

Holly says, 'I don't— Oh, I shouted at you, didn't I?' He tsks. He smiles. Since he's fucking with Valerian, he doesn't change his tone in the slightest when he adds, 'You didn't put me in my place hard enough, then. Best try it again.'

Holly waits for Val's blank look to begin to dissolve into a flush and only then does he clarify. 'Put me on my knees, lover.'

Val stands and paces away. 'That is your way of reminding me I have no high ground to be questioning power differentials in sexual relations, I suppose.'

Holly, mystified, says, 'That is my way of explicitly requesting sexual relations, since I enjoyed myself so very much last time.'

Val is over by the unlit fireplace; they don't much light fires in the stronghold nowadays, now the copperlits can heat rooms, and anyway, Val comes from the frozen north and couldn't possibly be burdened by Haven's clement winters.

He leans on the mantle. 'How could you have?' he mutters into the empty grate.

Holly straightens up off the desk and shoves Val's carefully organised paperwork onto the floor with a dramatic flourish. He's been blindsided.

That sort of bigoted opinion is rare in Haven; anyone who holds it has either long since departed for more receptive locations or at least has the decency to shut the fuck up about it. Val's fucking lucky the Mancer guards take their swords off for the run.

The gentle but telltale flutter of the papers through the air and down onto the rug makes Valerian turn around. He stares at the snowy chaos. 'All right, and what was that for, now?'

Incensing Holly further, he doesn't sound angry, or even particularly puzzled. He merely sounds resigned, as if accepting that this irrational display is just the sort of shit Rowan Holyoake does and there's not much to be done about it.

'How could a real man possibly enjoy having a cock in his mouth?' Holly seethes. 'You're coming at me with that shit? It was *your cock*, you hypocritical fucker.'

Now the lord's indignation spirals up after all. 'I meant because you don't like me and I made you do it.' He stomps over to the rug, eyes fixed on the mess Holly has made. 'As to your egregiously erroneous assumptions, I believe I would, in fact, quite enjoy having y— Oh, that's the quartermaster's inventory, I need that for my next meeting.'

He awkwardly stoops and starts collecting the papers, dropping to his knees after a moment as the magnitude of the job becomes apparent.

Holly is once again reminded that behind Valerian's aristocratic façade and coldly irritable manner beats the well-intentioned heart of a diligent and overworked bureaucrat who is currently responsible for planning the logistics of Haven's response to the Cristati threat. He taps himself on the forehead and kneels next to Lord Valerian to help him pick up the strewn papers.

'Please don't,' Val says tiredly. 'You're just further disordering them.'

'I really don't see how that's possible.'

'You can go. You're dismissed, captain.'

Holly sits back. Valerian tries to pull some of the paperwork out of his hands, and Holly catches his wrist, making him look at him. 'You didn't make me do it,' he says. 'I wanted you, badly. And I do like you.'

'You don't. You wouldn't even let me touch you.'

At this fairly fucking plaintive complaint, Holly smiles. 'I'll let you touch me now, my lord.'

The lord twists his wrist in Holly's grip. 'Are you entertained?' He still sounds weary, but there's a bite to it. 'Tormenting me, making me want you, making me unable to even *think* of anything but you? I trust I'm giving you the performance you're after?'

Since Valerian is making no move to seize him by his hips, push him to the floor, and take his cock hard and fast and deep, and never even mind the sweat from the aborted run, Holly is not, in fact, receiving the performance he currently desires.

Swallowing inappropriate laughter, he collects himself. He slides his hand from Val's wrist so he can link their fingers together instead. 'Tell me what you want, Val. I'll give it. You know I will.'

He tugs on Valerian's hand, and the lord, on his knees beside Holly, sways his torso over to him. Holly loops his arm around Val's waist and pulls him bodily closer so that their hips and thighs are pressed together, side by side there on the thick rug in front of the desk. It's a nice rug, plush enough to fuck on, if they push the paperwork aside.

He murmurs in his lord's ear, 'Tell me what you want, love.'

On a sigh, Valerian says, 'I want…'

'Hmm?'

'I want you to go back to ignoring me.'

That certainly breaks the mood Holly thought he was establishing. 'You stuck your head above the parapet and waved your flag at me, Val—'

'I most certainly did no such thing!'

'—you really want me to ignore it?' He presses his flank harder against Val's.

Val presses his lips together; he might be holding back a whimper. He closes his eyes and whispers, 'I think it's best, Holly.'

Holly looks at him, his eyes squeezed tight, his face drawn, and concedes that the poor fucker is probably not appreciating all this quite as much as Holly is. He stands and steps back as soon as he has the realisation. It's not one he often has to confront but he is also not one to take even rare refusal with anything other than consummate good grace.

Valerian opens his eyes, looking surprised, as he feels Holly's warmth retreat. He looks up at him, eyes so wide that Holly takes another step back, swallowing, because Val had *almost* said he thought he'd enjoy Holly's cock in his mouth but he hadn't actually said it, had he?

'All right, Val,' he says. 'I thought you were, ah, welcoming my attentions. I'll stop.'

He's surprised when Valerian laughs. It lightens his whole face; it's quite striking. 'I can't tell if I welcome it or not. Ask me later.'

Holly smiles back at him. 'Don't think I won't, lover.' He points a stern finger. 'But only once more, Lord Vee, I don't ever beg.'

Valerian tips his head back slowly. 'I don't imagine you ever have to,' he says.

There's no coquettishness in it at all and Holly knows Lord Valerian will be had at his convenience.

~Sixteen~

Haven held its breath. Everyone knew proud Cristati would come back; the only question was whether it would march openly with an army, or creep secretly with Mancer guards.

Them Upstairs were leaning toward the first option, Cristati testing its might against the combined strength of the five loosely allied coastal strongholds in an open breach of covenant protocol. The Haven militia were called up, while scouts and lookouts were sent out westward, to the far end of the estate and presumed direction of any siege force deployed by Cristati. The guard on the gates and around the walls was doubled. One of the older laundry staff had been a miner in a past life, and she was set to planning the defence against sappers. The artificer reinforced the bars on the main gate, consulting copiously with Albemarle to be sure it would not interfere with the moat. The estate's winter crops, normally sold off to the west and south, were stockpiled. The kitchen staff bottled and preserved and brewed as if their lives depended on it. Lady Fairhaven wrote letters.

At the same time, stronghold guards were permanently assigned to the Mancers. Albemarle wouldn't be able to tolerate so many newcomers, and they weren't experienced in handling zhem, so Evelyn assigned them to secondary guard positions and left her core eight in place. They doubled up into pairs on shortened shifts, so that they were all getting enough rest to stay alert.

The other Mancer guards begged Holly to increase their training time, and he scoffed and told them they'd been training for years and Cristati could *bring it*, those dozy fuckers.

'I've only been training for six months,' Titus pointed out mournfully.

'A-yah,' Holly said, and took her for extra tutelage, which involved sparring in the atelier hallway.

He wasn't wrong, but it didn't do much to reassure any of the under-croft staff who could extrapolate the motive behind that training location.

In these quiet, jittery days of Haven hunkering down for siege or incursion, Hazel used his free time to visit the stronghold staff, trading on years of being Hazel darling.

He made one last pie, the use of stores for frivolity being frowned upon now, and left it with the kitchen staff to thank them for letting him use their smallest oven so often.

He visited the laundry and congratulated the seamsters on the vest pattern they'd designed for Ash. Its cut was elegant without being definit-ive; they'd not sat the hem at the top of the hips in masculine style nor flared it out long over the hips in feminine style, but threaded their needles perfectly in between; and they'd made the cut of the chest fit both firm pectorals and firmly bound breasts. It suited Ash's deliberate androgyny perfectly and had started something of a fad—others in the stronghold had requested the same design, in all sorts of colours and sizes.

He walked the gardens with the head gardener, who had started as an apprentice in the grounds soon after Holly and Hazel had been recruited into the Mancer Guard. She seemed stolidly calm. Her people would join the militia on the walls, if siege came. When siege came.

He checked on Miriam, who gave him a long list which amounted to a demand for more supplies, more staff, and more space. He arranged for all three with Lord Valerian.

Titus, Haven-born, asked, 'Hazel darling, will you talk to my parents?'

He did, an awkward conversation designed to reassure them without outright promising them that their only daughter would survive the foreign incursion.

Nightingale found him and talked at him in circles: what Ash did—the [call it tinkering] that had turned out to have a real name, bricolage—was a sin and it must be wrong if they'd all collectively decided not to tell Albemarle about it, but also it had saved Ash and Hazel from the encroach-ing lieutenant, and anyway it was very hard to reconcile the quiet, sweet Mancer with such a dreadful taboo, and what did Hazel think?

Hazel thought that perhaps strong personal dislike for a thing, even from Mancers, especially from Mancers, whose strong personal dislikes were legion, did not necessarily equate to the thing being objectively wrong. He pointed out the bricolage continuum Holly had identified, the hazy line where an acceptable practice became an unacceptable taboo, and that Ash, isolated and alone and driven to survive, had no way of learning where that line was—hadn't even really understood there was a line, until Mithra tried to bite zheir earlobe off.

And, he gently added, the Mancer Guard's role was not to judge its stronghold's Mancer.

'I'm sorry,' she said miserably. 'I shouldn't be talking to you, of all people, about this.'

'Of all people?' he repeated, a touch wounded. He was exactly, of all people, someone that anyone should be able to talk to.

'You're…fond…of Ash.'

'Nightingale,' Hazel said. 'You're fond of zhem, too. That's why this is so hard for you.'

He didn't think he'd fixed it, not by a long way, but he'd helped her order her tail-chasing thoughts and she went about her duties with less staring in silent bemusement at Ash as the prejudices from her upbringing wrestled with her personal experience.

Some people left for the port. Some were newcomers who had never intended to stay long. Some were new, and had intended to stay, and now packed up and departed. Some old-timers went too.

Most stayed. The mood steadied, tilted, steadied.

Morano brought his wife up from the port. Second Jerome decided to leave his parents and siblings in the port. It was an obvious supply point for its local stronghold. It would be blockaded at best, attacked at worst. Some civilians, those with somewhere safer to go, left by ship or road.

On his slow, calm rounds of the undercroft just after lunch one day, Hazel visited the baths, and then the barber. He came back with tidied hair, still long, and his scruff turned into a short, well-trimmed beard. The barber found his work soothing, he supposed, like he liked baking pies and Valerian liked chopping wood, so he'd submitted to the chair when the man, fairly fierce in the beard department himself, insisted.

He went to the atelier, plotting kindnesses for Haven's Mancers now.

~What?

Ash had come out of the atelier, arching zheir lower back in a stretch, as Hazel entered the antechamber from the hallway. Hazel waited for more, but Ash just made [what] a few more times, as if zheir hands were caught in a loop, staring at him.

Holly, coming in behind Hazel, gave him a friendly and yet quite hard shove, testing him on his left again. Hazel gave him a cheerful elbow in the ribs in acknowledgement.

The Mancer captain was gleamingly sweaty from sparring with Titus and Nightingale. '~Scrubs up nice, doesn't he?'

Ash waved zheir hand to indicate Hazel's face and hair. *~What?*

'~Do you like it or hate it?' Hazel self-consciously touched his hair. He had that streak of white in his hair where the scar started; his beard had a slash of white too, where it ended. '~It made the barber happy.'

'~And see that? See how he's blushing?' Holly went on. He smirked at Hazel. '~He blushes all the way down to his *nipples*, Ash.'

'Holyoake!'

The Mancer looked rapidly between the indeed now very red Hazel and the smiling Holly, huffed out a tiny indignant squeak, and vanished back into the atelier, slamming the door with enough force that it caused a gust of ventilated air across the antechamber.

'A-yah, love the Mancer moods,' Hazel said. 'And *you*— You fuckster.'

'Oh, zhey probably don't even know the sign for nipples.'

The sign for nipples involved tweaking the air in front of one's nipples, so Hazel pronounced himself highly sceptical of this defence. Holly laughed and slapped his arse as he headed off upstairs for another meeting with Evelyn and Lord Valerian.

It was not as if sour moods weren't washing through the whole stronghold in waves. That was why Hazel walked his rounds, in between watches. And at least Ash's melodramatic retreat gave him a chance to set his surprise up in the antechamber.

Since the feast, Albemarle had surrendered access to all zheir journals to zheir new partner. Ash spent every evening, once the day's schedule was complete, paging through the journals. Zhey seemed to be savouring it, looking lingeringly at a design before slowly turning the page to the next. Zhey'd lie on a workbench in the atelier, or, less often, sit in the dining hall, immune to the noise of the full tables. But zhey never took the journals to zheir room to peruse alone.

Hazel had realised that this was because Ash was, in many ways, both a typical Mancer just like Albemarle, and yet Albemarle's diametric. Small and slim against large and broad; economical grace against stomping bullishness; deliberate neutrality against oblivious masculinity (if only because that was how extreme utility in dress and hairstyle happened to be coded in Haven); prickly temperament against one that steamed before it exploded; stubborn secrecy against blunt honesty; inclination toward wanted touch and conversation against resistance to any sort of physical or verbal interaction, and, therefore, gregarious against solitary.

For all zheir tendency to keep zheir secrets tucked close to zheir chest, Ash *liked* company, even if the company was just zheir guards, even if zhey didn't join in the conversations. Zhey were intent on the journals, and rarely glanced up for glimpses of hands and lips. It was probably tiring to follow half-obscured conversations for a long time, anyway. The mere presence of other people seemed enough for zhem.

However, despite Titus shyly presenting Ash with a cushion, zheir chosen reading spots were not comfortable. Hazel could see that in the way zhey grimaced and rolled zheir shoulders when zhey finished for the night.

Hazel had decided to fix it.

Morano and Kito were the guards on duty right now, the former stationed in the atelier hallway, the latter inside the atelier with the Mancers. Holly was with his sister and Them Upstairs, and the juniors were sparring, but the Jeromes had agreed to give up some of their off-watch time to help Hazel.

Those two came in now, with a couple of stronghold guards, staggering under the awkward bulk of a divan, its patterned upholstery old-fashioned in style but still in good condition. It'd been in one of the undercroft storage rooms, along with other heavy carved furniture out of favour with the purple and others of the collective Them Upstairs. A couple of the stronger laundry staff followed behind with a large rolled-up rug, which they'd beaten and spot-cleaned out in the kitchen gardens. Its dark red colouring was rich in the copperlit light.

That formed the bones of the new sitting area. The Jeromes and their helpers came back with a few side tables, an armchair, and a few smaller chairs, and the seamsters brought in fresh cushions and scattered them over the divan and armchair.

Hazel put the finishing touches on, setting out extra copperlits, and pulling the armchair a little further away from the divan. He placed a pot with a small red fern in the centre of the armchair's side table.

Then he called out the Mancers.

Albemarle emerged fuming. 'First you disturb me with all your noise and then you drag me off-schedule—'

Zhey stopped. Ash prevented zhemself from running into zheir broad back by the width of a hair, which was lucky given Albemarle was already tense. The smaller Mancer slid around Albemarle and beheld the sitting area.

Hazel patted the armchair. '~This is for you, Albemarle.' He smiled at Ash. '~The rest is for you, Ash. For reading of an evening.'

Albemarle harrumphed. 'I don't see the point of that.' But instead of returning straight to work, zhey picked up the pot with its lacy, curly fern. 'Unusual. I don't have one with red fronds.'

'~I know,' Hazel said. '~I found it in the garden where you never go.' It'd been at the foot of the moon gate. Albemarle didn't have time for whimsy.

Albemarle held the pot close. Then zhey set it down again and went back into the atelier without a word.

~Do zhey like it or hate it? Ash signed. Hazel couldn't tell if it was conscious or unconscious imitation of his question from earlier.

'~Zhey love it,' Hazel said with the confidence of many years of service. Albemarle loved it. Zhey just couldn't cope with loving it, hence the sudden retreat.

Ash's smile appeared. '~So do I. Thank you, Hazel darling.'

'~You're welcome, Ash love,' Hazel said, cheerily glib in the face of complete success.

He was suddenly conscious of Ash's deepening smile, zheir gaze lingering on his face, intensifying into Mancer focus in that way that made Hazel feel sliced open and dissected. He shifted under that long, intent, gaze, and zhey blinked and ducked zheir head, and awkwardly retreated into the atelier without another look his way.

'A-yah, Mancer moods,' Hazel said. 'Love 'em.'

~SEVENTEEN~

HAZEL WATCHED ASH CURL UP ON zheir cushions.

The Mancers had finished their project, and Ash was at an irritable loose end while Albemarle took zheir turn choosing the next one. Despite Valerian's brusque order, there was no pressuring zhem to choose a design that could be turned to the defence of Haven; the guards couldn't even hint at it. Knowing Albemarle, zhey'd choose something as benign and shakily useful as a butterfly net for the orchard. Hazel wondered what Ash would be able to turn that into.

After tolerating Ash pacing about for a hypocritically short period, Holly had practically shoved a new journal into zheir hands and shoved zhem bodily out of the atelier into Hazel's supervision before flouncing back inside to watch over Albemarle. Ash had retreated to the divan, now zheir favoured reading spot. Gradually, the severe lines of zheir face relaxed as zhey sank into the pleasure of browsing Albemarle's designs.

Hazel curled a hand against his chest, where the warmth, the desire for Ash, lived. Even now that he wasn't letting himself touch zhem, even knowing zhey wanted Holly, it was not going away. It was getting worse. The warmth was an ever-present glow in his core, blooming bright whenever Ash looked at him. Even when zhey didn't.

The divan had been a tactical error. It was long enough for Ash to stretch out on. Hazel could kneel over zhem, brace a hand on its curving back, use his other hand to cup zheir face and tip it back, gather up zheir lustrous hair, lean in, have that hungry mouth again.

He sucked in a breath and shifted. The movement might have caught Ash's eye; zhey glanced up. Hazel knew—*knew*—zhey'd surprised a look of naked longing on his face and he dropped his gaze immediately.

When he dared looked up again, Ash patted the space beside zhem on the divan. Hazel, sighing, obeyed the summons. He suspected he was about to receive a polite *You're lovely but Holly* speech. He would, by no means, be the first person in the stronghold who'd received the polite *You're lovely but Holly* speech.

He settled uncertainly—he perforce could not leave as much room for Ash as he would have liked to—and Ash adjusted zheir own positioning. Zhey were just barely leaning against him. It was a very deliberate move, as if Ash were saying, *You may have* this, *and no more.* Zhey went back to zheir journal.

Hazel, finding a disturbing amount of pleasure in the light brush of Ash's shoulder against his, began one of his slow, meandering ruminations.

Ash was wound as tight as when zhey'd first arrived, afraid and desperate to release the Mancy drive. Zhey were snappy with zheir guards, and even a touch impatient with Albemarle, and it might not all be to do with the tension of anticipating Cristati action or the enforced idleness of waiting for the next project. Or, at least, those things were exacerbating a need that would have already been growing.

He thought of the things people found soothing—he and the rolling out of the pie dough, Albemarle and the weight of zheir blanket, Holly and the grapple of a friendly body, Valerian and the rhythmic fall of the wood-axe, the barber and the rhythmic snip of the scissors.

Ash, when tense, found simple, safe touch soothing, a communication as vital and kinetic as the movement of zheir hands. The memory of their kiss in the atelier hallway made itself known, Ash's insistent mouth, Ash's warm, lithe body pressed against his and demanding ever more closeness.

Hazel wrenched his mind back to the topic at hand, his Mancer's needs.

Ash must have touched zheir Mancer partner all the time; at least one of the three, probably the unnamed third, had given Ash the affectionate touch zheir stilted story suggested zhey'd been sorely lacking otherwise. Hazel could see the shadow where the habitual touch had been, when Ash and Albemarle worked together: Ash's aborted reach, Albemarle's flinch, the convoluted workarounds they used so Albemarle never had to touch or be touched.

And Ash never got to touch or be touched, not by Albemarle, and not by anyone else, not now Hazel had forced himself to stop. He had not known that would be a selfish decision.

Ash hadn't even expressed zheir interest to Holly yet, who presumably would have been happy to do all the touching Ash desired. Hazel supposed zhey'd gotten too wrapped up in the projects. Albemarle would neglect zheir needs, food and rest and light. Ash was neglecting zheirs.

Zhey had to be starving by now, just for the press of a hand against zheirs.

It had taken Hazel some time to think this through carefully. He thought he was being fair, and helpful, and fixing a problem. He tapped the top of the journal for Ash's attention and said, '~Is it acceptable if I put my arm around you? It'll be more comfortable.'

Ash paused, eyes narrowing.

'~Or I can get someone else?' Hazel thought about who Ash liked best. '~Nightingale? Holly?' He glanced at the closed atelier door.

To be fair, he didn't think Ash actually liked Holly, as such. But Lord Valerian didn't seem to, either, and that had not put any sort of dampener on the coals of attraction for him. Hazel knew better than most how decoupled affection and attraction could be.

Ash assumed zheir Mancer blankness. ~You've worked out I'm used to more touch than I'm getting.

Hazel dipped his head in acknowledgement. '~I don't know how to tell a competent adult zhey might need a cuddle, but here I am, telling you I think you need a cuddle, you grouchy fucker.'

Their blankness broke into a small smile. ~And you're offering?

'~I'm offering. If you'd like it.'

~Hazel darling, Ash signed with some sarcasm.

'~A-yah, no need for it, Ash love,' Hazel said.

~People do like to touch you. A lot. Ash repeated that last sign with some emphasis.

'~People need touch sometimes, and they know I won't touch back.'

~Because you're not attracted to them.

Hazel half-shrugged. He was incredibly uncomfortable; he'd still failed to confess that zhey were the exception to his little quirk even as he suggested he wrap zhem up in his arms, even when he knew he'd just been caught out ogling. It felt like crossing a line from a lie of omission to a true deception to ignore zheir statement, given zhey'd made it with the subtle head tilt that indicated a question with no need for the literal [query] sign.

But, actually, his little quirk wasn't even relevant. He didn't touch back unless he'd been invited to, because he was a decent person who knew better than to jump to assumptions about what someone wanted just because of what they needed. Ash hadn't met too many of those, it seemed.

So he set his shoulders and blurted, '~Look, I am attracted to you. But don't fret yourself. I'd never touch you in any way you don't want. I'm safe.'

Ash sat up straight, a jerky motion quite at odds with zheir usual smooth grace. Zhey stared at Hazel with zheir lips parted. Quite plainly, zhey had not read the longing on his face as anything directed at zhem, after all.

'~Ah. There's the look I was hoping not to get.' Hazel stood and got some distance from where Ash sat wide-eyed on the divan, tension buzzing through his body. He hadn't thought it would go this badly. '~Pretend I didn't say anything. I didn't mean to scare you.'

Ash started to sign, lowered zheir hands, raised them again, shook zheir head. Hazel had shocked zhem into the Trade equivalent of stunned silence.

'~People touch me when they need it, and it doesn't have to mean anything,' he told zhem with growing desperation. '~I just meant, if you need it, I'm here and I'm safe, but actually any of us would be.'

~Holly.

Hazel had time to think, *Of* course, *fucking Holly*— before Ash finally managed to string a thought together. ~Holly doesn't mind?

To Hazel's justifiably blank look, zhey clarified, ~You've known him so long. Doesn't he mind when people touch you as much as they do? When you offer to cuddle people you're attracted to? I would mind.

Ash ducked zheir head as soon as zhey'd added that last, rather forceful, sequence.

Hazel realised that the Mancer, with zheir limited knowledge of basic Trade and poor understanding of Haven slang, was using [know] to mean something quite different to the way Hazel understood it.

Hazel was interpreting it literally. He had known Holly for a very long time. Ash was trying to imply togetherness beyond friendship. Another sort of knowing, the carnal sort.

'~We're not lovers,' he carefully signed. '~We have been, off and on. But mostly, we're friends.'

Ash stuttered zheir hands again, before dropping them into zheir lap, looking lost. Then, in a burst, zhey asked, ~Why didn't you tell me that earlier?

'~What? That we're not lovers? I didn't realise you thought we were.'

The look Ash gave him then was so savage that Hazel, laughing, had to add, '~Very close, physically affectionate, friends. Also verbally affectionate. And emotionally affectionate, if that's a real thing.'

~I think it is. Why not lovers, then?

He made a pushing away gesture. He didn't quite mean that he didn't want to talk about it. He meant: *That is a huge topic that I couldn't even come close to explaining to you even if you knew all the Haven slang.* He'd already made one difficult admission this afternoon; he was too raw to add that he gave away his heart like it was hot from the oven and burning his fingers, and Holly's tender hands weren't the right ones to take it from him.

What he expressed out of all that was, '~We're better as friends.'

Ash shifted restlessly; zhey'd be pacing, Hazel thought, if zhey were standing. Then zhey did stand, shoved Hazel surprisingly hard with both hands, and snapped out, even faster this time, ~Why the fuck didn't you tell me all of this earlier?

'~Why would I need to?' Hazel took the few steps backward that Ash seemed to want him to take. '~It's clear Holly isn't exclusively anyone's, isn't it? You could have had him anytime.'

Ash, looking outraged, kicked the floor and shoved him again. He rocked back on his heels obligingly, and then obliged further when the Mancer set both palms against his chest and steadily pushed. Ash wasn't strong enough to move him if he didn't want to be moved, but he let zhem have zheir way, allowing zhem to steer him until the backs of his legs hit the divan and he abruptly sat.

Ash leaned over him, silky hair hanging forward as zhey tilted zheir face over his. Signing slow and emphatic, zhey announced, ~Don't. Want. Holly.

Then zhey added, for good measure, ~You idiot.

Hazel considered this at length before saying, cautiously, '~You did apologise when you kissed me, so…'

~I thought you were Holly's!

'~Holly would've shared,' Hazel couldn't help but point out, though he drew the line at adding that Holly would've happily joined in.

With a rather enjoyable possessiveness, Ash answered, ~Mancers don't like sharing.

Again, Hazel put some thought into it before he ventured, '~Should I perhaps tell you that I'm all yours, then? I mean…you do mean me, yeah?'

Ash's knees settled on either side of his thighs. Zhey slid a hand into his hair, tugging so that his face was upturned fully to zheirs. Zheir eyes were intent. Zhey knelt over him, so close he could feel zheir warmth, but zheir hand was the only point of contact between them.

It was a little too close to the minor fantasy he'd been indulging himself with for his body not to react. Flushed, hard, breathing irregularly, he got out, '~May I kiss you now, Ash?'

Ash's mischievous smile peeked out. Zhey made the negatory fist with zheir free hand. Hazel drew back against the pull of Ash's grip on his hair. He'd had some pleasant interludes by answering the same question with 'Yes, but not on the mouth', so he appreciated the honesty. He waited to find out Ash's intentions.

Ash signed, ~You may take me to your room and fuck me, Hazel.

Hazel let out a breath. He stood, not without some effort, transforming a lapful of Mancer into an armful of Mancer. Ash showed willing by wrapping zheir legs about his waist and zheir arms around his shoulders. Zhey gave him an expectant look.

With all their hands occupied, communication was lacking; Hazel thought, *Isn't it a bit overdramatic to carry zhem through the hallways like a prize of war?*

He decided Ash's shiningly eager face was saying, *Yes but go ahead and do it anyway.*

He regretted his unthinking compliance when he had to walk past Titus and Nightingale, once again practising Holly's moves in the atelier hallway. Ash hid zheir face against his shoulder; Hazel thought from the slight tremor in zheir own shoulders that zhey were suppressing laughter.

Titus, looking delighted, nudged Nightingale, lowering her blunt practice blade. Nightingale looked more uncertain—she was still awkward around Ash—but she smiled too.

Ash lifted zheir head long enough to sign, with a ridiculously solemn expression, ~Do not be alarmed. Hazel darling is obeying instructions perfectly.

The other guards' Trade had come along. Titus giggled, while Nightingale touched her index finger to below her eye and briskly away again to silently indicate understanding.

'Shut up, both of you,' Hazel said.

'Didn't say anything, Hazel darling,' Titus said.

Ash was openly laughing by the time Hazel carried zhem around to the Mancer guards' quarters, little chirps of near-silent air against his ear. He kissed zhem up against the door of his room, groping for the latch and missing it repeatedly in the distraction of Ash's mouth moving under his, legs lithely wrapped around his waist, one hand burrowed into his hair, the other pressed by his against the door, spasming into the shapes of the signs for [Hazel], for [want], for [now], against his palm. He pushed zhem harder against the door and felt something like a growl vibrating through his mouth.

Zhey freed zheir hand and pushed his chest back a little so zhey could sign, ~Inside, or I'll tear your clothes off in the hallway.

This did not help Hazel's coordination. Ash reached down and flicked the latch zhemself and they stumbled through the door. Once Hazel'd finally managed to get it shut behind them, he let Ash slide to the floor, earning a great deal of squirming for his trouble.

Ash took a single glance around his chamber and zheir face went blank, all joyful anticipation instantly extinguished. Zhey took a step back, face clean of all expression but set in its strong lines.

Hazel, bewildered, looked about the room, trying to see it from a Mancer point of view. It was as small and plain as zheir own, a dungeon cell that had been plastered and furnished into forgetting its origins. The main difference was the small corner shrine, dedicated to quick and sly Kisane, guardian of the small, sudden squalls that didn't merit the attention of a true storm deity. Despite his general antipathy for some traditions, he couldn't quite abandon every childhood habit, and, anyway, Fair Haven by the Sea was a place of squalls, blown in over the water every spring.

But that was not where Ash was looking.

Hazel kept the rest of the room fastidiously neat; his clothes on hooks, his washbowl rinsed and dried, an ewer of water and clean washcloth folded beside it, the stool by the bed holding a copperlit, a book, and a potted fern, the bed tightly made to academy specifications—

It was this last that had transfixed Ash. Zhey had zheir hands pressed hard to zheir stomach. Zhey lifted them minutely to sign, ~You really are an academy-trained Mancer guard.

'~Yes,' Hazel said. '~You knew that. I told you I went to the academy. Just me and Holly, and Evelyn before us. Kito and Morano were due to go, but Lord Florian died and Lord Valerian discontinued academy training for initiates. Possibly rueing the decision now.'

Hazel realised as he spoke that Ash must have been inside an academy-trained Mancer guard's bedchamber before, to have become so discomposed by those militarily precise corners.

He lowered his hands, his breath giving a little hitch. He was thinking about the marks of a collar around Ash's neck. He was thinking about how Ash had told him zheir Mancer Guard were never protecting zhem, only keeping zhem prisoner. He was thinking about the naked hatred on the Cristati lieutenant's face when he'd laid eyes on his stronghold's former Mancer. He was thinking about Ash seeing a Mancer guard's bed and being very unhappy about it.

'~Ash, see that fern by the bed there?' he said slowly, feeling his way. '~Albemarle gave it to me. Zhey gave it to me after the accident. I think it was zheir way of apologising, for not stopping work while I was lying bleeding at zheir feet.'

~Some Mancers are just as awful as some Mancer guards?

'~Don't put words in my mouth, I have enough trouble with my own as it is,' Hazel said, and Ash's cool façade broke; zhey looked abashed. '~I want to say, zhey never needed to apologise. Zhey went on working, because zhey knew I wasn't mortally wounded and zhey heard someone coming at a run to provide the help zhey zhemself could not. I didn't need Albemarle. So zhey kept working. I didn't blame zhem. It's just what a Mancer does. And I know that. Because *that* is academy training, Ash.'

Unreadable, Ash met his eye. ~Along with how to murder someone with a sword.

'~That…is certainly one way to describe my ability to protect you unto death with any sort of blade, a-yah. But mostly, we're trained to—'

~You are trained to forgive the unforgivable.

'~*Not* what—'

~How very useful.

Ash closed the distance between them again and started to work on the buttons and loops of Hazel's coat. He put his hands between zheir face and zheir hands, made zhem watch the signs even as zheir fingers travelled nimbly downward. He was too busy concentrating on communicating his point to worry about Ash's actions for the moment.

'~Academy training is *not* what those Cristati fuckers did to you, Ash. It's not, never, how they treated you. It's not that they should have known better. They absolutely *did* know better. It's understandable that you hate them. Please don't hate the Havens because of it.'

The Mancer tugged at his coat's shoulders, pulled the coat down his arms and free. Zhey swivelled, put it on a hook.

Zhey went to work on the buckles of his sword belt next, and held the leather loop in both hands as zhey examined the tooled sheath with its ivy pattern, and partly drew the sword to feel the hexagonal grip, see the shine of the blade. Zhey put it aside, and then, slower, zheir own knives.

When zhey reached for him again, Hazel backed away. He wanted to outright leave, but he couldn't abandon his Mancer to this strange mood of zheirs.

Ash signed, ~I never hated my Mancer Guard, Hazel.

Zhey sat on his bed. Leaning down, zheir hair a momentary veil for zheir face, zhey undid the buckles of zheir pretty high-heeled boots and slid them off. Zhey sat up again to loosen the top tab of zheir vest, neatly parting the nested wooden button from the cross-panel. The air smelled like a storm, like a lightning strike.

Zhey met his eyes and undid the second tab.

Hazel found more words. '~You're allowed to change your mind.'

~But I haven't. I want you.

Zhey undid the third.

'~Ash, you were enjoying yourself a moment ago, and now you're not. You're allowed to change your mind.'

Looking him straight in the eye, Ash undid the next tab. ~How was that academy training, Hazel?

Hazel gritted his teeth. Albemarle needed patience. He reminded himself that Ash, for all that zhey appeared more controlled than Albemarle, needed patience just as much. '~I was taught to protect my stronghold's Mancer, Ash.'

~But you had a lesson on what you'll find under a Mancer's clothes?

They had, a seminar which was brief and to the point: do not expect the ways Mancers express themselves in clothes, hair, mannerisms, speech patterns and so forth to even slightly match each other, their self-regard, the physical presentation of their bodies, or their own local social cues. Do not expect what you have learned about your own stronghold's Mancer to generalise in any way to any other Mancer. There had been some technical data, and some anecdotes. For all that, there was only one real message conveyed.

'~It was a very short lesson entitled Mind Your Own Fucking Business.'

Ash smiled, a little. ~Hazel darling, it's about to be your fucking business.

Hazel shook his head. Ash slid open the last tab, and let the vest slide off zheir shoulders to the bed and then, in a slither, to the floor. Zhey wore now only the thin linen undershirt, their pale bronze skin a shadow underneath. The silver embroidery on the sleeves continued in elegant whorls over the rest of the material. Hazel looked away.

Ash stood, came to him, took his face in zheir hands and turned it so he was looking at zhem again. Zhey held up one finger, demanding his attention.

~Hazel, I never hated my Mancer Guard. Until I came here and saw what Mancer guards are meant to be. Until I knew I was meant to be able to trust them with my life. Until I met you.

Hazel tried to say, 'Oh.' It was just a breath of air.

Zhey came up on zheir toes and kissed him, an insistent claiming of his mouth that left him dizzy. ~I want you, Hazel. Every time you've touched me, I've wanted you. And then you stopped.

'~You always looked so agonised, though,' Hazel said apologetically.

Ash slapped him lightly across the chest, zheir impish smile suddenly back in full force. ~Agony is correct. You have no idea how attractive you are, do you?

Too embarrassed to examine that outlandish statement, he muttered, 'A-yah, if you say so.' He absently touched the scar on his face.

Ash caught his hand, briefly pressed it, trailed zheir fingers over his face. ~Hazel, you are *beautiful*. Beautiful to your core.

Hazel, rendered silent, felt the wash of heat from the roots of his hair to halfway down his chest.

~I want to watch you take your clothes off, please.

Hazel didn't move. He was beyond want now, paradoxically frozen within a fire of desire. Ash, seeming to understand this, ordered, ~Undo your top button.

He found he could obey that. He could obey the order to undo the next one too, and the one after that, and all the way down. He was ablaze.

Ash pulled his shirt off and stroked the fur on his bared chest, rubbed zheir face against it and licked his puckered nipples and the purplish scars down his left side, leaned into him to have his mouth again, kissed along his scar and down his neck, bit his clavicle. The light graze of the teeth sent a bolt of jagged response through Hazel; he shuddered and his hands slid over Ash's shoulder blades and up into zheir hair, silk over his fingers. He tugged zhem close, closer, the contact between zheir bodies burning at every point.

Zheir fingers pushed at his chest. Zhey were trying to get room enough to sign at him. ~Undo your trousers.

Zhey watched avidly as Hazel obeyed. Zhey were too impatient, and took his trousers and drawers to the floor zhemself, and knelt as zhey did it.

'~You don't have to—'

Ash wasn't looking up at his hands or mouth. Zhey leaned in, exploring with zheir tongue before zhey took him in, tentatively tonguing the tip before swallowing him down. Hazel half-sobbed with the feel of it, wet and tight and intense. He had done this for Holly plenty of times—Holly loved his mouth, and so had Miriam—as Holly had done for him.

As good as it had been, it had never felt like this, like the deep scald of a fire, the thrilling plummet of freefall. He would spend inside of a minute if he let Ash continue.

He pulled the Mancer up; Ash scowled and wriggled against his bare chest in something halfway between true protest and sheer incitement.

Hazel kicked off his boots and his tangled trousers and underthings with more haste than grace. He pushed Ash onto the bed—not hard, but Ash tipped on the small side of average as people went, and zhey bounced a little. Zheir eyes widened and zheir gaze locked onto his, the piercing look of a Mancer fixating on a project.

Zhey held up a hand; Hazel stopped.

~I want to look at you.

Zhey had not wavered in zheir fixated, fascinated stare. It was a more intense appraisal than he was used to. He felt his own nudity acutely, in a way he never had in the communal baths or with other partners. He'd never felt so *seen*.

He had a swordfighter's body, strong but not decoratively so. It was all he could do not to cross his arms over his chest; he straightened and put his hands on his hips instead, and let Ash drink him in because that was what his Mancer wanted.

Ash beckoned, smiling. ~You *do* blush down to your nipples.

Hazel, shaking his head in embarrassed amusement, knelt over zhem. He tugged at the hem of zheir thin embroidered undershirt to start lifting it up and off, but zheir breath caught. He let it go, set his hands on zheir waist instead, rubbing lightly with his thumbs and waiting on zheir cue. Zhey, with a little glance up at his face, ran zheir hands over his pectorals, flicked at his nipples as they hardened into nubs under the caressing.

Zhey relaxed again. ~Hazel, will you…

Zhey pulled on his shoulders, lying all the way back, silently asking for what zhey wanted. Hazel gently laid his naked body atop zheir clothed one. Ash curled hands into his hair and lithely hooked a knee over his hip, rocking up under him, a small formless noise escaping zhem as zhey burrowed zheir face against his neck.

Hazel set to worshipping Ash. He took zheir hands, kissed zheir fingers, kissed the blade tattoo on the left wrist, pushed zheir sleeves up and kissed the small white scars on zheir hands and forearms, the soft sensitivity of the crook of zheir elbows where the bigger scars lay.

He nuzzled his way back to zheir throat, lightly kissing and nibbling zheir skin and letting the soft prickle of his short beard tickle zhem. Slid his mouth over zheir collarbones, sucked lightly, and then, when zhey urged him on with zheir hands cupping his head, hard enough to leave marks. He pressed his tongue into the tender hollow in between, tasting zhem.

He looked up and got a nod, Ash's eyes bright, avid. He kept moving down.

Tongued hardening nipples through cloth. Sucked and nipped. Heard a gasp, felt zhem arch. Looked up, got a nod, kept moving down.

Pushed the shirt aside, just a little, and mouthed at the soft bared belly, feeling the hot skin under his lips, feeling the pulse of hands clenching in his hair. Looked up, got a nod, kept moving down.

Rubbed his face against the trouser front, pushing like a cat wanting a stroke, hearing Ash pant above him.

Stopped with fingers on the ties of Ash's trousers. Looked up.

Ash, propped up on zheir elbows, signed with tiny movements, ~Are you worried about what you'll find between my legs?

Zhey were trying to smile, but the lines of zheir face wore tension, the anxiety creeping back.

Hazel said the stupidest thing he could think of. '~As long as it's not a hamster, Ash, nothing much is going to surprise me.'

And suddenly, perfectly, Ash was laughing, relaxed and joyful again. ~But, Hazel, if it is a hamster?

'~I'll pet it and give it treats.' He wasn't Holly and dirty talk didn't come easily to him, so he was already blushing at the sheer nonsense of this byroad even before he added, 'With my mouth.'

He was rewarded with one of Ash's short sharp barks of surprised amusement. Zheir tension had ebbed away, at the price of only a little of Hazel's dignity. Ah, well. He'd never found sex to have much dignity anyway, when looked at objectively.

Zhey nodded and he undid the ties, tugged away the trousers, lightly bit zheir hipbone and found three small dragonflies tattooed in black curved lines in the secret hollow where hip became stomach. He kissed each one and looked up.

~Hope, Ash told him. ~They mean hope.

Hazel smiled. He caressed over the linen underclothes, stroked the lithe lines of the muscles of zheir well-shaped legs, ran his mouth from the crease of thigh to knee on one leg, back the other way on the other. He put his thumbs at Ash's hips, as if to draw down the last layer of clothing.

He could hear, from Ash's shallow and uneven breathing, both zheir excitement and zheir trepidation. He watched zheir face, and got neither nod nor shake of the head.

He didn't know what Ash had done before. He didn't know if zhey'd ever done it voluntarily. He didn't know if Mancer guards were a type for zhem, or a convenience, or a necessity. He did know that Ash would resist, strenuously, if he tried to pause here and talk about it. But Ash could not bring zhemself to nod.

Hazel had an idea. He propped himself on his elbows, gusting warm air over the fork of Ash's spread legs as he said, '~Here, love. Why don't you come on top?'

Ash looked puzzled, even slightly put out. Zhey'd requested Hazel fuck zhem; Hazel wondered if zhey'd assumed he'd literally put zhem on zheir back and do just that. He wondered if that's what zhey wanted.

He had more finesse than that, no matter how much of a brute he looked, and there were more ways to fuck than with a cock. They could get to that another time, if there was another time.

Hazel rolled and tugged, so that, abruptly, Ash was straddling his face. With hands on zheir hips, Hazel gently pulled zheir crux down to his mouth, touching there with lips and tongue through the linen, demon-strating for a moment before releasing zhem.

'~See? You lead. Your pace. Your choice. Including if you want to stop.'

Ash's eyes were wide, pupils dilated. Hazel could sense the flex of the strong thighs on either side of his head as zhey hovered. Zhey nodded. Zhey didn't take off zheir underclothes. Hazel admitted to a little dis-appointment that Ash didn't quite trust him so far yet, but just a little, because 'yet' could be a wonderful word.

Zhey lowered zhemself onto his mouth, tentative at first, supporting zhemself with hands on the wall at the head at the bed. Zhey shortly found zheir rhythm, rocking slow against his tongue, and Hazel found his to match, able to lick and suck hard and wet through the fabric without having to worry about his beard burning zheir most sensitive skin.

His hands were on zheir hips, supporting but not controlling; he slipped them back and under until he had his palms full of Ash's round biteable arse, clenching beautifully as zhey rocked.

Zhey'd shut zheir eyes; without hearing or sight, zhey must be lost in zheir other senses, the lingering taste of Hazel on zheir lips, the scents of storm and sex thick in the small room, the pure sensation of Hazel's mouth and tongue. Zhey began to make soft bird-like noises, intensifying.

It was too much. Hazel sacrificed one handful of arse to wrap an urgent hand around his cock. He moaned against the damp thrust of Ash's sex, and felt zheir rhythm speed up and stutter, zheir hips and thighs flexing strongly. His left hand was holding Ash's hip again, tightly encouraging zhem onward.

Ash released the wall to sign, ~that, that, that, a helpless flutter of zheir hands as zhey pressed against and into his mouth.

He felt the pulse of zheir pleasure. His hand worked frantically, and he came in convulsive jerks, feeling the hot flood spurt from him. Ash flung zheir head back and zheir hips forward, arching against his tongue. Zhey let out a keening cry that was loud enough to echo along the hallway and possibly spawn tales that a cryptid harbinger from any number of cultural tales had taken residence in the crannies of the subterrane walls again.

Ash sagged and fell forward bonelessly, half against the wall, before rolling to flop onto zheir back beside Hazel. Zhey were wide-eyed, pupils dilated, pleasure-drowned. Hazel had enough hubris to wonder if zhey'd ever actually had a climax quite as strong as that one; he was very good with his mouth. More likely, zhey'd just been missing sex for long enough to make this brief interlude especially pleasant.

Stirring, zhey made a face and shot Hazel a mock-offended look.

'~Sorry,' Hazel said. '~Fairly sure I soaked the back of your shirt there.'

Ash started zheir huffing laugh, putting zheir hands briefly over zheir face. Zhey signed, ~I'm sticky all over. And my thighs are shaking.

Hazel laughed too. '~Let me help you get your shirt off and clean up.' He paused. '~Is that…'

~Hazel, you just played me like a flute. I think I can let you see my torso.

He took zheir chin, kissed zheir mouth. He could feel zheir smile under his mouth. He couldn't stop smiling himself. He peeled off the bedraggled undershirt, baring Ash's upper body. Ash was watching him with slight anxiety again, and he wasn't sure if he was meant to feign disinterest or try to lavishly praise zheir body with his clumsy ineloquence. He settled for what he would do with any other lover and traced over the warm, smooth skin with his mouth. As he felt zhem dissolve under him again, he shifted to kiss zheir inner thighs where he could feel zheir muscles still trembling under his mouth.

He found round bruises on zheir hip where he had gripped zhem too tight. He kissed there too, slower.

Ash tapped his shoulder and shook zheir head. ~You didn't hurt me. I just bruise easily.

'~A-yah, me too,' Hazel said, thinking, *Here we are again, then,* in rueful concert with his heavily beating heart.

~I— That was not what I expected. I presumed…courtesy…from you, of course, but not like that.

Hazel brushed his fingertips over the bruises he'd left. He said, keeping his expression and signs as neutral as he could, '~People do expect a certain species of fuck from a man who looks like me.' Holly never had. Neither had Miriam. '~Did you… If you… I can… I mean, I *will*—'

Ash flashed zheir fierce scowl and reached down to poke his bare shoulder. ~Let me finish. Not what I expected, *and I loved it.*

'~Me too,' Hazel said again, and Ash mirrored his soft smile.

He got up, dampened the washcloth, stroked it over Ash's skin, kissed zhem some more. He handed zhem the cloth, and then a fresh linen shirt off a hook. Thus draped, zhey lolled with abandon, eyes glazed and sleepy. Zhey had been starved for touch; Hazel was quite, quite satisfied, bordering on smug, to have sated zhem, for now, and that was a lovely pair of words, too.

He had to sternly remind himself that *once* did not mean *again,* whether Ash had loved it or not. He imagined zhey'd love quite a few things, and he didn't necessarily have to be the one to provide those things.

He shrugged back into his own shirt, and his drawers, bringing himself to the same level of dress as Ash, before lying beside zhem. The bed was quite narrow, given the boundaries of the former cell, but he and Holly had long since sorted how to fit two adults comfortably together. He lay on his side and nestled Ash against him.

Ash pushed back the sleeves of the outsized borrowed shirt and used the flat of zheir palm to stroke over his arm. Zhey were, Hazel realised, rather enjoying the sword-honed muscles of his bicep under the cloth; he smiled and may have even flexed a little.

~Could you… —Zhey made a small gesture at zheir damp discarded shirt— ~Had it been a long time for you? Could you not wait for me to reciprocate? Sorry, did I insult you?

That last, rapid, signing, was because Hazel's face must have changed expression. If he'd been in bed with Holly, he'd have mocked him, a little, for the presumption, but instead he held up a hand, asking for time to think through what he wanted to say. He didn't want this to end with Ash feeling insulted in a way that Hazel certainly did not.

In one sense, no, he couldn't have waited, couldn't have kept himself from bringing himself off, overwhelmed by the sensations and sounds and taste of Ash's pleasure. In another sense… Well, he was not used to sex being coupled with attraction. Before this time with Ash, it had been an agreeable activity, undertaken, if at all, with someone he felt friendly toward. Holly and Miriam, in their different ways, had been generous partners in bed. But Hazel was very used to finding his true gratification, irrespective of any simple physical release, in the gratification of his partner.

And it was in his head, too, that Ash had come to Haven expecting to pay a price, and expecting that price to be sex, and expecting that sex to fit the shape of the other person's preferences, and expecting those preferences to be, on the whole, selfish. Zheir presumption of reciprocal obligation seemed part and parcel of that heavy chain.

'~Your pleasure is my pleasure,' he said at last.

Ash looked severe. ~That was an awful lot of thinking for a short answer. One day, I will order you to do the thinking aloud.

'~It really wasn't much thinking,' Hazel explained. '~It just takes me a while to get to the end of the thought. It's not… I know I'm odd in my way, Ash, but it's not all that unusual to take pleasure in, ah, pleasing your bedmate.'

~My prior bedmate did not—

Ash locked zheir hands together, the equivalent of clapping both hands over zheir mouth. Zhey looked momentarily aghast before zhey wiped zheir face clean of expression and stared straight up at the ceiling, Mancer blank.

He considered zhem. He considered zheir reaction to the regimented bed linens. He considered zheir anxiety about letting him see zheir bared body. He considered that zhey hadn't expected what he'd given zhem, and what zhey might therefore have expected. He considered the end of the thought zhey'd chopped off. He strongly suspected he could guess the end of the thought anyway.

Ash's last lover had not been as thoughtful—as courteous, per Ash's specific sign—as Hazel, he supposed. Ash's last lover had not been as kind as Ash deserved. They hadn't been the Mancer partner who'd taught zhem to appreciate safe, affectionate touch, that felt like a certainty.

He hated that the lushed-out look on zheir face was already gone. He asked, '~Would you like to talk about that a little further?'

~I would give all my worldly wealth to *not* talk about that a little further.

He bowed to Ash's tone and expression and tried to shift back into the light manner of only moments before. '~Oh, yes? And what wealth would that be, Mancer?'

He probably hadn't quite managed the right note. Mancers surrendered independent means and personal fortunes as well as their family name when they joined a stronghold. It was yet another thing that made them vulnerable if they did not choose their stronghold wisely, yet another hole in the foundation of the traditional covenant. It'd been so easy to dismiss, knowing only Albemarle and Haven, so easy to accept as just being how it had to be. It was what it was, but Hazel now wondered if it truly had to be.

Ash took his hand, ran fingers over his palm. Zhey sighed, slow. Tension seemed to seep into zhem with the gust of air, instead of out. Zhey huddled into the outsized shirt.

~There *is* something I need to talk to you about, Hazel darling.

'~Anything, Ash.'

Holding a tight fist against zheir sternum, Ash took a breath, then another. Zhey nodded, a quick and decisive message to zhemself. Zheir hand lifted and opened.

A single brisk knock gave scant warning before Holly leaned in and said, '~So sorry, my love. Cristati is marching on the walls.'

~Eighteen~

Hazel sat up. He brushed a thumb over Ash's cheek. The Mancer's glowing skin had taken on a sickly sallow tingle, and the groove of zheir frown was especially deep.

'~Ash, around to your room for fresh clothes, and then into the atelier with Albemarle.' He paused. '~Hold the course, love, and everything will work out.'

Ash licked zheir lips before managing a faint smile. ~Yes, Hazel. Everything will work out as it should.

Handing a hastily-dressed Ash over to Titus, waiting subdued in the hallway outside his room, Hazel followed Holly. Holly didn't say anything as they went up the shallow flight of stairs from the subterrane to the ground floor undercroft and through the dining hall. They were halfway up the corkscrew stairs from the dining hall to the first floor before he finally nudged Hazel, hard enough to tilt him sideways.

'Took you long enough.'

'I thought zhey wanted you.'

'Hah!' Holly said. 'By my lost relics, I'd've told you different if you'd mentioned that. I'm fairly fucking sure I did tell you, in fact.'

It was Hazel's turn to laugh. 'I think you'll find zhem a lot friendlier now zhey realise you don't have my cock in hand.'

'Don't I?' Holly purred, gliding over him with impudent hands. Hazel good-naturedly let him until he pouted. 'You're no fun. I don't think I'm ever going to get to fuck you again, am I? I'll miss that lovely mouth of yours.'

His tone was still flippant but he looked, just for a moment, impossibly forlorn. It occurred to Hazel—it had never occurred to him before—that, when he'd broken things off all those years ago to protect his own soft heart, he had hurt Holly exactly as much as Holly had hurt him in being unable to appreciate that soft heart.

Taking Holly's hand, Hazel said, 'One sparrow does not a summer make, Hols, and one fuck does not a love affair make.'

Well. Not for Ash, anyway.

'I believe you may truly be blind,' Holly said, the glimpse of sorrow gone as quickly as it had come. If Hazel didn't know Holly to his bones, he wouldn't've believed he'd seen it. 'Have you pair ever considered just openly informing people when you're besotted with them? You'd have got down to it weeks ago. The second Ash laid eyes on you, probably.'

Given that nothing would shake Hazel's conviction that Ash had started off truly afraid of him—zheir wobble when zhey'd remembered he was an actual proper Mancer guard didn't help—he vehemently, but silently, disagreed with this last sally from Holly.

Instead, he said, 'Shit timing,' as they reached the main floor of the stronghold.

'Plenty of time,' Holly said. 'We're under siege, what else are we doing now but fucking and drinking all the wine?'

'I don't think that how sieges go, Hols,' Hazel said mildly.

They went past the rear door of the great hall and up the servants' backstairs to the second-floor residential quarters. Holly finally dropped Hazel's hand and turned to business. 'Outrunners came in ahead of the first refugees. Cristati's coming in force, by report. They've torched a few farmhouses but are otherwise quite intent on getting here quickly.'

They went up the last set of stairs, a narrow switchback, and out on to the flat roof of the stronghold. From here, they were just higher than the walls. Evelyn, Lord Valerian and Lady Fairhaven were already standing at the low parapet, looking westward. The commanders of the stronghold guards and the militia stood with them, with their captains. A few more of the purple were about, chattering. Fa'avae the Artificer fussed over the fireworks array, her assistants and apprentices clustered at her side.

Holly leaned on the parapet, squeezing in beside Valerian, who rolled his eyes but did not, Hazel noted, shift away from the warm contact of long and lanky Holly pressed against him.

On the horizon, Hazel could make out smoke, or dust, or both, marring the beauty of the sunset. Closer, the road was choked with the estate's farming tenants, carrying children and cages of chickens, leading goats and milk cows on tethers, slowly moving in behind the protection of the stronghold walls. Lady Fairhaven was her usual serene self, watching sombrely but calmly as her people came to safety in the red rays of the setting sun.

The courtyard became crowded and the road became empty. As full dark fell, the last of the refugees came in. Hazel saw that Miriam and her new assistants were already moving among them, while stronghold guards shepherded them about to their temporary quarters. The undercroft accommodations would be bursting, but neither the Mancer Guard nor Mancer hallways would acquire new occupants, for security's sake.

The guards below shut the gates, and bolted them. They flicked the small latch that connected the paired Mancy panels on the back of the gates, which in turn completed the circle that ran all the way around the inside of the wall.

A silvery-white mist shimmered into being, enclosing the stronghold as if with a wall of rushing water falling the wrong way. The copperlits on the rooftop gave a single blink. A collective gasp rose from the watchers, echoed below.

'Albemarle's moat,' Valerian murmured.

'It's not lit up like that before, has it?' Holly asked. He glanced down and Hazel followed his gaze. Valerian had taken Holly's hand. Holly, smiling, squeezed.

'We have a clever Mancer,' the lord said. 'It only activates when they're latched together.'

'See, it's going to be fine, my love,' Holly told Hazel. 'That will hold them off till our neighbours send aid.'

Hazel thought, *a-yah, we have Albemarle, but they had Ash*, and wondered what sort of Mancy weapons that army out there might be carrying along with them.

Holly sang, 'Fucking and wine, Hazel darling.' He gave Lord Valerian a rather smouldering look, a little wasted in the fresh darkness of evening, and, since he was still casually holding the man's hand, kissed his knuckles lightly. 'You too, Val, if you like. And that's your once more, my lord.'

Valerian turned to look at him, expression lost to shadow. Over their heads, Haven sent up its fireworks against the first stars, bright green for a call on the covenant, Mancy-enhanced to extend the height and brightness for maximum visibility. The whistle and pop of it, like a shattering, made Hazel flinch, and Holly took his hand too.

One by one, the coastal strongholds in visual range answered with Mancy fireworks of their own.

Red.
Red.
Red.
The covenant treaties did not apply. They would send no aid.
Haven would stand or fall on its own.

~Nineteen~

Lady Fairhaven retreats to her study to write tiny missives to send by pigeon at first light; if only they could train owls, if only Albemarle's far-scry project could be made to work. Entwined in the flowery formal written language used among the purple, the message itself will be simple: *What do you know, that Haven doesn't know? What do you know, that Cristati made you too afraid to warn us of?*

Holly accompanies Hazel to the atelier, to ask Ash the same questions.

But Kito, in an attempt to keep Albemarle calm, has maintained the schedule and let the Mancers go to their chambers already. Holly is suspicious of this—Albemarle without fail retreats to solitude after zheir evening bath and meal, but Ash, before, has always stayed with zheir guards to read of an evening: hence, Hazel's gift of the antechamber sitting area, including the extra chairs for those guards.

Now Ash has bolted zheir chamber door and of course cannot hear a knock. Holly thinks zhey wouldn't have answered it anyway.

Hazel is not suspicious. Hazel is worried. His thick tousled hair's a dark cloud about his head because he's been running his hands through it, and his candid eyes are shadowed.

Hazel's heart is too big for his body; he gives it away with the slightest of provocations because it cannot be confined within its natural bounds. Holly thinks he may have made a very bad mistake, in endorsing his dear friend's infatuation with a Mancer whose habit is secrets. They're all so used to Albemarle's unwavering honesty. They'd forgotten that it isn't a universal Mancer trait.

There's only one universal Mancer trait: the need to create Mancy. Whatever it takes, for the freedom to do that.

What does Ash think it will take, for that freedom?

Holly sighs, looking at the closed door. He thinks about how weak the bolts on the Mancers' doors are, deliberately so that a Mancer guard can break in, in an emergency.

'Get some sleep,' he tells Hazel.

Neither of them is on watch till tomorrow morning and there's no point hanging about bothering the other six Mancer guards, who will take it in pairs overnight to guard the Mancers' hallway.

There exists a small chance that the army on Haven's doorstep is merely a distraction for an incursion by the Cristati Mancer Guard. There exists a vanishingly small chance that such an incursion would make it through Albemarle's moat. There is still, however, a surfeit of stronghold guards between every ingress and the subterrane. But only the Haven Mancer guards are allowed this close to the Mancers.

He adds, 'Do you want me to stay with you, love?'

Hazel waves him off. This might be genuine, or it might be because he heard Valerian's low-voiced command—or acquiescence, or request, or invitation, or plea. Holly does not know how to categorise it.

'Are you sure?' he asks, because he's attracted to irritable Lord Valerian but he loves Hazel more, far more, than he loves sex with people who just can't bloody help themselves.

'Yes. Go enjoy yourself, Holly. I will sleep, don't fret.'

Holly doubts this, but up he goes, to Lord Valerian's private apartment on the floor above the great hall, where only the purple and their honoured guests are granted accommodation.

'Lord Vee,' he says with deep insolence as he enters his patron's suite. It's elegant, a touch bare. Reminders of his wife must have been too painful; he's removed all traces.

Behind him, the lord closes the door, locks it. That's suggestive, but Holly tries anyway. 'The situation downstairs—'

'I'll get my report from Commander Holyoake in the morning,' Valerian says. 'You know why you're here, the night before the siege starts. What was it, captain? Fucking and wine?'

'A-yah.' Holly makes a delicate pause. 'You don't seem to have any wine, my lord.'

Holly's quite pleased with this sally; he flashes the smile he knows makes men weak at the knees. Lord Valerian does not, however, look moved in any way. He hasn't followed Holly further into the room. Back against the door. Arms folded. Mouth set. Eyes cold—

'Are you going to get on with it? I didn't bring you here to be stared at.'

—Irritable.

Holly supposes it's better than the soft look he was wearing after the first time, and even the near-friendliness they'd seen on the far distant horizon in his office after the feast night. This shouldn't bog either of them into difficulties, then.

Smiling, he steps into Valerian's space, close enough that the other man is forced to tilt his head back to keep glaring at him. He does not even slightly look like a man intent on embarking on a tryst, but he takes a fistful of Holly's thin braids, wrapping them twice, holding him tight, and Holly likes that. He likes that. He kisses Valerian.

Valerian's mouth is warm and willing but his body against Holly's is tense and stiff and, though the hand trapping Holly's braids does not relent, his other hand stays inert at his side, even while Holly slides his own hands from Valerian's face and over his shoulders and chest.

He is not, Holly realises, fighting Holly. He's fighting himself.

Holly pulls back. Valerian's mouth tightens; he is furious that Holly stopped. 'Get on with it,' he says again, snarling, hand taut in Holly's hair. 'Do you need me to say it aloud? Fuck me. I want you to fuck me.'

Holly is decidedly confused. Valerian is saying one thing. His body is saying another. Holly, for now, chooses to obey his words. He draws the man through to the bedchamber and lays him on the bed, which is wide and pleasantly soft.

Valerian's breathing is rapid as Holly unbuckles his sword and strips them both with more efficiency than spectacle. He says only, 'Leave the skirt on.'

Holly laughs and kisses and bites. He runs his hands over the man's broad and bulky shoulders and biceps and down his back, all those muscles from the axe-work flexing and bunching under him, Valerian's tension ratcheting up and up and up till, suddenly, it breaks.

He goes limp, submissive, pale eyes dazed. Holly has his mouth on his and a hand around his meaty thigh, expertly positioning, and the other hand slips an oiled finger into his hole; he'd brought along a vial, but Val had a flask waiting.

Valerian grunts and squirms against the invasion. Holly pauses. Valerian is not making good sounds, good movements. He is fighting again.

'Don't be nice,' Valerian bites out, as Holly eases back, withdrawing to sit on his heels between the lord's spread legs. 'You're not nice and I don't want nice. I want you to do what you're best at.'

'I don't think you're ready for this, lover,' Holly says, his first words for some time but the thought he has been having repeatedly.

Valerian has his hands clenched, fists so tight his knuckles are white, laid beside his head as if in a surrender his body is very much not feeling. His eyes are squeezed shut. Tears are leaking from their corners.

'I need it to be different,' he says. 'I need my first time since her to be different from her.'

'Oh, love,' Holly says, at his rare softest. He wipes a tear away with his thumb. He understands now why Valerian is so distraught over something he is insisting he wants. It's not over that at all. 'Anyone would feel different than her. You should find someone you'd actually like to be with.'

Valerian cries in earnest then, nearly silently. Holly, after a moment of deliberation, lowers his full body weight onto the man and holds him. Valerian doesn't resist. Holly thinks more people than Albemarle need a heavy blanket to cozen under sometimes.

This is what Hazel did for him, at the academy.

Haven for Hazel is his place of belonging, his nest. He'd needed a firm nudge to get him out of it, but like any good fledgling, he'd opened his wings and flown. He'd been homesick at the academy, but not wrecked. That had come when he'd come home, and Maya had been gone.

Haven for Holly is his place of safety, his cocoon, wrapping him securely away from the memory of watching his family butchered during the civil war. Crouched under the industrial Mancy loom that was their family's wealth. Evie, her hand over his mouth, her arms locked around him, keeping them both from bursting out of hiding to fight a hopeless battle. That was a memory.

She'd eased opened the trapdoor leading down to the hidden printing press that was their family's revolutionary contribution, and dragged him out the runner's tunnel, him fighting her all the way, a wretched silent struggle they'd taken a long time to stop having.

He'd thought he'd finally burst out at the academy, transformed, but instead the mummifying shell had dissolved and his grief had unfurled, preserved shiny and fresh. If Hazel hadn't been there to comfort him, to do exactly this, hold him secure and let him grieve, Holly would have fractured.

Valerian is fracturing now. Holly encases the lord's stocky, wracked body in his long limbs, holding as tight as he can, pushing him down as hard as he can with his ropey strength. He presses his mouth into Valerian's soft hair and weathers the storm.

When the man is finally calm again, his breathing steady and slowing, he says, voice thick, 'I miss her. I know it's been years, but I still miss her every day.'

'That's grief, Val. That's the way it is.' Holly takes a leaf from Hazel's book and chastely kisses his temple. 'I'll go.'

Valerian's hand locks around his bicep, holding him in place laid out atop him, their naked chests pressed together. 'I *did not* invite Rowan fucking Holyoake to bed on our last night of freedom so I could cry and cuddle,' he says fiercely. 'I *am* ready, Holly, and you *are* who I want to be with.'

Holly considers him again. He is still marked by tears, ragged in the aftermath of his storm, and yet tense at his core.

But this is where Hazel's dispassionate kindness has the advantage over Holly's impulsive generosity, because Hazel would absolutely not be aroused right now. Holly is. Holly is hard against Valerian's muscular thigh and only barely stopping himself from rutting against him.

Holly's an easy mark for strong but vulnerable, controlling but needy.

He rolls easily, pulling Valerian on top of him, Val swallowing the end of a startled protest.

'How about you tell me all about what you want, love?' Holly runs his hands over Valerian's back, smoothing the long muscles there. The lord is burying his head against Holly's shoulder. 'Or what you might have wanted, when you were quiet young Val, if that's easier? We've played that game before, haven't we? What would he have liked?'

Valerian scoffs at his adolescent self. 'To cry and cuddle, probably. I was shy and innocent, Holly. I don't think my imagination ever really got beyond what it might be like to kiss you. Boring, I know.'

'How very dare you suggest that kissing *me* would ever approach boring.'

Val makes one of those half-amused, half-irritated sounds Holly is proving adept at eliciting from him.

'How did you imagine it?' Holly asks. 'Did I come to you gently with soft and tender kisses, like in a romantic novel?'

The lord slowly shakes his head, still not lifting off Holly's shoulder.

'Ah,' Holly says. He laughs. 'Even back then, even in your own head, I had to overcome your better judgment with assertive seduction? I do so adore a consistent heart.'

Holly does kiss him then, drawing his mouth to his with a hand on his nape, fingers tangling with that silly floppy hair. Valerian's tentativeness gradually transforms into surety, and the man presses his weight onto

Holly, trying to take control of the kiss. Holly doesn't let him. Holly breaks off and smiles to hear the frustrated noise he makes.

'You weren't shy and innocent when you were telling me to get on my knees,' he points out. 'Would you like that again? You seemed to enjoy yourself well enough, right up until you decided to poke yourself in the eye with your own propriety.'

'My propriety showed up far too late,' Valerian said ruefully. 'Even now…'

Holly tuts at himself. He's reminded Valerian of his misplaced guilt over their previous encounter. 'Nah, too early and unwanted, like the very worst of uninvited guests.'

Holly's been running his palms over Valerian's broad back, caressing flesh, stroking the tense muscles. He can feel the strength there. It's given him a hankering.

'Are you truly not concerned with the power differential between us?' Lord Valerian says, oblivious to Holly's ever-rising arousal, despite hard evidence. 'It was very wrong of me to summon you here so cavalierly.'

'This has taken a somewhat unexpected bureaucratic turn,' Holly says. 'By my holiest of relics, Lord Vee, you know how to sweet-talk a fellow, don't you?'

'No, really,' Valerian insists. 'Stop laughing, Holyoake.'

'Have you considered,' Holly says, valiantly trying to obey, 'that I have all the fucking power, Val? You did not summon me. I made you plead for me to come. And you will plead with me to let you come, not so very long from now.'

Valerian does not take the bait. 'I'm a lord and you're my subordinate.'

'Ooh,' Holly mocks. 'Your subordinate. A-yah, I'm under you.' He rocks his hips.

'Fuck off, you utter dick,' Valerian says, finally starting to laugh too. 'I have genuine concerns.'

'Your genuine concern is that you don't actually like me and this is just another excuse to avoid fucking me,' Holly tells him.

It pangs, a little. He likes Valerian, irritable and duty-bound and all.

'Not true, Holly.'

'Stop talking, then, and actually get between my thighs. Get on and fuck me if you're going to, Vee.'

That arrests Valerian's attention, for sure. 'Do you— Do you do that?'

'Lover, I do everything.'

'But you said you like to—' Valerian flushes, and his voice is hoarse as he continues. It's delightful. '—spill buried deep inside your lovers.'

Valerian, Holly notes, has quoted him exactly. 'Or them, me. I like many things.'

'Except incompetent fumbling.'

And he's still quoting him, holding him uncomfortably accountable. The man puts far too much weight on what comes out of Holly's mouth instead of what Holly could be doing with it.

'Better make it competent, then, lover,' he says slyly, before pressing another kiss against the man's stern mouth.

It's not one of his better efforts, open-mouthed and chaste, but Valerian responds. Holly finds himself held down to be kissed with savage intensity. Valerian's let go at last. Holly lets go with him.

He's not usually passive in bed but now he stretches out his long limbs and permits Valerian to ravage him, lips and teeth and tongue over his hot skin, the man's calloused hands over his ribs, at his hips, pushing up the skirt. He groans, he arches, he demands more. The first touch of Valerian's mouth on his cock genuinely leaves him writhing, his fingers scrabbling over the linen.

There's not a lot of technique to it, but there doesn't have to be, with Valerian both zealous and thorough. He's ricocheted from being timid about offering his hand, to downright enthusiastic about offering his mouth, a silver lining to the siege, Holly supposes, or to Holly's unrelenting goading. He fights not to thrust his cock down the man's throat; Valerian swallows him to the root anyway, and moans like he's tasted heaven.

'Fuck,' Holly says to the ceiling when he hears that moan, and he spends, great spasms jerking his hips up without volition, feeling Valerian's fingers press into his skin as he rides through it.

Holly drags Valerian back to his mouth, kisses him and tastes himself. His fingers are already oiled, he's reaching down and fucking himself open for Valerian. The lord is thrusting against his thigh, leaking and ready. He groans, heartfelt, as Holly takes firm hold of his cock to oil him up and guide him in, and groans again as Holly takes him to the hilt. He doesn't move.

'Come on, love,' Holly murmurs in his ear. He's hooked one leg up so his heel is set in the small of Valerian's back, and now gives him a nudge like encouraging a horse. 'I want to feel you for a week.'

Valerian thrusts with a grunt in his throat, and again. Holly tilts his hips to meet him, angling to take him deeper, to make it good for himself and better for Valerian. The man is over him, hands in claws at his shoulders, braced hard, pressing him down, taking him mercilessly, nothing but sweat and grunt and weight. Holly laughs—this is fucking delightful—and pushes up with his hips, revelling, and hears Val's soft exhalations change in timbre.

'Not yet,' he admonishes. 'Beg me for it, lover.'

Valerian says his name, a gasp, a protest, a plea, the desperation Holly wants to hear. He grips the man's thick arse and slides his finger down his crease.

When Valerian comes, he digs his fingers in and curses robustly, teeth against Holly's neck. He collapses fully onto Holly and lies there, panting, until Holly taps him on the shoulder and suggests he needs to breathe. Valerian pulls out without finesse and rolls to lie next to him, forearm slung over his eyes.

'All right, love?' Holly asks. He stretches, with a small wince. He's not as young as he was, not quite as flexible; he *is* going to feel that for a fucking week.

'You can go,' Valerian says from under his arm. His chest is still flushed and pebbled with his arousal, but he's regained his cool tones.

'Excuse me?' Holly says, more amused than offended, but still offended. His breathing hasn't even returned to normal yet. 'Is that permission or a lordly command? Did you not have some kind of genuine concern about that, not so long ago?'

'I understand why you were a shit to me that last time,' Valerian says. 'Not looking to give you the excuse this time. Go ahead and get out.'

Holly is nothing but contrary. 'I want to stay.'

'As you like,' Valerian says crisply. He doesn't move.

'Ah, I like affection after someone's fucked me, Lord Vee.'

It's true enough, though the person doing the fucking and the person providing the affection are usually not the same, being, respectively, whoever's caught Holly's eye and the always sweet and obliging Hazel, who sleepily rolls over and wraps his arms around Holly, no matter the unsociable depths of the night it might be when he crawls into his bed.

'You do not,' Valerian says, sounding mutedly outraged.

Holly swallows a smile. He says, 'I would like a cuddle, please, my lord.'

He's managed to inject enough sincerity into his voice that Valerian uncovers his face and looks at him cautiously. The lord, indeed, is trying to hide the same soft look he wore the first time Holly had his way with him.

Holly opens his arms. He knows he shouldn't. He knows he's just encouraging Valerian in an unwise infatuation.

But he likes him and he wants to hold him and, also, he wants to be here in the morning because he thinks he'll get another bout and he thinks it'll be even better than this one. He loves the way Valerian is restrained and controlled, right up until he's not.

Holly thinks he might be able to coax this staid and dutiful man into being the best fuck he's ever had, if Cristati doesn't kill them both first.

Valerian, looking suspicious, edges over into Holly's arms. Holly pats him. 'There we are, that's not so bad, is it?'

'Shut up, you dick,' Valerian mumbles into Holly's shoulder. 'Did I hurt you?'

'Nah,' Holly says, running the tips of his nails over the skin of the man's back and feeling him shiver. 'I like my play rough on occasion.'

Valerian makes a dissatisfied sound. He's worked his hands down, and is stroking Holly's thighs, pushing under his leather skirt, which is still rucked up and sticking to his skin. Valerian's rubbing in circular motions with his thumbs over Holly's thighs; Holly realises he's absently trying to massage away any remnant discomfort. It's sweet. Holly shifts under him, opening his thighs to him.

He wonders if he'll have to wait until morning for the second bout. He wonders if he'll even have to wait an hour.

'When are you going to tell your boy you're fucking his crush?' he asks mischievously.

'Are we fucking? Or have we fucked?'

'Now it's a grammar lesson from the bureaucrat?'

Valerian squeezes his strong hands over Holly's inner thighs and Holly lolls back, purring his appreciation. The lord clarifies, 'I'm asking if we're done, Holly. You've had me.'

'I most certainly have not,' Holly informs him. 'You better tell him. Or are you just going to let him catch us over your desk one day and hope he's too embarrassed to ever mention it?'

'That would be exemplary parenting on my part, compounding the already spectacular job I'm doing by fucking his crush in the first place,' Valerian says dryly.

'Be fair, I was your crush first,' Holly points out, drawing lazy circles on Valerian's skin.

'I went and checked on him earlier, to make sure the siege wasn't scaring him. He's with his friend. He said he was fine, like I was an idiot for even asking. He asked if *I* was all right. I didn't tell him I was so sick with nerves I couldn't think of anything else to do but give in to my worst impulses.'

'I've been described as a lot of things in my life, and that might be the most accurate.'

'He's not quite as terrible as that feast night episode makes him seem.' Valerian sighs. 'I sometimes wonder what Margarite would have thought of how I raised him without her. He lost her at such a vulnerable—'

He cuts himself off. Holly watches him flush with some confusion before he understands.

'You can talk about your family, Val. You can talk about your wife. I'm not going to be a dick about that.' When Val says nothing, Holly gently takes his face in both hands and repeats, 'You can talk about her, love.'

Valerian evidently decides he can take Holly at face value, which is exactly where Holly can always be taken. 'Lorian lost her when he was only twelve. She was the one he talked to. She was the one who… Well, she was the light-hearted one of the two of us. I wish— There are many things I wish.'

'It was the cancroid disease, wasn't it?'

'It was a slow and painful death,' Valerian says bitterly. Holly slowly tightens his hold on the man as he goes on. 'She could let her son see her suffer, or spend her days in the twilight of Miriam's poppy concoction and not know him at all. That he had to see any of that…' He coughs, and adds in a deliberately altered tone, 'I don't know how it affected him. It's made him…younger…than I was at that age.'

'He'll be a good man. He just needs the same growing up we all needed.' Holly nudges Val, deftly switching his own tone to something lighter. 'Except you serious dutiful types who are born good and grown up. Yes, I just insulted you, you can stop wondering.'

Valerian makes his delightfully annoyed grumble in the back of his throat. 'While we speak of our lovers—'

'Don't ask me to name them, it'd waste the rest of the night.' Holly's teasing again; he knows what Val's going to ask. Also, there is a large question mark over his ability to conjure up the names of even a proportion of his previous lovers.

'—what the fuck is going on with you and Hazlemere?'

Holly laughs. Val says to the ceiling, 'Oh, such a dick.' Setting his jaw, he pushes on. 'He seems infatuated with the new Mancer, and I can only assume he's not bothered by you taking other men to bed in your turn?'

'Hazel *is* a lovely fuck, and I indeed adore the man,' Holly says, and he's watching Val's face closely. 'But it's never infatuation with him. He's built to fall in love. I'm…not. I've hurt him, in the past, because of that. So we mostly avoid fucking these days.'

Valerian hesitates. Then he grows a spine and says, 'I'm sensing a warning there.'

'If you would like to take it that way, my lord.'

Again, Val pauses. He's wearing a thoughtful look that Holly is moved to erase by biting his neck suddenly and making him yelp.

'You like the skirt?' Holly teases, because Valerian's hands have been repetitively sliding over his thighs just where the leather hem caresses them.

'I like the skirt. I like the trousers, too. Your arse, Holy Mother.'

'A-yah, my arse knows you like it, intimately.'

Valerian nestles in further, sighing against Holly's neck. His hands have come to rest, curved about Holly's hips. 'Are you Rowan, when you're in trousers?'

'I'll answer to Rowan, but I'm always Holly,' Holly says. 'Though it'd be nice if the Mancer pronoun wasn't just for Mancers, sometimes, I suppose. Just sometimes. Mostly I'm just a man who likes to wear an excessively short skirt.'

'That's ironic.' He sounds endearingly sleepy now. Holly touches his ridiculous hair, runs his fingers through it. 'Albemarle told my father zhey didn't care what we call zhem when zhey first arrived. He, she, they, zhey, it, one, you, no difference to zhem.'

That is quite the taboo, actually. Nightingale would be shocked all over again.

After a long silence, Holly asks, 'Did you ask because you prefer Rowan?'

But Valerian's asleep. Holly thinks about sliding out from under him, going to his own bed. He stays.

He wakes, hours later judging by the dim state of the copperlits, wrapped in the same sense of warm safety that sleeping with Hazel inspires, but with the feel of a decidedly different body, softer, more tucked in against him than enveloping him. He opens his eyes to find Valerian staring at the ceiling. He doesn't look around when Holly stirs.

Holly rubs his palms over Valerian's shoulders and is unpleasantly surprised. 'Tense? My lord, tell me what a fellow has to do around here to get you to relax?'

'Scared,' the lord says, and abruptly rolls to hide his face against Holly's chest.

'No shame in it.' Valerian says nothing—the silence has a certain quality to it—and Holly nudges him. 'Everyone's scared, Vee.'

'Are you?' Valerian asks pointedly.

'Nah,' Holly says. 'Not enough imagination for it. What's your what-if, Vee? Let me have a try at reassuring you.'

'What if I haven't prepared the stronghold well enough for this siege?' Val whispers after Holly has outwaited another weighty silence.

'On the one hand,' Holly says, lazily spiralling his thumb over bare skin, 'Lady Fairhaven trusts you to do your job right, and you can hardly call her trust misplaced, can you? And on the other hand, she trusts a lot of other people to have also done their jobs right. It's not all on you, love.'

'That will be of great comfort when Haven falls.'

'Pessimist,' Holly says. 'Haven falls over my dead body, and I'm not dying today.'

He's already decided: only one Mancer Guard captain dies during this siege, and it's not him.

'It's not all on you, love,' Valerian mimics, quite well, and his shoulders release.

Holly flicks the side of his face to make him look up. He's smiling, if not wholeheartedly. Holly kisses his nose fondly and then stretches, long and luxurious, watching Valerian's pupils dilate as he stares.

Holly says, 'You fell asleep while you were groping me. If I didn't have an ego the size of the stronghold, I'd be insulted.'

'Hmmm. How shall I ever make it up to you?'

Holly's eyes narrow. Valerian's abruptly sounding far too in control. He can't be having with that.

'It's early,' he murmurs. 'Let's go down to your office.' Val frowns but before he can ask why, Holly goes on, 'I'll wager you have plans for me and that desk of yours.'

There's a distinctly fraught pause before Valerian gets out, 'How are you such a dick, and yet so perceptive?'

'I'm the gift that keeps on giving,' Holly enlightens him. 'Are you going to bend me over it, lover? Push my skirt up over my hips?'

As Holly speaks, he's sliding his hand down; he finds Valerian's cock, already hard, and runs a thumb over the head. Valerian gasps and thrusts against him, eyes closing to slits. Holly tightens his grip and pumps, pushing his own erection against Valerian's strong thigh.

'You going to fuck between my thighs, Vee? You going to wrap my braids around your fist and ride me hard? I'm going to feel your hot breath on the back of my neck? You going to make me say your name? Valerian.' He says like a prayer. 'Valerian. Let's go, lover, let's— Oh. That was fast.'

He wipes his hand on Valerian's soft stomach, matting the thatch of chestnut hair there. He's grinning.

'You fucker,' Valerian says weakly, and that's much better. 'Stay still for once, I'll have you,' and that's even better.

But while Valerian is laying a strip of wet along Holly's cock, the question from the night before comes out. 'Do you prefer Rowan?'

Valerian pauses. He doesn't look up. He runs his neatly pared nails along Holly's length. 'What?'

'I know you don't like Holly. Do you prefer Rowan?'

'No,' says Valerian.

'You don't like either?'

'You're always Holly,' Valerian says, 'and I always like Holly. You just send me wild sometimes.' He pauses. 'All the damned time, actually.'

'Good answer,' Holly says. He's unaccountably relieved. 'And so, circumstances aside, why did you not just proposition me sometime before now, then? Ask, and you will definitely have received. You didn't need to be shy about that.'

'Yes, Holly, *you* do not need to feel shy about propositioning a man who looks like you, because you fucking look like you.'

'Gorgeous?' Holly asks, since he meant it when he said his ego was robust.

'Unbelievably gorgeous. Who the fuck would ever say no?'

Holly does not point out that Valerian is, in fact, the fucker who said no. He says, 'Ah, and have you seen your thighs, my lord? The very definition of mighty thews.'

'Only if you don't actually know what thews are, captain.'

Holly sniggers and tangles his fingers into Valerian's hair. 'I'm going to write my name on the canvas of your inner thighs and you're going to think about me all day.'

Valerian gives him a stern look, making Holly shove a hand into his floppy hair and twist meaningful.

'Get back to it, Lord Vee, or do I have to remind you how it's done?'

Valerian surrenders to the tiniest of smiles. He's laving his tongue over the very tip of Holly's cock when a knock sounds, rapid, urgent. Holly feels even more acutely the pain of having to interrupt Hazel with Ash, now it's happening to him.

Valerian answers the door in a robe, and comes back to sit beside Holly. He looks sickly.

'Lady Fairhaven is calling for us,' he says. 'Lady Cristati is for parley at the gate. She's got a Mancer with her.'

~TWENTY~

Hazel waited outside Ash's chamber. He wouldn't sit down, but he'd bent enough to lean his shoulders against the wall. He'd been there a while now. Holly had come flying down the stairs, racing to wash and tie his braids back and change into trousers and his dress coat in between telling the rest of the Mancer Guard the news.

'They've brought their spare Mancer,' he'd said. 'They're really rubbing it in, how untouchable they think they are.'

He'd run back up the stairs to join Evelyn and Lord Valerian. Kito walked Albemarle to the atelier and had zhem lock zhemself in with a breakfast tray, with the certain knowledge zhey wouldn't eat it.

The other guards arrayed themselves in pairs, in the atelier antechamber, in the subterrane lobby, where Hazel's directional chalk drawings had long since been scrubbed off, and at the top of the subterrane stairs. The undercroft staff were going about their duties, subdued and nervous.

They were all waiting for the outcome of the parley, which naturally could include a trick to get at the Mancers, and Hazel was waiting for Ash.

He'd thought of asking Albemarle to make the copperlits flicker, the way zhey had when zhey'd funnelled Mancy into the moat at the feast night, and again when zhey'd activated it last night. He supposed it would, indeed, snag Ash's attention, but only in so far as zhey'd stay locked away in zheir room for even longer.

The small bolt on the chamber door was for privacy, not for security. Any Mancer guard could break it down. Hazel had considered that, too. He desperately wanted Ash safe behind the secure lock and thick bolts of the reinforced atelier door while that parley went on upstairs. Privacy won, for now.

He heard, in the thick silence of the Mancer hallway, the shot of the bolt he'd been musing on. Ash stepped out of zheir chamber. Zhey were wearing zheir coat and shawl, and the trousers and boots zhey'd arrived in. Zhey didn't look surprised to see Hazel waiting for zhem, just resigned. Zhey closed the door behind zhem and gave him a long, unreadable look.

They'd just finished making love, the last time Hazel had seen zhem. It seemed an eon ago.

Hazel straightened. He pointed at Ash's clothes, asking a silent question.

Zhey nodded. ~Lady Cristati will be coming for me soon.

That was chilling. '~You tried to leave, before,' he said. '~You said it wouldn't be a matter of the covenant. And now the coastal strongholds are saying the same thing. But how can it not be? You asked for sanctuary and we granted it.'

~I'm sorry, Hazel, Ash signed. ~I wish this could go differently.

'~But what does that mean?' Hazel waved at Ash, at zheir clothes. '~Lady Cristati's come knocking, and you knew she would. Help us. What does Haven need to know?'

~Everything is happening exactly as it must happen.

'~Ash,' Hazel said. '~Stop with the cryptic Mancer bullshit and give me a straight answer.'

Ash stood frozen, face set in that haughty expression of offended pride. Hazel almost grasped where he'd seen it before. Then zhey cracked a smile, reluctant but genuine.

~You're about to get the full brunt of cryptic Mancer bullshit, I'm afraid. Everything will work out. Trust me.

Hazel took a step closer. '~Can't you trust me?' he asked. He heard the note of pleading, but Ash wouldn't; zhey'd have to read it in his expression instead. '~Please, Ash, trust me?'

He was reaching to touch Ash's face, and Ash, eyes closing, was tilting zheir face to be touched, when Hazel heard the thunder of boots on stone. He whipped about.

Coming down the hallway in a storm were guards in the green Mancer Guard uniform, but lighter than the Haven bottle-green. Ash made an indescribable noise and Hazel put zhem behind him.

The parley was a ruse. They'd come through the stronghold guards; Kiselyova and Devi were on watch at the top of the corkscrew stairs at this time of day. They'd come through Nightingale and Titus at the top of the subterrane stairs. They'd come through First Jerome and Second Jerome in the subterrane lobby. Maybe they'd picked the Mancer hallway by lucky accident. Or maybe they'd already been down the atelier hallway, and gone through Kito and Morano in the antechamber and were now looking for someone with the knock-code to get the door open.

He heard Holly say, *You're the last guard standing between Haven's Mancer and an invading Mancer Guard. May you surrender?*

No, he fucking may not.

His sword had cleared its sheath before he'd even finished cataloguing how a foreign force had reached this far into the subterrane. He had, for the moment, the advantage. The hallway was narrow enough that they couldn't use their full numbers against him, and they hadn't expected a single fighter to launch straight into them. They were only just drawing their swords.

He'd already killed the first two, hard blows slamming through the slight resistance, when the thought occurred to him: to be in the subterrane, they'd have had to come through Holly, and Evelyn too.

It made killing the next two a whole lot faster and more savage. He ripped his sword out of a butchered chest, wiped his mouth and eyed off the next four, who'd learnt a little caution. He stepped over the bodies and waded in.

'Hazel, hold! Hold, for fuck's sake!'

Only when Evelyn's bellow finally penetrated did he recall that no one got through the Holyoakes unless the Holyoakes had to let them.

There were six bloody bodies in a trail down the hallway behind him, one injured guard at his feet, and another beating a retreat to where a cluster of people stood.

There were the Havens—Evelyn, looking blankly soldierly, her commander face; Holly, seething; Lord Valerian, face coldly set; Lady Fairhaven, ever serene.

And there were the Cristatis. A woman who had to be Lady Cristati, given the shade and sheer quantity of purple. Around Lady Fairhaven's age, maybe a year or two older, an inch shorter but with a frosted elegance to her, she looked like she had ancestors from a region adjacent to Hazel's. She seemed familiar in a niggling way.

Captain Tassone, as furious as Holly, his whole face mottled with it as he looked at the bodies of his fallen men. Another few Mancer guards were with him, expressions appalled as they viewed the outcome of Hazel's defence.

And the Mancer zhemself, age and sex made irrelevant by the depthless, luminous eyes and androgynous features, but, that said, one of the more feminine-cued ones he'd seen, so much so that he had an irregular moment of trouble in wrenching his mind into the right pronoun.

Zhey had long hair in an elaborate plait that read as female, and wore a robe that read as female, and dangling earrings, and even looked as if zhey wore cosmetics in the shades and style reserved for women rather than those for men in this part of the continent. Zhey had the same olive skin and height as zheir Mancer guards, and Hazel remembered that Ash had said that zhey were local to the Cristati region, that zhey'd knocked on the door of zheir nearest stronghold. Zheir hair was lighter, though, brown instead of black, and zheir eyes were a dark but limpid blue, clear pools of starlit midnight. Zhey had not a patch on Ash's severe beauty but compelled the eye in the otherworldly way that Mancers often did.

Zheir body language, however, bespoke fear.

'Sheathe your weapon, lieutenant,' Evelyn shouted.

The storm in his head ceased at the order from his commander. He mechanically wiped the sword clean and put it to rest. He had blood all over his coat, and his face, where his skin was beginning to itch as the gore cooled and dried. He scrubbed at it with one cuff, then put his hands behind his back, settling into the trained stance of a soldier awaiting orders.

Behind him came the soft noise of Ash picking zheir way through the bodies. Aside from the laboured breathing of the injured man at Hazel's feet, zheir slow progress was the only sound. Ash reached his side, and he turned his head and looked at zhem.

Zhey looked down at the bloodied mess he had made and, as expressionless as he'd ever seen zhem, signed, ~Academy-trained Mancer guard.

For the life of him, Hazel could not tell if zhey approved of the slaughter or not. He repeated zheir own sarcastic signing back to zhem. ~How very useful.

Zhey nodded. Zheir fingers clasped his left wrist, comforting him or anchoring zhemself, he did not know.

Evelyn took a deep breath. 'Lieutenant Hazlemere,' she said. 'The covenant does not apply. Release the Mancer.'

Hazel didn't move. He thought that perhaps he now understood how Albemarle felt, when zhey'd had a demand made of zhem that zhey could not answer. His core was frozen, his tongue was frozen. The frustration made his limbs want to thrash.

He slowly put his hand back on the pommel of his sword. If he drew, here in the presence of a visiting lord, it would amount to an act of war. He finally noticed that Holly was intently fingerspelling the same three letters over and over again.

P-Y-S-P-Y-S-P-Y-S-P-Y-S-P-Y-S-P-Y- S-P-Y-S-P-Y-S

The sign for it surely existed in Trade, but none of them had ever had occasion to learn it.

Hazel, helplessly, looked at Ash again, and Ash made the loose fist of the negatory sign but it was slow, an unconvincing whisper of a movement. Zhey were frowning, just a little. Zhey let go of Hazel's wrist.

He looked at Evelyn. If she gave him the nod, he would draw his sword and kill the Mancer and that would certainly be not just an act of war but an entire cursed theatre production of it, and it might still be better than letting a spy with a knack for weapons and the ability to change other Mancers' designs walk out of here with all of Albemarle's work in zheir head.

He remembered Ash reluctantly telling him, *Albemarle's designs are particularly suited to it* and the way zhey had looked at that wasp gun schematic, amusement fading.

Evelyn shook her head, and Hazel took his hand off the hilt, the sickening mix of anger and confusion and relief making him shaky.

Ash started to sign; the first sign was unknown to Hazel, but familiar, the same sign zhey'd used when speaking of zheir Mancer partner. The second sign was [ask].

'*No*,' the lady of Stronghold Cristati said. 'You know how I feel about it, Silverthorne.'

Ash must have been watching her lips; zheir hands immediately dropped to zheir side. Zhey'd been watching her, but the signing had been aimed at the other Mancer, who, guards on either side, did not respond beyond a tightening of zheir facial muscles.

Captain Tassone stood very close behind zhem. Zheir shoulders were tight and drawn up in a way that suggested the captain might not be standing there by coincidence.

Lady Cristati beckoned, an arrogant crook of the finger. 'Come, Silverthorne. Now.'

No, Hazel thought, and put both hands to tight, angry fists angled for a fight to disguise that he'd signed the thought as well.

Ash walked stiffly down the hallway, Evelyn and Lord Valerian parting to let zhem through, Evelyn tugging Holly aside with her, outrage inscribed on his every jerky step backward. Zhey stood before zheir lady, back and shoulders rigid under zheir coat, hands still. Lady Cristati bent close and said something, inaudible to Hazel.

Holly had sharp ears. He looked up, a flash of shock cutting through his anger.

Ash had read her lips again; zhey nodded, once. The look of triumph on her face made Hazel's stomach roil.

One of the Cristati Mancer guards stepped forward. He raised what looked like a small copper box with squat square handles on the sides. As Hazel watched, he easily extended the handles into a circle, so that the box was set like a jewel atop a ring meant for the finger of a giant. It was not, however, jewellery.

Ash bowed zheir head. The guard fastened the collar about zheir neck, the box secured against the hollow of zheir throat. The snick of the clasp was very loud in the quiet Haven hallway. The collar looked tight.

'That's not—' Hazel said, and cut himself off. It was part of the Cristati covenant if Ash had agreed it was, back when the covenant was formed, a covenant that somehow overrode Haven's later claim.

'Takes his job seriously, doesn't he?' Lady Cristati said, making it an insult.

Ash stalked to the other Mancer, glanced up at zhem, and slowly turned to stand beside zhem. They both stared straight ahead, the depthless stares reminiscent of soldiers performing an unpleasant duty, like turning their backs while treachery was committed.

Without looking, the other Mancer took Ash's hand and squeezed. Hazel watched as Ash squeezed back, some of the tension easing from zheir shoulders. Zhey took a breath. Zhey still would not meet his eyes.

'This is a pretty mess, Tashi,' Lady Cristati said to Lady Fairhaven, eyeing off the dead bodies of her Mancer guards as if they were the detritus of a city street about to smear her pretty shoes.

'Lieutenant Hazlemere is certainly very methodical in his duties,' Lady Fairhaven said.

Evelyn stiffened. 'I warned your people not to run too far ahead. Hazlemere was acting according to regulation. Your captain should have—'

Lady Fairhaven silenced her with a raised hand. 'As you say, my people take their jobs seriously,' she murmured to her Cristati counterpart.

'I suppose I can chalk it down to Captain Tassone's error, then,' Lady Cristati said, 'given you've been so cooperative in correcting your own errors.'

Tassone's face flushed even darker. He looked like he might want to murder someone, preferably Hazel. Hazel struggled to keep the same expression off his own face. Only the fact that the purple could see him provided sufficient motivation to do so.

'I expect you will be disciplining those of your servants who decided to hide a Mancer from you. Acting according to regulation. Quite the daring claim, under the circumstances.'

That was right. Together, Valerian, Evelyn and Holly, with the strong implicit support of Ash, had made the call to not formally announce Ash's arrival to Lady Fairhaven and her senior advisors, so that Lady Fairhaven could save face if an aggressive stronghold came for zhem.

It was meant to let them hide Ash, or help zhem escape if zhey chose. It wasn't supposed to be an excuse to give zhem up. Once again, a tangle of emotions, confusion and shame and anger, roiled inside Hazel; once again, he obeyed the signalling from Evelyn and Holly warning him to hold.

'I trust I know how to manage my own stronghold, Adelma.' Lady Fairhaven's tone hadn't wavered from her usual mildness.

Lady Cristati sighed. 'You were like this in Glelissi, too. Do you remember when you first arrived at school? So soft, Tashi. Crying for mummy in the middle of the night. Giving the younger children treats so they followed you about like strays. Giving coins to beggars until we couldn't move for them at the gates. I had to set you straight, didn't I?'

'Kindness isn't weakness,' Lady Fairhaven said. 'My father taught me that, and nothing in my life has changed my mind. And nothing ever will.'

Lady Cristati smiled wickedly. 'No? Take a look at this, dear. Makes for interesting reading, if you can decipher the runes.'

She tossed a notebook, the large and sturdy amatl sort Mancers favoured, to Lady Fairhaven. It was a contemptuous gesture. Lady Fairhaven, outwardly unperturbed, passed the notebook to Valerian.

Hazel, still watching Ash, saw zheir eyes widen. Zhey signed, fast and frantic—he hadn't noticed how fluent zhey'd become—keeping zheir hands low and slightly toward the other Mancer. ~Did you tear the pages out?

The other Mancer signed, slower, ~I didn't know they'd found it till she made me read it to her.

Ash shut zheir eyes. Zhey kept them shut as zheir lady brushed past zhem, but she stopped and put her hand on zheir shoulder. Hazel saw a shudder run through Ash, before zhey opened zheir eyes and obediently watched her lips.

'I'm so glad to have you home safe, sweetheart,' she told zhem. 'I was so worried about you while you were away.'

For a long moment, Ash stood poised in Mancer blankness. Then, hands curling into light fists at zheir side, zhey curtly nodded.

She squeezed zheir shoulder. 'Use the collar. It was invented just for you.' Ash nodded again. 'Oh, I forget how obstinate you can be.'

Ash raised a hand as if to reply, but Lady Cristati lightly tapped it and shook her head. It was playfully chiding. It sent ice down Hazel's spine. He found himself thinking of Ash's broken ring fingers, twin injuries, neatly matched, crookedly healed.

'See to that,' Lady Cristati said to Tassone, with a jerk of her head at the bodies, and the one injured man, who obligingly moaned as if to remind them of his existence. She turned back to Lady Fairhaven. 'Tashi, dear, my son tells me you host wonderful feast nights. I wonder if you might hold one for me tonight?'

'Certainly, Adelma,' Lady Fairhaven said, walking away with Lady Cristati. Again, her tone gave no indication that she knew that Lady Cristati was baiting her. 'We shall be happy to host Cristati again. We are, after all, very old friends indeed.'

Tassone looked at the bodies of his fallen men. Hazel expected him to mouth off to him, or to Holly, to relieve his simmering anger. He moved up to stand with the other Havens, ready. But Tassone instead poked Ash in the chest, bristling, looming over zhem.

'Captain Olivette died, after what you did to him.'

Ash did not try to sign a reply; either zhey knew Tassone wouldn't understand, or zhey knew the captain would make the same complaint Lady Cristati had, or possibly follow up on the implicit threat twisted inside the complaint.

Instead, zhey put zheir hand on the box attached to zheir throat. 'That's what happens when you put a knife in someone's heart,' it said.

Hazel blinked. He felt the ripple of surprise go through the Havens. Despite understanding that the Mancy collar was transforming Ash's subvocal vibrations into audible speech sounds, he wanted to demand, *Fuck, was even that a lie?*

Zheir collar's voice was colder than zheir signing. It sent a frisson of distaste through him. The person he'd taken to bed was serious, watchful Ash with the unexpectedly mischievous sense of humour. This person was Silverthorne, cold, calculated. There was nothing playful about zhem.

Then the words struck him.

Tassone shoved Ash, hard, and zhey fell back against the other Mancer, who immediately encircled zheir arm about zhem, tugging zhem a few steps away. The brown-haired Mancer's evident fear was enough to bring the Cristati captain back to his senses, even as Hazel started forward, hand back on his hilt.

'Not Haven's Mancer,' Valerian snapped.

Hazel subsided, the habitual obedience like swallowing acid. Evelyn had her arm locked around her sibling; Holly had moved when Hazel had, because Holly always would. Tassone glanced about, and Hazel saw him clock the tension.

He grunted. 'You see what zhey are? You're lucky your purple is sensible. Otherwise we'd have razed Haven to the ground, and for what? This treacherous little fuck?'

Ash's gaze finally drifted to Hazel. Zhey were utterly blank, in a way zhey had never quite achieved in Haven before. Hazel wanted to sign something. He couldn't think of a thing to say.

Zhey drew zheir thumb across zheir heart, dipped zheir head. Hazel shook his head, not at Ash, but at the very idea that an apology could touch this.

Tassone said, 'Do it again. Lady Cristati's given me permission to break your thumbs.'

He pushed his way past the Mancers, delivering a brusque order to a couple of his Mancer guards, who moved slowly toward the bodies.

Ash turned in unison with the other Mancer and plodded after the captain, moving like Albemarle instead of with zheir usual understated grace. The Cristati Mancers were surrounded by their guards. They were holding hands again.

~Twenty-One~

Hazel contained himself while he, Holly, Evelyn and Lord Valerian walked around to the antechamber, gathering the other Mancer guards as they went.

Only then, when he was absolutely sure the foreigners were out of earshot, did he say, 'What. The. *Fuck*?'

'What's going on?' Kito demanded. She was pacing.

As First Jerome quietly told the junior guards of the Cristati party, coming in force, leaving with Ash, Evelyn shook her head, Valerian looked uncomfortable, and Holly put his hand on Hazel's arm.

His warm gaze was painfully sympathetic. 'Did anyone else notice that Ash has zheir looks from zheir mother?'

At last Hazel understood why the expression Ash got sometimes, proud and imperious, was familiar. Not that it made zhem look like Lady Cristati, who Hazel had never seen before, but that it more generally resembled the expression the lordlings had worn when he'd met them in the capital during his years at the academy.

But, yes, more specifically, and now it'd been pointed out, Ash did look like Lady Cristati, who had the same stern features reminiscent of ancestors among the northern mountain people.

'Ash is Lady Cristati's third child,' Evelyn confirmed. 'Zheir family never renounced zhem, Hazel. Zhey weren't in Stronghold Cristati under a covenant that zhey could revoke. Zhey're a family member.'

'A family member who is well and truly beyond the age of majority,' Hazel said.

Valerian sighed and started to speak. 'Don't you start,' Holly growled. 'You could have backed us, up there. You stood there and made me swallow shit from that fucking Tassone.'

The lord folded his arms, letting the notebook from Lady Cristati slip. Evelyn retrieved it as he said, 'Captain Holyoake, there is more at stake here than your overweening pride.'

Holly set his hands on his hips. 'It's like you want me to punch you, Val.'

'Go ahead, see what happens,' Valerian said, with a mild bravado that may or may not have been founded on true intent.

Holly flashed his savage smile, delighted. Evelyn, exchanging what would have been an eyeroll with Hazel if Lord Valerian couldn't see her, cupped one of Holly's elbows, drawing his arm down.

'Holly,' she said softly. 'None of us had any choice in the matter. We did try, Hazel. We tried all the arguments you're thinking of. But the fact is—'

'Ash is deaf,' Hazel said. 'Ash is deaf and under law, that makes zhem subject to guardianship regardless of zheir age or actual competence or wishes.'

'Exactly.'

'Not in Haven.'

'True,' she said, 'but zheir legal guardian has to accept that zhey belong to Haven for that argument to work. Fair to say, she does not.'

'And now we've given a hostile stronghold all of Albemarle's designs,' Valerian said. 'Which, correct me if I am wrong, Commander Holyoake, they can use in some way, yes?'

Evelyn, of course, could not correct her patron, because he was entirely not wrong. She gave a single nod, and withdrew, looking through the notebook. It wasn't like her to deflect; something there had caught her attention.

Nightingale shuddered and wrapped her arms about her own chest. 'They all have their own projects. Why take another's?' she said as if to herself.

If what they had learned from Ash and Nightingale and Albemarle in the last few weeks was true, spying was indeed as possible as Albemarle had assumed it was when zhey'd tried to bar Ash from the atelier. Zheir guards had assumed zhey were being unreasonable, and brushed off zheir concerns, mostly because Albemarle was often unreasonable, but also because of Nightingale's dilemma—what Mancer needed to steal another's designs, when zhey were constantly bombarded with zheir own ideas that wanted singing into life?

A Mancer whose stronghold was forcing zhem to. A Mancer who couldn't translate zheir own songs into designs. A Mancer whose stronghold had three other Mancers' design journals, and still didn't have the weapon they wanted for their aims, whatever those might be.

Hazel tried it out, carefully. 'I don't think Ash intended to be a spy. I think zhey're being coerced.'

'That is infatuation talking,' Valerian said flatly.

'That's Hazel darling,' Holly corrected him. 'Did you catch what Lady Cristati said to Ash? I can't be sure—she didn't say it loud, just enough so Ash could lipread it, but it looked to me like, "We can always get you another partner, again".'

The Mancer guards looked at each other, shocked. The very concept that the stronghold pledged to protect a Mancer under the covenant could use zhem as a bargaining chip... Hazel had told them what Ash had said, about Mithra and Inigo, and the Havens still hadn't recognised what that implied, for Ash and for zheir third Mancer partner.

Kito's pacing intensified, and Titus and Nightingale clustered with Morano, who was a generally mellow and fatherly presence, comforting amid Kito and Holly's tense energy, and Hazel's aura of stoic misery, too, no doubt.

The Jeromes stood by the atelier door, taking turns to knock the all-clear pattern. It would take a while for Albemarle to respond, if zhey were lost in zheir project, and there was no if about that.

'That's worse, Holly,' Evelyn said, glancing up from the notebook. 'If zhey were just a spy, accidental or otherwise, we could perhaps hope some fondness'—not looking at Hazel—'would make zhem hold zheir tongue. But if zhey're coerced... Well. Zhey'll spill out every design zhey saw, and let's face it—that's every last one, isn't it?'

All those evenings, Ash lying on the workbench or companionably curled up on the divan Hazel had set up for zhem, gazing at each page of each journal. Enjoying browsing a clever Mancer's ingenious schematics? Or memorising them for zheir mother?

He couldn't accept it. 'This can't be. Ash shot the Cristati lieutenant when he came to get zhem. Zhey were frightened.'

Holly hissed through his teeth. Something had occurred to him. 'Zhey'd only seen one journal then,' he said. 'Zhey knew there was at least a dozen others stashed in the cupboard. Zhey wouldn't want to walk away from that. And Hazel—were zhey truly frightened? You said Dimitriou was frightened of *zhem*. Maybe he was horrified to find their spy wasn't ready to be retrieved—and with how zhey were choosing to stay undercover.'

Hazel thought of the way Ash had clung to him in the dark. He thought of the ruthless way zhey'd shot the lieutenant in the back. 'Zhey tried to leave, after.'

'We persuaded zhem not to,' Kito said, with dawning dismay. She made forefinger curls in in the air as she repeated, '"Persuaded".'

We. Not *you.* Hazel noted that kindness, clinically.

Holly smacked his forehead. 'And after that, Albemarle let zhem look at *all* the journals. It was perfection. Zhey just had to sacrifice a guard. Well played, you tricky little fucker.'

Hazel shook his head at the appalled expressions of the other Mancer guards. They were talking themselves into believing the worst of Ash, when zhey were quite plainly as badly trapped as Haven was. Zhey had *quite plainly* been threatened by Lady Cristati herself in that hallway. Holly had said that himself, so—

Hazel caught himself.

He had done this with Maya too.

When she had left Haven, she would have come under guardianship again as a legal incompetent due to her deafness. Her husband took precedence in that regard over her brother, and Hazel didn't know her husband. He'd read and re-read her letters in the early years after her departure, looking for any clue, any subtle sign or codeword, that she was being coerced, trapped, held prisoner by this new guardian, who she could not have truly known any better than Hazel did, given the whirlwind of the courtship and marriage.

He'd even, with great guilt, poked at the legality of the marriage, since the happy couple had not received the approval of Maya's nominal guardian before their near-literal elopement. In Haven, that hadn't mattered, because she'd been beyond the age of consent, but outside Haven the lines were far murkier, given Maya's legal incompetence in most other jurisdictions.

It would have been a travesty to challenge a love-match on those grounds. He'd eventually had to accept that she was not under any sort of duress which prevented her from visiting or from writing more often. She was just happy, and young, and busy, and did not have much time for her brother, her parental figure. It probably hadn't even occurred to her that he would be hurt; she'd freed him from a responsibility she might have assumed he didn't want, after all.

He was now doing the same thing, combing Ash's behaviours and words and expressions so he could clutch at any hint that zhey'd been coerced, because that was what he preferred to believe, over the idea that he'd been tricked and used and discarded.

He thought he'd seen true relief in the sag of Ash's body when Haven had granted sanctuary. Was that an honest reaction from a refugee, or a performance disguising the satisfaction of a spy achieving the first step in a plan that ended in treachery?

Ash had refused to tell Haven where zhey were from. Had zhey been trying to protect zheir new stronghold, or merely protecting zheir own secrets?

Zhey'd killed the Cristati lieutenant when he'd come down from the feast to take zhem back. Was that driven by true fear, or a calculated move to send a 'not yet' message back to zheir people?

Zhey'd indeed tried to leave. Had zhey truly been concerned about bringing Cristati down on Haven, or had it been another ploy to garner sympathy and worm zheir way deeper into all of their confidences?

Zhey'd given Hazel a carefully edited version of the truth, leaving out the true identity of zheir mother. Was that because zhey'd been too cautious to reveal it to a stronghold zhey still didn't quite trust, or because zhey knew exactly what she had planned and wanted to preserve her surprise?

Zhey'd… Zhey'd fucked Hazel with every appearance of enjoying zhemself and was that because zhey *had* enjoyed zhemself, or because it was useful to let Hazel think zhey had?

Evelyn snapped shut the notebook, jolting Hazel from his circling thoughts. 'We need Albemarle to read this to us,' she said. 'Too many Mancer runes.'

She looked at Hazel then, and he was disconcerted to read pity in his stern commander's eyes.

'My stars, if zhey'll ever open the door,' Kito said.

They all turned to the locked atelier door. Second Jerome shrugged and tapped out the all-clear pattern again.

Hazel tugged a hand through his hair, refusing to get lost again in walking a labyrinth to defend Ash. In the end, it didn't matter if zhey'd acted willingly as spy for zheir stronghold, or been coerced into it, or even had no idea Cristati was going to make this play—though Hazel could see no way someone as clever as Ash would not have anticipated it.

None of that mattered. The result was the same. Every last one of Albemarle's designs, walking out of the stronghold tomorrow morning. Ash's partner able to bricolage any of them so that zhey could sing them into being. Ash able to transform any of them into weapons from there.

Albemarle's designs are particularly suited to it. There was really only one course of action.

'So,' Hazel said. 'We'll get Ash back during the feast tonight, yes?'

'Yep,' Holly said.

'What?' Valerian said. He looked shocked. Most of the Mancer Guard didn't, but Titus gasped.

'My lord, we can't let zhem take Albemarle's designs away. We have to retrieve zhem.' Evelyn was still frowning at the notebook, but she did not sound any less certain than Hazel did.

'That means all-out war with Cristati,' Valerian said. 'I utterly forbid this reckless—'

'I'll be going up alone,' Hazel said. 'I'll be the scapegoat, my lord.'

This got a chorus of protests from the others, and a 'Fuck off with your own self, Hazlemere,' from Holly.

He held up his hand, and turned to Valerian. 'It'll be the action of a lone rogue Mancer guard, outside the knowledge of the purple. You can go ahead and blame it on infatuation. Cristati can have no grounds to attack Haven if the Manc— if their liege is not within the stronghold, and zhey absolutely will not be.'

'They may very well attack anyway.' The lord had already regained his cool composure, and Hazel could see him turning the plan over in his mind. 'For pride, if no other reason.'

Evelyn nodded, tapping on the notebook. Hazel wondered if she knew she was making the all-clear pattern in rhythm with First Jerome taking a turn on the door.

She said, 'It is a risk, my lord, but less so than meekly giving over Albemarle's designs so they can come back at us with those designs turned into weapons courtesy of their Mancers.' She addressed Hazel. 'You'll take Ash to the port?'

'You cannot be considering letting him do this,' Holly said to his sister. Hazel had never seen him look so serious.

'I caused this, Hols, let me fix it.'

'You did not—'

To Evelyn, Hazel said, 'I'll take zhem to the port, and away on a ship.'

In fact, he intended to head north by road, back to his home region, with its remote and forested valleys. He'd need to borrow the atelier of one of their coastal allies, to keep Ash sane, but move zhem onward quickly, to keep zhem safe, before Lady Cristati could swoop down and cast the net of her guardianship over her child again.

There was no real solution here, except the obvious, the greatest of taboos, the knife in the throat of a Mancer.

'Cristati will expect the port,' Evelyn said musingly.

Hazel shrugged. 'I'll have my sword.'

He met his commander's eyes. He meant he'd die to protect Ash and get zhem through a Cristati blockade. She silently communicated that Ash would have to die, too, if Hazel could not prevent recapture.

'You won't be able to come home, Hazlemere,' Valerian said. 'Cristati will demand execution. We'd have no choice but to comply.'

'I do not intend to come home, my lord,' Hazel said. He turned to the other guards. 'I'll ask your help, tonight, but none of you can be seen to assist me, or the rogue excuse won't work.'

Holly said, 'Nah.'

Hazel stopped. He took a breath. He tried not to look as if Holly had just kicked him in the guts.

'Oh, stop with the puppy eyes, love,' Holly said. 'Cristati is bold, we know that. Let's be bold, too. Let's go get Ash right now.'

Evelyn made a noise. The other Mancer guards exchanged looks.

'Val, where's Lady Cristati this morning? You met her. What do you think she'll do now?'

Valerian, after a moment, said, 'She'd be with Lady Fairhaven, wringing reparations out of her while she's got an army camped outside.'

Nodding approvingly, Holly translated, 'She'll be gloating. Will the Mancers be with her, my lord?'

Again, Valerian paused, before he said, 'Probably not. Not Ash, anyway.'

'The other one might be. That one was compliant enough.' Holly and Valerian exchanged a look, then, and Hazel wondered what else had happened in the meeting this morning that they and Evelyn were not sharing with everyone. 'But Ash is a spiky little fucker, and did not appear overjoyed to see zheir mother again. And she gave zhem a verbal voice. She misplayed her own spite there, I think.'

'Lady Cristati would be greatly sensitive to embarrassment in front of Lady Fairhaven,' Valerian agreed.

'So she's busy gloating. Ash is locked in a guest chamber in the west wing upstairs where zhey can't cause a fuss. Cristati don't have many surviving Mancer guards right now.' Holly turned back to his commander. 'Evie baby, have you considered that they'll be expecting us to act at the feast tonight?' He was smiling again, fiercely. 'That's why

Lady Cristati asked for it, right? Not just posturing, but temptation. So they can catch us out and kill a few of us, or all of us, with impunity. Might even take Albemarle at that point, though good luck to them.'

'Their Mancer Guard will be smug and lazy right now,' Kito said. She was playing with her trishul knives, running her fingers over the banded hilts.

Hazel rather thought the Cristati Mancer Guard would be pissed off and looking for an accounting for its six dead members. Kito was never going to rein Holly in, of course.

He looked to Evelyn, and Evelyn said, 'Yes. Hazel?'

Hazel paused. 'I trust your assessment, Holly, but, by Kisane's tail, it feels much riskier to go by day. What about once Ash and I get through the gate, and have to run for the port in broad daylight? You know we can't wait for nightfall to get Ash out of the stronghold, or Cristati will still have reason to attack this morning.'

'Here's the play. Where's the other Mancer Guard?'

When Hazel just frowned, Evelyn stepped in, reading her sibling's intentions expertly. 'Only one Mancer Guard set accompanied Lady Cristati and near-half of them are dead. They presumably have two sets for two Mancers, but the other must be out in the camp. If Lady Cristati is sensible, and she is, she'll want reinforcements to bolster security on her Mancers and set a trap for tonight. She'll call the other Mancer Guard in. They'll be arriving soon.'

'Perhaps there can be difficulties in lowering the moat when they do,' Valerian murmured, and looked reluctantly chuffed when Holly bumped his hip into him in approval. 'But not for long, captain,' he added sternly. 'I won't risk Haven on this venture more than is necessary.'

'Oh, there he is,' Holly said, giving him another fond little nudge. 'If we time Ash's *exit* out the postern for when the reinforcements gain *entry* through the main gates, zhey'll have a relatively easy path to the port. But we have to move fast. We have to move *now*, Hazel.'

'*We'll* have a relatively easy—'

'A-yah,' Holly said, in a tone of voice which was very much one of his cheery *nah*s. He refused to back down when Hazel gave him a look.

For all he'd suggested using the moat as a delaying tactic, Valerian appeared unconvinced, all frown and folded arms. It seemed he, at least, would be a second voice of reason.

He said, 'I'll join Lady Fairhaven, make sure Lady Cristati stays occupied, help with the timing of lowering the moat. Act fast, Mancer Guard, and if you're caught, I'll disavow the lot of you.'

'Thanks for the support, Vee,' Holly said, and blew him a kiss.

'Holy fucking Mother, you people,' Lord Valerian said, already heading out of the antechamber to make good on, in fact, the very real support Holly had no call being sarcastic about.

Holly caught him by the arm and hauled him back. Valerian startled, expecting the worst; even so, he held his ground as Holly leant into his space.

Holly touched his forehead to his. 'Sorry for swearing at you, Val. I know I fuck up.'

There was really nothing like an apology from impetuous, generous Rowan Holyoake. It wasn't so much the words as the intent. Hazel had been on the receiving end of the sincere black-eyed look himself. He didn't blame Valerian for looking struck.

Holly, of course, saw it, and smiled. 'I'm very good at making amends, though,' he added in a purr. 'Take me up on it sometime.'

The lord backed off, brushing his coat down. 'All right,' he muttered. 'I am very uncomfortable right now.'

He all but fled. Holly turned back to the rest of them, still smiling, and made a *carry on* wave.

'I may be coming back down a-pace with Cristatis on my tail,' Hazel told Evelyn. 'Deploy as best suits, but remember we can't leave any witnesses that I wasn't acting alone.'

'And *you* remember what you need to do if it turns out Ash was indeed a willing spy and won't come quietly.' She hesitated. 'Maybe—'

'Well, fuck, Evie, I liked zhem, too,' Holly said. He was cheerful again, now action had been decided on. 'But yes, Hazel darling, if you need me to do it...'

'I'll do it,' said Kito.

'I can do it,' Hazel said. 'If it's needed.'

He felt in control, calm, but the false composure almost cracked when Titus flung herself into his arms. 'Come home,' she whispered through tears. 'Come home. We'll find a way.'

Then he had to hug all the rest of them, too. None of them said anything. Technically, he'd be back with them within the hour. But he'd have Ash with him, and none of the others' emotions would be on display then, not in front of someone who had turned out to be a stranger.

Holly came with him. On the stairs to the undercroft, they met Miriam, carrying her medical bag.

'Their injured Mancer guard,' she explained, hoisting the black leather bag higher in corroboration. 'They wouldn't leave him down in the subterrane with you fuckers.'

'Stay safe,' Hazel told her. 'Have some stronghold guards with you.'

Miriam checked, just for the barest second, and Hazel knew she'd noted the irregularity, his failure to volunteer himself or Holly or Kito as a shield equal to the angry foreign Mancer Guard. They weren't meant to extend their care to any other than their stronghold's Mancer, but everyone in Haven knew they did and would.

As they crossed the dining hall, her lips were pressed together, her eyes watchful. She catalogued the way he and Holly were walking. She catalogued the drying gore on Hazel's coat, and that he hadn't bothered to change out of it. She catalogued the almost ceremonial donning of his leather gloves.

'Why are you going upstairs, Ari?' she asked at last, when they reached the base of the corkscrew steps to the upper stronghold.

'No reason anyone needs to know about, Dr Vo,' Holly said, and smiled to her flat look.

She looked between them, holding her bag in both hands, wearing her coldly assessing expression. 'Give me a few minutes,' she said, and hurried up the stairs.

Hazel watched her go with some trepidation. He didn't want more of Haven's people drawn into this than had to be, and Miriam had a scheme in mind. She was probably the best placed person in the stronghold to successfully pull off a scheme, given how icy calm she was under pressure. Not a person in Haven could match her for that.

Except, perhaps, for Liege Ashlin Silverthorne Cristati.

Hazel wriggled his fingers, seating the gloves properly. 'Holly…am I dragging the whole stronghold into jeopardy for the sake of my own stupid heart?'

'Likely,' Holly said. He truly had no mercy, that one. 'But the logic is sound—we can't let Cristati have Albemarle's designs.'

Hazel asked the question he didn't want the answer to. 'I should kill zhem, shouldn't I?'

'Nah,' Holly said. 'This is Fair Haven by the Sea. We don't do that here.' Hazel had a moment to feel unalloyed relief before Holly added, 'It'd bring war on down on our heads. Do it as soon as you get zhem to the port instead.'

'Holly!'

'Pin it on a pirate,' Holly said with a casual shrug. 'It'd certainly be handy for trade if Cristati decided they had a vendetta against the scourge of the seas instead of us.'

Hazel gaped. Holly finally couldn't keep a straight face. Laughing, he hugged Hazel. 'Your face, by my lost relics. *No*, Hazel, you are not killing Ash.'

'Unless zhey don't come quietly,' Hazel said grimly. He was not much inclined to join in with Holly's good humour.

'My love, you are going to crook your finger and watch your Mancer come to heel, don't you bother yourself about that.'

'A-yah, we've given Miriam long enough.'

Holly squeezed his shoulders. 'One more thing. Watch out for a, ah, Mancy pet,' he said. 'It was at the meeting this morning.'

Hazel huffed out. 'Springing that on me.'

'Springing is right, I think the fucking thing can climb. Keep your eyes up, love.'

Hazel signed [expletive] at his captain, but he was smiling now, and much calmer. Holly knew what he was about. They went up the interior stairs to the upper stronghold. It was still early, and Kiselyova and Devi were still on shift. They exchanged nervous looks when the two Mancer guards came off the small landing and into the back hallway.

'You stay here now, Hols,' Hazel said. 'You only saw me, right?' he said to the stronghold guards.

'What if they saw no one?' Holly said.

'No, Holly, Cristati needs someone to blame if they're not to blame everyone.'

'They can blame Ash.'

Devi put her hands over her ears. 'We can't hear this conversation.'

'Too bloody right, you can't,' Holly growled at her, and then grinned. 'Good. Are you sure I shouldn't come along further with you, Hazel darling?'

'A-yah, fuck you, Holyoake,' Hazel said. 'I killed six of them from a standing start, what've you done?'

'Day's not over.'

Hazel smiled faintly. He was taking his first steps down the hallway when Holly grabbed him. His friend put his forehead on the crown of Hazel's head, and held there for a long moment. Then he shoved him hard away.

'Eyes up, my love. Have fun.'

Shaking his head, Hazel loped off down the hallway. It was the quiet time of morning, the servants having completed the earliest of the chores and served breakfast, the retainers and minor lords having settled to their daily routines, all falling into the soothing predictability as the threat of siege ebbed, as readily as Albemarle cleaving to zheir schedule.

Still, he passed quite a few upper household staff and some undercroft staff and nodded to them without furtiveness, with, in fact, very much an ostentatious sort of soldierly march about him. He had to be seen, noticed, acting alone.

He went straight up the backstairs to the second floor, where the guest residences were. Here he paused. He had never had much cause to explore this area, but he knew the layout and knew that Lady Fairhaven and the rest of the purple had their quarters on the east side, facing the ocean, while guests were situated westward. The backstairs brought him up on the north side, overlooking the bailey. He turned toward the front of the stronghold.

He dropped from his deliberate stride into a silent stalk as he approached the designated hallway. It was the only choice for guest Mancers, because it had a large alcove where Mancer guards could station themselves. It was also rather better set up for Haven to advance on than for visitors to defend, due to its poor sightlines, though Hazel had to doubt that was on purpose.

He knew how Evelyn would have organised a guard there—two in the main hallway, around the corner from where he collected himself, a pair down the guest hallway in front of the Mancer's door, and more in the alcove in between.

He'd killed six, and dropped a seventh, who would be under Miriam's care by now on the floor below, in more lowly accommodations. Captain Tassone would probably be with Lady Cristati. That left eight of the sixteen-strong Mancer Guard, and Hazel expected to find all eight of them between him and Ash, and all of them alert to his presence the moment he stepped around the corner into the eyeline of the first pair.

He'd had worse odds. He glanced up, reassuring himself that the mysterious, and terrifying, Mancy pet wasn't hanging about, and stepped around the corner, announcing himself with the song of his sword sliding out of its sheath.

~TWENTY-TWO~

No one awaited him. Hazel again looked about for the Mancy pet before prowling toward the alcove, expecting the Cristatis to charge him without warning. Or something to come scuttling at him.

'Thanks, Holly,' he muttered. 'Oh, Hazel, I think the thing can climb, have fun with that thought.'

He rolled his wrist, idly ticking his blade through the air. He could not deny that he was indeed having a specific sort of fun with that thought. He'd needed his mind taken off rescuing Ash, and put on to recovering Silverthorne, and the idea of a Mancy pet that could climb the fucking walls had certainly done it.

And that, Lord Vee, is why Holly is the captain.

He came into the alcove fast and low. After a pause, he straightened up. He felt ridiculous.

One of Albemarle's Mancy tea urns, a direct offshoot of zheir projects for the laundry, softly emitted steam in the corner, sounding like someone singing under their breath. A teapot was still sending out its own tendril of steam in the middle of the small rectangular table at the centre of the room. Six delicate teacups, soft-edged pale blue birds decorating their rims, sat before the six chairs around the table.

So far, this was standard practice in Haven. No matter who the guests were, welcome or not, they received a tea service, a gesture of comfort.

The bodies under the table were not standard practice.

Two of the chairs were still occupied. Even as Hazel watched, one slow-blinking guard gradually slid to join his four fellows on the thick rug under the table. He recognised him as the unscathed survivor of the earlier debacle. The other guard still in a chair slumped further, head lolling.

Hazel sheathed his sword. He assumed he was looking at the result of Miriam's scheme. She must have marched herself into the alcove on the pretence of looking for the injured guard, and swapped the tea leaves or dosed the water in the urn under the eyes of a Mancer Guard who very well knew it was in enemy territory.

As brave as that was, she'd surely had help, one or two upper servants quickly commandeered to distract the guards, draw in the two who should have been standing guard in the main hallway, keep all eyes distracted. That meant pretty, and young, and prepared to flirt, and tolerant of lewdness and groping for a greater cause.

It meant someone in Haven had made a pot of tea for the foreign set of guards now sleeping on the floor, leaving a rather obvious clue sitting in the middle of the table.

He was reluctantly impressed at Miriam's efficiency, yet chagrined that it made his own scheme much harder to pass off as the work of a solitary rogue. Not even the most rosy-eyed of people would believe the Cristatis had let a big scarred brute with a sword serve them tea.

Two more teacups were still stacked, clean, beside the urn. From the guest hallway opening out from the alcove, a voice said, 'You all right, lads? You've gone quiet. The pretty thing gone, has she?'

Hazel guessed he had another minute or so before one of the pair in front of Ash's door, who had stayed professional and eschewed the charms of the teapot, came to investigate the suspicious silence. He carefully lifted the pot, poured its contents back into the urn, wiped it out, and set it down beside the urn. He turned to collect the teacups, and noticed, on a spare chair in the other corner, a familiar coat, familiar daggers atop. He poked at the folded pile underneath, and saw that it was indeed Ash's clothes.

Mouth tight, Hazel, quickly but still careful not to make a clink, picked up the cups one by one to wiped them clean and set them by the teapot, trying very hard to concentrate on removing as much incriminating evidence as he could, trying very hard not to see, in his head, a circle of large men surrounding Ash, making zhem strip to zheir underthings, jeering over zheir pitiful weapons, deliberately humiliating zhem. They might have let zhem change in private. He didn't think they had.

It made what he'd have to do next a good deal easier. The Cristatis were, after all, only sleeping, and had a story that could not be told.

As he reached for the last teacup, the slumped guard slid sideways like a sack of potatoes, knocking the cup so it clattered over, splattering the surface with the dregs of the tainted tea. Hazel caught the cup before it could roll all the way off the table and shatter, but missed his lefthanded grab for the scruff of the guard's neck. The unconscious man thudded onto the stone flooring, right beside the rug that might have muffled it.

'Lads?' came the voice, closer, and Hazel took a purposeful step, hand dropping to his pommel, body dropping into the stalk years of training had drilled into him.

Then a rapid series of noises sent him sprinting before his brain had finished decoding it.

The slight scuff of a door opening.

The concussive pulse that was a modified copperlit discharging.

The boneless thump as another body hit the floor.

The rather familiar aggression of a Cristati Mancer guard swearing at the Cristati Mancer. 'You goddamned motherfucking dastardly runt!'

Hazel ran into the hallway in time to see the surviving Cristati pick Ash up by the metal collar and slam zhem into the wall next to zheir chamber door. A tall, broad man like the rest of them, he held the Mancer crushed against the stone, both hands tightening at zheir throat between chin and collar. Zheir feet were well off the floor, dangling by the head of the deathly still body of the guard who'd taken the brunt of the copperlit.

'You gave me the excuse Tassone wanted you to give us,' the guard said conversationally. 'You know who gets the blame for this? Haven gets the blame for this. We're going to burn them to the ground. You've slaughtered an entire stronghold, Silverthorne. Die thinking about it.'

Ash kicked weakly, one hand clawing at the whitening knuckles of the guard. With zheir other hand, zhey swung the discharged copperlit—zhey must have been allowed only one inside the chamber, on suspicion of exactly this, because surely zhey'd have otherwise started zheir ill-advised break-out better armed—in a poor and panicked blow.

It slipped loose from zheir hand, completely missing the guard currently throttling zhem, and jangled on the door opposite.

That door instantly opened; the brown-haired Mancer looped what looked like the sash of a nightrobe about the Cristati's neck and pulled hard.

The tactic of only coming at a trained Mancer guard from behind was well thought out, but the Mancer didn't have a hope of strangling the man, especially when he dropped Ash and managed to work his fingers between his neck and the loop of the sash, at the same time jerking backward to bruisingly jounce the Mancer into the other wall. Zhey grimly held on, just.

It had only been the scant moment it had taken Hazel to run down the hallway. He arrived at speed, starting to draw his sword.

Ash left off coughing and clutching zheir neck to sign, emphatically and with both fists, ~No!

Hazel jerked his hand off his hilt. He supposed, in the breath he wasted to think about it, that Ash wanted the other Mancer to finish the job zhemself. Shrugging, he yanked the guard forward off the Mancer and pulled the man's fingers out from working the loop loose.

Hazel told the Mancer, 'Now twist that sash till it's really tight.'

Ash snatched another copperlit from the wall and hummed into it, the same reprise zhey'd used before, but much faster. Then zhey shot the guard. The other Mancer dropped the body and leant forward with hands on knees to suck in air as if zhey were the one who'd been choked.

Ash ducked down to look at zheir face, lightly brushing knuckles along zheir cheekbone. Hazel was reminded again: this was who had taught Ash to appreciate affectionate touch, or safely indulged zheir need for it, or both.

The other Mancer straightened, raising a hand and nodding. Zhey were calmer already. Zhey'd re-arranged zheir robe somehow and plaited zheir hair into a different style, and washed zheir face, too, so that zhey presented far more neutrally than zhey had in the subterrane. Zheir nose was a little large for zheir face, now that zhey were not so exactingly styled. Zhey had a silver band about one wrist, a tight cuff of etched metal.

Zhey tugged at zheir robe, and then started as if zhey had only just noticed Hazel. 'You are substantial,' zhey informed him.

Hazel looked down the length of his body and back up again. 'Thanks?'

'The tidal wave does not wait for the shore to invite it in.'

Hazel blinked at zhem. Ash waved for his attention. ~I'll only come with you if you bring [unknown name] too.

'Izidore.' Zheir voice was light, high, still a little gasping. Zhey made the unknown sign zhemself, that messy combination evoking a baby owl. Zhey smiled, displaying crooked teeth that again subtracted from zheir conventional beauty but multiplied zheir charm.

'Fuck's sake,' Hazel said. He was both offended and alarmed. '~You must know what I've been told to do if you won't come without a fuss, Silverthorne.'

Ash's name sign was the same either way, but zhey were good enough at lipreading that zhey'd know the name he was saying aloud. He might have imagined the flinch, so quickly did Ash make zheir expression blank.

Zhey measured him with zheir head on one side. ~But you're not going to do that, are you, Hazel darling?

Both zheir signing and the head tilt had a cold sort of insouciance to them, alien to Hazel. Because this truly was the Cristati named Silverthorne talking, not Ash. Even the formal Mancer robe and silver wristband zhey now wore, matched to Izidore's, took zhem further from the person Hazel had thought he'd known.

He made himself pause long enough for the slightest flash of anxiety to break through the nonchalant mask before he admitted, '~A-yah, you know I'm not. And you know I wouldn't leave your friend behind too, so why even make the threat?'

Ash's face was set in the defiant yet resigned expression zhey'd worn when zhey'd put zhemself under his hands and told him to take his price. ~Because I couldn't assume you would still be willing to be helpful.

'~I'm here, aren't I?'

~You didn't need to come. It'd be better if you hadn't.

Hazel swung an indignant look zheir way. Zhey shook zheir head. ~I intend to escape in such a way that no blame can attach to Haven. Therefore, it would be better if I were not literally accompanied by a Haven Mancer guard. At least you've left no evidence you were here.

Zhey followed up with a wave at the two guards dead at zheir feet, the cauterised copperlit wounds. That must have been why zhey'd blocked him from using his sword, so he wouldn't leave the incriminatory marks of a blade—in much the same way Miriam had left the incriminatory crockery of her dosed teapot.

He glanced involuntarily at the alcove. Ash frowned in that direction—it should have long since spilled out Cristatis responding to the sounds of a fight—and huffed, glaring at him.

'~Oh, sorry, is my rescue fucking up your escape?'

Ash, hand on hip, considered him for a long moment before scathingly signing, ~Actually, yes, it is.

Hazel slapped his leg and turned a circle in sheer frustration. By the time he'd turned back, Ash was only just getting zheir impish little smile under control. When zhey met Hazel's eye, it broke out again. Hazel couldn't help a small laugh of his own. He was angry, and betrayed, and hurt, he was here to take care of a blatant spy—and Ash had peeked out from behind the mask of Silverthorne.

He forced himself back to severity. 'There's six sleeping guards in there, thanks to other Havens. We'll have to drag them into the hallway and make it look like you shot them before they got to you. Given how fast they'd come at you, I really can't see how to make that convincing...'

Ash was watching him with a growing expression of amusement on zheir face. The other one, Izidore, had come to stand at zheir shoulder and was giving him a particularly blank Mancer look.

'A-yah,' Hazel said. '~So how *were* you planning to get past six alert Mancer guards when you can only charge one copperlit at a time?'

Ash pointed upward. Hazel followed the finger, heart already sinking, to behold a coppery lump attached to the ceiling over his head. Even as he watched, the Mancy project—the pet—lazily extended a limb from its perfectly round carapace, like a dog stretching in its sleep, if a dog had at least one attenuated and multi-jointed leg. The leg softly clicked and whirred as it scrabbled idly over the plaster of the hallway ceiling.

Oh, you think it can climb, Holly, you absolute fuckster? Hazel went for his sword. Ash leapt at him and slapped both zheir hands over his, violently shaking zheir head.

'The song of the killing blade awakens in those who hear the melody a lust that may be slaked only in hot red blood,' Izidore intoned. At his blank look, zhey took pity on him and signed, not fluently, ~It defends me if it hears a sword being drawn too close.

'And Cristati let you create that? And *keep* it?'

'The wind cannot argue with the forest, nor the forest with the wind.'

Hazel took a breath to answer and could find no words. He said, 'I still have to hide that these guards were drugged.'

Ash nodded and arced two fingers between the alcove and the hallway. Working as swiftly as they could, Hazel and the two Mancers followed the plan, hauling the sleeping guards from the alcove into the hallway. Ash did not seem to think any special arrangement of the bodies was needed. Apparently, the tableau zhey were leaving for zheir mother would be quite naturally jumbled.

Then Hazel stood with Ash in the alcove; Ash collected zheir daggers but didn't touch the rest of the clothes. Izidore, in the hallway, drew one of the unconscious Mancer guard's swords before scurrying into the alcove in an undignified flurry of robes. Hazel caught a flash of the coppery carapace descending—it had at least ten spidery legs and some looked sharp and others looked barbed—before Ash pushed him and Izidore the other way, out into the main hallway.

~Don't need to see that.

'~Can fucking hear that, Ash.'

Indeed, the noises that drifted through as the Mancy pet mindlessly responded to its design were wet and meaty. Hazel knew the Cristati Mancer guards deserved a nasty fate, for their deliberate and ongoing abuse of the Mancers gifted to their care, for their plan to murder Ash and blame it on Haven. He'd killed quite a few of them himself not so long ago, before he even knew the extent of their cruelty. The quiet, damp sound of this particular nasty fate was still the stuff of nightmares.

'~Will it follow us?' He managed an even tone both verbally and visually.

~It's busy for now, Ash signed placidly.

Izidore screwed up zheir face in a way reminiscent of Titus, reminding him that zhey were quite young, younger than any of zheir guards. Ash looked unmoved. Zhey couldn't hear the filthy noises. If zhey could smell the distinctive tang of blood in the air, zhey looked neither guilty nor satisfied about it. Zhey took a couple of fresh copperlits and sang the altered song, handing one to Izidore when finished.

'~Come along then, Mancers.'

Hazel kept his hand by his hilt, dropping into his quietest walk as they approached the corner around which enemies might lurk. Unless Lady Cristati had managed to bring in the second Mancer Guard already, Captain Tassone was now the only threat inside the walls.

Except Izidore's fucking pet.

Lady Fairhaven and Lord Valerian had evidently managed to keep Lady Cristati and her captain occupied so far. Once again, the only people they met on their way back downstairs were strongholders.

The first time they ran into one, a young man carrying linens, Ash levelled zheir charged copperlit at him. Hazel knocked the tube aside, and matched Ash's scowl with one of his own.

'~Don't threaten my people, Silverthorne.'

~I just want to tell him he didn't see you.

Ash put zheir hand to the collar, and used its cold Mancy voice to say, 'You only saw me, you didn't see Hazel.'

The servant very slowly turned his head and looked at Hazel queryingly, who rubbed a hand over his eyes. '~Someone has to be the Haven scapegoat,' he told Ash.

Ash answered with a fist in the negatory. 'You did not see Hazel,' zheir collar repeated.

The next time they passed an upper staffer, Hazel grabbed Ash's arm before zhey could start waving the copperlit around again, and dragged zhem on past, ignoring zheir stiff annoyance. With Izidore hurrying along behind, they reached Kiselyova and Devi at the top of the corkscrew stairs. Holly wasn't there, but Kiselyova leaned into the stairwell and gave a mighty whistle, long and shrill.

A few moments later, Holly came bouncing up. He had an odd look on his face, one Hazel couldn't recognise.

He realised it was true, deep rage when Holly snarled at Ash, 'You absolute fucking treacherous piece of dirt-eating *shit.*'

~Twenty-Three~

Holly waits with Devi and Kiselyova, idly rocking on his heels. He knows he's making the stronghold guards tense. He's not good at standing still. He wishes he could chase after Hazel, start evening up the day's tally.

He's trying to distract himself by thinking about the parley meeting this morning, though all it's really doing is making him angry again. Or angrier. His feelings are unrefined, but complicated.

Lady Cristati was self-satisfied as she laid out her child's identification papers in front of Lady Fairhaven, revealing exactly why the other coastal strongholds refused the call on the covenant, reclaiming Ash—Liege fucking Silverthorne—under guardianship.

The question of legal competence was, ironically, one of the reasons families had to formally renounce their Mancer children under the covenant. They could otherwise make the same guardianship claim against adult Mancers who could not live independently and were therefore, technically, legally incompetent.

But in this case, Ash's deafness counted for more than zheir Mancy, and Lady Cristati had the precedencies in hand to prove it, had delayed her retrieval long enough to prove it to Haven's allies, and now proved it to Lady Fairhaven, who serenely nodded to the explanations and then bent over the papers and read them closely and keenly while her visitor sipped tea and simpered.

The other Mancer, introduced as Izidore, was quiescent. Zhey kept zheir gaze on a tight silver bracelet around zheir wrist, slowly stroking the engraved metal, not looking about Lady Fairhaven's comfortable reception room, not meeting anyone's eyes, not speaking or looking up, even when spoken about.

This passivity was made even more disconcerting by the spidery Mancy creation that followed zhem about on twelve angular copper legs, of which at least half seemed more like weapons than a mode of transport. Joints hissing softly and claws clicking sharply, it inched up the wall to squat in the corner just by zheir head, tucking its legs under its carapace so it looked more like a giant tick than a spider. It didn't seem to have eyes, yet Holly felt observed.

How a Mancer who had that sort of creepy pet could still act so cowed by the guards escorting zhem was fairly fucking telling, in Holly's unconsidered opinion.

The guards themselves hid their own smugness imperfectly behind professionally neutral faces, except Captain Tassone, who wasn't bothering to hide it at all. He smirked at Holly from the other side of the room, so blatant in the challenge that at one point Valerian felt obliged to press Holly's hand to make him break eye contact.

The Cristati Mancer guards were perfectly matched in their light green coats and their imposing heights, and even their appearance, so that Lady Cristati glanced pointedly between the dark and lanky Holyoakes and pale, stolid Lord Valerian, side by side and very different to the round face and light brown skin tones of Lady Fairhaven, the only born local in the room.

'You recruit from far and wide, don't you, Tashi?' she asked in the snidest possible tone.

'Yes,' Lady Fairhaven said, imperturbably. And then, 'Didn't your father do the same, when he married your mother from the northern mountains? In line for the throne, wasn't she? It must have warmed his heart, how well you took after her.'

Lady Cristati's eyes narrowed—there were some politics or other history here that Holly wasn't privy to—but Lady Fairhaven's tone and expression remained nothing but friendly.

Her guest said, 'Will you take me to my darling Silverthorne, then, dear? I have greatly missed zhem, you understand.' And then she got her own back with, 'Well, you'd understand better if you'd ever had children of your own, of course.'

'I believe I understand well enough, Adelma.' Lady Fairhaven gently set down her cup and rose.

Holly caught her subtle signal to Val, the slightest brush of a finger on the papers, the slightest shake of the head. She didn't have grounds to fight the claim.

'Zhey'll have such a story to tell, won't zhey?' Lady Cristati said. 'Hiding in your basement, all unbeknownst to you.' Her tone was sincere, her eyes cold. She knew it was a face-saving—a stronghold-saving—fiction. Her false smile widened. 'The people zhey've met, the things zhey've seen.'

Lady Fairhaven's warm smile faltered, just for an instant. Only then did Holly grasp that Ash, deliberately or not, had effectively stolen Albemarle's designs for Cristati.

It was Valerian, the patron of the Haven Mancer Guard, who had to turn to Evelyn and stiffly order her to escort the foreign Mancer Guard to the subterrane. He looked as collected as ever, but colour burned in his cheeks and his grey eyes were wintery, ice and storm.

Evelyn would never give the Cristati the satisfaction of seeing her displeasure. She wouldn't even let herself frown. She dipped her head and gestured for them to follow her. Lady Fairhaven's reception room was opposite the great hall. Evelyn led them through the hallways toward the corkscrew staircase. The purple walked out after the cluster of guards, with Izidore.

'Leave that behind,' Lady Cristati said to the Mancer, nodding at the Mancy spider, which was skittering along beside zhem, treating floor and wall much the same.

The Mancer hummed a few notes, a Mancy song that sounded like warming up a fiddle. The pet appeared to go dormant, pulling its legs in and becoming a perfect round mound on the floor. Izidore easily picked it up, and held it out to Captain Tassone, who in turn handed it off to a couple of his Mancer guards, jerking his chin up, at the accommodations above.

'Quick,' he murmured. 'Remember it only sleeps for ten minutes. Lock it in Izidore's room before it wakes up.'

The guests had already been assigned quarters. They intended to stay overnight. Holly began to make calculations.

Captain Tassone lingered to walk beside him. Holly could feel the captain's smug regard as they walked, but he ignored him in favour of turning over possibilities and probabilities, weighing the likelihood of Ash's innocence and finding it wanting, weighing the chances of keeping zhem from decamping with the designs and finding them slim.

'No hard feelings,' Tassone said eventually. 'Don't lose any sleep over giving up Silverthorne. You made the mistake of trusting zhem, easy to do.'

His tone was mild; Holly didn't believe it. Unwilling to risk speaking in case he lost the last fingerhold on his temper, he waited for the sting. He watched Lord Valerian walking just behind Lady Fairhaven and Lady Cristati, his pace slowing.

Holly didn't blame Val for rolling over, giving the order to fetch Ash. And he did blame Val for rolling over. He wanted the lord to be better than Holly himself was, who was also going along with this travesty.

'Or maybe,' Tassone continued, and now his complacent arrogance was leaking through, 'your mistake was playing it safe in Haven in the first place. Every stronghold wanted you, and you came back here. Why?'

Holly wondered if he was being recruited. Valerian was walking even slower now, lagging well behind the others. Valerian, Holly realised, was getting ready to stop Holly from drawing his sword.

Valerian had no idea how fast Holly could be, if he thought he could stop that from a few paces away.

His silence was only egging Tassone on, which was exactly the point he'd tried to make to Valerian at the feast. 'Nothing mouthy to say now, Holyoake? Maybe you and me should have a drink, revisit that cocksucking conversation. I think you'll like being forced to your knees. You'll pretend you don't, but you will.'

Lord Valerian turned around and caught Holly's wrist, an easy enough achievement because Holly, *actually*, hadn't so much as twitched for his hilt. If anything, it was Valerian's assumption that he wouldn't be able to control himself that tipped him over the edge, and so it was Valerian who got the brunt of his simmering rage, its magnitude unsuspected.

'Hands off, you fucking son and heir of a mongrel bitch,' he snapped, jerking his arm free to the counterpoint of Tassone's mocking sniggering.

It was awful language to use at and in front of the purple. This was the point where everyone's attention slipped and somehow Evelyn let some of the Cristati Mancer Guard run on ahead of her down into the Mancer Guard's hallway and onto Hazel's sword.

Hazel, Holly muses now while standing at the corkscrew stairs, acquitted himself well. Indeed, Ari Hazlemere fell upon the enemy like a bearded, beefy avenging angel from the pages of Second Jerome's bleak mythology and hadn't even raised a sweat.

Hazel is, no doubt, nursing a broken heart and refusing to think about it. Holly shifts restlessly and curses himself for ever encouraging his friend.

He hears, from below, the low whistle that's Evelyn's summons. 'Call me back when Hazel comes,' he tells the household pair, and goes on down the stairs.

Evelyn meets him halfway. 'Don't panic,' she tells him, and then hugs him fiercely.

The Holyoakes don't do this. If either of them needs a hug, they turn to others—he to Hazel, and Evie to… Well, that's her private life and he isn't supposed to know, so he pretends he doesn't. They certainly do not turn to each other, a habit, probably not a healthy one, from the time after they'd escaped the civil war, before they'd reached Haven. Holly had, for a long time, hated his sister with fiery adolescent passion for saving him from dying with the rest of their extended family. The hate settled into a gleaming habitual bitterness that meant everyone except Evelyn got the best of him, his good cheer and generous impulses, while he fed her only sullen resentment.

Only when he and Hazel went to the academy did Holly understand that the rest of the world was not as kind as Haven, that Evelyn must have paid, not in coin, for every scrap of food and shelter and passage they'd grovelled for on their way north, that Evelyn had sheltered him from every vile drop of the price she'd paid even while he spat nasty invective at her for the injustice of surviving when everyone else was butchered.

Upon return to Haven, it took all his courage to ask her if the sword-master they'd lived and trained with for several months before heading to Haven had really taken them in because he'd been awed by the Holyoakes' innate talents with a blade.

She'd looked at him with uncharacteristic compassion. 'I paid him for our lessons and our board. You don't need to ask how.'

If he'd tried to hug her then, she'd have ripped his head off.

Now she's hugging him hard and scolding him. 'I saw how quick you were to volunteer yourself for exile with Hazel, Ro. You are forbidden from doing that. We'll find a way to bring him home, under a new name like us if we have to. But you're not allowed to leave.'

Holly rests his head on his sister's shoulder. He's already laughing, because he knows what she's setting him up for.

She pushes him away and adds, giving his own wicked smile right back at him, 'I need you to die right here so my children can have your useless bones as relics for the new reliquary.'

'Are these children still hypothetical or has Miriam finally asked you to help her out?'

'Apparently sieges make people think of their own mortality,' Evelyn says. 'So *if* we survive, and *if* she doesn't change her mind…'

Holly gives a twirl. 'I'm going to be the favourite uncle.'

'And *if* the poor little mite survives you and Kito competing over who's the more fun and irresponsible one…'

'And *if* you remember what to do…' Holly says, cheerily inappropriate since it's just the Holyoake siblings. 'Doesn't it wither away from lack of use?'

'I wouldn't know,' she says, eyes narrowed. 'Doesn't it drop off from overuse?'

'Ooh, bitchy!'

He skips down the stairs in front of her, mood lightened. It's good news. He hopes Hazel will be cheered by it too.

Evelyn is once again the sombre commander by the time she exits the stairwell behind him. The dining hall is still empty, other than the rest of the Mancer guards, looking grim. Oddly, Albemarle is there, too. The Mancer should be locked back in the atelier, but zhey're sitting at the guards' table, mechanically ploughing through a pile of baghrir. That's the usual offering if Hazel can't do a pie. Zhey like them plain. The kitchen staff must be frantically preparing tonight's feast from their siege provisioning; Kito has burnt a few favours to win those soft little semolina pancakes.

'Albemarle, please read the journal to Holly. The relevant pages only, thank you.'

'Again?' zhey complain. But Evelyn, like Kito, has always had a way with Haven's Mancer, and so zhey irritably push zheir plate away and open the journal, paging through.

Some of it's in Mutual, mostly the headings. Holly recognises a few stronghold names, written at the top of some pages like a title, the rest of each page covered in Mancer runes in two hands, one usually using blue ink, the other a darker purple, almost black. Albemarle slows, and Holly sees more familiar names—the coastal strongholds, all five names written within one large circle, representing the loose alliance they form.

Underneath the circle, the two rune hands go back and forth in written conversation. Albemarle taps the page here. 'This is where they decide the coastal alliance will suit best.'

'Suit what?' Holly asks, and Albemarle shrugs.

When Holly glances at his sister, she merely directs him back to the journal with a sharp jut of her chin. There's pages devoted to each of the five strongholds, and the notes become more detailed. The names of the Mancers are written there, in runes, and the names of some of the associated Mancer guards, with commentary, all in Mutual and not all of it complimentary. Quite a lot of it, actually, is aimed at identifying the weaknesses of these Mancers and their guards.

Each assessment is followed by the two sets of runes, which Holly assumes must be Ash and Izidore, discussing the findings.

Albemarle stops on the page dedicated to Haven. Haven's name is circled. Lady Fairhaven's name is there in full, Tashi Diasha of Stronghold Fair Haven by the Sea, with a single comment in the blue runes.

There's Albemarle's name, written in Mancer runes, with a rune discussion below it, no Mutual words at all. Albemarle glances over this without reaction. Holly makes a guess that it doesn't say anything Albemarle was greatly surprised to read. Albemarle's never cared what's said about zhem. Zhey only care about zheir projects.

And anyway, Haven earned a circle. Albemarle must have passed the other Mancers' assessment.

'I researched Haven, before I came,' Albemarle says. Zhey're staring past Holly's ear. 'And if there'd been a Mancer here already, I would've researched zhem, too.'

'A-yah, Albemarle, we know,' Morano says, his mild tone fighting to disguise a darker emotion. 'That's not…where the harm lies.'

'Look,' Albemarle says, more eagerly. There's a loose sheet folded in the pages, like a bookmark. Zhey unfold it. 'It's a schematic of Second Jerome's Mancy leg. They liked my design, but they've changed it. It works fine, but they changed it. Blatant bricolage. Very rude. They should at least wait till I'm dead. Exequys.'

Then zhey tsk like a maiden aunt, looking down at the schematic with zheir pale unreadable eyes. It's been drawn all over in both colours of ink, and the runes are very dense over the rest of the page as the two Cristati Mancers work through their edits to the design.

Holly looks at zhem, and looks at Evelyn and the other Mancer guards. All of them had fully expected Albemarle to have paroxysms if zhey ever found out that Ash's mensuration crossed the inviolable line.

Nightingale gives an embarrassed shrug. She'd warned them it was a sin among her own people and among Mancers. But not every Mancer reacted the same way, it seemed. If Albemarle didn't even care about the Mancer pronoun, maybe zhey truly weren't bothered by this other great taboo either.

And anyway, zhey've raised a very good point—if Mancers never use bricolage, what happens to all those journals when one dies? For that matter, what would have happened to Holly's family's loom, if it hadn't already been smashed to pieces, when its Mancer couldn't travel from the local stronghold to recharge it anymore, through death or other inconvenience?

There is a very real possibility, it occurs to Holly, that it's taboo solely because it's associated with Mancer death rituals—exequys—and when Nightingale's people decided it was a sin, they'd simply misunderstood the reason for the taboo.

'Relevant pages only, Albemarle,' Evelyn repeats.

Albemarle folds the paper and tucks it away, expressionless. Zhey turn the page. The names of the Haven Mancer guards are written here. Holly glances around at the faces of his comrades, his friends. He's not sure he wants to read what Cristati spies thought were their weaknesses, weak enough to be the atelier chosen for infiltration.

'If I might save you the bother,' Kito says, voice low. She's deadly angry. 'I drink and gamble too much, Morano may be got at through his wife, Second Jerome's a cripple, and First Jerome will be effectively neutralised by the modesty injunction if her veil is ripped off. Nightingale and Titus aren't in there. It's old information.'

Holly meets Kito's eyes. He rather suspects the two youngest guards, or Nightingale at least, have their cruelly efficient summaries on the next page. Otherwise the information would be at least two years out of date. The baghrir must be in aid of keeping honest Albemarle distracted from turning over the page.

The juniors know it. They're looking miserable, in addition to angry.

'And me?' he asks lightly.

'Oh, you fuck around, boy,' Kito says.

Albemarle pats the patch of runes that must discuss him. 'They decide you'd be easy to seduce but there'd be no point doing it, because you're too whorish for sex to affect you. Not like Hazel.'

And now, now Holly understands Kito's deep rage, the grim fury of the rest of them. Until then, what they'd read was insulting. It hurt. But there was nothing there with any true power to harm them beyond the sting of eavesdropping on a discussion of weaknesses it'd be easier not to hear. Haven itself would have paid spies to reveal similar flaws, if it had ever felt inclined to raid another atelier.

But there's a fucking mark next to the name of Ari Hazlemere in this fucking Mancer journal.

He reads the Mutual entry about Hazel, but most of it doesn't sink in. What does is the reference to Maya. What does is Albemarle's indifferent translation of the runes.

'The one with the neat runes in blue says he has a deaf sister, he will be sympathetic. The one writing in purple says he's the most promising candidate so far, and Haven the most promising stronghold. The one writing in blue agrees that Hazel of Fair Haven is the target.'

From out of the stairwell, Holly hears a piercing whistle. Hazel's back.

~Twenty-Four~

Hazel stepped in front of Ash, barring Holly. 'Not helpful, Hols.'

'Zhey targeted us. Zhey deliberately picked Haven for whatever shit zhey're pulling here.'

'I'm not quite following how this is different from zhem choosing to spy on us, which we already knew about?' Hazel said slowly.

Ash folded zheir arms, once again looking both defiant and resigned. Zhey lifted zheir fingers to Holly, not Trade, but eloquent none the less—a *go on, then* motion. Holly transferred his focus from zhem to Hazel, his expression transforming accordingly from deeply hostile to the same pitying look his sister had given Hazel before he'd gone to fetch Ash. It was not a look the Holyoakes often wore.

'We'll show you the journal. Zhey targeted *you*, Hazel. Because Maya would make you sympathetic to zhem.' He hesitated, but truly, the Holyoakes did not wear pity. 'Because it would make you a soft touch. And it did.'

While Hazel was still contemplating that, running a hand through his already unruly hair, Ash shot the wall just above the heads of the stronghold guards. Both guards dived away from the entrance to the stairwell at the sudden burst of light and heat.

Having demonstrated the weapon, Ash spun on zheir heel and yanked the other one from Izidore, who sighed heavily but did not otherwise protest.

'We're going downstairs,' the collar's voice announced as zhey pointed it at the guards and began to edge toward the stairwell, pulling Izidore with zhem. 'You did not see anyone with me but the other Mancer.'

Kiselyova had fallen to the floor, eyes wide, Devi crouched next to him, half-shielding him. They both mutely nodded. Neither attempted to rise.

Holly, on the other hand… Holly only ever had one reaction to a fight. He took a smart step back, blocking the archway, and set his hand on his hilt. Hazel instinctively glanced upward, but the spidery pet was not in view.

Again he moved between Holly and Ash. '~Don't,' he said sharply, not entirely sure which of them he was addressing. To Holly, he said, 'The plan holds, Holly. We still have to get zhem out of the stronghold and away from Cristati.'

'We can slit zheir throat and dump zhem outside the walls,' Holly said. If he'd been joking when he suggested murder in the port, he definitely wasn't joking now. 'That'll do it.'

Ash swung the copperlit from the stronghold guards and levelled it at Holly. Hazel knocked it aside. ~Don't ever wave a weapon at Holly.

This was not his love for Holly talking. It was the remnant of his care for his Mancer.

'~If you want to go downstairs, we're going downstairs,' he told zhem. '~You don't need to carry on like…whatever the fuck this behaviour is.'

Ash's shoulders hunched. Zhey swayed, rubbing zheir wrist where the silver cuff dug in, looking disconsolate and uncertain. Then, straightening, firming, zhey put the copperlit into one of the capacious pockets of the robe, took Izidore's hand and marched past Hazel, past the guards only just picking themselves up, and past Holly, through the archway and down the stairs.

'I think,' Holly said to Devi, 'that when questioned, you can safely say you witnessed the Mancers rescuing themselves without perjuring yourself.' She nodded. 'Pass that along, would you? No one saw Hazel.'

'And pass along that no one is to draw a weapon on the Mancy project, or impede it in any way,' Hazel added. He touched Holly's arm as they hurried down the corkscrew steps after the two Mancers. 'I appreciate the thought, I really do, but Haven still needs its scapegoat. Those two will still have to have help getting to the port and away.'

'Will they, though?' Holly said. 'By my lost relics, Hazel, Ash is…'

'Cristati,' Hazel finished.

'A-yah,' Holly said heavily.

They found Ash in the dining hall, standing motionless beside Izidore, progress blocked by the other Havens. Hazel assumed zhey'd head straight for the south door, for the postern gate, but instead zhey'd been on zheir way to the subterrane. The guards looked at Hazel, and he saw pity again, and their anger.

'If the Mancers need to go to the atelier, let them go to the atelier,' Hazel said, reluctantly walking across the hall to break the tableau. He expected Ash to pull the copperlit again, but zhey didn't.

Holly shot past him, over to their table where Albemarle sat with zheir head lowered. From the stiff set of zheir shoulders, zhey were absorbing the tension. One of zheir Mancer guards should be with zhem, helping zhem breathe, keeping zhem calm, taking zhem out of this confrontation.

Snatching up the incriminating journal, Holly brought it over to Hazel. He silently held it out, open to a page with Hazel's name circled, the indisputable evidence that he'd been deliberately picked for manipulation and exploitation.

His thoughts were trying to spiral, stuttering *That's why*— repeatedly. He thought of the newly arrived Ash, exhausted, tense and stiff in Evelyn's office, pretending zhey couldn't read lips, pretending zhey couldn't read Mutual, all to engineer the summoning of the most likely user of Trade, Ari Hazlemere, brother of a deaf girl. Zhey'd been working to zheir plan from the moment zhey'd arrived.

Ash had stared at him with such wide-eyed fixation. He knew zhey'd been frightened of him—of course zhey had been. Zhey'd taken one look at him and thought, *Oh shit, I have to pretend I want to fuck* that?

It was almost funny, really, if it hadn't been so fucking painful.

Hazel ran his hand through his hair, and again. He breathed out. He thought, *a-yah, you've got through this before and you can do it again. It is what it is, so get your shit together and deal with it.*

The other guards, and even Evelyn, had laid their hands on his back and shoulders. He recognised they were trying to comfort him, but he also read their fury in the tension of their fingers, the stiffness of their bodies as they clustered about him. It felt—only a little but a little was enough—like the stormy tension in his village after blight destroyed the first promising crop after the drought, and the villagers' thoughts had turned toward a scapegoat. It cut through his tangle of feelings and made him want to wrap Ash up and flee with zhem.

He gently shook the others off. To Evelyn, he said, 'Commander, this doesn't read like people planning a spy mission, so I suggest you question the Cristati Mancers as to their true aim.'

He knew he wouldn't have had to point that out if she, like the rest of them, had not been distracted by the damning contents of the journal, instead of paying attention to the overall implication of it—the search for a stronghold with characteristics that in some way suited what Ash and Izidore were trying to achieve.

He finally steeled himself and turned to Ash—but the Mancer had taken advantage of the distraction and was already marching off to the subterrane stairs, towing Izidore with zhem.

Hazel did blink at that; he realised he'd expected Ash to be waiting on his reaction. He'd expected to see Ash looking at least slightly guilty, slightly apologetic. Slightly like zhey cared what he thought of zhem now. But why would zhey?

Dropping the journal, Holly sprinted after Ash, catching zhem by the collar of the robe. Ash reacted badly, of course, twisting hard and snatching the copperlit from zheir pocket. Holly ripped it from zheir hand and threw it away. It clanged to the floor and rolled under the table where Albemarle still sat alone.

'What's that noise?' the Haven Mancer asked, voice slow and thick.

'Holly, let zhem go.' Hazel hurried over, pulled Holly's hand off Ash. 'It doesn't change anything. We still have to let Ash escape the stronghold before zheir mother has grounds to attack. Let zhem have the atelier. Let zhem have whatever zhey need so zhey can leave. Otherwise, we're shooting ourselves in the foot for petty payback.'

'Petty!' Morano said. 'Hazel, what zhey did to you, it will not stand.'

The rest nodded. They had defaulted into protecting one of their own. That wasn't right. A Mancer Guard didn't protect anyone other than its Mancer. A Mancer Guard certainly didn't turn on its Mancer. He'd reminded Nightingale that it was not their place to judge their stronghold's Mancer, and he'd meant it.

Hands on hips, he said briskly. 'All right, all of you. Did you forget?'

'Forget what, Hazel darling?' Kito idly twirled one of her trishuls, eyeing Ash.

'What a Mancer is. We all know this, don't we? Maybe we all got used to Albemarle's variety of—'

'Not giving a shit about anyone else.'

Hazel overrode Holly's angry interjection. '—preoccupation with Mancy, but we should never have expected anything different from any Mancer. That is what a Mancer *is*.'

Ash had been closely watching his face, reading his lips. At this, zhey huffed and tapped zheir foot, once again bring the glares of the Havens down upon zhem.

'That is some nerve.' Second Jerome sounded reluctantly impressed.

'No wonder the whole fucking Cristati Mancer Guard hates you,' Holly said. Ash shot him a scathing look before turning smartly for the stairs again.

'Oh no, you don't, you fucker.' Holly hauled zhem back. 'If Silverthorne wants the atelier, zhey give us answers in exchange. Ask what you need to ask, Evie.'

Evelyn held up her hand, taking effortless control. She nodded at Holly to release Ash, and he did, though the two of them were then left standing side by side, mutually seething in accidental concord.

'What is your goal?' Evelyn asked, facing Ash and speaking clearly. 'What are you trying to achieve here, Silverthorne?'

Ash rubbed at the silver band on zheir wrist, frowning. Zhey glanced longingly at the stairs.

Izidore, clasping zheir own cuff, said, 'The wheat submits to the plough not knowing if it shall become chaff or bread.' Zheir hands added, ~Just tell them the plan.

Ash tapped zheir partner's cuff. ~We don't have time for this.

'The tide comes in no matter the opinion of the grains of sand on the beach,' Izidore said. ~You're not thinking straight. Trust me when I tell you it'll be faster to explain to them than to argue with them.

Ash started to sign. Izidore shook zheir head once. 'Heated metal melts and collapses into the mould.' Meanwhile, zhey signed, frowning down at zheir own hands as zhey struggled against the limits of zheir fluency, ~Ash, you are under strain and falling back on poor habits. Tell them. They will help.

'Fuck, will we, though?' Holly said.

Izidore squeezed Ash's shoulders, tucked zhem under zheir chin for a brief hug, then turned zhem to face Evelyn.

Puffing a sharp breath out in frustration, Ash nonetheless obediently signed, ~I intend to break Cristati, commander.

Zhey formed [break] with no little relish: it was meant to be a sharp gesture like snapping an invisible twig with both hands. Ash did it like zhey were snapping a spine.

~They are my family and they will not renounce me. There is no provision for me to renounce them. My only path to be free is to break them.

Then zhey looked at Hazel for the first time since they'd all come downstairs, expectant. Zhey were waiting for him to be zheir voice to the less fluent Evelyn.

Holly saw the presumption and instantly bristled, even while his sister tried to settle him with another upheld hand. 'Are you fucking telling us this is all in aid of winning a spat with your *mother*?'

Ash's eyes widened. Zhey smacked zheir hand over the collar around zheir throat. 'Are you fucking stupid?' howled the metallic voice from the box on the collar, grating and grinding as it tried to keep up with zheir outrage. 'I *told* you Cristati is ambitious. I *told* you the only kind of Mancy weapon they want from me is something that can be deployed on a large scale. Do you think Lady Cristati is just going to give me a pat on the fucking head for effort when I finally manage it? Or do you think, maybe, just maybe, she'll start picking off other strongholds? Do you think she'll stop at one city-killing weapon, when she holds Izidore hostage to force my compliance? Or do you think she might just keep me churning out weapons till she's camped outside the capital, politely requesting the crown from her cousin? It's a little bit more than a fucking spat with my fucking mother and it's a good deal more than a Mancer acting like a shit just because zhey can.'

Zhey snatched zheir hand back off the collar, shoulders heaving. Zheir eyes flickered for a single second to Hazel before zhey directed zheir full fierce glare at Holly.

A resounding silence had fallen. Into it, Albemarle said, 'What's that noise?' again, louder. Zhey put zheir hands over zheir ears and keened, high and terrified.

The modified copperlit. Ash had warned Hazel that Albemarle would be able to hear that it'd been altered, bricolaged.

Kito dashed over and threw herself under the table. She rolled out holding the copperlit tube, which she hurled all the way to the other side of the room, near the south door to the gardens.

'To the atelier, Albemarle,' she said brightly.

'No, what is that *noise*?' Albemarle said, voice rising even higher.

Zhey were shaking.

The Mancer guards moved like the well-oiled cogs they were. First Jerome persuaded Albemarle to stand up, and she, Titus and Nightingale walked with the sweating, panting Mancer past Ash and Izidore to the subterrane stairs. First Jerome's voice was soft and calm as she instructed Albemarle to breathe and step, breathe and step. Kito walked along behind, alert to any shift in Albemarle's posture or lumbering gait that might indicate zhey were falling into paroxysm.

Ash watched zhem go with a look of open yearning, which zhey swallowed when Morano and Second Jerome stepped into guard position on the stairs. Hazel guessed they weren't actively intending to block Ash from making a dash for the atelier. They'd just calmed down enough to remember that they existed to guard Haven's Mancer, not protect their friend's inappropriately tender feelings.

Ash shuddered in a breath and cast Hazel, Holly and Evelyn another hotly indignant look, stubbornly picking up the argument where it'd been dropped while they soothed Albemarle.

'Quite the speech,' Holly said. He sounded more cheerful, as he often did after being challenged. 'Were you always this grouchy and keeping it reined in so we'd like you, or are you just having a particularly stressful day?'

The tight set of Ash's shoulders released slightly. Zhey juggled zheir open hands in a gesture evoking weighing apples and oranges in the pans of a scale.

Holly snorted. 'You still haven't told us the plan, lover.'

Ash turned to his Mancer partner. ~Ask for sanctuary.

'Oh, ancestors save us, why not dig ourselves in deeper?' Evelyn blurted. She clapped her hand over her mouth. 'My apologies, Izidore. You are, of course, entitled to request formal sanctuary of Stronghold Fair Haven by the Sea.'

'The sunbird's beak is perfectly suited to the curve of the trumpet flower,' Izidore said sulkily. Zhey tapped Ash. ~We are escaping on a ship together. That's the plan. We're running for the port.

~That was never going to work. I can manage almost three weeks without Mancy now, you can barely go three days. You can't survive the journey to a new stronghold far enough away.

Izidore looked hurt and bewildered. 'The ant lifts much more weight than—'

Ash tapped zheir foot in an impatient staccato. ~Ask for sanctuary or I will not remove your cuff.

Izidore's eyes widened. Zhey clutched zheir wrist and gave a hard twist on the silver band; it didn't move. Zhey shook zheir head at Ash. ~I am appalled at you.

Ash shrugged. ~I am my mother's child. *Ask.*

The brown-haired Mancer huffed and turned to Evelyn. 'The corn stalk bows when its ears grow too heavy,' zhey said. 'I request sanctuary.'

'And Fair Haven grants it,' Evelyn said, with a sigh of her own. 'What, precisely, is your endgame, Silverthorne?'

A new voice rang out from the corkscrew stairs. 'Indeed, I would quite like to know that, myself.'

~Twenty-Five~

Lady Fairhaven glided across the dining hall, flanked by Lord Valerian. He shot the briefest of looks at his senior Mancer guards but his expression was stiff, giving nothing away aside discomfort.

The lady of Fair Haven offered Evelyn a small smile. 'Lady Cristati has departed back to her camp,' she said. 'Apparently there's quite the mess to clean up in the guest hall.'

'She's already gone?' Evelyn said.

They'd been expecting more time. They'd been expecting her to stay to keep threatening Lady Fairhaven. They'd been expecting her to call in the second Mancer Guard so it would be misdeployed when Hazel took Ash out the postern. They'd expected her to turn her attention to recovering her escaping Mancers, not retaliating against the stronghold that had sheltered them.

Ash, it appeared, had expected none of that. ~How long do we have before she attacks?

'Ash,' Izidore said, zheir light voice trembling. 'Ash, the leaf cannot only fall with the first winds of autumn.' And zheir hands said, ~I tried, I tried, I tried.

Zhey pulled back zheir sleeves, showing Ash the bandages wrapped around zheir arms. The linen strips were stained dark at the crooks of zheir elbows where zhey'd ripped zheir skin, trying to release the Mancy drive in any other way than creating whatever project Cristati had dictated.

Ash brushed the bandages, stroked down zheir forearms, pulled the sleeves of the robe back down. ~I know, Izidore. We knew you'd have to, didn't we?

'Well. As encouraging as that sounds,' Lady Fairhaven said when Hazel finished voicing the unsettling exchange, 'I need to know what's happening, Cristati Mancers. You have a plan. What is it?'

Ash glanced at Hazel. Then, looking at the floor, zhey set zheir hand to the box on the collar. 'Cristati will assault your walls. You will call on your allies. Your allies will destroy Cristati.'

'You have gravely misunderstood the nature of the coastal alliance if you think our allies will march for us for anything less than a covenant violation.'

'It will be a covenant violation if I am not within Haven but Izidore is. It will be in direct contravention of zheir request for sanctuary.'

Lady Fairhaven's face remained placid, but she did pace up and down, slow and stately. Musingly, she said, 'Your mother will argue that she thought you were within, of course.'

'Since I will be within her camp instead, it will be very difficult to sustain that particular defence.'

Hazel took a breath. Even Holly blinked. Lady Fairhaven gave them an interested onceover before she once again addressed Ash, who was watching her lips intently. 'Why would she continue to attack Haven if she has you back? I do not wish to give offence, but surely she sees your Izidore as replaceable. Particularly if she has Albemarle's designs in exchange. Lord Valerian informs me they are eminently useable.'

She raised her eyebrows at Ash, all mild enquiry.

'I intend to convince her that one of Albemarle's projects is suited to become the large-scale weapon she has always desired. Should the Cristati Mancer Guard retrieve both this project and Izidore, then together we could bricolage it to that purpose before your allies arrive, and therefore my mother need have no fear of them.'

'I doubt she does, regardless,' Lady Fairhaven murmured.

'Which project?' Evelyn asked. Her tone was professional; whether she thought to destroy it or set Izidore to work on it immediately was entirely unclear.

Ash shook zheir head. 'I will be lying. I'll draw her one of Albemarle's designs if I have to and pretend it already exists as a project. But there is no weapon inside Haven that will save you.' The Mancy collar wheezed into the dismal silence before zhey said, 'There's only me.'

'We are taking a little upon ourselves, aren't we, young Mancer?' Lady Fairhaven said. 'Haven does not stand nor fall on the back of a single person.'

Lord Valerian, for his part, said, 'You are taking a great risk with all of our lives on the expectation that you can bluff your mother.'

'I am aware. But I anticipate success for the simple reason that she *wants* the excuse to come at Haven. She feels insult greatly, and Haven has insulted her. Also, she still nurses a grudge against you personally—'

'My word, does she?' Lady Fairhaven said, looking amused.

'You were kind to her at school and that is unforgivable.' Ash frowned. 'And her cousin liked you more than her?'

'Ah yes, Adora. We were very close. Such fond memories.' Lady Fairhaven smiled minutely. Evelyn folded her arms.

'She *will* continue the assault on Haven, it *will* appear like a covenant violation whether she intends that or not, your allies *will* respond.'

Lady Fairhaven made a thoughtful noise. 'I can notify them by pigeon today of the new covenant with Izidore. We can formally call on them the moment you are back with your mother and she does not call off the attack.'

'Or this whole plan is a tale spun to get zhemself out of enemy hands,' Holly muttered.

'Then zhey would have waited safely in zheir room for the Cristatis to take zhem home,' Hazel said. 'Yet zhey were well on zheir way to escaping before I even got th...'

He trailed off. Why hadn't Ash simply waited and allowed zhemself to be taken back to the Cristati camp, if that was the goal anyway? The plan to goad zheir mother into violating the covenant for the sake of a made-up weapon would have worked even without Izidore; Albemarle, creator of the fictional weapon, could serve as the bait and switch just as well.

'Which you didn't,' Valerian interjected dryly, 'according to every single witness. Astonishingly, no one served the visitors tea, either.'

Hazel turned to Izidore, realisation dawning. 'A-yah, I see. Ash didn't leave when zhey could have, not when the lieutenant tried to retrieve zhem, and not when zheir mother *did* retrieve zhem. Zhey wanted to get you out first.'

'The lever,' Izidore said.

'Izidore may be replaceable to my mother but zhey are irreplaceable to me, and she knows it,' Ash said. 'As long as she holds a knife to Izidore's throat, I will obey. That is the other reason she will risk breaking the covenant, and why she even brought Izidore with her today. Izidore is the lever that forces my compliance...' Zhey shrugged. '...but levers have two ends.'

Hazel nodded, not looking at either Mancer. They were fond of each other, he'd seen that from the way they turned to each other for comfort.

He'd already guessed that, even before Izidore had arrived, from the way Ash missed touch.

'And Haven is the fulcrum upon which the lever moves the world,' Lord Valerian said, expression abstracted.

'I am the fulcrum,' Ash's Mancy voice said. 'Haven is the solid ground on which to place me.'

Lady Fairhaven turned to Valerian. 'Cousin, I will hear your thoughts.'

'The closest stronghold is a full day's march away,' Lord Valerian said immediately. 'But they must muster first. I doubt they can arrive much before sunset two days from now at the very earliest, and even then, they'll have to wait on the others before breaking the siege. Cristati obviously knew that open warfare was a possible outcome when they first marched on us. It is clear Izidore, willing or no, built Cristati something helpful. What's to say they're not strong enough to destroy us *and* our allies without even needing to get their hands on Ash's fictional weapon?'

Lady Fairhaven seesawed her hand. 'Juniper is reportedly rather more useful in that regard than dear Albemarle. Stronghold Mollymawk will bring zheir Mancy to bear, I am sure.'

'If we can hold out long enough for Mollymawk to reach us.'

Ash touched zheir collar again. 'You have the moat now. I believe you can hold out long enough.'

'We didn't have the moat, though, when you made this plan,' Evelyn said. Her arms were still folded. 'You knew the Mancy drive would force Izidore to make whatever this thing is zhey've made but you didn't know Albemarle had anything like the moat to defend against it.'

Again, the Mancy hiss of the collar was the only sound. Izidore took Ash's hand and squeezed. 'They cannot decry the arena, who know not the lion.'

'I see.' Lady Fairhaven nodded slowly. 'You assumed Haven would fall and our allies would be left to get the job done. Just another one who has mistaken kindness for weakness, I suppose.'

That answered all of Hazel's questions, his desperate groping to exonerate Ash from the worst of zheir deceptions. Zheir lies had never had anything to do with protecting Haven, and all to do with keeping a trap baited for Cristati.

When Ash remained silent, Izidore signed, ~Please do not judge us harshly. We did not know you.

'You fully intended to sacrifice our stronghold. We'll judge you as harshly as we like,' Holly said flatly.

Hazel'd noted the 'us' and the 'we' in Izidore's defence. But until only a few moments before, zhey'd thought the plan was to escape by ship.

Indeed, Ash set a hand on Izidore's chest and pushed zhem slightly away, other hand on the collar. 'No blame attaches to Izidore. It was my plan alone and I stand by it. One stronghold balanced against the entirety of the east coast from here all the way up to the capital.'

'Didn't have to be Haven.'

'I stand by the choice,' Ash repeated. 'Haven was my highest chance of inciting Cristati to violate the covenant and my lowest chance of falling into the hands of another brutal Mancer Guard.'

Holly leaned over Ash, eyes very dark. 'Oh, was it, lover?'

Ash set zheir shoulders. 'Yes, it was and is.'

Hazel took Holly's arm and gently pulled him back, thus proving Ash's point. He shook his head at his friend, saying again, 'It's not helpful, Holly.'

'Not trying to be helpful, Hazel.'

'Albemarle would have weighed the same choices and made the same decision.'

'Good point, lieutenant,' Lady Fairhaven said. She set her hands on her hips and breathed out in one long exhale, her only sign of any level of distress so far. 'Well, then. I never could abide bullies. Cristati Mancers, you have my blessing to proceed.'

Ash set zheir hands together and offered a bow, shallow and stiff. Hazel felt Evelyn, Holly and Valerian exchange glances around him, but didn't raise his gaze to partake.

Lady Fairhaven swept a look over them all, her cousin, her commander, the Mancers and their guards. 'I have faith in my people. Fair Haven will hold.'

There came a scuttering, clicking noise from the stairs. Hazel felt his teeth tingle like he'd scraped metal tines across them. At his side, Holly got even tenser.

'Also, I would very much like someone to deal with that thing, please,' Lady Fairhaven added.

'Pet,' Izidore said in delight, and clapped zheir hands. Zheir arachnoid creation scuttled out of the stairwell and across the ceiling at speed.

'Don't touch your swords,' Hazel said sharply, glancing over his shoulder to ensure Second Jerome and Morano knew they were included in that recommendation.

The Mancy pet descended from the ceiling in a complicated spiral of far too many legs and came to rest at Izidore's side like a dog at heel.

'Yes, we rather found that out,' Valerian said. 'Luckily, your warning percolated in time to stop the incipient carnage.'

'We found it difficult to come up with any other reliable trigger.' At the grate of the cold voice from Ash's Mancy collar, the pet extended a couple of legs, probing, and Ash stepped away. Watching it suspiciously, zhey added, 'We will attempt to adjust the song now we need not imminently fear blades drawn against us.'

Lady Fairhaven nodded briskly. 'I also require more details of this Mancy project Izidore has built for Cristati. I shall update our commanders. I suspect we do not have long before the assault begins.'

She patted Evelyn's hand. Very softly, she said, 'My dear, I'm surprised and disappointed you didn't trust me with the full details of what was going on instead of your carefully edited accounts.'

'I was trying to protect you,' Evelyn just as quietly answered. 'The less the purple knew, the more you could honestly deny to Lady Cristati. *Especially* this rescue.'

Ash, who could, of course, lipread very well, gave Holly a particular kind of pointed look in the aftermath of this exchange.

'I want to slap zhem so badly right now,' Holly said. Hazel slung his arm around his shoulder in fond comradery and yet firm restraint.

Lady Fairhaven patted Evelyn's hand. 'We will discuss it at length at a more convenient time.'

Evelyn very rarely acted like her sibling, but at this she pulled a heartfelt *do we have to* face. Smiling fondly over her shoulder, Lady Fairhaven swept away, Valerian with her, leaving the rest of them standing in a semi-circle about Ash and Izidore.

Once the purple were gone up the corkscrew stairs, Holly said, 'Fine, good plan, wonderful plan, well done you, but at what point did you consider telling us what you needed and letting us choose to help you?'

~You cannot understand how hard it is for me to trust Mancer guards.

'Bloody easy for you to fuck them, though, apparently.'

'A-yah, Holyoake, enough,' Hazel said, tightening his hold. He was wincing and trying not to look at Izidore. He had no idea how much of Ash's intentions zhey'd been party to, though both Mancers had discussed him in the diary without qualm. 'It wasn't easy. Zhey had to force zhemself. Didn't quite recognise that at the time.'

Though he fucking had, hadn't he, really? He'd seen the anxiety and tension and let himself believe it was still all right to continue. He turned to Ash. ~Sorry for that.

'By my *fucking* relics, Hazel, did you just *apologise* to that treacherous shit for making zhem seduce you?'

Ash, for zheir part, wildly signed, the equivalent of shouting, ~I *did not* have to force myself. Stop taking my decisions away from me. I didn't drag Haven into the shit because I'm a Mancer and I couldn't help myself, *I decided to*. I didn't take you to bed because I needed to have you on my side, I did it because *I wanted to*.

Holly yanked free of Hazel, who was guiltily looking for Izidore's response to that confession—there was none except a small smile—and crowded into Ash, who did not give an inch.

Looming over zhem, Holly snapped, 'Maybe you could not yell at the person you've fucked over, how about that one, Liege fucking Silver-thorne?'

~*Do not call me that.*

Evelyn clapped her hands together in one sharp concussion, which at least made Holly blink. 'Back it up, Ro,' she said. Holly sullenly obeyed as she went on, 'We have a lot to get done before the attack begins. Let's go to the atelier.'

~Twenty-Six~

They trotted in train after Evelyn. Izidore, flanked by zheir pet, walked beside Second Jerome, fascinatedly watching the Mancy leg propel him along. Hazel was reminded, painfully, of Ash when zhey'd first arrived, the innocent charm of a Mancer admiring a superlative Mancy project.

'The pink-hued diamond is rare indeed,' Izidore mused.

'Oh, no, I was born with two legs. I fell under a cart as a child,' Second Jerome explained. 'The wheel rolled over my lower leg and crushed it, and they had to amputate. Albemarle noticed me trying to get up the stairs with my crutch one day.'

'The sun's ray are welcome after winter.'

'I'm not convinced that zhey're kind so much as offended by inefficiency, to be honest.'

Izidore pointed at the leg. 'A cloud may be a rabbit, a cloud may be a dragon?'

'Sure,' Second Jerome said, 'if you like. It already works well, though, and Albemarle might not like it if you start messing with one of zheir projects. Apparently…'

He stopped talking. It must have occurred to him, as it had to Hazel, that Izidore, young and isolated in Stronghold Cristati, could only know that bricolage was taboo if Ash had told zhem.

Given zhey'd just openly offered to bricolage Second Jerome's leg—or so Hazel gathered, because he completely lacked Second Jerome's ear for Izidore's speech patterns—it seemed Ash had not done so.

Ash came to Hazel's side and thrust zheir hands into his line of sight. ~Will you ever speak to me again?

Perhaps around the time Ash dared look at him again. Zhey still weren't. Zhey were plodding along next to him with zheir eyes fixedly on his hands. ~When I have something to say to you.

~I think you probably have quite a lot to say to me, Hazel.

He shrugged. He probably did. But it was all so jumbled he didn't have a hope of getting words out about it.

~I know how awful and selfish that sounded just now.

~Which part? Hazel asked. ~The part where you're risking the lives of almost all the people I love, or the part where you knew you were going to and fucked me anyway?

Oh, look at the words lining up, after all.

Ash clasped zheir hands together and walked mutely beside Hazel before finally signing, ~The latter. I am sorry. It had been a very long time since I had taken anything for myself.

Hazel shook his head.

Ash touched his arm. ~Please. Still awful and selfish, I know. But I need you to know it wasn't a ploy.

Holly caught Ash by the elbow. 'Let's play a game where we don't act like our victim is hurting our feelings, shall we?' he said. 'Stop trying to make my friend feel guilty and go walk with your friend, Cristati.'

'Holly, I'm fine,' Hazel said, though not with any great conviction.

Ash tugged zhemself loose from Holly and caught up with Izidore, carefully coming up on the side furthest from the scuttling Mancy pet. Izidore took zheir hand and tucked it under zheir own arm, first giving that comforting little squeeze that seemed habitual between them.

Inside the atelier, Albemarle was wrapped in zheir weighted blanket and restlessly sorting wires and springs and cogs.

'Forget about it, dear,' Kito was saying. 'Don't bother yourself.'

'I could hear it.' Albemarle sounded distressed. 'What was it? Why won't you tell me?'

From zheir tone and zheir dazed expression, the purposeless flex of zheir hands over zheir favourite materials, it was catatonia zhey were sliding into, not paroxysm. Kito might even have been hoping for it, because it would effectively and safely remove Albemarle until all the unpleasantness was over, no matter the direction of the resolution of the unpleasantness.

'Right,' Evelyn said, after a long assessing look at Haven's Mancer. 'I'm going to see if I can't pry loose a few extra stronghold guards to reinforce the security of the atelier. Izidore, draw out that design and neutralise your pet. Ash, help zhem and do whatever else you need to do here, then get out the postern gate.'

If she had misgivings about Ash's plan, Ash's chances of paying back Lady Fairhaven's trust, she didn't betray them.

Ash's collar said, 'Cristati Mancer guards will more than likely be waiting by the gate for exactly that possibility. They may use the opportunity to force their way in and try for Izidore. They may have Mancy weapons.'

Izidore piped up. 'Water level equalises across connected vessels.' That one was particularly obscure. Zhey explained, ~I drained as many as I could, Ash. They won't have projectiles, anyway.

Evelyn was silent. Hazel thought she might have been wondering just how conniving Ash was, that zheir previous Mancer Guard would be anticipating that zhey'd abandon zheir new stronghold to its fate.

Eventually she said, 'Hazel will escort you out. Hazel, take a couple of the others.' Her voice gentled. 'You understand that you don't go through the gate with Ash, yes? Zhey're walking right into the arms of the Cristati Mancer Guard, they'll kill any Havens with zhem.'

'A-yah,' Hazel said. 'Though…'

'Nah,' Holly said. He waved to Evelyn, who nodded and marched off to chase down Valerian, satisfied that her sibling would handle Hazel. 'Love, don't even think it. I won't let you.'

Hazel shoved his hands through his hair. He was feeling managed, and he hated it, and he hated that Holly, their captain, felt he had to devote thought to it right now, too.

Taking a breath, forcing calm, he addressed the two Mancers. '~Ash, I'm going to fetch you a change of clothes. Izidore, are you comfortable in the robes or do you want fresh clothes too?'

'By the lost relics of my ancestors, stop being nice to them.'

'For fuck's sake, Holly, just let me do my fucking job!'

After a beat of shocked silence across the whole atelier—Hazel never raised his voice—he saw, from the corner of his eye, Ash duck zheir head, covering zheir face with one hand.

A-yah, he thought, you *did that, you shit.*

He immediately reproached himself. He did it himself. His reactions were under his own control, not Ash's.

Holly said, 'I see. You're just going to shout at me instead of the person you're actually angry with.'

'Like you do all the time, mate?' Morano asked mildly.

'A-yah,' Hazel said, hand worrying at his hair. 'That's how we're playing it.'

Holly came to him, caught his hands, stepped in close. 'My love, I understand you're having a hard day, but you're not the only one, yes?'

Hazel nodded, thoroughly ashamed. Holly smiled and chuffed his arms. 'I *do* do it all the time, love, Morano's not wrong. I hate it when other people aren't wrong.'

He sent a narrow-eyed look past Hazel at the offending party.

'I'm…' Morano said. 'I'm going to the kitchen to get some trays of food. Breakfast was a while ago. Some of us didn't even get breakfast. Want to help, Titus?'

Titus went with him, and Nightingale breathlessly said, 'I'll fetch some changes of clothes,' and hurried out after them.

That left Kito and First Jerome helping Albemarle breathe, and Second Jerome showing Izidore to a workbench. He laid out loose amatl and a couple of pens, and Izidore began to sketch. Zheir Mancy pet squatted at zheir feet under the table, idly shuffling a few of its legs in turn. The scratch of the pen and the chittering of the metal points along the stone floor were the only sounds.

'I'm going to pull rank on you now,' Holly said to Hazel, who once again mutely nodded. 'Lieutenant Hazlemere, assist Second Jerome with Izidore. I'll be helping Silverthorne. And you can shut it,' he added over Hazel's shoulder. 'I'll call you by any name I like and you'll be glad it's not more accurate.'

'Maybe I should work with Ash,' Second Jerome said.

'Nah,' Holly said. 'We're good here, aren't we, Silverthorne?'

Hazel joined Second Jerome and Izidore. The young Mancer was a fast sketcher and had already produced a couple of different schematics of the same design, showing different perspectives and cutaways of the insides, all springs and cogs, pistons and pipes.

While pretending he wasn't, Hazel watched Ash rummaging through a drawer, Holly leaning idly nearby. Zhey pulled out the project zhey and Albemarle had completed together after the moat project was done, the small lever-like tool zhey'd chosen when zhey couldn't do the far-scry mirror.

The two Mancers had finished it, and Albemarle had tossed it into a drawer without either of them ever mentioning what it was meant to do or what it might be made to do. For all that the materials had included wire and oilcloth and cogs, it looked mostly like a small crowbar.

'I think Izidore likes the insect theme,' Second Jerome said, tapping one of the sketches.

Hazel turned back to the workbench and rotated one of the papers his way. 'What's the scale on this?'

A flash of Mancy made him, and everyone bar Albemarle, look up. Ash was shaking zheir left hand, lever in zheir right. The silver cuff fell to the ground at zheir feet. Zhey quickly tugged zheir sleeves down and pulled on each end of the little lever. It extended and fattened. Zhey set one end of this new, stronger version of the lever under the edge of the collar about zheir neck.

Then zhey went still, staring straight ahead, hand tight around the lever. Zhey'd gone blank in a way that would have made Hazel go to zhem, if things had been different. He looked back at Izidore's sketches.

Izidore squatted down and hummed at zheir pet. It drew its legs in and settled to the floor with a hiss from its inner workings.

'Sleep closes thine eyes but morning inevitably dawns,' Izidore warned them.

'Let's be quick, then,' Second Jerome said agreeably. He and Hazel hoisted it up onto the workbench.

Izidore turned zheir pet onto its back and pulled a Mancy tool like a screwdriver from zheir robe. The carapace and underside appeared to be a single smooth half-dome except where the legs came out, but Izidore poked gently and hidden panels slid open, responding to the low hum of the Mancy tool.

From the look of the design to inexpert eyes, Izidore had been very careful to make sure the Cristatis couldn't easily destroy this thing even when it was made temporarily dormant. It couldn't even be taken away from zhem, lest it wake up and come searching like it had from the top floor of Haven: Hazel bet it would batter its way through any locked door between it and Izidore.

'Clever,' he murmured, upon that realisation.

Izidore gave him a pleased smile. Zhey patted Hazel's arm and said soothingly, 'We're born without skin and the protective shell we grow is not always in the best pattern. We can grow a new pattern.'

'A-yah,' Hazel said, sighing.

Ash walked over to Izidore and caught zheir wrist, dislodging zhem from zheir task and making zhem drop zheir screwdriver.

'The purple is showing through where the gold is cracking,' Izidore murmured, making [rude] with zheir free hand, knuckles to cheek.

Ash ignored Izidore's chastening. Zhey were still wearing the collar, and had made the lever small again. For a moment, Hazel thought zhey hadn't been able to dislodge the collar, but then he understood—if Ash's mother had refused to let zhem learn Trade, she certainly had not learned any signs herself. As much as zhey must want it off, Ash would need the collar's voice to play out zheir bluff.

Ash hooked the lever under the silver cuff on Izidore's wrist. With a twisting motion that flashed another burst of Mancy through the copperlit atelier, zhey split the band and pushed it off Izidore's wrist. It fell to the ground, jingling into two pieces.

Izidore rubbed at the skin where the cuff had been clamped. It was red, sore-looking. 'The fire burns hotter the further one gets from the hearth.'

Ash tapped the pet's underside. ~Attention. Are you changing the trigger, or turning it off completely?

'The mouse is not sensible, if it assumes the cat cannot catch it.'

~But what trigger can there be, that will not risk the Havens?

Izidore turned. 'Albemarle? The candles' flames are pale in the glory of the sun's rays.'

'Good idea,' Kito said. 'Zhey need something to keep zhem occupied. The Cristati Mancers need some help, Albemarle.'

She briskly herded the fretting Mancer over to the other two, positioning zhem on the opposite side of the workbench. Ash quickly slipped the lever into zheir pocket, perhaps concerned Albemarle would demand zheir project back.

Izidore folded zheir hands together, and with complete lucidity explained, 'My pet is triggered to defend me if it hears a sword being drawn. We need a different trigger, but one that will only be tripped by the Cristatis.'

Albemarle said, 'You cannot sing it a song.'

It wasn't a question; zhey were giving the other Mancers the courtesy of assuming the solution was too obvious for them not to have thought of it. Zhey already sounded calmer. Zheir gaze was fixed on the opened underside of the pet, ticking over all the elements of its inner design.

'I can, but there must also be an automatic trigger, for there will be no time to sing a song if a Mancer guard is trying to kill us.'

Albemarle blinked once, as slowly as a lizard. 'My Mancer guards would never try to kill me.'

~How very fucking lovely for you, Ash signed.

Without looking, Izidore reached over and pushed zheir hands down, out of sight below the benchtop.

Morano and Titus returned with trays of food then, and jugs of clean rainwater, followed shortly by Nightingale and a few seamsters carrying armfuls of clothes, which they dumped on a workbench before scurrying out. Ash collected zheir usual outfit, and slunk to the other side of the atelier to change. Izidore tapped the tips of zheir fingers together and looked delightedly through the choices. Zhey liked layers when zhey weren't being forced into Mancer robes, it seemed, and took various jerkins and undershirts and petticoats and pantaloons and skirts and overskirts over to Ash. Everyone turned their backs while the two Mancers dressed, except Albemarle, who was too busy fixating on the pet to even notice.

For all that the rest of the stronghold must be preparing for the impeding assault, the Mancer atelier settled into an odd serenity. The three Mancers clustered about the pet's carapace, poking at it and bickering about how to redesign its trigger. Every now and again, Izidore would hum the dormancy song, keeping zheir pet asleep.

The Mancer guards ate, and Morano and Titus slid plates onto the active workbench too, so that the Mancers absently picked at the food in between their discussions. Holly paced about, into the antechamber and back again, until Albemarle lifted zheir head and gave him a cold stare.

'Fine,' he said, and flounced over to stand with Hazel.

Hazel put his arm around him. Holly before a fight was a nightmare of anticipatory energy; not all his tension was anger at Ash on Hazel's behalf. Holly eyed him speculatively; Hazel shook his head. No, he would not be taking Holly somewhere private to help him take the edge off.

Albemarle turned back to the Mancy. 'It can be made to respond to the shade of green the Cristati Mancer Guard wears?'

'It cannot see, Albemarle,' Izidore said patiently to this latest suggestion. Zhey looked less imposing in zheir scarecrow layers, but far more comfortable. 'It navigates by feel. It responds to sound.'

~Vibrations.

'To patterns of vibrations.'

Albemarle went still for a time, before stirring to say, 'Your initial premise is based on outdated information and is not correct. You do not need an automatic trigger because you will have time while the Havens hold off the Cristatis. It will need to be a short, distinctive sound for brevity and for Ash. Can you both whistle?'

They both could, it seemed, and the three Mancers turned to designing the new trigger into the pet, making short trills as Albemarle and Izidore decided on the melody of the two-note whistle and taught it to Ash, zheir hand on Izidore's throat, repeating the notes until the other two were satisfied.

'How are you going to make sure it only attacks Cristati once activated, though?' Second Jerome asked.

The Mancers paused. They had all plainly gotten lost in the design and forgotten that this was a criterion. The Haven Mancer Guard would be with Izidore, unless zhey used the pet only as a last resort if the Cristatis broke down the atelier door. Even then, zhey'd have Albemarle to think of. The pet could not be allowed to attack too indiscriminately.

'The Havens can whistle a safety tune,' Albemarle said.

'The Cristati will notice and learn it,' Izidore said.

'Also, a bit hard to fight and whistle in tune,' Morano said, from where he leant against the far workbench, finishing his bowl of noodles. 'I imagine it better be in tune.'

'I can't whistle at all,' First Jerome added.

Albemarle tapped the workbench with each forefinger. It made a dull pitter-patter sound, rhythmic as footsteps. 'The pet responds to vibrations. Let it attack a particular set of vibrations, then.'

'Like the vibrations when every Cristati shouts "you little fucker" the moment they spot Ash?' Holly asked. He flashed a vicious smile. 'Oh, wait. I don't think that phrase is unique to Cristati anymore.'

Ash had been scrupulously watching Holly's lips, looking for a real suggestion just like the other Mancers. Hazel expected another bout of sarcasm in response to Holly's nastiness, but Ash merely looked down at the workbench, smiling a small, sad smile and shrugging.

It tilted Hazel, balanced precariously atop his pile of emotions, toward anger; if anyone had the right to be looking sad and hurt, it was him. But he also tightened his arm around Holly's shoulder, tight enough that Holly whacked him lightly and extricated himself.

Albemarle blinked at Holly without smiling. 'Their boots thump, when they move.'

'All our boots do that, Albemarle!' Nightingale blurted. '*Your* boots do that!'

'You would all have to stand still, then, if it is triggered,' Izidore said. 'Cristati will notice that, too, eventually, but in the short term, they will be trying too hard to get away from it. Vibrations.'

~The short term may be all it takes.

Izidore nodded to Ash for that grim wisdom.

'First Jerome can't whistle, I can't stand still,' Holly pointed out.

Indeed, as soon as he'd escaped Hazel's hold, he'd started swooping from one side of the atelier to the other, making sure only to stay out of Albemarle's sightline this time.

'But at least it will no longer be triggered by the sound of a sword being pulled,' Hazel said quickly, before Kito could point out the obvious: if the Mancers needed to whistle the pet into action, Holly—all of them— would more than likely already be dead. Albemarle, on the other hand, was adept at staying still.

The Mancers set to work again, Izidore singing zheir Mancy, zheir eerie voice rising a cappella into the mournful sob of the violin, as Albemarle made minute adjustments with the borrowed screwdriver tool.

Albemarle's large, steady hands paused. 'Yes, it is very lovely,' zhey said. Zhey looked up from the work, turning zheir meticulous focus onto Ash. 'It must have been dreadful for you.'

It had been long minutes since zhey'd just as gravely informed Ash that zheir Mancer Guard would never kill zhem and Ash had made zheir sarcastic riposte. Hazel had always assumed Albemarle'd picked up at least a little Trade. Whether zhey had only just now deciphered the signing, or finally had time to think about it, or whether the implication had taken this long to percolate through zhem and turn into sympathy, he couldn't guess.

Albemarle bent back over the pet's workings, prodding at some complicated cog arrangement under Izidore's fingers. Ash stood by as if still intent as well, but after a few moments, zhey stepped back. Zheir luminous grey-green eyes were wide, wet.

Zhey gave a sharp nod to no one in particular, then turned on zheir heel and walked out of the atelier.

Hazel knew what this was. He'd seen it before, in grieving people. He'd seen it in Evelyn, when Lady Fairhaven had been told the Holyoakes' circumstances by some well-meaning retainer, and come to welcome them to Haven personally, a kindly gesture. She'd only just finished the death rituals for her own father.

Evelyn had been holding the pieces of herself and Holly tight for months without cease by then, and the unexpected featherweight of sympathy broke her—much to Lady Fairhaven's dismay and devoted efforts to help her pull herself back together.

Holly blocked Hazel from following Ash before he even knew he was moving. His friend pressed in close, hands over his wrists, holding him still.

He spoke in Hazel's ear. 'I don't want to see you hurt more than you already are, love. Let one of the others go after zhem.'

Hazel bowed his head and stood in Holly's arms while he tried to work out how to persuade him that it would hurt more to not go after zhem.

'Holly,' he said. He wrapped his arms around his friend, hugging him tight. 'Hols, love, I can't help but think this is not so much about Ash hurting me as about you hurting me, all those years ago.'

Holly straightened. He looked both indignant and chagrined. 'Well, how very dare you peel back my layers like that,' he said, but lightly. 'They're there for a *reason*, Hazel darling.'

'A-yah, I'm about to do it again. I'm sorry I hurt you, too, and I'm sorry I never acknowledged that I did.' Since Holly then suffered a rare moment of speechlessness, Hazel pressed his advantage. 'I know you hate to see me hurt again. You were like this with Miriam, too. I got over you, you know, and her, and I'll get over Ash. But I need to do it my way. I don't need protecting. I need—I need to fix something. Let me fix this.'

He waved at the door. Holly sighed at the ceiling and then kissed Hazel, stepped back and flicked his fingers for him to go.

Hazel had feared Ash would be halfway to the postern gate by now, but zhey were standing in the middle of the antechamber, very still, zheir back to the atelier door. Zhey seemed to be staring at the reading spot Hazel had set up for zhem.

Even as Hazel came through the doorway, zhey took two jerky steps, picked up Albemarle's pot with its rare red fern, and hurled it with all zheir strength at the opposite wall.

The pot shattered like a crash-bomb, shards and soil and ragged fronds flying everywhere. Hazel, flinching, felt the rush of response behind him, and waved the others back. When Ash turned around, it was still just Hazel standing there. He shut the atelier door.

Ash looked momentarily shocked to see him, before zhey smoothed zheir face into unreadable blankness. Zhey hadn't been expecting anyone to come after zhem. Izidore was zheir only ally, and zhey were lost to Mancy.

'~For future reference,' Hazel said, '~smashing things makes a really loud noise, if you hadn't realised.'

Ash made a helpless little huff, half a laugh, half a sob. Just a day ago, zhey might have given Hazel a playfully rude gesture for the patronisation.

Zhey wiped at zheir cheeks, zheir eyes. ~I need to go out to the postern now, so you can lower the moat for my egress before the attack begins.

Hazel waited, watching Ash's face. Zheir expression shifted from blank, to stubbornly blank, to distressed under his silent regard. Zhey started to sign like a whirlwind.

~Albemarle will die in a place like Cristati. Haven will fall, every one of you will die defending zhem, and they'll take zhem back to Stronghold Cristati and zhey'll either die or the Mancer Guard will kill zhem.

'~That's…dire,' Hazel said. '~Let's assume Haven will stand, instead.'

~What have I done? Ash was rocking on zheir heels suddenly. ~What have I done, Hazel, what have I done?

Zhey locked zheir trembling fingers together. Zhey were trembling all over. Hazel wanted to cross the space between them, hold zhem, soothe zhem, forgive zhem. He wanted to walk back into the atelier and lock the door behind him and let Ash drown in zheir guilt.

He did neither. '~Exactly what you set out to do. And now you have to keep right on doing it. It's a little late to be squeamish.'

Ash nodded, wiping frantically at zheir face again. ~I really did want to leave, after the Cristati found me, after he killed that guard—'

'~Her name was S-H-A-O. Shao.'

~I told myself I had to keep to the plan. But I just took the excuse to stay in the warmth and the sweet.

Head bowed, Ash pressed zheir knuckles against zheir mouth. The movement made zheir embroidered sleeves fall back further, exposing zheir tattoo on one wrist, and the skin the silver cuff had clasped on the other.

Zhey fought and fought and fought for calm, and then finally, the swoop of zheir hands was tranquil as zhey signed, ~I'll go out the gate now, Hazel.

Hazel pointed, an abortive gesture. He made a strenuous effort to keep his voice even, even though Ash couldn't hear it. '~When Izidore said the fire burned hotter the further from the hearth…'

Izidore's wrist had been reddened, as if zheir cuff was too tight. Ash's wrist, visible since zheir sleeves had ridden up, was an angry, violent scarlet, with blisters and weeping and soughing skin all the way around, as if the touch of the cuff had scalded worse than hot steam, worse than acid.

Ash breathed out a concussive puff of air. Zhey tugged zheir sleeves back over zheir wrists. ~Lock device. The further one gets from the key, the more it hurts. They made us create it from Inigo's design. The range on mine was set quite a bit tighter than Izidore's.

Zhey glanced down, gently touching the cloth covering the abused wrist. Hazel could see, now he knew to look for it, dark spots marring the snowy linen and silver threads where blood and pus had rubbed onto the embroidered material and soaked through.

Ash added, blank-faced, ~I taught them how to treat me.

Hazel thought of Ash's growing tension and unexpected aggression as they'd descended through the stronghold. How much pain the cuff must have been causing zhem every step zhey took further from Captain Tassone or zheir mother, whichever of the sadistic Cristati fucks held the key. How desperate zhey must have been to get to the lever tool in the atelier. How patiently, then, really, zhey had stood for Evelyn's questions.

He was, suddenly, standing beside Ash, wrapping an arm around zheir shoulders, taking zheir hand so he could see the wrist. '~We better see to this before we go.'

Ash returned compliantly into the atelier. Despite the askance glances from the other Mancer guards and the exasperated eyeroll from Holly, Hazel did not remove his arm from zheir shoulders. He guided zhem across the room to the cupboard holding a basket stocked with Miriam's burn salve and other simple medical supplies. He set the basket on the nearest workbench. It was where the two Mancers had changed clothes, leaving their Mancer robes draped on the bench. Hazel cut strips from the abandoned robes and soaked them in a rainwater jug.

In between washing the wounds, Ash hissing through zheir teeth at the first touch of the cloth but otherwise grimly still and silent, he asked, '~Why did you try to hide this? Can't bluff your mother if you're coming on feverish from a nasty infection.'

That was ridiculous; it'd take days for a fever to set in. That was just his natural concern making itself known because it had nowhere else to go.

Ash signed in very small motions, like a whisper, ~If you'd seen it and not cared, I couldn't have borne it.

Holly had walked up behind Hazel. 'Really digging in on that line, aren't you, Silverthorne?' he said. Nevertheless, he examined the injuries and said to Hazel, 'We should call in Miriam, probably.'

Ash shook zheir head, fisted the hand they were both staring at. ~No time now.

'This is done,' Izidore announced. Zhey dropped back into the speech patterns zhey used when not intent on Mancy. 'Even the youngest of dragons will stretch its wings and roar when the knight comes.'

Predictably, Kito said, 'I'll dance with it,' and Holly shot across the room to join in.

Hazel paid a great deal of attention to laying out the disinfectant solution, the salve, the clean bandages. He said, '~Of course I care. You're my Mancer.'

Ash set the back of zheir hand on the table, offering the injured wrist again. Zheir eyes were downcast, zheir expression determinedly neutral. Zheir other hand signed, [of course], a double-shake of the index and middle fingers pressed tight together.

Izidore said, 'Stand still,' and whistled the notes.

Hazel looked over his shoulder to see the pet rise up on its spindly legs. Kito stamped and it skittered in a circle and homed in on her, fast. She dodged it and Holly tapped a foot on the floor to flick its attention his way.

'Ooh, I like this for the spar,' he said as he skipped backward, only just quick enough to avoid a slash of one of its limbs. It came on, inexorably following the light bounce of footsteps.

Kito drew her trishuls. 'Hoi, boy, give it back.' She hopped up and down, trying to make her vibrations outdo Holly's.

The Mancy pet scuttled at her, but halfway, it stopped and once again rotated with minute adjustments of its limbs so it appeared to be facing Second Jerome, in so far as a thing without a face could face anything. Second Jerome's eyes widened. He eased his Mancy leg off the floor, balancing on his meat one.

They were all still. The pet shifted its carapace back and forth, like a dog sniffing the air. Holly tapped his toes on the floor, and it spun and jittered at him. He crouched, looking like he was planning to close in and make a fight of it. He and Kito pulled disappointed faces when Izidore whistled again, different notes, and zheir pet immediately folded its legs and settled.

'I want it on record that I don't like it for the spar,' Morano said.

Hazel turned back to tending Ash's wrist. Ash stayed subdued as he salved and dressed it, murmuring his people's traditional incantation. When he was done, zhey pulled aside, fossicking through zheir discarded robe. Zhey collected zheir daggers, and the lever tool.

Hazel nodded to the lever. '~Did you have a Mancy project like this yourself, back in Cristati?'

Ash shook zheir head.

'~But you had to get a lock cuff off to escape then, too, didn't you?' He thought of the abrasions around Ash's neck when zhey'd first arrived. '~And you got a collar off, too.'

The Mancer sighed, deeply. Then, very deliberately, zhey looked Hazel in the eye and told him, ~It took me six months to persuade Captain Olivette that I was so in love with him that he could trust me and have more fun if he removed the cuff and collar while he fucked me. Once he was asleep, I put a dagger in his heart and escaped out his window. No bars on the Mancer Guard's windows.

Zhey spread both palms at him in a gesture both angry and ashamed. ~Satisfied, Hazel? Tell me I did what I had to do.

~Six months, Hazel echoed stupidly.

His thoughts were tangled rat tails, twining together in pity and anger: he mused on how long those months must have felt, waiting on someone else's whim to unlock the shackles, even as he also thought, *Well, fuck, didn't you hone your technique this time around.*

After a moment, he said, not really knowing what he was saying, '~At least you didn't have to target an officer holding keys here. You could just…' *Aim straight for the weakest of us.*

~Enjoy myself, Ash signed, with a savage glint in zheir eye that dared him to say different.

Olivette had been the bedmate who hadn't cared for Ash's pleasure. The bedmate who had seen Ash's need for touch and taken advantage of it…while Ash was taking ruthless advantage of him in turn. And why else would zhey have ever turned to a Mancer guard when fond and doting Izidore existed? Ash did not flinch to fuck for ulterior motives, for sure.

'A-yah,' he said aloud to Ash and to all his useless thoughts.

They were on dangerous ground. He shoved a hand through his hair, breathed, decided on a change of subject. He nodded to the lever as Ash dropped it into zheir pocket. '~I thought that was going to be a weapon that would help Haven? You told me as much.'

Ash flicked another fleeting glance his way, and away. ~Anything that helps me at this point will help Haven.

Hazel shook his head, more resigned to than surprised by the further deception.

'What did you just say?'

Albemarle. Hazel shut his eyes and said, 'Shit.'

'A weapon? Ash makes *weapons*? And you all knew this.' Albemarle pointed wildly at Kito. 'That's what the noise was, a bricolaged copperlit. A *weapon*. You all knew and you made me make weapons.'

'Technically, no to that last question,' Holly said. 'You made a lever that turns into a bigger lever.'

Albemarle's shoulders were heaving. Kito said, 'Hmmm, not the time for levity, boy. Albemarle dear, take some slow breaths for me.'

'Show me.' Zhey tore a copperlit from the wall and pitched it at Ash's head. Ash instinctively raised zheir hands to catch it before wisely ducking instead. It smashed hard into the opposite wall. 'Show me!'

'Probably don't want to arm you, at this stage,' Second Jerome said.

Haven's Mancer stamped zheir foot and struck the workbench with both fists. 'You pack of *hypocrites*.' Zheir voice was rising. 'You're all hating Ash for lying to you and you did exactly the same thing to me.'

Hazel winced; Albemarle, even spiralling into paroxysm, was not precisely wrong.

'You're meant to protect me and you cozen me and lie to me and force me to your schedule—'

Morano made the cardinal error of being drawn into arguing. 'That schedule helps you!'

'It helps *you*,' Albemarle roared.

Holly murmured to Hazel, 'Me and Kito'll deal with this. You have to get Ash out of the stronghold. Take the Jeromes with you in case of trouble at the postern.' He flicked a finger for Morano's attention. 'You run Izidore's design up to Evie and Lord Vee so they can show it to the militia commanders.'

Morano, looking quite relieved, grabbed the design and headed for the door, muttering, 'What *is* the scale on this?' as he went.

As Holly and Kito closed in on Albemarle, the Jeromes followed Hazel and Ash out to the antechamber.

Here, Ash baulked. ~I will go alone. I do not need you.

Hazel turned to the Jeromes. 'Clear the way.' Once they'd gone on ahead, he said to Ash, '~You do. The guards on the postern gate aren't going to open it on your say-so. And I won't have you threatening them to try and force them to do it. We've had enough of that.'

Ash's mouth took on that stubborn line. ~I don't want you with me.

'~Shouldn't have collected yourself a conscientious Mancer guard, then.'

Ash glared at him. Zhey probably only didn't stamp zheir foot like Albemarle just had because it was beneath the dignity of a fucking Cristati lord.

Then zheir shoulders slumped. ~That's why you're helping me. Because you were trained at the academy to help the stronghold's Mancer in all circumstances.

'~Is there meant to be a different reason I'm helping you?'

Ash looked down, hunching as zheir shoulders bowed even further. ~I want you to forgive me for what I've done to Haven, to Albemarle, to all of you. But not because I'm a Mancer and you assume I can't do any better. I want— I want you to understand that I chose to do it and, and forgive me for it anyway because, because…

'~Because you deserve to be forgiven? Not because I've been trained to forgive you whether you deserve it or not?'

~Yes! Yes, that's exactly it, Hazel.

So Ash wanted to stick zheir elegantly deft fingers into the tangled knot inside Hazel's chest, did zhey? '~You know what you've done to Haven and you'd really like to hear my current feelings about it?'

He'd be quite interested to hear his current feelings about it, too, to be fair.

Ash covered zheir eyes. Then, face averted, zhey made the negatory fist. ~It appears I am not brave enough for that right now, no.

Hazel pushed his hands into zheir sightline and briskly snapped out, '~Then how about you have a wee bit of gratitude that your oh-so-fuck-ing-awful academy-trained Mancer guard can't stop thinking of you as his Mancer, and take the fucking gift that that is, and let's go fix this.'

Zheir gaze flashed up to his. ~I'll fix it. I—

The copperlits in the antechamber flickered, a blink off and then on again.

They both glanced up instinctively, and Hazel leapt to the door, fearing the worst for Albemarle. Inside the atelier, Albemarle was standing frozen, looking at the ceiling on the western edge of the room. Izidore, beside zhem, was looking there too, blank-faced. The copperlits did the split-second blink again, and both Mancers blinked in unison. The next time, Hazel became aware of a faint vibration under his feet in time to the flickers of the Mancers and the Mancy.

The Mancer guards were looking at each other in silent query when Ash tapped on Hazel's back. He turned to look at zhem.

~The assault has begun. Izidore's creation is hitting Albemarle's moat.

The copperlits and the Mancers blinked again as their Mancies clashed.

Ash signed, ~It won't hold. I *will* fix this, Hazel.

Zhey ran. Hazel ran after zhem.

~Twenty-Seven~

Collecting the Jeromes, they went through the undercroft's south door and around to the central courtyard. Hazel only became aware the others had followed when he stopped dead and discovered Holly at his shoulder.

Holly had wrapped his braids in his favourite silk cloth. He was expecting the hand-to-hand to start either soon or without warning, then.

'Oh, *that's* the scale on that,' he said.

Like Hazel and Ash, he was looking up. So were the other Mancer guards. So were Albemarle and Izidore, zheir pet at docile heel; those two should have stayed locked in the atelier but had chased Ash anyway just like Hazel had. So were the stronghold guards assigned to the outside defence. So were the militia soldiers, who couldn't take their places on the walls because Albemarle's moat shimmered up from the inner wall and blocked access to the top of the ramparts. So were Evelyn and Lord Valerian, and Morano, still holding the design sketch made moot by the actual project in the metallic flesh.

'A-yah, Izidore likes the insects,' Second Jerome muttered.

On paper, Izidore's design had struck Hazel's inexpert eye as flea-like, but the gigantic Mancy creation looming over the wall resembled more a locust in its swivelling head, gleaming body and great mandibles. Its coppery carapace was longer than it was wide; unlike Izidore's dog-sized arachnid pet, the carapace was not one smooth piece, but made of tight latticework. At first glance, it seemed taller than Haven's walls, but Hazel realised from the way its front legs were hooked over the parapet that it must be clinging to the outer wall.

With mechanical rhythm, it struck Albemarle's Mancy barrier with its spiked head, trying to batter its way through a solid mist that rippled like water but repelled like rock. For all the violence of the motion, it was near-silent, since the collision of Mancy locust with Mancy moat made no sound. The only noise was the scrape of metal on stone as the locust adjusted its grip. Dark shadows, close by its point of attack but independent of it, were moving about on top of the rampart, obscured by the moat's thick shine.

Hazel heard a melody that was both familiar and strange, and familiar in its strangeness. He tore his gaze from the Mancy insect, and saw that Ash had both hands laid on one of Albemarle's wall panels, directly under where Izidore's locust rammed its head against the mist moat. Zhey were humming Albemarle's panel song, except, of course, it was twisting as zheir own Mancy interfered.

Red light flashed under Ash's hands, and it geysered up, crimson through the white like ink through water, like fresh blood over stone. The next time the locust struck the moat, it sizzled and steamed. The locust swivelled its head and fell back, the hot reek of scorched metal suddenly strong in the air.

Ash looked left and right and an expression of extreme frustration crossed zheir face. Only the narrow section above the panel zhey'd sung zheir Mancy into had transformed from shield to weapon. Zhey'd expected, or at least hoped, that zheir taboo bricolage would flow through the entire ring of panels installed along the inner wall.

The locust had already shifted away from the change, skittering along the wall. It paused at the gateway, but the thick oak must have been more permeable to Albemarle's moat than the stone of the walls, because the locust explored the gates with an articulated leg and then crawled back the other way, rushing across the red section of moat to follow the curve of the wall south.

Pacing along below it, Ash leant on another panel, already humming.

'Albemarle, calm!' Kito cried.

Heedless, Albemarle roared up to Ash and ripped zheir hands loose from the panel, Ash's face contorting with pain as Albemarle's fingers tightened on zheir damaged wrist.

'No weapons,' zhey bellowed. 'How dare you?'

Zhey shoved Ash hard enough to put zhem on the ground and stomped to the bricolaged panel. Zhey'd performed a sleight of hand when zhey'd pushed Ash over—zhey now held the Mancy lever. Albemarle must have heard the quiet hum of zheir own Mancy emanating from Ash's pocket, and snatched it back on possessive instinct.

In almost a single coordinated motion, Albemarle expanded the lever, inserted it into the panel's decorative fretwork, and pried the despised bricolaged Mancy out of zheir moat. It fell off the wall in two pieces.

Like a curtain being drawn open on a stage, the misty screen of the Mancy moat winked out in a wave rushing both directions along the wall.

'Whoops,' whispered First Jerome.

The dark shadows they'd glimpsed through the mist turned out to be Mancy creations about the size of cats, as numerous and fast as the cockroaches Izidore must have drawn inspiration from. Now the moat was down, they came over in a great undulation of scuttering limbs and clicking jaws. Some waved longer limbs, tentacles.

They swept off the wall and crashed upon the defenders, who quickly found that their swords were useless against hard carapaces and their leather gloves and linen armour were useless against strong and biting mandibles. Shouts of alarm and pain rose from all about the courtyard.

Meanwhile, the locust darted back the other way, settled on top of the gates, and began to rip great chunks out of the hardened oak with its mandibles.

'I may have overreacted,' Albemarle said in zheir slow, deep voice, standing stock still in the centre of the sudden eruption of chaos.

Hazel pulled Ash to zheir feet, and Nightingale guided Izidore over. The rest of the Mancer Guard, tugging on their pliable leather gloves—except for First Jerome, who wore them habitually—marshalled around the three Mancers and drew their swords. Evelyn joined them, sword drawn too, her free hand around Lord Valerian's elbow.

The lord was looking overwhelmed, but he was also carrying his wood-chopping hatchet, its long handle slid through his belt, its head encased in a leather sheath. Lady Fairhaven's senior vassal should have been up with the rest of the purple, safely out of the way, and had evidently elected to stay, armed.

Izidore caught one of the smaller Mancy roaches with deft expertise as it careened past. Zhey flipped it over and pointed to a seam along the underside. 'Stab here.'

Titus obeyed, and it cracked open and fell still. Lord Valerian grabbed the carcass and slipped out of the cordon, dodging his way across the hectic courtyard to the militia commanders. A moment after he'd reached them with his demonstrative cargo, the new instructions were bellowed out.

A contingent of soldiers managed to break free of the Mancy roaches, flipping and stabbing their way clear to the steps on either side of the gateway up onto the walls. They rushed the locust, striking it about the head with their swords. It scraped with its forelegs and threw them back.

Hazel glanced at Ash. The Mancer was raptly watching the locust shrug off the defenders and resume eating its way through the gates. He wondered if not being able to hear the shouts and clangs of the battle meant zhey were less scared. Then a cloud of dust and debris huffed over all of them and Ash flinched and turned zheir face away.

Hazel called himself an idiot. Ash was white about the lips and zheir eyes were wide and wild. Zheir shoulders heaved as zhey gasped for air. Zhey were terrified.

Zheir eyes met his. The stricken look did not leave zhem. ~Hazel, I will fix this.

Hazel took zheir arm, drawing zhem with him as the Mancer Guard began to fall back to the south door. Kito and Holly ranged ahead to kick and stab a clear path, the others closing in to make an even tighter ring about the Mancers.

Ash shook free of Hazel and caught Izidore's sleeve. Hazel eavesdropped as zhey signed, ~Did both my half-brothers come with my mother?'

~Marco is in command of the soldiers, of course. I never saw Paolo. But they wouldn't have let him near me even if he is here. They know he is sympathetic.

Ash nodded. Zhey pointed back at the locust. ~Did you create it exactly to its design? Exactly?

Izidore said, 'Exactly as designed, interior.' Zheir hands added some slow and uncertain signs that Hazel took a moment to interpret as, ~I skipped the digging legs. I thought it would be best if it couldn't burrow straight under the wall.

Again, Ash gave a small, set nod. Zhey grabbed Second Jerome by the back of zheir coat. ~Give me your Mancy leg.

The forward motion of the Mancer guards stuttered as Second Jerome fell out of his position, or was tugged out by Ash's insistence. 'Um, I sort of need it?'

Izidore tsked and tapped Ash on the arm. 'The fox raised by scorpions must learn it cannot sting amid the lions.'

Ash looked like zhey wanted to seethe before deciding not to waste the time. Gritting zheir teeth, zhey signed, ~Please, Second Jerome, may I borrow your Mancy leg for just a moment. I promise to return it.

Once Hazel had voiced the plea, Second Jerome looked around for Holly. Their captain had become a touch distracted chasing down the Mancy roaches; he and Kito had competing kill counts going. He looked at Hazel instead.

'Give it to zhem.'

Second Jerome loosened the straps and handed his leg over, giving it a last pat as he reluctantly released it. Morano positioned himself by his side to help his balance.

Ash started to crouch over the leg before shaking zheir head, straightening, and addressing Albemarle. ~Please, Albemarle, may we bricolage your design? Not a weapon. Not.

Izidore tapped Ash's shoulder, smiling zheir crooked smile. 'Ah, the fox can learn where the scorpions will not.'

Ash pulled a face and gave Izidore a little shove before looking back at Albemarle.

Albemarle slowly nodded. 'I saw,' zhey said, rumbling the words deep in zheir chest.

Zhey looked down at the lever zhey were still holding, that zhey had used to bring down the defence of Haven. Zhey nodded again and held the lever out to Ash.

Ash took it. Zhey and Izidore bent over the Mancy leg, prodding and adjusting with their respective tools. For all that Albemarle had given permission, zhey stood as far away as the cordon would allow, back turned, hands over zheir ears. Nightingale looked very much like she wanted to do the same.

Izidore was working quickly, but Ash kept pausing to sign at zhem, insistent sequences that Hazel couldn't make out past the two Mancers' hunched bodies. Izidore nodded and nodded again to whatever Ash was rattling off to zhem with scant regard for zheir lesser fluency.

Izidore clicked the panel shut. With barely a pause, still crouching low over the leg, zhey sang zheir own Mancy into it, that eerie thrum so reminiscent of a stringed instrument.

Albemarle's face screwed up tight as zhey fought zheir instinctive dislike of zheir changed project and the new song that went with it. 'Inefficient,' zhey muttered.

'This is done,' Izidore said.

Ash wrapped zheir arms about the leg and slid between First Jerome and Hazel's rear guard, heading back to the wall.

'~Hold up,' Hazel said, reaching for zhem. Exasperatingly, zhey jigged neatly past him.

'Get the other two to the atelier,' Hazel told the rest, and ran after Ash.

Ash nimbly threaded through clusters of soldiers and roaming Mancy roaches, but about halfway to the gates, the packs of roaches clotted too thickly to avoid. Ash stopped, tightened zheir hold, and smacked one palm against the leg's sole.

It shot up into the air, taking Ash with it.

Hazel grunted with surprise. He watched Ash arc through the air, clear the wall, and land on the back of the Mancy locust still tearing its way through the thick hardwood of the gates. Zhey slid sideways before bringing zhemself to a jolting stop with a fingerhold in the latticework of the carapace.

Zhey hung for an agonising moment before managing to draw zhemself to zheir knees. Keeping one hand locked into the latticework, zhey flung the Mancy leg back toward Hazel with more hope than accuracy. Then zhey started to crawl up the pitching back of the locust with the grim determination of a sailor crossing the tossing deck of a ship on a stormy sea.

Hazel turtled and stabbed a couple of roaches before he managed to retrieve the Mancy leg. He backed toward the other Mancer guards, who had not obeyed his injunction to go for the atelier. He should have been shepherding them away. He couldn't take his eyes off Ash's agonising struggle to clamber up the length of the Mancy locust, even as he handed Second Jerome his upgraded leg.

At length, Ash reached the top edge of the carapace, where the juncture between back and head formed a gap in the latticework. Hooking the fingers of one hand onto the edge, zhey drew one of zheir daggers with the other. After one glance into the gap to establish zheir target, zhey stabbed the blade forcefully down into the gap.

The locust continued to eat.

Ash pulled the dagger back out and laid it across zheir thighs. Head bowed, zhey stared fixedly into the gap even as zheir body rocked along with the lunging movements of the locust, hand and knees jammed into the lattice.

Izidore gasped. Zhey said, 'The heart is buried too deep for the touch of the lover's tongue to reach it.' Their hands echoed, ~Bad design. Bad design. Bad design.

On top of the carapace, Ash stirred. Zhey pulled out the Mancy lever, losing zheir dagger over the wall in the juggle. Barely sparing a glance after it, zhey extended the lever to its full length and plunged it downward in another confident jab.

The locust remained unaffected.

Ash grimaced. Zhey raised the lever to zheir face. Hazel couldn't hear it, but he guessed Ash was humming zheir Mancy, to see what it might turn the lever into.

Zhey fumbled along its side. A white light blazed at one end like a knife blade made of liquid metal. Ash recoiled dangerously from the sudden glare, then steadied enough to inspect it. Zhey nodded and began to cut into the carapace. The locust instantly reacted this time, rearing and lurching to toss Ash, clinging like a limpet, wildly back and forth. The modified lever flew from zheir hand and all the way across the courtyard. First Jerome swooped in to grab it, and threw it down again.

'White hot,' she said, shaking her hand. It was hot enough to burn even through her gloves.

Ash stared after the lost lever and slapped the carapace, looking, as far as Hazel could tell from this distance, enraged. The locust settled back to its work. The top of the gates were rent with splits, chunks of splintered wood tumbling out. So far, the panels on the inside were intact; the locust was actively targeting the wood and ignoring the copper.

Ash clung to the carapace, peering into the aborted cut, zheir second dagger in zheir free hand. Zhey reached in up to the shoulder, strain in every line of zheir face.

Hazel saw zhem shake zheir head, a small gesture meant only for zhemself, because Ash never presumed help from any other quarter.

He woke up.

'Atelier,' he shouted at the others, and started running for the stairs up the wall.

Ash needed a longer blade. He was fucking *holding* a longer blade.

'Zhey need a longer blade,' Holly said, suddenly lobbing up to Hazel's side. 'Stairs?'

Holly took the lefthand, Hazel the right.

Hazel ran along the top of the rampart and took a flying leap onto the back of the Mancy locust before he could think too hard about his general lack of Holly's sort of dramatic athleticism. He crabcrawled along, locking his gloved fingers into the lattice of the carapace as the locust lurched again.

The spasm of its forelegs batted Holly, racing in from the other set of steps, off the wall.

Hazel craned to see how badly he was injured, but couldn't find him in the frenetic anthill movement. Cursing steadily, he started climbing up the carapace again, feet scrabbling because his boots were too big for even the tips of the toes to slip into the lattice holes. The thin metal slats bit into the joints of his fingers each time he wedged them in, even through leather gloves thick enough protect him from sword nicks.

He reached Ash. Zhey had zheir eyes tight shut, lying flat and forcing zheir arm as deep as zhey could into the workings of the Mancy locust. The larger opening zhey'd started to make with the modified lever was not clean cut. The jagged metal sawed through zheir vest and bit into the meat of zheir shoulder as zhey forced zhemself to press harder.

Hazel nudged zhem. Zheir eyes snapped open and zhey flinched so hard zhey almost lost zheir hold. He steadied zhem, locking his arm about zhem as an anchor. He proffered his sword, sliding it across the carapace and not letting go until Ash had relinquished zheir dagger and wrapped zheir fingers about the sword's hilt.

Ash poked the sword down into the gap between head and carapace. Concentrating fiercely, zhey peered in, sighting along the blade, and then thrust, putting all zheir wiry strength into it.

Sparks flew. The locust's head jerked and swivelled all the way around, the mandibles brushing over Hazel's back where he lay protecting and securing Ash, his body the harness that held Ash firm to the carapace.

Ash, trusting to Hazel's hold, let go of the carapace and locked both hands around the hilt. Grimacing, zhey twisted. A sour grinding assailed Hazel's ears, and the locust convulsed under them, bucking like a wild horse.

It began to tip sideways off the top of the wall.

'Shit,' Hazel said in his eloquent way, and pressed down hard onto Ash, fingers manacled into the carapace as tight as he could.

The locust toppled off.

Hazel and Ash fell with it.

~Twenty-Eight~

H OLLY IS STRUCK BY THE LOCUST creature's flailing limbs and falls off the wall. By sheer luck, he hits the steps he ran up, but he hits them knee-first, and feels it pop. By the time he rolls to his feet and staggers back to the top of the wall, it's clear he's done himself some damage, and Hazel has fallen outside the stronghold into a scattering mass of Cristati troops, which almost immediately begin to regroup.

Holly limps down, spitting the pain out on every step. He finds a stronghold guard. 'Open the sally port.'

'No.' Valerian is there, suddenly, taking Holly's elbow, trying to take his weight.

'Get the fuck off me,' Holly says. 'I'm going after Hazel.'

'No,' Valerian says again. 'Gates stay closed,' he adds to the guard. 'Do your duty.'

That might have been addressed to either of them, but Holly takes it to heart because he discovers his Mancer Guard, and the Mancers, surrounding him.

'Why are they not in the atelier?' Holly snaps at Kito.

'Izidore refused,' she says.

Izidore is holding the lever Ash dropped. Holly saw it flash from the top of the wall, and saw First Jerome fling it aside when she tried to pick it up. It must have cooled off. Zheir pet is still squatting by zheir side, as close as if it's chained to zheir ankle.

'All rivers can be crossed, be it by ford or bridge,' zhey say soberly. ~I can repair the broken panel, if Albemarle will assist. We will raise the moat again.

Holly takes another look at the sally port. Hazel is already dead. If the fall hasn't killed him, Cristati certainly has.

He thumps his knee with his fist. The white-hot bolt of bright agony penetrating the deeper throb is better than the feeling in the rest of his body as he turns his back on the sally port.

'Mancers to the atelier,' he orders.

Izidore shakes zheir head. 'The onrushing water cannot be diverted unless the channels have been dug deep.' Zheir hands clarify, ~We can save Haven.

'That's not the covenant,' he tells zhem. 'That's not your job.'

Albemarle stirs. 'Then what is our job, Holly?' zhey ask slowly.

Holly looks at zhem in surprise. Albemarle says, 'If the stronghold protects the atelier, why does not the atelier protect the stronghold?'

'It's not the covenant,' Holly says blankly. He can barely think past the pain, but he rallies. 'You know the rules, Albemarle. Mancers in the atelier when the stronghold's under threat.'

In his distracted state, he has forgotten: like any other Mancer, Albemarle is not, in fact, a follower of rules. Albemarle is a follower of zheir own strong sense of justice, with which zheir Mancer Guard makes sure the rules align.

Albemarle says, 'You treat me like a child. You could have asked me for defensive projects at any time. You must have known this siege was coming and you let me make a *lever*.'

'Ash picked that project,' First Jerome points out.

'It's seeming pretty useful so far?' Second Jerome adds.

'My point holds,' Albemarle says. 'Ash knew the siege was coming, and zhey chose something useful within the narrow bounds allowed to zhem. I did not know the siege was coming, and I am in the middle of making something to keep pies warm. You have been illogical and not made use of your best resource.'

Kito has her hands on her hips. She's looking indignant. 'Albemarle, you would've had a paroxysm if we tried to direct your designs or tell you which project to create.'

'Once I was like that,' Albemarle says. 'I can grow and learn, like any other. You have spent many years teaching me so, and then you did not give me any opportunity to act differently.'

'Have we considered that this argument would be more comfortable in the atelier?' Holly says lightly. He makes an ushering gesture with both arms. 'Mancers—'

A reverberating blow shudders the gates—the Cristati soldiers have brought up a battering ram. Both sides of the massive double entrance shed chunks under the blow. The Mancy creature weakened it enough that it won't take long to pound it open.

Evelyn's beside him. She says, matter-of-factly, watching the shiver of the gates, 'I don't think I can watch everyone I love slaughtered again, Demi.'

It's a sobriquet he's not heard since they left Asaano, when they'd been children of the prosperous Aumona family, the proprietors of a profitable Mancy loom and an illicit Mancy printing press, both making the family targets for counterrevolutionary forces when the civil war broke out.

He looks at his sister's weary face and feels the rage Ash had provoked in him earlier, but this time it twists till it lands where it belongs— Cristati.

Pigeons take flight from the stronghold roof and Holly watches them scatter across a sky rapidly being writ to grey. Ash's plan is working. Cristati is attacking Haven, with Izidore under covenant. Lady Fairhaven is calling on her allies. All Haven has to do now is hold.

Holly looks at the Mancers, standing edgily apart. Izidore looks mutinous. Zhey're fidgeting with the lever. Albemarle is slump-shouldered, blank-faced as only a Mancer can be, and yet zhey'd just told off the Mancer Guard for not letting zhem help.

He's the Captain of the Mancer Guard, and the Mancer Guard has one role and one role alone: protect the Mancers. The rest of Haven has the stronghold guards and the militia, all competent and trained to their own roles. The Mancer Guard should be taking Albemarle and Izidore to the atelier, forcing them if they won't go voluntarily.

He turns back to Evie. 'You won't have to, Neshi,' he says. 'Promise.'

He gestures. Izidore gives a *finally!* sort of sigh, and crouches by the broken panel, Albemarle shambling over to join zhem. The Mancer Guard makes its cordon, Evie joining the line in Hazel's stead, the two Mancers between the half-circle of bodies and the wall.

After a moment, Holly nudges Valerian and puts him inside the cordon, too. The lord looks annoyed by that, and Holly spares a moment to wink at him.

Albemarle and Izidore work quietly and efficiently together. For all that Izidore must be used to taking the lead as Ash's partner, zhey readily take zheir cues from Albemarle. Albemarle, for zheir part, is calmer now zhey're working, and has the practice of interacting with Ash to make working with this new stranger slightly easier.

Albemarle sings zheir Mancy into the broken panel in zheir throaty murmur while Izidore uses the hot light Ash sang into the lever to soften and weave the metallic edges together. Zhey'd wrapped the lever in layers and layers of cloth ripped from zheir skirts. The cloth is singeing; every now and again, zhey discard the smouldering padding and wrap the lever in new layers. Zheir skirts are in tatters.

Holly's knee is sending sharp stabs up and down his leg in time with his heartbeat. He can neither fully straighten the knee nor properly bend it without a pulse of pain that he experiences as a blinding white burst under his skin and in his head.

'This is going to make things difficult,' he says to himself, and catches a wry look from Second Jerome. 'All right, but you have a flying leg now, SJ.'

The Mancers finish repairing the panel and start to lift it to the wall.

'Wait,' Valerian says. 'The commanders might want the militia on the walls before the moat goes back up.' He pushes through the cordon, calling back, 'Just wait one moment.'

Holly appraises the courtyard. The soldiers have taken care of most of the flood of Izidore's Mancy roaches now, only a few still scuttling about. Miriam and her assistants are moving among the injured, establishing a triage centre by the bailey wall. Quite a few soldiers are running up the stairs onto the wallwalk already, carrying bows. Now that he listens for it, he can hear the regular thrum of arrows, Haven's archers shooting at the Cristati soldiers sheltering under the shielding around the battering ram.

Valerian jogs back. 'Give them a little longer to get up,' he calls out as he gets closer, confirming Holly's own conclusion.

The battering ram strikes again, and both gates bow under the blow, bars and bolts creaking.

'I'm not convinced we've got *any* longer,' Morano says uneasily.

A Mancy roach whirls out of nowhere. It's one of the ones with tentacles, as if a giant cockroach wasn't quite nightmarish enough for Izidore's imaginings. A tentacle whips out and snatches Valerian to the ground in an instant. The roach swarms on top of him, mandibles clicking, before he can get hold of his axe.

Holly breaks the cordon. It doesn't even cross his mind that Valerian isn't within his purview. He only remembers that his knee is damaged when the pain of moving fast tries to drop him, but he pushes through it.

He strikes the tentacle wrapped about Val at the join with its body. It's more hastily constructed than Izidore's pet, and the blow severs the joint and sends the tentacle flying. He'd kick the roach off Valerian, but that would mean either standing on his bad leg or kicking with it, and neither appeal. Instead, he flips it off with his blade and stabs at the weak point Izidore showed them.

Valerian's injured and trying not to show it when Holly pulls him up. 'Where?' Holly asks brusquely, checking him over.

'I just went down hard, it's nothing,' Val says. 'Why'd you leave your Mancers, captain?'

It's accusatory. 'I don't know,' Holly says sulkily, reacting to the tone. 'Already lost Hazel, can't lose you.' Valerian stares at him and Holly snaps back to business. 'Or anyone else. Let's go.'

He drags Valerian back to the cordon. He's at a hobble, and Val's moving stiffly like his hip caught the brunt of his fall.

'Take Lord Vee inside,' he tells his sister. 'You know that's where you both should be.'

Valerian looks irritated even through the grimace of pain he's trying to keep off his face. Holly heads off any argument he might wish to make with, 'Bet you're really wishing you granted the budget increase for more Mancer guards now.'

He's diverted, but Evelyn isn't. She draws herself up; she's not quite as tall as her rangy younger sibling but she's broader. 'That's where you're supposed to be, too, Ro.'

Holly glances at his fellow guards. Second Jerome is bouncing a little; that's the new Mancy in the leg. Titus has tear tracks on her face—they all saw Hazel go over the wall—but their youngest member is looking fiercely determined. They all look set and steady, ready to fight.

If Holly had his way, he'd send every one of them inside with their commander.

'We'll follow as soon as the moat is done,' he assures Evelyn. 'Go.'

He turns back once he's seen them safely get through the south door. The last of the militia assigned to the wall is up there now, attending the parapets with bows and arrows. Albemarle holds the panel in place, humming, and Izidore uses zheir screwdriver tool to attach it. Even before zhey're done, the Mancy is rising, connecting with the other panels, sending up the shimmering white shield.

A ragged cheer goes up around the courtyard and from the wallwalk, notwithstanding those soldiers are now on the wrong side of the moat. They can at least answer back, and Holly can dimly see the rhythmic pull and release of the bows through the mist. The militia soldiers are doing their utmost to drive back the enemy soldiers wielding the battering ram. The moat will hold against any other Mancy insects, and will negate any Mancy amplifying the ram, but Holly's not sure it can hold against the massive momentum of the simple physical weight slamming into the weakened gates.

Izidore evidently thinks the same. Zhey touch Holly's arm. 'If a sheep won't serve, perhaps a goat will.' Zhey sign, ~I can make the moat repel equal to the force exerted against it. The harder they try, the harder it will push them back.

Holly glances at Albemarle. He knows Izidore has approached him with this idea, not the other Mancer, for good reason. Albemarle's desire to be useful, and zheir ability to control zheir reactions, are independent variables.

But he thinks the Haven Mancer Guard has a lesson to learn, and he better start showing he's learned it.

Albemarle shifts closer. Zheir face is screwed up with discomfort. 'You don't mean bricolage the design,' zhey say flatly. 'You mean change the song itself. You mean bricolage my Mancy. Like Ash just did.'

'It's taboo,' whispers Nightingale. 'Ash shouldn't have done it.'

Kito catches Holly's eye. 'That's not what bothered Albemarle though.' She turns to the Mancer. 'You didn't say "no bricolage" when you broke Ash's song. You said "no weapons".'

'Every tree has its place in the forest,' Izidore says, signing, ~No weapons.

Albemarle stares into space. Another thud comes, and the great gates shake momentously. The Haven soldiers still in the courtyard are readying barriers to funnel the invaders onto their blades when the gates break open.

Haven's Mancer nods to Izidore, and then quickly turns zheir back, crouches, and wraps both arms around zheir head, trying to block zheir ears. Holly picks out Kito, Titus and Nightingale with quick stabs of his fingers, and gestures for them to take Albemarle inside so zhey don't have to suffer through it.

'We'll follow as soon as Izidore's done,' he says.

Izidore's already at one half of the double gate, feeling out the song with zheir hand on the panel. The spooky thin wail of zheir voice copies Albemarle's melody in a different key, swings across Ash's reprise, and then steadies into zheir own version. The Mancy barrier on the side zhey're touching flashes instantly from Albemarle's white mist to a speckled deep blue like a starry midnight. Zhey quickly repeat the song on the other side, faster this time.

Holly notes that Albemarle, for all zheir distaste, has stopped, hands over zheir ears, to stare in fascination, ignoring Kito's chivvying. Nightingale is watching too, her face wearing a mix of revulsion and pensiveness. It's taboo, a supposed perversion, and it looks and sounds just like any other Mancy.

Izidore turns, hands still spread on the panel. 'The hours pass in but a blink if we do not watch the clock,' zhey point out.

Holly looks up and down the length of the wall. Izidore is correct; it would not take so very long for zhem to sing zheir version of the moat song all the way around the wall.

He'd have said it'd take longer than Haven had to stand, only a moment ago, but when the battering ram hits the gate this time, there's a concussive boom, and shouts and screams. The soldiers over the gate, shadows beyond the dark sheet of Izidore's repellent shield, cheer wildly.

The circumference is less than a mile around. Izidore may not be able to run it, but then, neither can Holly. They could limp their way around, and then every blow Cristati tries to make against them, main gates to postern gate and back around again, will rebound like the battering ram did.

As half the guards finally get Albemarle away, Izidore moves briskly from panel to panel southward, passing from the courtyard gravel to the grass that heralds the edge of pleasure gardens. Morano's keeping pace with zhem, the two Jeromes just behind. Holly hobbles last, looking down at his knee. He's still wearing trousers, from the meeting with Lady Cristati this morning. He can't see the injury but the sensitised brush of the cloth across his skin suggests it's swollen to the size of a melon. It feels like it'll burst like rotten fruit if he keeps trying to limp along on it.

First Jerome points over to where Miriam is diligently triaging by the bailey gate.

'We three can handle this. You should wait there or go to the atelier,' she says gently. 'I know you don't want to be sidelined from the fight, Holly, but there is no fight.'

Naturally, this is when Cristati soldiers erupt out of the pleasure garden.

~Twenty-Nine~

THE MANCER LOCUST SMASHED TO THE ground, landing on its side. The reverberating crash tore Hazel's hands free, and he and Ash slid and dropped from its back, their metal latticework floor now a steep wall with no viable handholds.

After a sickening but mercifully short plummet, Hazel hit the ground. His shoulder took most of the impact, but his vision whited out as his head cracked on a rock. Bright lights danced circles in his head, and then mercifully extinguished.

He opened his eyes. He'd blacked out, he muzzily realised, but it couldn't have been for more than a moment or two. His vision was still blurry, and he blinked. His whole side felt bruised, his shoulder ached, and his head throbbed.

He also couldn't catch his breath, but that was because Ash was fairly well crouched on his chest, clasping his face. As soon as he, still hazy, met zheir distraught gaze, zheir hands flew to sign, ~Thought you were dead!

Zhey collapsed forward to hug him fiercely.

Hazel muttered, 'Hit m'head.'

He waveringly made a stylised slap in mid-air. Ash, sitting up, caught his hand and kissed it, smiling through tears. ~Yes, I get it, Hazel darling. Why did you follow me like that?

Hazel smiled back, tracing a somewhat shaky finger over zheir cheek. He spoke the unassailable bedrock that sat as foundation below the more temporary emotions tumbling confusedly about his head.

'~Ash. You're my Mancer. I'd follow you anywhere.'

Ash checked. ~I'm your Mancer. You're trained to protect me. You're trained to trust me. You're trained to forgive me.

Hazel squinted up at zhem, head pounding. '~Why do you keep acting like it's a bad thing?'

The emotion drained from Ash, zheir expression turning remote and cold. ~It's not a bad thing. It's a useful thing.

Zhey rose, then, and Hazel, following the direction of zheir gaze, became aware that Cristati soldiers were closing in.

'Hoi there, soldiers,' Ash's collar announced. 'I am Liege Silverthorne. Fetch Commander Cristati. I want to be taken to my mother. Touch this man *at your peril.*'

It was quite something to see several armed and physically imposing men stopped dead in their tracks by fear.

Hazel didn't quite lose his grip on consciousness then, but he jolted in and out of awareness. He'd lost his sword, and couldn't stand even if he'd had it. He was heaved into the back of a cart under the harshly barked orders of the commander, Ash's half-brother, who seemed none of pleased, surprised or dismayed to meet his sibling in the field.

In the cart, Ash sat cross-legged and straight-backed, as serene as if zhey were riding in state in a carriage, ignoring Commander Cristati walking next to zhem and Hazel, prone and foggy, lying beside zhem.

Beyond zhem, he glimpsed more soldiers tying ropes to the felled Mancy locust, getting ready to drag it away, while others, under shields, were drawing a battering ram up to the gates of Haven, coordinated by the shouted chants of an overseer. The greening fields on either side of the road had already been trampled to dirt and dust by the march of the besieging army.

He slumped back. His head ached. His mouth tasted of dirt. The sky was very blue above him, but the air glowed with an ominous yellow underlight.

As the cart rattled off, the walls of Haven rose into Hazel's field of vision and a boom came, the first strike of the battering ram. The gates, pockmarked on this side with deep bites and gouges, shivered like paper screens in a breeze.

As if frightened from their roosts, a flock of pigeons scattered overhead. The soldiers shouted and sent arrows after them, and hawks. Some fell, but most sped away, a few south, the rest north.

The messages to the other coastal strongholds, repeated across the whole flock. Ash was out of the stronghold, Izidore was within, Cristati had hit the gates, Lady Fairhaven was calling on the covenant. After dark, she might risk send up green fireworks again, to find out once and for all if their allies would answer the call this time—Cristati would get the news at the same time, of course, so Lady Fairhaven would have to be very sure she'd see green in return.

Hazel wondered sleepily if he'd still be alive by then. He wasn't entirely sure why he was still alive now.

He looked up at Ash's face, set in imperious impassivity. Ash, as if feeling his gaze, squeezed his hand and nudged zheir leg into his side.

His vision was hazing grey at the edges, limning the receding Haven in the eerie gloss of storm light. White mist was rising again. He couldn't tell if his senses were bowing out, or if one of Kisane's sudden squalls was sweeping in from over the ocean.

Another thought was trying to make itself known, and he kept shying from it. *Holly*, the thought started, and Hazel stared up at the sky and mused on the weather in spring instead.

Ash nudged him again, a firm press to his thigh that drew his scattered attention. ~Holly is alive. He only fell a little way. I saw him land on the stairs.

Hazel raised one shaking hand and signed a thanks far less emphatic than he'd have liked. Ash caught his hand and held on tight.

By the time the cart creaked into the Cristati camp, the sky had clouded over and rain was spitting. He didn't think the weather would hamper either pigeons or fireworks, though if the wind picked up beyond the current occasional blustery gust, it might. It'd hamper Haven's archers, though, if the rain got much heavier.

Ash let go of Hazel's hand. Soldiers marched him into a command tent and roughly pushed him to his knees before manacling his wrists around a thick support pole. Ash's hip brushed him; zhey were standing very close. Hazel sank back onto his heels and rested his head briefly on Ash's hip. He felt dizzy, a little nauseated.

'Leave us,' he heard someone order. The voice was familiar. It was Lady Cristati.

He raised his head. The tent was large, rectangular and of heavy leather, a far cry from the smaller round linen ones he was more familiar with. It had a foldable table in the centre, with a map rolled out and tokens scattered on it, lit by lamps bearing the telltale steady glow of Mancy. The air was redolent with incense, masking a heavier, muskier smell, the scent of wet leather and soldier.

While there were several chairs, and several goblets on the table, the command tent was currently empty except for Lady Cristati. Presumably Commander Cristati had already returned to the field.

'Why is this Haven not dead?' Lady Cristati asked. She was still dressed in the formal purple regalia she'd worn to fetch Ash this morning, though her hems were muddy now.

Hazel had been pondering the same. Ash's collar said, 'I asked Marco for his life and he granted it.'

Ash slid a hand into his hair and caressed him, making zheir reasons blatant. Zheir eyes, when Hazel looked up at zhem, were blank, indifferent. The gesture was a taunt aimed at zheir mother, not a reassurance aimed at him.

'I see.' She sounded very cold, as cold as the Mancy voice did. 'Behave, then, lest I ungrant it.'

Ash nodded zheir head and zheir fist. 'Understood.'

'I act only out of love, you know that,' she added.

'Understood.'

Lady Cristati sighed, a theatrically burdened sound. She looked zhem over, mercilessly measuring zhem. 'Your complexion,' she chided. 'Too much sun, I suppose. And you've ruined your family tattoo. And your beautiful hair. Hacked it off and washed the dye out and look at the mess.'

Ash's hair, normally silk-smooth, was a wild tangle after zheir day's adventures. Zhey pushed the snarls back behind both ears, and then flicked zheir fingers as if annoyed zhey'd risen to the bait.

Zheir mother tutted and touched her own earlobes, where pearl drops hung. 'And I suppose you traded your lovely silver and jade earrings to fund your excursion. Heirlooms, they were, your grandmother's bequest. She wanted those passed down from mother to—'

With a shudder of self-control, she cut herself off. The collar hissed into the silence that followed.

Ash said, 'I will not feel grateful for a gift I did ask for nor want. The funds it provided were appreciated, however.'

Zhey ran light fingers over zheir uninjured wrist, where the Cristati feather was inscribed, with its overlay of knife blade.

An image flashed through Hazel's head, Ash, fugitive, intent on reaching Haven, nonetheless stopping as soon as zhey felt safe enough to replace zheir robes and cut zheir hair and transform zheir family emblem. Zhey'd swapped a family heirloom for a disguise against said family. At the same time, zhey'd shed the trappings of an unwanted family identity, the costume zheir mother made zhem wear.

Lady Cristati tsked again and now raked Hazel from head to toe, or not quite, since he was resting back on his heels. If she recognised him as the Haven Mancer guard who had killed half of Tassone's men, she didn't say so.

Instead, she said, 'This is the one who put those marks on you, I presume.'

Ash traced two fingers along zheir skin below the collar. Hazel winced. Just yesterday, he'd sucked love bites into Ash's collarbones and left bruises on zheir hips, never imagining he'd be judged by his adult lover's *mother* for it. She must have been there when the Cristati Mancer Guard forced Ash to strip for the formal Mancer robes. Perhaps zhey had been able to undress privately, after all, and had handed that neat pile of zheir favourite clothes directly to zheir mother's care. Somehow, it was not the comforting thought it should have been.

'He did nothing to me I didn't ask for,' the Mancy voice said in its monotone.

Hazel wished zhey'd been able to sign it, if zhey had to talk about it at all. Zheir signing had warmth and sincerity the collar lacked. Its flat voice sounded like a defensive lie.

Lady Cristati scoffed. She strode to Ash and pulled zheir hands to her. The bandage around zheir injured wrist was still in place, if filthy, but zheir palms and fingers were sliced and nicked from zheir struggle with the Mancy locust, and a scarlet band of blisters across zheir left palm marked where zhey'd tried to hold onto the modified lever as it heated up. Ash had not been wearing gloves. She touched zheir shoulder, too, where the ragged metal had ripped zheir skin as zhey craned to destroy the locust's heart.

'Oh, Silverthorne, must you be so addicted to hurting yourself in so many unsavoury ways?'

Hazel cleared his throat. 'Zhey didn't put that cuff on zhemself. Nor that collar.'

Zhey hadn't broken zheir own fucking fingers and left them to heal badly as a reminder to stay silent, either.

Lady Cristati looked astonished to be addressed. 'The cuff does not harm zhem if zhey stay where zhey are safe, and Izidore offered many times to re-do Inigo's collar design to make it fit more comfortably.' She raised her eyebrows at Ash. 'Silverthorne refused because zhey like to suffer—'

'A comfortable collar comforts the master, not the servant,' Ash's collar said.

'—which tendency is quite plain when zhey subjugate zhemself to a brute like you.'

Coherent words were coming harder than usual. 'I didn't— With respect, my lady, consenting adults—'

Still looking at her child—and if only Mutual had a word that didn't infantilise the adult offspring of possessive parents—she said, 'Only an ignorant boor would assume you can truly consent to anything. I warned you how the world would treat you, didn't I? And you indeed paid the price.'

Hazel said, 'What?'

He looked to Ash, who tapped zheir ear. ~Deaf means incompetent, remember?

Hazel jerked on his chain, signing against the constraint. ~But she doesn't actually—

Ash widened zheir eyes dramatically and gave a quick shake of zheir head. Hazel, taking the hint, faced back to Lady Cristati, who was indeed drawing herself up in indignation to see someone communicating with her child in a way she did not approve of.

Hazel said it to her. 'But you don't actually believe that, do you?'

'Believe what? That you took advantage of zheir vulnerabilities so you could use zhem for your own selfish pleasure?'

Hazel risked another glance at Ash. ~Did I do that?

Ash made the negatory fist, smiling, before popping zheir forefinger and little finger into rabbit ears for a cheery, ~You idiot.

Hazel snorted, lifting his chained wrists in general agreement with the sentiment. Ash's smile vanished and zhey looked down. Hazel leaned his shoulder against zheir thigh. He hadn't been trying to make his Mancer feel guilty about his current predicament. He'd chosen to follow zhem on to the back of the locust, after all. He'd chosen to follow zhem anywhere, and here he was.

'I see you don't understand.' Lady Cristati said. She spread her hands on the table, leaning heavily. 'Of course not, you're from Haven. The world's different outside Tashi's naïve little paradise. It's not kind to those who are different. It will take and use someone like my Silver. Zhey need protecting, as much as zhey think zhey don't. Did you really think Haven could protect zhem? Look what happened when you tried.'

That struck Hazel as distinctly circular reasoning. Ash tugged on his hair, a warning. This was, Hazel could well guess, an argument zhey had engaged in many times with zheir mother. It was not an argument inarticulate Hazel would win, if Ash couldn't.

He tried, anyway. 'Lady Cristati, my sister is deaf. I understand these fears, I really do.'

'You understand nothing,' she retorted. 'Your sister is not a Mancer. Silverthorne's father tried to take zhem from me the moment zhey were born, just for the Mancy. My father *did* take zhem from me for the Mancy. And then to be deaf, and reliant on other Mancers. And yet to be able to transform any Mancy into a weapon. By all the furious gods, man, Silverthorne's a target for every single stronghold once that's widely known, and it *will* be widely known after this palaver, thanks to zheir own ridiculous obstinance.'

Hazel could see exactly what Izidore meant by Ash falling back into maladaptive habits under the influence of zheir family. Zhey set zheir hand on zheir hip and huffed out, every inch the sulky juvenile version of zhemself. But where was the incentive to act otherwise?

Zheir mother pointed an accusing finger at zhem. 'Cristati is acting to your benefit, as always, and you will never even admit it, you ungrateful, recalcitrant creature, because you deliberately will not recognise what's good for you.'

Hazel nudged Ash with his shoulder again, willing calm. 'Are you saying you're going after other strongholds to keep Ash—Liege Silverthorne—safe, my lady?'

'They will come after us,' she said. 'We're merely making the first move.'

'It is ambition,' Ash's collar corrected coldly.

'It is *love*,' Lady Cristati shouted. 'Every time, with you. It's like hitting my head on a brick wall, trying to make you see what I do for you. I blame your father's blood. He was stubborn, too. I traded him the right to name you and he thought it meant he owned you.'

The collar hissed and grated. 'And you *don't* think that?'

'A-yah, as much as this is a constructive conversation…' Hazel rattled his chains and Lady Cristati's attention snapped to him. 'My lady,' he said politely. 'I believe you intend to act in Ash's best interests as you see them.'

She smoothed her hands over the bodice of her dress. She was once again coolly calm when she said, 'Gracious of you. Just what I needed, the approval of a strange man from a weak stronghold.'

Hazel dipped his head in acknowledgement of the justified sarcasm.

'But you've made zheir situation in Cristati untenable. The Mancer Guard, for starters—'

'Those guards are academy-trained,' she told him. 'They act always for the good of the Mancer, whether Silverthorne knows it or not.'

'Ah.' Hazel paused. 'I see now.'

She tried very hard not to ask. 'What do you see, Haven?'

'You'd rather trust an ideal than your own child's actual experience of the reality. Against all evidence, you really, truly, don't believe Ash is capable of making decisions about zheir own life.'

'How dare you?' she cried, storming over to stand over him, bristling.

'I don't doubt you love zhem, in your own way,' Hazel told her earnestly.

~Fuck, Hazel, she will stab you!

She did stab him, with her finger, repeatedly jabbing at him. 'You will never understand what it means to raise a vulnerable but valuable child. I do everything for zheir own good and zhey spit it back in my face. Do you know what it costs me, to have my own child hate me just because I must raise zhem to look strong in this world!'

She had tears standing in her eyes. Hazel saw the pure sincerity of the emotion behind her words.

'You raised zhem strong,' he said. He rose to his knees; he would have gone to his feet if he could. 'By Kisane's tail, how could you doubt it? You raised zhem strong. You raise them strong, but then you let them go. And, yes, they might walk away and never look back, but you made it so they could, and that was your only goal, so you take the consolation for what it is. *That's* love, Lady Cristati. *You let them go.*'

Hazel's chest was heaving. He lowered his gaze and controlled himself, feeling Lady Cristati staring down at him. After a moment, she stepped away, to the table. She lowered her head, ostensibly shifting the tokens on the map, her back to them as she touched a handkerchief to her eyes.

Ash pressed against him. ~Hazel darling. I appreciate your defence, but I don't need it and she will not heed it. Do not think I came to this pass without first trying less dramatic means.

Lady Cristati, discarding her handkerchief and her distress, rapped the table. Hazel jerked his chin, bringing the summons to Ash's attention.

'It is apparent you care, "in your own way",' she said to Hazel, and to Ash, 'You may keep him as a pet if you're good. You can start by repairing Izidore's monster. Off you go.'

Ash hesitated. Hazel watched zheir gaze flicker uncertainly, darting from zheir mother's face and away. He assumed zhey were trying to gauge how much more defiance she would take.

'You went to so much trouble to remove Izidore as your guarantor of good behaviour, and you handed me another one straight away, Silverthorne. And so, off you go and do as you are bid or I will have your Haven killed right in front of you.'

Not much more, then.

Ash nodded. Zhey approached the table, Lady Cristati tensing as zhey came close. Zhey took her beringed hand.

'Mother,' said the collar. 'I refuse to be grateful for forcibly bestowed gifts. But I know how hard you worked to be sure I would not be driven insane by the Mancy, and for that, you have my undying gratitude. Your work is done now, though. I do not have to be your burden anymore. You can renounce me.'

'A mother's work is never done,' she murmured. The response had an unthinking reflexiveness to it. 'It is not safe to renounce you.'

She did not say zhey weren't a burden.

Ash bit zheir lip. Zhey very much looked like zhey wanted to tell zheir mother something else. Hazel tensed. If Ash was going to go back on zheir own plan and either capitulate to Cristati or doom Haven, or indeed both, now would be the time.

Zhey bowed and kissed her hand in stiff obeisance.

It was a tradition among the purple, not held to in Haven, to kiss the hand of the high lord in obeisance. Hazel could tell, from her expression as Ash bowed over her hand, that this was not a tradition much respected between Lady Cristati and her truculent youngest child.

Ash walked out, not looking again at Hazel. Balled in zheir right hand was an embroidered linen cloth. They'd taken zheir mother's damp handkerchief off the table. Lady Cristati was too busy staring down at the back of her hand as if it defied the adage to notice.

Hazel's presence, his defence of Ash, had waylaid zhem from zheir stated goal of ensuring Lady Cristati's forces kept attacking Haven, heedless of the covenant violation. On the other hand, she showed no sign of ceasing the attack now she had her Mancer child back in the traces, Hazel as her leverage in the whip hand. She still wanted, and expected to get, Izidore back. She still wanted, perhaps, revenge on Lady Fairhaven for long-ago slights.

Therefore, Hazel held his tongue. He didn't need to mention some fictional weapon to provoke an attack already underway, and he certainly didn't want to accidentally dissuade Lady Cristati from continuing it, as much as he would have liked to do such on purpose.

Lady Cristati gave herself a shake and eyed off her prisoner. 'You are wondering about the covenant, I suppose,' she said. 'Tashi will call on it, of course, for Izidore's sake.'

A response did not seem required. Hazel watched the lady pace about the command tent. The sound of the rain on the leather roof abruptly seemed loud.

'Silverthorne has misled you, if you think we won't be done here before your allies even start their march.' She paced over to him. 'The Cristati Mancer Guard is already inside. Don't think for a second Silverthorne didn't know it would be.'

With that revelation, she marched from the tent, leaving him alone.

Hazel, head aching, weighed his options. Though his instinct was to wait till dark, that would be when most of the soldiers would have returned to camp, squeezing into the tight rows of smaller tents that lay beyond this one. Now, while the camp was quiet and curtained by rain, with only a handful of servants and cooks about, was his best opportunity to escape.

They'd have to skirt wide about the field to remain unnoticed on their way back to Haven, perhaps hide in the forest to the south until after nightfall. In fact, they'd have to, so that Haven could legitimately send up its covenant signal while Ash, the sole lawful reason to attack, was outside the stronghold.

The Cristati Mancer Guard is already inside.

The soldiers had checked him for additional weapons, but they hadn't taken his Mancer Guard coat and hadn't guessed about the hidden pockets the innovative Haven seamsters had developed. Hazel directed his attention to one of the buttons. His chained wrists gave him just enough play to yank the button loose and unravel its thread.

A short length of wire tugged out with the thread. Hazel used it to probe the lock of the manacles, bending his hands and fingers awkwardly to reach. It had been a while since they'd practiced this. He wasn't sure if Titus had ever practiced it. He'd have to give Holly a nudge when he got back.

The Cristati Mancer Guard is already inside.

The first lock clicked open. He freed that wrist. The second manacle was quicker. He left the irons on the floor and now delved into one of the secret pockets to extract a stiletto in its sheath. It was deliberately light and narrow, so it didn't distort the sit of the coat or lend itself to discovery under a perfunctory frisking.

He thought about slicing his way out of the back of the command tent, but the leather was thick and there was no guarantee that way would be any clearer of Cristatis than the front entrance. He pushed the flap aside and stepped out, stiletto held at chest-height.

The Cristati Mancer Guard is already inside.

He punched the stiletto through the base of the skull of the single sentry without hesitation or remorse.

Hazel briefly considered—*don't think for a second Silverthorne didn't know it would be*—heading straight south for the forest.

Then he scanned about until he saw the hulk of the Mancy locust, deposited by Cristati soldiers. He marched through the camp like he belonged there. He wore a Mancer guard's coat, and the Cristati green would darken to nearer the Haven shade in the rain.

He dodged several servants but killed one more sentry before he reached the locust, leaving the body inside an empty tent so his path would be less obvious. He buckled on the man's sword. It was less well-made than his own, which was a cursed expensive piece of equipment. Lord Valerian would sigh when he found out Hazel had lost it.

The wax and wane of a familiar glow drew him to where Ash and a Cristati sheltered from the light but persistent rain in a small cave formed by the curve of the locust's neck. Ash was reaching up into the workings with a tool like Izidore's, luminescent with Mancy, while glancing down to watch lips and hands while the Cristati talked to zhem.

The man, somewhere in age between Ash and Hazel, wore the light green of the Cristati Mancer Guard, and had the same look as them, olive skin and curly dark hair. But he didn't wear their coat—it looked more like a stylised dress uniform, which marked him as a patron—and he was too short besides, from what Hazel had observed, and much more relaxed and friendly in his body language toward Ash.

In fact, the pair were casually chatting while Ash worked and the Cristati handed zhem bits and pieces from a spread oilcloth, in a way far more reminiscent of Haven than anything Hazel had previously seen of Cristati.

'Yes, but I did miss you, you know, Ash.'

Ash ducked down to grab a cog out of his hands, casting him a wry look. Zheir head and shoulders vanished into the open panel on the underside of the locust while zhey attached the part, the splash of warm white light bathing the man waiting at zheir feet.

'I did,' the man insisted when Ash had emerged again and could see his lips. 'I could have come with you, if you'd told me what you were doing. I definitely would have been able to delay the chase more, if you'd told me what you were doing.'

Tucking zheir tool out of the way, Ash signed, ~[unknown name], you had plenty of time to choose my side.

'I know, I know.' As he spoke, the man grabbed hold of Ash's hands, which Hazel bristled at; it was the equivalent of gagging zhem. But he merely turned them to look at the cuts and scrapes and pulled a sympathetic face before letting go. 'I do wish you'd let me treat those. I have salve and bandages right here.' He patted his capacious pockets.

~Need my fingers unencumbered.

It was an argument they'd already had; the man did not pursue it, in favour of pursuing their current one. 'And I did choose your side, as much as I could. I slipped you and Izidore every scrap of information I could get hold of, didn't I? But she's quite scary to openly cross, and we aren't all as brave as you.'

Ash gave a single shake of zheir head. ~I understand why you didn't. But the fact remains that you didn't. Pity doesn't open locks, [unknown name]. No matter your good intentions then and now, I cannot trust you not to fall straight back into line with what our mother wants as soon as she realises you're helping me again.

Their mother. So this was Ash's other half-brother, Paolo. Zhey had specifically asked Izidore if he'd come, but not, apparently, to draw him into any schemes.

Ash was still rapidly signing. ~You claim you delayed the chase, but they found me rather quickly, yes?

Paolo was squinting at the fast sequences, nose wrinkled. To his credit, he didn't ask zhem to repeat zhemself with the collar. He finally worked out that Ash was, very mildly, accusing him.

'That wasn't my fault! And look, I promise, this time,' he said eagerly. 'I guessed you were going to do something for Izidore and I didn't say anything.' He pulled a small velvet bag out of his pocket and waved it. It rattled. 'Look. I bought along zheir button collection so zhey wouldn't lose it if you helped zhem escape.'

Ash looked at the bag, dismay on zheir face. ~Paolo, do you think Izidore is going to thank you when zhey find out you took zheir antiques out of all those carefully labelled cases and jumbled them up together?

Paolo shook the bag experimentally. Hazel could hear the discordant jangle as glass and metal and bone chimed and clicked against each other. 'Yes?' Paolo said eventually.

Ash patted zheir brother's hand. ~I know your suddenly unshakeable loyalty is more to do with Izidore than me.

'What? No!'

~But you do understand zhey're a Mancer, not a woman? I know our mother likes to feminise us both, and Izidore doesn't mind that as much as I do, but zhey're still a Mancer.

'All the heavens, Ash, stop! I'm practically old enough to be zheir father.'

~Age does not matter to a Mancer.

'It matters to me! Zhey're a baby. An itty fluffy baby Mancer who needs taking care of. That's all.'

Ash went still. Hazel wondered if zhey were contemplating pointing out that zhey could've used some taking care of, when zhey'd been a new Mancer under Cristati control. But that, of course, was precisely what happened when you were raised to show no weakness lest the world forced you to your knees: no one knew when you needed taking care of.

Instead, zhey firmly signed, ~Not a woman, and not a child either. A Mancer.

Paolo was nodding. 'Yes, yes, and Mancers don't feel gratitude and they don't fall in love, I didn't even imagine it.'

Hazel, watching from the shadows along the line of the locust's body, looked briefly down, struck. Then he started edging forward. It seemed as if Ash got along well with this brother, for all that he was not a reliable ally. Therefore, it wasn't in Hazel's mind to hurt Paolo, but it was also clear that Ash didn't want to have to trust him. Hazel intended to knock him out.

Ash made [expletive]. ~Why does everyone— Mancers are *human*. We're capable of right and wrong like everyone else. We're accountable for our choices like everyone else. And we fall in love like everyone else. What appears impossible is for people to not weight us with their prejudices.

Hazel bit his tongue to stop from saying aloud, 'Well, that's not true *at all*,' and starting an argument he didn't have time to continue, or possibly the moral high ground to win, as well as giving himself away to Paolo.

He took another slow step toward Paolo's back while the man was intent on trying to follow the rapid Trade and, really, get a word in edgewise.

The movement caught Ash's eye from over Paolo's shoulder. Zheir signing smoothly changed. ~You may incapacitate him, but don't hurt him.

'What?' Paolo turned around and saw Hazel. He started violently, hand to his chest. 'Oh, you surprised me. Are you Ash's Hazel?'

A touch nonplussed, Hazel nodded. He'd put the stiletto behind his back. He didn't want Paolo to take fright and raise the alarm.

Ash signed, ~I was about to come and get you.

Hazel smiled. ~Oh, sorry, is my escape fucking up your rescue?

Zhey gave zheir little bark of laughter, looking pleased in that endearingly shy way Hazel now knew was mainly driven by surprise.

'Please, can I come, Ashlin?' Paolo said, hands tucked together; the Cristati prayed to their deities. 'Please? I won't get in the way and I won't help Mother, and I won't—'

~Incapacitate him.

'Oh, Ash, you're such a…' Paolo, sighing heavily, held out his wrists to Hazel. 'Could you tie me up without hitting me? I do so hate getting hit. Marco used to hit me all the time, growing up.'

'Chatty,' Hazel commented. He collected a length of wire from the oilcloth.

'Taciturn? Are we playing a word association game? Such fun!'

~Take his coat, Ash ordered.

Paolo obligingly stripped off his light green coat and handed it over. 'Can I have yours?' he asked Hazel. 'It's cold.'

'Ah,' Hazel said.

He was quite attached to his Haven Mancer Guard uniform. Apart from anything else, the detailed and intricate tailoring and the linen armour panels meant it probably cost more than the sword he'd already lost.

'Ash means you to wear mine, you see.'

Hazel glanced at Ash and got a nod. He wrapped his bloody coat around Paolo's shoulders, before looping Paolo's wrists to a strut on the Mancy locust, careful not to let the thin metal wire bite into his skin.

Ash touched zheir brother's cheek. ~Thank you for…being as decent as you could be, under the circumstances.

'Damned with faint praise!' Paolo exclaimed. 'I will do better, Ash. If I get the chance— oh, you look just like her when you pull that face, you know. *And* that face.' He chortled.

~You can hit him.

'Ashlin Silverthorne Cristati!'

'I'm going to gag you,' Hazel told him. 'Otherwise it won't be convincing and your mother's going to know you let us escape.'

'Oh, I think she'll know that anyw—' Paolo managed before Hazel shoved a balled-up rag into his mouth.

~THIRTY~

IZIDORE AND MORANO ARE AT THE wall right on the edge of the trees when the Cristatis boil out. One of them strikes Morano so hard in the chest that he flies backward, and the only reason his ribs don't cave in is the linen armour panels sewn into the front of his coat.

He's still knocked flat and gasping for air when Captain Tassone steps out of the trees.

'Gotcha,' he says, and grabs hold of Izidore.

His men, a full complement of Mancer guards backed up by soldiers, divide around them and rush at the Jeromes and Holly. Holly grasps that they've come in through the postern while the moat was down.

Ash warned them it would be so—Cristati probably used one of the small modified Mancies Izidore couldn't drain to get the gate cracked open, or their injured and marooned colleague slipped out and opened it—but between the Mancy attack at the front gates and losing Hazel over the wall, the risk slipped his mind.

He feels flattened by how unaware they've been taken, all their training and procedures for nought.

Holly can't move properly to fight; he'd be at Izidore's side already if he could. Zhey're left defenceless as Tassone drags zhem back into the trees.

Except zhey're not.

Zhey whistle, two strong notes, and zheir pet, placidly at zheir heels this entire time, springs into life. Tassone lets go of zhem and stumbles back in alarm. The pet follows, chasing his footsteps.

'But no one drew his sword near it,' Tassone shouts indignantly, backing up faster as some of the limbs, long and sharp, begin to thrash the air.

He parries its first strike, but its second cuts into his side and he swears and falls. It immediately loses interest in favour of chasing the beats of the boots of the other scattering Cristatis. The soldiers are thrown into panic and quite a few are killed or vanish back into the trees.

The Cristati Mancer Guard, however, must have practiced how to deal with Izidore's pet. They stay calm, dodging it, leading it this way and that. The pet struggles, chasing one set of vibrations before getting distracted by another.

Izidore's trap would have worked magnificently inside, with walls to ricochet off and corral its targets and keep the levels of chaos high. The fight would have been over before any of the Cristati could have worked out what was triggering the pet to chase them.

But out here, it's taking too long, and the Havens have stopped moving. Second Jerome was halfway to Izidore, who sensibly sat on the ground and covered zheir head, when he had to freeze. First Jerome, meanwhile is standing over the prone Morano, who either can't get up because he's injured, or won't get up for fear of drawing the pet.

But it's Holly who gives it away, Rowan Holyoake, the best fighter of his generation, who never stands still and never refuses a fight—who is, fairly fucking conspicuously, standing still and refusing a fight.

Holly watches Tassone notice him not moving, and then the others, not moving, and then he's shouting to his men, 'Stand still, stop moving, it'll only attack you if you move.'

The Cristatis obey, the Mancer Guard instantly, the remaining soldiers slower and paying for it. The two forces, some two dozen surviving Cristatis and the four Havens, look at each other, the pet shuffling slowly between them, some of its limbs idly tasting the air as it swivels about.

It's by far the strangest stalemate Holly's ever been in.

He and Tassone gaze at each other with what Holly recognises as near-identical longing.

By the south door, Kito and the others have paused to watch. With a word, Kito orders the two youngest Mancer guards inside with Albemarle. As soon as the door is closed behind them, she stomps toward the fight, deliberately banging her boots down.

The pet swarms at her; she catches two limbs on her trishuls and a third on the thick padding of her coat's sleeve. She uses the momentum to swing the pet with her, and hurls it into a clump of Cristatis. They cannot help but break ranks and run, and the pet tracks their vibrations and falls on them, slashing.

'Oh, wait!' Second Jerome says, delighted, and slams the heel of his Mancy leg into the ground.

He lurches crookedly into the air, and when he lands, behind a couple of Cristati soldiers, the pet scuttles his way at top speed and rips the legs out from one of the soldiers while Second Jerome blasts off again, whooping. Every time he lands, he pulls the pet his way, skittling Cristatis. Kito, meanwhile, plunges into the soldiers and drives them at the pet. She and Second Jerome are the pincers of a claw with the pet the cutting edge.

Holly wishes with lightning intensity that he could join in their game of speed, but the knee has made him too slow. He shakes his head in impotent frustration, and notices that Izidore is moving, slowly, slowly, crawling over to First Jerome and Morano, watching zheir pet intently in case it reacts.

Tassone's still looking at Holly. Holly smiles at him, mocking. The Havens are outnumbered, but they have the upper hand.

Tassone suddenly lunges, crashes into the crawling Izidore, and rips the lever from zheir hand.

The Cristati force must have been watching the Havens for some time, from the shelter of the pleasure garden—Holly thinks that after this, Lady Fairhaven may have to order the bloody garden razed with fire—for he unerringly slides his finger along it until the hot white light shoots out.

He cuts the pet in half with a single silent stroke of the lasering light. Izidore shrieks.

Tassone seems poised to turn the beam on zhem, but grunts and flicks his hand, dropping the lever; it heats up too fast to hold for long. It rolls into the undergrowth, which begins to smoulder. He makes a grab for the Mancer, but zhey skitter backward, still wailing, and then Second Jerome lands beside zhem, parries a blow from Tassone, and jerks himself and Izidore away in a scuttering series of leaps that ends with a dismal hop.

'Leg's out of Mancy,' he pants to Holly. He crouches by Morano, unstrapping the dead weight of the artificial leg. 'New design's not as efficient as the old. Sorry.'

First Jerome assumes a guard position in front of both men. 'I'll stay with them. You get Izidore to the atelier.'

By rights, she should abandon her colleagues and friends; by rights, Holly should order it. The Mancer Guard protects the Mancer. That is their sole duty, their reason for existing.

Holly whistles to Kito, who is still having a grand old time amid the Cristati soldiers despite the loss of the pet. She extracts herself with a last slash and stab, and reaches his side in an instant.

'Izidore to the atelier,' he orders.

She flashes a disappointed look but takes Izidore's arm without demure. Izidore shakes her off. It's started to rain, cold spits of drizzle, and zheir hair is growing frizzy where it's escaped from zheir simple plait. Zheir clothes are in shreds. Zheir composure is in shreds. Zhey clutch zheir sides. Zheir face shows the marks of tears but zheir expression is ferocious and stubborn. Zhey are far from the docile creature sitting demurely in Lady Fairhaven's reception room this morning under the eye of zheir vicious fucking Mancer Guard.

'The fox—' Izidore cuts zhemself off. Zhey're frowning horribly, fighting zheir own words. Zhey manage to clearly say, 'Ash told me zhey need a far-scry mirror.'

'Ash is, at best, captured,' Kito says. She tugs at zheir arm. 'Whatever idea zhey had…'

'Ash needs a far-scry mirror.' Zhey set zheir feet. 'Ash needs a far-scry mirror.'

'We have one but it doesn't work,' Holly tells zhem, simultaneously recognising and trying to break the characteristic obstinacy of a Mancer with a fixation.

Again, Izidore concentrates fiercely. 'Ash needs me to bricolage it and make it work.'

When Holly says nothing, zhey say, enunciating every word, 'Zhey need it. I must fix it.'

Holly takes a deep breath. He knows what he wants to do. He wants to tell Izidore to shut up and have Kito drag zhem to the atelier.

'You go to the atelier with Kito,' he says. 'I'll bring you the mirror.'

Izidore sags with relief, and offers a formal little bow, reminiscent of Ash. Kito runs with zhem across the courtyard. Holly pivots about on his good leg so he can face the gathering Cristatis.

'Right after I take care of these fuckers,' he adds under his breath.

Second Jerome is on his feet, First Jerome supporting him so that they are side by side, arms wrapped around each other's waists. Holly regularly had the Mancer guards fight in tandem with Second Jerome with his Mancy leg removed. The pair have assumed that stance, a two-armed, three-legged unit, moving as one.

Morano has tried to rise. He's in a crouch, his breathing laboured, his colour poor. The rain is glinting on his scalp as he gasps, head lowered. He holds up a hand. 'Help. Me.'

Each word sounds like agony. First Jerome frowns, but she plants her feet and hauls him up. He can't prevent a yelp, but he shakes it off and sets himself, and then the surviving Cristati soldiers fall on them.

To people who aren't familiar with swords, Holly describes swordplay as a dance set to the music of clashing steel; he glides through the movements at his own tempo. He's forced to a more human pace now, but the dance is still his. He blocks and slashes and swings and stabs, pivoting and spinning on his good leg, letting the pain of the other leg drive him to greater ferocity whenever he must put weight on it. He's pushing forward trying to reach Tassone, who he lost sight of in the rain, and falling back to cover the others, pulsing through the Cristatis like licks of lightning.

It's the most fun he's had all day, Valerian's mouth on his cock this morning notwithstanding.

There's more bodies moving around him now, coming up behind him, and he spins into the new front before he recognises the colours through the misting rain and realises it's some of Haven's militia belatedly joining the fight.

In the chaos, and without a Mancer to protect, the remnant Mancer Guard falls back. Holly sees the Cristati soldiers divide, some melting back into the pleasure garden, drawing Havens after them, others dodging away to dash off across the courtyard.

Morano is struggling, hand pressed to his side. Second Jerome is exhausted, and First Jerome is exhausting herself in turn trying to keep him on his one foot. Holly steers them to Miriam's hospital near the bailey gate. First Jerome helps Morano lie down. Holly doesn't think he'll get up again today. Miriam's already abandoned her current patient to come check on him. Second Jerome leans on the wall, trying to pretend he doesn't want to be on the ground next to his friend.

'Stay with them,' Holly murmurs to First Jerome. 'There's too many Cristatis about to leave any of the wounded unguarded.'

'But the Mancers,' she says.

'I'm getting the mirror from Val's office and then I'll be with them. Kito's with them, and the juniors. All will be well, Ayala. Hold here.'

They clasp hands through their gloves. Holly squeezes Second Jerome's hand, and Morano's; he seems barely conscious of the touch.

Miriam is at his side. 'Hazel,' she says.

'I know,' he says.

She looks like she can't decide if she wants to cry or slap him. Holly wonders if he wore the same expression when Val blocked him from the sally port.

Her professional poise fortifies her. 'You're injured, Rowan. I can tell from how you're moving.'

Holly looks down at his knee. 'Can't stop now, Merry,' he says cheerfully. 'I've got a stronghold to save.'

He tries very hard not to hobble as he crosses the court.

~Thirty-One~

When Hazel tried to guide Ash out of the camp southward, zhey shook zheir head and insisted on the corral. They pulled each other to a stop in the disagreement over direction.

'~We have to hide out till after the fireworks signal,' Hazel explained.

They were standing behind a tent, out of sight of the boundary guards, but he was feeling acutely exposed anyway, even wearing Cristati green. Paolo was shorter than Hazel, but almost as broad, and barrel chested—the coat was short in the sleeve and sat at his hips instead of lower like he was used to, but he could button it and his shoulders weren't too constricted. The persistent misty drizzle was dampening its shoulders already.

Ash held up both hands. ~Please try not to hate me, Hazel. There is a change of plan.

Hazel drew breath to answer, stopped.

The Cristati Mancer Guard is already inside. Don't think for a second Silverthorne didn't know it would be.

'~Is it a change of plan? Or is it what you've intended all along? Don't lie to me, please.'

Ash shut zheir eyes, hands closing momentarily to fists. ~Fair. Yes, I have had this plan in mind all along, but it did not become necessary until…until Albemarle brought the moat down. Yes, I know I should have handled that better so zhey weren't provoked into it!

Hazel caught zheir flying hands. '~Calm,' he said. '~I'm listening. Go on.'

~Cristati will have broken through the postern gate as soon as the moat failed. They would've been waiting for that exact opportunity.

Hazel looked up into the drizzly rain, letting the drops kiss his face. He said, '~Like the exact opportunity afforded by lowering the moat to let you out the postern gate so you could go to your mother's camp?'

Ash looked completely blank, not in the Mancer way. Then zhey looked indignant. ~I warned you they'd be there! That's why you and the Jeromes were going to escort me out. I hardly need that sort of underhanded trick to bring the stronghold down if that's my plan.

They looked at each other.

~Which it's not!

Hazel grimaced. '~Yes, I know,' he said. '~Aside from anything else, letting in Cristati risks Izidore in a way I don't think you're prepared to do. Ash, I trust you—

Eyes flashing, Ash inserted, ~Because you're trained to.

He bit down on a retort; he was getting slightly tired of the accusation, and besides, what difference did it make what his motivation was, if Ash got what zhey wanted? As zhey'd said, it was useful.

He patiently said, '~Because if you really wanted to watch Haven fall, you'd pretty much have to do nothing at this point. And you're not intending nothing. So what *do* you intend?'

~I need to return to Haven. Izidore is working on zheir half of this new plan. I now hold the key.

Ash took from zheir vest pocket zheir mother's handkerchief and showed it to Hazel before tucking it away again. It hadn't exactly given Hazel any further clue.

~I'm— Hazel, I'm trying to save Haven, I promise you. This new plan does not need Haven to hold out until its allies arrive. This plan involves obliterating Cristati if my mother will not back down.

Hazel was no great admirer of Cristati, but even with its forces camped at Haven's gates and its Mancer guards actually inside, he still must have looked taken aback at the particular verb Ash's signing suggested: a Trade sign to do with wiping out rats, eradicating them, exterminating them.

Ash smiled grimly. ~It is, as you say, too late to be squeamish. If this comes to a choice between Haven and Cristati—I will wipe their stronghold off the face of this world.

'~The stronghold?' Hazel repeated in surprise. He glanced around the camp reflexively.

~That's why I wanted to be sure Paolo wasn't back there. Very many innocents will die if I do this. I do not want Paolo to be one of them.

While Hazel was still frozen, thinking about rats, zhey pointed at the horses in the corral. ~We ride across the field, Hazel. I may be a Mancer, but I'm also Liege Silverthorne, and you're wearing the coat of my

Mancer Guard. I'll look like I'm under escort. The only ones who would dare accost me are Mother and Marco, and if we're fast enough, we'll avoid them. But we must be fast. So, please. Will you come?

Hazel followed Ash to the corral. He stood silently by, flummoxed, as Liege Silverthorne peremptorily ordered a startled groom to saddle zhem a horse and was indeed obeyed. Privilege couldn't save zhem from zheir Mancer Guard but it had its silver lining anyway.

Ash flashed one of zheir small smiles. ~You're thinking, zhey really are a purple-wearing noble scion. See—there *is* a difference between knowing it and actually seeing it with your own eyes.

'~It's disturbing, quite right,' Hazel said.

Already gracefully up in the saddle, Ash looked down at him and held out a hand. ~Can you ride, Hazel?

He'd learnt at the academy, but since Albemarle would not leave the stronghold—never joined the purple in any jaunts into the surrounding countryside, never allowed any of zheir projects that would need recharging with zheir Mancy to be sold or gifted outside the stronghold, never travelled afar for research or pleasure—he hadn't overly much practiced since then.

'~Probably,' he ventured, entrusting his hand to Ash's and finding himself half-heaved and half-scrabbling into the saddle behind zhem, much to the snorted disgust of the horse.

It was big, war-trained, Hazel presumed, and he wrapped his arms around Ash's waist without hesitation and held on tight. He'd defer this task to the expert. He felt, in the same moment, safe under the sure guidance of Ash's hands on the reins, and secure with his arms around zhem, keeping zhem safe with his body in turn.

The drizzle cut visibility as they rode across the muddy field—he'd have to lay fresh flowers on his shrine to Kisane at the earliest opportunity for this convenient squall—and, exactly as Ash had predicted, they were not challenged.

He saw ahead, to his immeasurable relief, that the warm glow of Haven's moat had been re-established. A small section of it was glowing a different shade, not Albemarle's pearlescent white, and not Ash's throbbing red, but a deep blue, near black. That, as far as he knew, would be Izidore's contribution, and he silently blessed zhem for whatever zhey had done to talk Albemarle around.

The soldiers with the battering ram had fallen back, and Hazel saw why when they rode closer—the entrance gates were protected by

Izidore's modification, and it looked like that was more along Ash's more assertive protection than Albemarle's passive shield. The front of the battering ram, the heavy iron cap, was in shards.

That made it easy to ride right up to the gates. It made it a little harder to get in.

Ash sent the horse off with a light tap to its flanks. Zhey turned to Hazel. ~We should hurry. Knock on the sally port and make them let you in.

'~They'll be under orders to not open for anyone.'

~They'll let *you* in, Hazel darling.

Hazel glanced around, pushing wet hair from his face. Visibility was poor. For all he knew, just beyond the haze of the rain, a whole army was waiting for him to accidentally betray his stronghold. For all he knew, *that* was Ash's plan.

He hammered his all-clear signal on the sally port, thumping it hard to make it audible.

The wood sparked under his fist like metal in an electrical storm, but it was more of a tingle than anything painful. The gate was too thick for him to hear more than muffled noises on the other side; it felt interminable before he saw the moat blink as the latch between the sally port panel and its neighbour was lifted. He heard the scrape of the bolts. The small gate was pulled open an inch.

On the other side were a lot of Haven militia with drawn swords, and Miriam.

'See, I told you,' she informed someone coldly over her shoulder, and tugged him through.

He pulled Ash after him, and the guards quickly slammed and barricaded the sally port again, bringing the Mancy moat back up.

'You let me in?' he said to Miriam, genuinely surprised that someone as cool-headed as her had risked overriding the soldiers, even for him.

'Always, Hazel darling,' she said, coming up on tiptoe to kiss his freckles.

Haven militia were swarming about, mopping up the last of the Mancy roaches and rounding up a few prisoners. The cloy of wet smoke hung in the air, and bodies were everywhere, though it looked like Cristati had had the worst of that. The injured on both sides were laid out in rows between the wide entrance stairs and the heavily blockaded gate to the bailey.

He looked queryingly at Miriam, who, having shaken off her temporary slide into emotion, rattled off a report as crisply as any seasoned soldier. Hazel struggled to keep his horror off his face as he heard the litany of ills.

Cristati soldiers inside the walls. Holly, injured, severity unknown because he was still on the move. Morano, injured, severity known and high. Second Jerome back to one leg and exhausted. First Jerome diverted into protecting them. Whereabouts of the Mancers, unknown, at least to Miriam.

She pointed across the courtyard to where the wounded were laid out, and Hazel hurried over, dragging Ash in his wake.

First Jerome crouched over Morano. 'Do you mind if I cut loose your binder?' she was asking. 'It'll help you breathe, I think.'

She glanced up as Hazel's shadow fell over them. 'Hazel,' she cried, and threw herself into his arms for a fervent hug. 'We saw you go over, we thought you were dead.'

She paused, then, and gave him a onceover. He stripped off the Cristati coat and dumped it on the ground. Otherwise Holly would skewer him before he slowed down enough to look beyond the colour.

'Did everyone else make it to the atelier?' he asked as he acknowledged Second Jerome's pat on his ankle; the younger man had lain down next to Morano, who looked half-asleep, probably due to Miriam's poppy concoction.

'Yes, the atelier, go,' First Jerome said.

Ash got Hazel's attention. ~The mirror? Did Izidore get the far-scry device?

'Holly's going for it,' First Jerome confirmed once Hazel had conveyed the question. She wasn't being precisely cold to Ash, but she hadn't included zhem in her pleasure over Hazel's safe return.

The Mancer nodded, signing to Hazel, ~We'll need it.

With one last look to his fellow Mancer guards, Hazel brought Ash safely across the courtyard to the south door.

He'd just tripped over the bodies of some Haven stronghold guards and recognised what that meant when enemy soldiers thronged from the alcove leading to the undercroft staff quarters.

He'd walked Ash right into an ambush.

Hazel kicked a bench and skittled a couple of the soldiers; they were mostly Cristati Mancer Guard, he realised, and there was at least a half-dozen of them, Tassone included. He weighed his chances against theirs and decided he couldn't protect Ash properly if Ash was trapped in the middle of this fight.

Shoving the Mancer away from where zhey were pressed against his side, he signed, ~Atelier.

Then he launched bodily at the Cristati guards, beating them back into the hallway so that Ash would have space to get away. When he battered the cheap stolen blade too hard against a Mancer Guard sword, it shattered, leaving him unarmed and outnumbered.

Hazel gripped the hilt with its stump of broken metal, eyeing off his large, armed and determined opponents.

He just had to buy Ash enough time to reach the atelier. He could hold out that long.

~Thirty-Two~

CRISTATIS HAVE MADE IT INTO THE undercroft via the south door, overpowering and killing the Haven guards stationed there, but, as Holly shortly learns, they did not head down to the subterrane and the atelier. They went up the corkscrew stairs to the upper stronghold, because the inner door has not been bolted; the stairs are too much the convenient thoroughfare for the Havens, and the Mancer guards were not the only ones taken unawares when the Cristati force broke through the postern.

Holly catches up with the incursion after he's finally managed to haul his throbbing knee up every last step—he even tries hopping, but that jostles the injury in a way that makes him nauseated, so he just doggedly pulls himself up through the pain instead.

The Cristatis are in the hallway outside the great hall, assaulting a strong contingent of stronghold guards. They are not Mancer Guard, which explains their mission—they are, or were, on their way to try to capture Lady Fairhaven. If any Cristati Mancer guards are inside, they'll be the ones who targeted the subterrane.

Holly comes up behind the pinned enemy soldiers. Even with the knee making him slow and unsteady, there's no real challenge in dispatching them. That doesn't make Holly even slightly less ruthless about it.

It's an easy matter, then, to nod to the victorious stronghold guards and continue to Valerian's office. The lord is not there; Holly trusts that he and Evie are both safe up with Lady Fairhaven.

Holly retrieves the dead far-scry mirror as per Izidore's impassioned plea and retraces his steps. Coming back down the corkscrew is even harder on the knee because the mirror is heavy enough that he has to use both hands to carry it, and can't lean on the wall to ease his steps. He grits his teeth and forces himself through it. He can taste blood and smoke, making him want to spit.

He reaches the undercroft dining hall just in time to see Hazel and Ash enter through the south door, sodden.

He doesn't have time to feel the joy Hazel's survival merits, because they run smack into a Cristati ambush.

Carefully, Holly sets down the mirror. Then he's running, hobbling really, through the trestle tables as Hazel kicks a bench flying and flashes [atelier] at Ash before forcing the enemy back to clear zheir escape route.

The Mancer does take a step toward the subterrane stairs. One step. Then zhey spin and duck under a table and come up with a copperlit— the weaponised copperlit Kito threw across the dining hall to keep it from Albemarle's attention. Holly has time to wonder if zhey can somehow sense the Mancy in it, hearing the soft buzz with something other than ears.

Zhey shove off the table, over to the wall by the south door, reaching up to snatch another copperlit on zheir way after Hazel. This is zheir mistake. In zheir moment of distraction, Captain Tassone rushes out of the alcove and slams zhem face-first down onto the table.

Holly was already moving to help Hazel, and he only has to divert his trajectory slightly, but he's going to be too late. Tassone has a knife in his hand. He's buried his other hand into the wet snarls of Ash's hair and is holding the Mancer down hard with all his body weight. Ash's hands are trapped under zhem and zhey can't get them free.

Holly's the fastest fighter Haven's ever seen and he's not going to be fast enough. The Cristati captain is going to cut Ash's jugular right in front of him.

Tassone hasn't noticed him, though. Tassone can't resist the gloat. He wrenches on Ash's hair, pulling zheir head up and around so the Mancer can read his lips.

He leans down nice and close. 'Do you know how much it pleases me to be the one to slit your throat, Silverthorne?'

Ash's collar hisses a long whistle and then says, 'I'll wager it's less than it pleased me to kill Olivette and Dimitriou.'

Tassone swears and yanks again on Ash's hair, hard enough to arch zheir upper body off the table. Ash wrenches a hand free and discharges the copperlit over zheir shoulder, right into Tassone's face.

Zhey miss.

It had to be a hard, fast motion, to pull zheir hand out from under zhemself and swing the copperlit up and around to fire at Tassone before the man's reflexes kicked in. Ash didn't have time to aim, and couldn't see to aim anyway, and zhey miss.

The bolt of hot light does graze Tassone's ear; he flinches before smashing back into Ash even harder, slamming zheir head onto the table with a snarl.

It's all played out in something less than fifteen seconds, and Holly's still only halfway there.

Ash, held pinned, is wearing the same infuriated face as when zhey fumbled the lever while zhey were atop the Mancy locust. But zhey don't stop trying. Tassone's bringing his blade around for the kill stroke, and Ash is holding the copperlit across zheir throat to block it even as zhey hum zheir Mancy to recharge it.

The sheer stubborn courage of it is enough to dissipate the last of Holly's anger over Ash's plots against Haven and replace it with only the helpless rage of having to witness zheir murder.

But between the copper tube and the collar, Tassone is momentarily stymied, slicing and stabbing the knife with only the tinny clink of metal on metal as his reward. In this fraught moment of mutual struggle, Ash finally notices Holly, frantically hobbling toward them.

If zheir face had registered relief to see him, Holly might have ratcheted his outrage up again, at the presumption of thinking any Haven Mancer guard—who wasn't Hazel—would still be prepared to help zhem. Holly would have still helped zhem, of course, but he wouldn't have been gracious about it.

As it is, he practically watches zhem add him to zheir very full to-do list: *Deal with Captain Tassone*, that look says, *and then deal with Captain Holly*.

Which is optimistic, but again, Holly can't not feel a dollop of admiration at the can-do attitude.

'Hoi,' he says as he arrives, and Tassone looks up in the middle of shifting the knife around to stab Ash through the back of the neck.

Holly's indignation is directed at Ash, however, not Tassone. He is highly offended. He's suddenly suspecting that Ash's antipathy has been only partly due to jealousy over Hazel, and mostly to do with the fact that Ash has mentally categorised him with the Cristati Mancer Guard. Ash is assuming Holly is the type to hate zhem just like the Cristatis hate zhem.

That Holly said something very much to that effect does not factor into his offence.

He whacks Tassone solidly in the face with the pommel of his sword, only not using the blade because he doesn't want to risk cutting Ash.

Tassone lurches from the force of the wallop and falls off Ash. He's quickly on his feet again, circling around another table, watching Holly closely. He's dropped the knife, drawn his sword. He touches the side of his face with his free hand. It's already swelling.

Ash is up off the table, rubbing at zheir chest. Zhey're still holding the discharged copperlit. Zhey didn't have a chance to finish zheir song. Zheir face is swollen too, where Tassone smacked it into the table.

'~Atelier,' Holly orders zhem, and repeats the sign when zhey don't move.

There's still something of that dangerous assessment—*deal with Captain Holly*—in the way Ash stares at him as if weighing up all zheir varied options. Then zhey give one firm shake of the head, snatch up Tassone's discarded knife, and rush off down the staff hallway, humming into the copperlit in zheir other hand as zhey go. The grunts and clashes of battle are still going on down there.

'Hazel doesn't need your help!' Holly calls after zhem. 'Oh, zhey're deaf, why am I shouting?'

'See?' Tassone says. He's still got a table between him and Holly, and he's looking quite relaxed, if cut up and singed and bruised. 'That one is nothing but trouble. Does as zhey please. Won't ever listen. Endangers everyone with zheir defiance and disobedience.'

'Lover, you just described the general state of being a Mancer,' Holly says.

He feels the faint pulse in his ears that is the soundless yet forceful discharge of Ash's copperlit weapon, and smiles.

'Bullshit,' Tassone scoffs. 'The atelier serves the stronghold.'

Holly squints at him. 'Did we attend the same academy?'

The Cristati gestures lazily at Holly with his sword. 'I saw how docile the Haven Mancer is. Albemarle. You got zhem under the thumb, Holyoake.'

Holly is brought up short. He considers, like a man finally seeing the forest past all the trees, the traditions that have accreted around Mancers and Mancer guards, ateliers and strongholds. Those traditions, in trying to protect Mancers, have made them utterly dependent on the temperament of their Mancer Guard.

He thinks of the bolt on Ash's door, all the Mancers' doors, designed to be breakable if a Mancer guard needs to get in. The only reason he or Hazel didn't break in when Ash was hiding in zheir room was because of basic decency and respect for privacy. That could change, even in Haven.

Mancers could never be truly safe, if safety relied on dependency. Ash, a privileged purple protected by zheir own mother, is a quintessential case in point, but any Mancer could fall afoul of a hostile Mancer Guard.

Any Mancer could fall afoul of the opposite problem too. Albemarle had been careful in choosing Haven, but zhey'd point blank said the Havens were treating zhem like a child, and zhey weren't, apparently, the only one who'd noticed it.

He says, slowly, 'We help zhem regulate zhemself, that's all.'

'Yeah,' Tassone says. 'Regulate. Good word. You would be so useful for *regulating* Silverthorne.'

'Ew,' Holly says. 'I don't have anything more articulate to say about that than just—' He shudders theatrically. '—*Ew*. Are we going to fight, or what?'

'You're being stupid about this. You're the best, Holyoake. Come *be* with the best. Don't waste yourself.'

'Talking, talking, talking.' Holly twirls his blade. 'You'd rather recruit me to your side than face me on mine, is that it?'

'Your yon man just got ambushed by half a Mancer Guard. He's dead. Silverthorne's coming back out of that corridor a prisoner. If zhey're lucky. My men hate zhem, and we've still got Izidore. See sense. Take your last chance to join a big stronghold with bigger plans. We'll make use of your talents instead of frittering them away in a basement.'

'I am fairly fucking appalled that somewhere, somehow, I've behaved in a way that makes the swamp you call your brain think of me as belonging in your nasty narrow little box. I don't and I never will. Now come fight me so I can kill you, you fuck.'

'You're crippled, Holyoake,' Tassone says. He's dropped the falsely confiding tone and is circling back around the table, raising his blade. 'You couldn't beat me when you were fast, you don't have a hope now.'

Holly saw Tassone fight, outside. His statement could very well be true; the latter half of it, at least. 'I could kill you lying on my back with my eyes closed,' he says anyway.

Tassone crouches into the slow stalk of a man about to attack. 'Sounds like you're threatening me with a good time, honey.'

'I feel sorry for your lovers, then. Come at me.'

Tassone lunges, and Holly gladly throws himself into the fight. He can't move like he normally would, and it puts him at a disadvantage, but he pivots and parries, strikes fast at Tassone, who dodges and comes in on Holly's left and makes a jab at the knee. As Holly hops back in an embarrassingly clumsy fade, he flashes on the memory of unrelentingly targeting Hazel's weak left side. It irritates him enough that he flings his body into a rapid series of thrusts and slices that makes his knee scream at him.

He's forced to drop back but he's lucky; the Cristati captain pauses to catch his breath instead of noticing how close Holly's knee is to buckling.

'Silverthorne is a serpent,' Tassone says. 'You've taken a serpent to your breast, do you understand that? Maybe even literally.' He raises an eyebrow. 'It's zheir usual method.'

Holly, annoyingly, glances at the alcove, but there's no movement and no more audible noise. Tassone catches the look and smiles knowingly. 'Oh, the big one, is it? Makes more sense. I saw that look zhey gave you. Zhey've decided to get rid of you, you mark my words.'

'Are you really so afraid to fight me, you'd tell nursery tales of a monster under my bed?' Holly snaps. 'I'd trust Liege fucking Silverthorne over you anytime, arsewipe. If zhey don't trust me in return, that's on me.'

He takes a breath. Hazel and Ash are emerging from the hallway. Ash is staying slightly behind Hazel, Hazel holding one arm out to keep zhem shielded, bloodied sword at the ready in the other.

Tassone performs a satisfying double-take. 'What the fuck?'

He is referring to the incontrovertible fact that Hazel walked back out, alive and unharmed, if daubed with fresh blood, and none of the Cristatis did.

'Academy-trained Mancer guard,' Hazel tells Tassone in his unassuming way.

'So were mine. And there were five of them and your sword was broken.'

'You can still stab people with a broken sword,' Hazel says.

He's deliberately sporting his mildest expression, as he did when facing Tassone over his lieutenant's body. He's probably feeling pleased with himself, this being the second Cristati Mancer Guard he's decimated today.

He holds up the blade he's now carrying, which is definitely not broken. 'And then you can take *their* sword. Because they don't need it anymore.'

If Ari Hazlemere wasn't congenitally modest and also hadn't had the exquisitely bad timing of attending the academy in the shadow of Rowan Holyoake, Holly is fairly certain he'd be the Haven with the famous reputation.

And he'd have been happy as a gardener.

Holly one-handedly signs, ~I love you, and Hazel gives him the slightest of smiles, more a creasing of the eyes than a movement of the lips. A-yah, fairly fucking pleased with himself.

'I had some help,' he adds, giving Ash a fond little nudge.

Ash glances up at him, unsmiling. Holly has been assuming that Ash, despite all zheir plotting, could not resist diverting off-plan to assist Hazel; it made him think better of zhem. Now Ash's carefully blank expression as zhey look between Hazel and Holly forces him to consider if zhey aren't doing *exactly* as zhey planned—dealing with Captain Holly.

Dealing with Captain Holly, by keeping the useful, pliable Hazel alive to stand between him and zhem.

Even as this thought occurs to him, Ash raises the discharged copperlit and starts humming Mancy into it. Zhey meet Holly's eyes as zhey arm zhemself, and the fight at the centre of Holly's being flares high: *threat, threat, threat*, it tells him, and it thrums right through him.

'Warned you,' Tassone says softly.

Ash shifts further behind Hazel, charged copperlit loose in one hand, still watching Holly. Ash, Holly realises, is once again remembering that Holly is like the Cristatis, and hates zhem.

'~I trust zhem over you,' he repeats, making sure Ash can see his lips and hands.

He impulsively salutes the Mancer with his sword, and only then reflects that it very well may look like he's either acknowledging an adversary or, standing more or less beside Tassone, actually opening hostilities.

Ash, however, finally blinks, and then offers him up an elegant shallow bow and tilt of the copperlit in return.

It is with no little relief that Holly says, '~And are we letting Tassone surrender, or are we engaging in some payback, Ash? I know where my vote lies.'

'Cristatis don't surrender,' Tassone shouts.

'You're all in for a shit of a day, then,' Holly tells him.

Tassone leaps at Holly; Holly catches the swing of his blade on his own sword and shoves him back, but stumbles backward himself when his knee finally gives way. As Tassone recovers, Ash shoots him with the copperlit. It again misses and Ash gives it a disgusted look and throws it away; it's dented, Holly realises, that's why it won't reliably shoot straight.

Across the dining hall, the remnant Haven Mancer Guard run up the broad subterrane stairs, Albemarle and Izidore with them, coughing.

'The atelier's full of smoke,' Kito calls when she sees Holly, who's caught his balance on a table. 'It's spreading through the subterrane. I think the venting must be pulling air in near a wildfire. We can't breathe down there. Everyone else and their cat has gone out into the kitchen gard—'

The south door flings open and men in the Cristati colours pour in, shouting to their captain about fire and smoke driving them from their hidden position in the garden.

Then they notice the Havens.

Hazel tips a table into the onrushing soldiers, while Ash throws Tassone's own knife at the captain's face and looks enraged when zhey miss yet again. Holly snags zheir sleeve and hurls zhem toward the others.

'Go up, go up, go up,' he shouts over his shoulder, joining Hazel to provide cover for the retreat.

He cursed the tables on his slow way across the dining hall before, but now they provide a much-needed labyrinth to stop too many of the Cristatis coming at them at once. As with the initial attack outside, there are a mix of Cristati Mancer guards and general soldiers in this cluster, around half and half. These men must have fallen back into the pleasure garden to act as rearguard when the others made the dash into the stronghold. The fire's driven them inside, the same way it's driven all the Havens from the subterrane.

Holly spares one thought for Miriam and the injured men and women of the stronghold. With the greenery damp from the rain, it will be a smoky fire out there. He hopes the soft mist and the stone of the courtyard is enough to stop the fire and heat from reaching them, and that the air outside stays clean enough to breathe without hazard.

Hazel jams in tight on Holly's injured side, bolstering the knee. Together, they parry and slash and stab, falling steadily back to the corkscrew stairs.

'Don't *wait* for us,' Holly is incensed to be obliged to add to his previous order, when he risks a glance and see that the others have clustered at the bottom of the stairs.

'Mirror?' Izidore calls back.

'Table,' he says, leaning on Hazel so he can plant a solid kick into the midriff of a Cristati.

Titus and Nightingale dart about the nearby tables, Titus quickly spotting the mirror and swiping it up to carry back to Izidore. A Cristati breaks through Holly and Hazel's shield and goes for her, but Nightingale is there, strong and fierce.

'Pretty throat,' she mutters as she stabs him in it, spraying hot blood all over herself without a care. 'Looks prettier with my sword in it.'

Which is the only way Holly realises that at least some of these intruders are the same men who'd come to the feast night. They'll know their way about, then.

Nightingale grabs Titus's arm and hustles her and the mirror back to Kito. The three Mancer guards begin to shepherd the three Mancers up the stairs. Hazel and Holly fall back behind them.

From there the fight gets both much easier, because only so many swords can come at them within the narrow corkscrew, and much, much harder, because if Holly thought the stairs were hard on his knee the first time he'd tackled them, he'd woefully underestimated the agony of trying to take them fast, and backward, and while wielding a sword.

By the time he reaches the top, leaning hard on Hazel's inexhaustible strength, he's spent. The knee will barely hold his weight anymore. He collapses against the wall, beside Albemarle, who is shaky-legged already. Holly regrets not making Haven's Mancer do the daily stair run.

'Keep going up,' he says to Hazel, pushing him toward Kito and the others. 'I'll hold them here.'

'A-yah, sure, you do that.' Hazel slams shut the stairwell door, and bolts it. 'The fucking door will hold them here, and the stronghold guard.'

Indeed, the guards Holly ran into earlier, Devi and Kiselyova among them, are waiting, strung along the hallway in a funnelling formation.

'I can't walk, love,' Holly explains. 'I'll just slow you down.'

'Fuck off, Holyoake, I'll carry you.'

In the brief moment of catching their breaths, Kito hugs Hazel. 'Oh my stars, my dear, I thought you'd abandoned us to Holly's tender mercies.'

The junior guards converge on Hazel for their own fast display of affectionate relief. Even Albemarle gives him a single pat on the arm.

'We'll help Holly,' Titus says breathlessly, pointing rapidly between herself and Nightingale. 'You and Kito get the Mancers up, Hazel. Izidore needs a safe place to stop and fix the mirror.'

Holly takes the compromise; he knows Hazel will dig his heels in if he thinks Holly's going to stay behind. 'Get up to Lady Fairhaven as fast as you can,' he says. 'Her location will be the safest place for the Mancers now.'

'She'll be on the roof,' Kito says. 'The door there's the strongest in the stronghold, bar the atelier's and the saferoom for the children, and she'll be looking out for signals from our allies.'

Ash looks satisfied when zhey lipread that. He tugs on Hazel's sleeve, pointing up and nodding. Hazel looks between Holly and Ash.

'Go on, Hazel,' Holly says. He catches Ash's eye. 'Your Mancer has a plan, and if you trust it, I trust it. If you trust zhem, I trust zhem.' He then takes a moment to grab Hazel's arm and say, 'Glad you're not dead, love. Keep it that way.'

'You too, Hols,' Hazel says, giving him a hard hug before turning back to Kito and the Mancers.

When the small group is out of sight, Holly addresses the two juniors. 'Have you considered that I can barely move and these stairs are an excellent chokepoint to make a stand? Leave me to it. You don't have to tell Hazel.'

'Have you considered that we don't abandon our captain?' Nightingale counters.

'The switchback to the roof is pretty narrow,' Titus adds. 'Let's make the stand there, shall we, if we're going to?'

'Pair of puppies,' Holly murmurs. He looks then at the stronghold guards, waiting to face down a foreign Mancer Guard, the most elite fighters in all of Eldemira.

'Don't even try it on, Holly,' Devi says. 'We'd never tell you to step away from Haven's Mancers.'

Holly nods. 'The door will hold,' he says, more to himself than them.

A beam of light pierces the top of the door and carves a char-edged path downward. Tassone must have snatched back the bricolaged lever from the smouldering undergrowth before coming inside, or sent one of his men for it. He's cutting through the wood as easily as unlacing a boot.

That bloody lever. If this is the sort of thing Ash produces on a regular basis, no wonder Lady Cristati will risk all to get zhem back, regardless of how heavy a mother's love lies on the scales.

The beam reaches the thick iron bar and slices through it like butter.

Holly lets Titus and Nightingale nudge themselves under each arm, and they make progress toward the rear of the stronghold. Behind them, they hear the first clash of the battle, and Holly starts to turn because the sound is a siren song.

The others pull him onward. They do not belong with the defence of Haven. They belong to Haven's Mancers.

The next set of steps, the backstairs up to the purple's residential floor, taxes Holly again and leaves him panting. There are no stronghold guards waiting here. They'll be at the main doors, unaware of the incursion, or with the injured at the bailey gate, or on the roof with Lady Fairhaven—the ones who aren't dead at the postern gate, or dead at the south door, or dead at the top of the corkscrew stairs.

By the time the two youngest Mancer guards have got Holly to the switchback stairs to the roof, Captain Tassone and his remaining men have almost caught up with them.

'Go on up,' Holly tells his people. 'Make sure the rooftop door is as locked as it's going to get. Make sure you're on the Mancer side of it.'

'Holly—'

'I've got to get that lever off Tassone or he'll come straight through that door, too.'

'But—'

'We've got three Mancers and only two Mancer guards with them. Go to them.' Holly looks at his junior guards. 'It's your duty and it's an order. Go. *Go.*'

Holly limps in their wake to stand alone on the lower half of the switchback. Behind him, at last, he hears the thump of the door closing, the bolts shooting.

He's far enough up that Tassone's men will have to come at him one at a time. There's a small landing just behind him, and the switch up the roof, making a useful corner for an ambush. But he doesn't want Tassone to get even a sightline on the last door between him and the Mancers while he's still holding that fucking lever with its cutting beam of light.

Holly's never been much for ambushes anyway.

The Cristatis come into sight, moving briskly along the residential hallway, Tassone at the fore. Holly hops down a few steps, making sure they can see him. It doesn't look like Haven's stronghold guard managed to cut their numbers down by many. On the other hand, they seem out of breath, a combination of the many sets of stairs and the fighting on the way. Swordfights, even brief ones, were more exhausting than non-combatants realised. So were stairs.

'Hoi, Tassone,' Holly says. 'That job offer still open?'

He's watching the Mancer guards among the soldiers as he says this, and catches the flash of disgruntlement before those consummate professionals can hide it.

Tassone doesn't appear to notice his men's annoyance. 'I knew you'd reconsider.'

He's sounding smug but looking contemptuous, as he should be. Who would take on a Mancer guard who laid down their sword in these circumstances?

'Nah,' Holly says. 'Just fucking with you.'

Tassone rolls his eyes and waves his men forward. It's a couple of mere soldiers that come at Holly first, and he braces his bad leg and beats them back. They're attacking with brute force and he's using the same to counter them. Tassone is trying to tire him out, make the knee give way, and it will work. But for now, he holds the high ground and a solid defensive position.

One of the soldiers falls back, clutching a spurting cut to his shoulder. 'May a demon fuck your mother!'

'One did,' Holly says. He winks. 'I'm the result.'

He finishes that one off and pauses to mentally apologise to his long-dead parents; he'd gotten a bit carried away there and they are indubitably two of those ancestors he's meant to revere. Then, leaning on the wall and working his good leg hard, he manages to cut down the second soldier and pushes the body off the stairs.

A third attacker, a Mancer guard, approaches with more care. This one's had coaching from Tassone, and aims for his knee, which means he's too busy to notice when Holly reverses his blade and puts it through his neck in a flash.

The assault pauses then, while Tassone comes to terms with the simple truth that Holly's still faster than his people, even when standing mostly still. Holly blows him a kiss; he wants the fucking captain to attack before he's too tired to hold.

Behind the clustered men, a door to one of the purple's apartments opens; Holly thinks *ambush* and therefore expects Kito—it would have been a fantastic idea, if they all hadn't been moving too fast to think of it. To his astonishment, Valerian emerges, towing a sulky Lorian by one arm.

They're in the midst of an argument, evidently a long one, which Valerian is trying to shut down. 'That is quite enough. I am done discussing this, you are joining the other children in the saferoom.'

An ambush *was* a fantastic idea. Except it seems it's the hot-headed adolescent who had it, and then didn't mention it to anyone else. He's got a dinky little sword in his free hand, glinting in the copperlit light. Valerian's got his bare axe dangling from the hand not dragging his petulant son.

Plainly, Val found his son hiding in his chambers with a weapon and the door ajar to listen for the invaders. Plainly, once the door was fully shut for an intense father–son conversation, it was fairly fucking sound-proof in those well-appointed apartments, unlike the rooms in the sub-terrane. They have no clue what they've walked into.

The Cristati turn in impressive, if disturbing, unison and watch as Lorian wails, 'I'm not a child!'

'If you could only hear how much like a child you sound like when you—'

Valerian finally glances up the hallway and, pale face turning ashy, notices the enemy soldiers. His grip on his son tightens so much that Lorian cries out in protest, and then he too cuts off into appalled silence as he follows his father's gaze.

Lorian, the little idiot, brandishes his sword at the invaders. The Cristatis automatically shift to answer the threat, facing an ill-trained and shaking child and all. Valerian growls and drags the boy behind him. He stands firm, gripping the axe two-handed.

Holly is obliged to intervene. 'Non-combatants,' he shouts, the axe and sword notwithstanding. Valerian lifts his gaze to meet Holly's and looks so relieved that Holly feels sick. That is misplaced hope if ever he's seen it. 'They're non-combatants, Tassone, come on, you know the rules. Prove you have some honour and let them go.'

The Cristati captain eyes Holly appraisingly; Holly, without noticing himself do it, has come down off the stairs.

'Well,' Tassone says. 'And which one did you give up your defensive position for?'

One of the Mancer guards looks over his shoulder at his captain. 'Sir, Lieutenant Dimitriou said that boy told him he's the Haven heir.'

There's no chance to claim Lorian was engaging in empty boasting; into the struck silence, the lad gasps, 'Sorry, Father!' with fervent and honest dismay.

'Take him and kill the father,' Tassone orders.

Even before he's got the words out, Valerian has reacted, sinking his axe with startling force into the chest of the nearest Cristati with a furious cry of, 'For fuck's sake, Lorian.'

He rips the axe free and violently backswings it into the next man's throat, almost severing his victim's head from his neck with the blow. He doesn't miss a beat in his paternal commentary. 'This is precisely why strongholds keep their heirs a secret!'

As he shouts at his son to run, he makes the mistake of hurling the axe at a third guard—not that it doesn't hit its mark with a satisfyingly meaty squelch, but he's now left unarmed.

If Holly is asked, he does call swordplay a dance, because he knows that's what others will understand—it doesn't matter what sort of traditions they left to come to Haven, all cultures dance in one way or another. They see his skill and speed and imagine him progressing merrily through the steps faster than his opponents, and the metaphor suits a simple fight well enough.

But he's from a family of weavers; he played under the Mancy loom as a very young child and was set to work untangling threads as soon as his fingers were nimble enough. And so, in his own mind, swordplay, especially swordplay as complicated as the sequence he is about to undertake, is not a dance at all, but instead a tapestry, woven from disparate threads, wool and silk and gilt and metal, weft together to make vibrant blocks of colours through the warp.

He looks at the arrangement of swords and their wielders, and he sees how the weft and warp will interleave to make the whole. It is this, more than mere physical ability, that gives him such phenomenal speed. He can even see where a broken thread, a broken knee, will best fit the emerging pattern.

He smacks into the Cristatis only a second or two after the tableau broke, Tassone shouting his order and Valerian swinging his axe. The pattern unrolling in his mind's eye means he only gets one strike at Tassone as he whips past him, and he feels from the bite and recoil that he didn't put enough force into it; he couldn't, it would have tipped him on his arse when his knee finally made good on its threat to collapse under him.

In fact, his knee is why he moves in an erratic zigzag, pushing off bodies he should be pivoting around and resting on walls he should be bouncing off. He's slower than he'd like but he has inexorable momentum as he shuttlecocks his way down the hallway, matching the tapestry he's woven in his head to the most efficient pattern for dispatching the Cristati Mancer guards and soldiers, flashing sword a counterweight to his aching knee, so swollen now that it's going numb and that is not the best of signs.

He's not quite to Valerian when the lord makes the fatal mistake of throwing away his weapon. Lorian has turned to run, obedient to his father's order, but he swings back as a Cristati piles into Val. The three bodies go over in a threshing tangle.

Holly reaches them. He's panting, his knee will no longer let him bend his leg at all, he's splattered with blood, his own and others, and Valerian is lying on his back with his eyes closed and a nasty cut on his chest. The soldier who launched at them is dead on the floor next to him. Lorian kneels over him, own bloodied sword in hand. It still looks like a tin toy.

The boy looks up at Holly. Holly looks down at him, and at his father, motionless on the ground.

Then the tapestry weave snaps back into place and Holly whirls back down the hallway to take care of the Cristati he missed on his first pass.

He ends up at the base of the stairs, every last Cristati bar one dead on the floor behind him, and he is shaking. He feels the soundless throb in his ears that he's beginning to associate with Ash's Mancy. He hears the grind of tortured wood beyond the switchback. He let Tassone get past him, to the door, and the man is wasting no time cutting it open.

Holly tries to take the stairs at a run, and he ends up pulling himself up one by one. When he rounds the small landing of the switchback, Tassone has turned from the door and is looking down at him, lever in one padded hand, sword in the other. He's paused his assault.

Holly can guess why. He's still dangerous, and Tassone is probably torn between turning the lever on him or saving whatever is left of the Mancy—there can't be much—for the door and for the fight beyond the door. Holly guesses that the man's sole aim now is simple vengeance; he can't possibly hope to kidnap the Mancers alone, but he might get lucky and kill one of them. Holly knows which one.

'You can't win this,' the Cristati captain says, almost kindly. 'You made a good go of it. I'm impressed, truly. But you don't have to die today, Holyoake. Just stay there. Let me have Silverthorne. You hate zhem too, and zhey know it. Get rid of zhem before zhey get rid of you. It'll save you and your stronghold so much trouble.'

Holly faces the dismal truth. He is exhausted. His leg has seized up so badly he can barely move and barely think from the pain. Tassone has the high ground. Tassone has a sort of sword made from light that will cut him in half if he comes a single step closer.

The other captain is correct. Holly cannot win this.

And so Holly does what Holly always does in a fight.

Holly doubles down.

He doesn't bother with backchat; he just launches off his good leg and lands halfway up the stairs, just close enough that the utmost stretch of his arm and swipe of his sword connects with the lever and knocks it flying from Tassone's hand.

Tassone jumps down the first few risers, attention split between tracking the arc of the lever and Holly. He swings his sword two-handed at Holly, knowing how off-balance he is; indeed, when Holly parries, he falls against the wall and has to scrabble miserably along it, his wrists locking up as he tries to hold back Tassone's blade with his own without the power of his braced back and legs. Tassone is backing him up toward the door, where any speed he has left to him will be neutralised by the narrowing space.

Tassone batters through his guard and kicks him in his bad knee. Holly shouts in true agony and falls back again, only just having the where-withal to parry Tassone's hard strike at his head. His back hits the door and the impact jolts his sword from his weakened grip.

He is unarmed and has nowhere left to dodge. He's done.

~THIRTY-THREE~

KITO SLAMMED THE ROOFTOP DOOR SHUT behind Hazel and the three Mancers and bolted it. 'Cristati on the way,' she reported tersely to the others on the roof.

Those others included Lady Fairhaven, most of the other Haven purple, Evelyn, the artificer, and a smattering of commanders, retainers and guards. The rest of the non-combatant Havens would be hiding in various lockable locations under tight guard. Any in the subterrane would have escaped out into the kitchen gardens, which was walled off from soldiers and from fire, and so was not such a bad location.

The air still had the feel and taste of storm, but the rain had stopped, the low clouds rushing away westward in a stiffening breeze that blew the lingering taste of smoke away too. The flagstones underfoot were slippery. Izidore, with blithe disregard for the cold damp through zheir tattered skirts, immediately knelt and laid the dysfunctional far-scry mirror flat on the ground.

Zhey glanced questioningly at Albemarle, who was panting and red-faced from zheir exertions, and a touch wild-eyed from Kito's unrelenting prodding to get zhem up all those stairs. But zhey merely nodded to the expectant look and pulled from the capacious pocket of zheir loose robe one of zheir journals. Zhey opened it, displaying the page with the original design of the mirror.

Hazel, despite the frantic sense of an inevitable tip toward disaster, took a moment to marvel—it felt like only yesterday that Albemarle would have had a paroxysm to be so bluntly confronted with zheir failure.

Ash got Izidore's attention. ~Izidore, you do not have time to add legs.

'Every little creature on the green earth functions better with mechanisms of motion,' Izidore said. 'Lots of them.'

Ash crossed zheir wrists, both hands in the negatory fist, and even mouthed a no with a puff of air.

Izidore, for the first time in this whole long day of being manipulated and pushed around by zheir friend, looked very cross. Zhey slapped zheir hands on the ground and stuck out zheir bottom lip and finally said, 'No legs and be damned to you, then.'

Ash had the gall to assume an offended expression before hurrying over to Lady Fairhaven, leaving the other two Mancers to their work. Hazel heard Izidore say to Albemarle, 'You forgot the focus. You forgot to consider how to connect to your location.'

And miracle of miracles, Albemarle still did not have a paroxysm.

'Well,' Lady Fairhaven said mildly. 'Things appeared to be going to plan, except you are back here and now it's not a covenant violation.'

~It's too late. Cristati will have Izidore and me back before your allies reach us.

As if to underscore Ash's point, a Mancer Guard code sounded from the door. Sword in hand, Kito cautiously opened it, letting in Nightingale and Titus.

'The door will hold them,' Lady Fairhaven said. She looked north. 'It's still a siege, just on a more intimate scale. We'll hold for Mollymawk.'

Hazel knew from seeing some of Albemarle's letters that Juniper liked wings like Izidore liked legs and tentacles. Lady Fairhaven was looking out for reinforcements from the air. It was a faint hope; anything light enough to fly here on a single charge of Mancy would not be of much use.

'No,' Titus blurted. 'My lady, they can cut through this door in seconds.'

~The lever? Ash asked.

'They've got a thing like a hot knife that can cut metal and wood,' Titus went on, oblivious. 'Holly's going to try and get it off them. He's holding the stairs.'

Hazel took a step toward the door, and stopped himself. Evelyn had done the exact same thing. They looked at each other. Evelyn looked back at the door, her feet inching.

Lady Fairhaven said, 'Let's trust to Holly, then, and bolt the door he's trying to protect. *Evie*. Please, sweetheart. Trust to Holly.'

There was more than just a touch of command in her voice this time, and a plea. Evelyn turned back from the door, face a silent curse. Hazel made himself follow her.

Ash signed to Lady Fairhaven, ~I need Lady Cristati to come up here.

When Hazel, not without a blink, voiced this, Lady Fairhaven said, 'What?' with a clear note of incredulity. It was the first time Hazel had ever seen her completely abandon her façade of impervious serenity.

Ash repeated zhemself.

'My dear, I can only engender that with surrender.'

While her people made noises of quiet shock, Ash glanced to where the two other Mancers worked. Zhey stamped zheir foot twice, which was evidently a familiar signal, because Izidore immediately looked up, face tight in concentration.

Zhey nodded to Ash. 'Almost.'

~But you can make it work? For sure?

'For sure. I won't go back, Ash.'

~Whatever happens, I won't let you go back.

Izidore appeared to have a level of faith in Ash that was either touching or terrifying, depending on perspective. Zhey nodded again and returned to zheir task.

Ash turned back to Lady Fairhaven. ~Yes. Surrender.

Zhey had a reciprocal level of faith in Izidore, it seemed.

She set hands on hips. 'Young Mancer, I need more information than that.'

Ash shifted, half-turning as if to stalk away, face set. Hazel caught zhem by the elbow. '~Calm,' he said. '~There's no other way but through Lady Fairhaven. Tell me what I need to tell her.'

Ash swayed forward, resting zheir face on his chest as if drawing strength. Hazel absolutely did not feel the urge to pull zhem all the way into his arms, stroke zheir hair, and lend zhem every drop of strength he had.

Gathering zhemself, Ash began to rapidly sign. ~The far-scry mirror will give me access to Stronghold Cristati. My mother needs to see that I have that access, or this plan will not work.

'What plan?'

Here Hazel paused for his own aside. 'Zhey told me zhey will obliterate Stronghold Cristati, my lady.'

Her eyebrows went up. She looked again at Ash, a long, surprised look. Zhey nodded. ~I must prove my intent to her, or my threat against her stronghold will not work. She needs to come up here.

Lady Fairhaven looked at Hazel. 'Hazel darling,' she said. 'If we allow Lady Cristati up those stairs and Ashlin does not come through, we are handing all three of our Mancers over. Do you truly trust that zhey can do as zhey say?'

Hazel took a breath. How easy it would be, to say no. To say, you betrayed me. You used me. Go home to Cristati, where you so plainly belong.

Lady Fairhaven's face was compassionate. She knew intimately how much faith it took to extend kindness. How much faith it took to trust so very many lives to a single slender and overburdened back.

But that was Haven. Not a place, but just people, people who chose to be kind, and strong with it.

'Yes,' he said. 'Can and will.'

She flicked a look at Evelyn. Evelyn said, 'If Hazel trusts zhem, we trust zhem.'

'The academy training has much to answer for,' Lady Fairhaven murmured.

'Yes,' Hazel said, heartfelt. 'But not in this case, my lady. Please. I trust zhem completely. Zhey have a plan. Zhey'll see it through.'

She threw up her hands. 'Then we surrender.'

Her advisors made a muttering, but she merely nodded to Evelyn, who raced to the rooftop door, flinging back the bolts. A low hiss the only warning, the hot light of the modified Mancy lever pierced the door, narrowly missing her hip. She threw herself aside and drew her sword as the light began to slice the door in half.

The Mancer Guard tightened around the Mancers; Hazel stepped completely in front of Ash. That would be Tassone coming single-mindedly through that door.

Holly, he thought.

The light winked out. A couple of muffled thuds sounded on the other side. Evelyn, swearing under her breath, yanked the door open.

Holly, all his weight on the door, tipped backward and hit the ground hard enough to audibly lose his air. Tassone, in the middle of lunging forward to stab him, overextended. He fell onto Holly, only not stabbing him as he landed because Holly grabbed his arms and redirected the sword tip over his own head.

Holly had always been fast, and not just on his feet. While the other captain was still trying to recover enough to get his legs under him, while Kito was still leaping forward with one of her trishuls angled for the back of his neck, Holly wrenched the blade from Tassone's hand, flipped it, and skewered him under the ribs. Kito's blade followed a scant second later.

Tassone coughed blood and died.

'On my back with my eyes closed,' Holly said to the sky. 'And your own sword, you utter *fuck*.'

He wiped his face and grimaced. He was fairly well bathed in blood and gore. Hazel dreaded the state of the hallway below them.

Evelyn leaned over him, pushing the body off. 'We're surrendering to Lady Cristati.'

'Oh, for fuck's sake,' Holly said. He tilted his head back until he had eyes on Ash. '~I suppose that's your doing?'

Lord Valerian, inexplicably, stepped out of the stairwell and helped him up. Hazel saw Holly wince a little, which meant he was in a great deal of pain. The lord had lost his axe, gained a gruesome cut across his shoulder, and looked as contained and practical as ever, as though he weren't unsteady on his feet and splattered with blood. Lorian hovered at his shoulder, wan and tear-streaked, holding a decorative sort of sword in a white-knuckled death grip.

Holly said, 'You're alive, then?' He shoved Valerian with both hands, making himself wobble quite dramatically and the stolid lord move not a whit. 'Don't ever fucking do that again, you selfish shit, you should have seen the look on your boy's face.'

'Like you can fucking talk,' Evelyn shouted at him. 'I am so angry with you! A last stand, what were you even thinking?'

She clipped him over his ear like he was still sixteen, and he said, 'Evie!' like he was still sixteen, and, 'You're ruining my righteous tantrum with yours, you know.'

'You're welcome,' Valerian put in mildly, and strolled off to the other lords with his arm around his son, looking both highly pleased with himself and also somewhat guilty, while Evelyn hauled her sibling into a short, hard embrace and then smacked him again.

Ash looked down at the dead body of the Cristati captain, face neutral. Then zhey turned to Holly and made [thanks] with the scantest of movements before launching off into, ~Do you have the lever?

'~Fuck, give a fellow a moment to catch his breath.'

Nevertheless, he started off in a limp, a shift of his jaw suggesting he was gritting his teeth. Evelyn tsked and ran the errand for him, vanishing into the stairwell, sword still drawn.

Hazel pulled Holly into his arms for a long hug, letting him lean on him. 'Let a fellow catch his breath!' Holly repeated, before giving Hazel a loud kiss on his ear. 'Love, I'm all right.'

Evelyn came back with the lever and tossed it to Ash.

Zhey, using the lever as benignly as Albemarle intended, extended it into its longer form and placed one end under the collar around zheir neck. With one savage jerk, zhey had snapped it in two. Zhey flung the pieces off the roof with prejudice.

Lady Fairhaven followed the twin arcs with a calm eye. 'Don't you need that to talk to your mother?' Unspoken was the question: *Have I misplaced my trust in you?*

Ash appeared unconcerned. ~Hazel will voice for me.

Rubbing at zheir neck, zhey stood at the parapet and looked over at the ground below. It might have been an innocent glance, idly checking where the two parts of the hated collar had fallen. But Hazel thought he knew Ash rather well by now. Hazel thought Ash had plans upon plans.

Whatever happens, I won't let you go back.

Ash had proven ruthless, and Hazel didn't think zhey would flinch if it came to turning that ruthlessness on zhemself. And so, an obvious alternate plan, should the mirror fail, would be to remove zhemself from contention so that the covenant would snap back into place over Albemarle and Izidore, and never mind that it would do nothing to stop Cristati before Haven's allies arrived.

A *very* obvious way to remove zhemself from contention, that would mortally wound zheir mother as an additional boon, would be to take a walk off the top of the stronghold right in front of her.

Having meandered his way to this appalling conclusion, Hazel shared it with Evelyn, who had a short discussion with one of the commanders. Guards spread out around the circle of the wide parapet.

Ash had hastened to Izidore and Albemarle, but when zhey glanced up and saw the new arrangement, no part of the parapet wall out of arm's reach of a guard, zhey shot one of those unreadable Mancer looks at Hazel. He looked back as blandly as he could manage.

Not quite being so unsubtle as to shake zheir head, zhey turned back to the other Mancers, who appeared finished using Izidore's screwdriver tool on the mirror. They had added a few bits and pieces from their pockets to it, loose notions they must have snatched from the atelier during the smoke-induced evacuation. An oblong arrangement of coils garnished the top now, almost decorative in its coppery scrolls.

Together the three Mancers lifted the mirror so it was leaning against the western parapet. Izidore opened zheir mouth and sang a Mancy song. If Hazel had shut his eyes, it would have sounded exactly like a violin. He wasn't sure if it would ever become less strange to hear that sound coming out of a person's mouth.

~This is done, Izidore told Ash.

Ash knelt by it. Zhey pulled out the stolen handkerchief and threaded it through the coils along the top. Zhey fidgeted with the placement, minutely adjusting it, and then pressed along the side of the mirror, deft fingers finding knobs set into its wooden frame.

The mirror's surface hazed and cleared, and they were all looking into a lavishly furnished bedchamber, devoid of occupants.

Ash sat back on zheir heels and heaved out a long breath. Izidore knocked zheir hip into zheir shoulder, and they exchanged smiles.

~Steer it to the atelier.

Izidore leaned over, pressing on the knobs. 'This is the biggest scorpion's nest, yes?

~Neither of us have anything intimate enough to connect us to the atelier. Mother's chamber was as close as I could get.

As Izidore pressed the various knobs, the view through the mirror changed, rapidly swooping this way and that and to and fro. Hazel, seasick, had to look away, and was not the only person who did.

'Wherein lies the atelier from there?' Izidore casually asked, and Ash put both hands into zheir hair in sheer frustration.

As Izidore and Ash bickered over steering the mirror's viewpoint, Lady Cristati and her guards and retinue strolled onto the rooftop. Havens had been working to clear the bodies here and below, so she did not have to step over the corpses of her own people, but her disdainful expression suggested she wouldn't have cared either way. Her oldest son, Marco, must have been left in charge of the soldiers in the field, but Paolo was with her, his open face worried. He was still wearing Hazel's blood-spoiled coat over his shoulders.

The Havens, Mancer guards and stronghold guards, snapped to attention as the Cristati contingent walked in. Holly was on his feet, weight on his good leg, sword in hand, watching Lady Cristati like she'd murdered his lastborn.

Ash took one look at zheir mother and rapidly tapped zheir palms together by Izidore's ear. ~Atelier, atelier, atelier.

Izidore smacked zheir hands away. 'Shouting doesn't help!'

~It helps *me*!

'Let me,' Albemarle rumbled crossly, and pushed them both aside. 'This knob makes it go this way, and *this* one…'

Zheir voice trailed off as zhey sank into fierce Mancer concentration, Ash signing the directions and Izidore whispering zhem into Albemarle's ear. Lady Cristati watched them with contemptuous amusement before flicking an idle hand at Lady Fairhaven.

'So glad you came to your senses, Tashi. I'm owed reparations, of course.'

Lady Fairhaven sighed. With one last look at Ash, she smiled and said, 'I'll call for refreshments.'

'Surely we can retire somewhere more comfortable.'

'Apparently your stubborn child thinks not.' Summoning a retainer with a gentle crook of her fingers, Lady Fairhaven gave a few quiet instructions, not all to do with tea.

Lady Cristati waited for her to be done before saying bitingly, 'You needed a firmer hand, Tashi. Not your first mistake, of course, but one of many in this matter.'

The viewpoint of the mirror opened up from a brightly lit and carpeted corridor into a neat and spacious atelier. As Ash had told Hazel, it was high up in Stronghold Cristati, the wide vault of the sky visible through its wide windows. It would have been a light and airy workspace, if not for the thick iron bars on every one of those generous windows. The sky glimpsed through the bars was grey; the squall had swept inland.

'I feel very bad about housing you in the dungeon now, young Mancer, renovated or no,' Lady Fairhaven remarked to the air, having taken a close look through the mirror.

She watched the scene with her usual serene attention, but she was gently pinching the cloth over her wrists, worrying at the frills on her cuffs.

Ash rose and tapped Izidore on the shoulder. Zhey, hands on the mirror, began to sing a Mancy song, different to the one that had charged the mirror.

'Oh!' Hazel said, alarmed. '~Ash, aren't you going to try talking to her first?'

~Threats don't work. I am going straight to the proof.

Zhey faced zheir mother, setting zheir hands together as zhey waited for Izidore's song to end.

Which it did not.

Still singing, Izidore tugged the bottom of Ash's vest one-handed. ~Too far.

'Well, Silverthorne? Do you have something you wish to say?'

Ash was staring at Izidore in the aftermath of zheir urgent message. Zhey flashed a look of sheer defiance at zheir mother, and crouched to put one hand on Izidore's throat, the other on the mirror. A scant moment passed before zheir melodic humming joined Izidore's trembling a cappella in harmony.

And again Izidore signed, ~It's too far.

'Really, you two,' Albemarle said. 'Second Jerome's leg, and now this. Learn *efficiency*.'

Zhey set zheir hand on the mirror, and began to sing the Mancy song too, zheir vocals interweaving effortlessly. Ash shook zheir head at Albemarle, but had no hands spare to express what zhey wanted to tell zhem. Albemarle sang on, drawing the other two with zhem.

Hazel felt the hairs on his arms and nape lift as the vibrating beauty of the three Mancers' otherworldly harmony made an exultation that brushed his soul. Others about the rooftop wore expressions of awe.

'This is quite enough,' Lady Cristati said, voice like a whipcrack. 'Stop your nonsense. Paolo, fetch your sibling.'

Something like a cannon boomed, loud even through the medium of the mirror. The view of the empty atelier shook itself into silvery pieces. A moment later, it cleared, now showing nothing but thick black smoke and bits of debris, with the red hint of flames beyond.

Again, Ash sat back on zheir heels and looked at the sky. Hazel could see the deep relief on zheir face, underlaid by a deep dismay. Slowly, zhey rose, turned to zheir mother, and pointed imperiously westward over the parapet.

Lady Cristati followed the pointing finger; they all did. A tiny plume of black smoke rose, a barely visible smudge against the pale grey sky. Hazel would've thought nothing of it, if he hadn't seen the mirror.

Meanwhile, Izidore was trying to steer the mirror's viewpoint somewhere else. Albemarle was sitting inert at zheir side, hands in zheir lap, face slack.

'Albemarle,' Izidore whispered. 'Albemarle, steer.'

It had been a bomb, Hazel realised. Ash and Izidore had created a Mancy bomb, and left it in the atelier, and used the mirror to reach it, to sing Izidore's triggering Mancy song, detonating it and destroying their atelier.

A bomb was a weapon. Albemarle had helped set off a weapon.

In the mirror, loose scraps of paper began to drift down like a minor blizzard. Amatl wouldn't properly burn, but it did smoulder and char, and wasn't immune to being blown apart.

'No one was in the atelier,' Izidore said. 'No one is even on that floor when the purple are away. Please help steer.'

Albemarle shook zhemself, all over like a dog. Zhey set zheir hands on the knobs.

Ash had told Hazel that Stronghold Cristati was located in the middle of shallow lake. Hazel could see, in the dizzying spin of the mirror's gaze as it rapidly withdrew and shifted, that it was an artificial lake, created by damming a river from one side of a valley to the other.

The retainer Lady Fairhaven had dispatched returned with one of Albemarle's small Mancy tea urns, and also a small fold of coloured silk which she discreetly handed to her lady before calmly laying out the tea service with complete disregard for the tension.

The pause gave Lady Cristati time to compose herself. 'You exploded your atelier. That is neither here nor there. You will merely have to get by with a lesser alternative, and that is your own petulant fault.'

'And all the journals,' Izidore said, very clearly, knuckles white on the frame as zhey helped Albemarle. 'You'll not force another Mancer to use those.'

Haven's Mancer, without losing zheir focus on the mirror, said, 'The journals of dead Mancers are a memorial and a shrine and you are both heretics of the worst sort.'

Albemarle did not sound particularly upset; if anything, zhey were teetering on the edge of admiration.

Ash huffed out air, shaking zheir head. ~It was not petulance; it was a demonstration.

Hazel, having voiced this to zheir mother, added, 'Look at the mirror, Lady Cristati. Look at the next target.'

The Mancers had reached their goal. The mirror's viewpoint was now at the substantial dam structure that sluiced water from the massive reservoir cradled by the valley walls into the lower outflow lake where Stronghold Cristati sat squatly on its island.

Izidore whispered rapidly in Albemarle's ear, hands hovering over zheirs without touching. Zhey were, Hazel assumed, trying to talk Albemarle into detonating another bomb, this one guaranteed to hurt people.

'But.' Lady Cristati looked about her in confusion. 'But that amount of water breaking all at once would wash out our foundations. It would destroy the stronghold.'

~Yes.

'Half or more of our people would die in such a cataclysm.'

~Yes.

She drew herself up. 'You are an obstinate, sullen, ungrateful creature, but I know you would never do such a thing.'

Ash's face stayed blank. Zheir hands moved in zheir easy grace. Zhey looked at Hazel, the furrow deep between zheir dark brows.

'You raised me,' Hazel said on Ash's behalf. 'I am my mother's child. So you tell me. Will I really do it?'

Lady Cristati stared at her child, eyes narrowed. Her decision was in the thickened air, a knife's edge which could slice in any direction.

'I did raise you,' she said eventually. 'And no, you won't.'

Ash looked up at the sky again. Zhey gave zheir mother a tight smile and nodded to Izidore, who exchanged a long look with zhem. Izidore bent over the mirror and began to vocalise zheir unearthly song, Ash's hand on zheir shoulder.

Albemarle shook zheir head, moving in little jerks, toward them and then away. Hazel knew zhey couldn't bring zhemself to help use a weapon against innocent people. But if zhey didn't help, Lady Cristati would realise the Mancy detonation song, attenuated by the mirror, couldn't reach far enough with only two of them.

For now, she was too intent on her own child to notice Albemarle. 'This is a bluff,' she said flatly. 'When did you ever get out to the reservoir wall to plant a bomb? And I'll wager you didn't risk the detour when you left—'

'Escaped,' said Holly from where he stood with Kito and the others. Hazel couldn't imagine the amount of pain he must be in to have stayed so quiet for so long. 'Be honest.'

'—And so. You are bluffing, child.'

Ash's face was set into its sternest lines, which meant zhey were at zheir most vulnerable. ~Please. Please, Mother, do not make me do this. I do not want to be the monster my Mancy tries to turn me into.

Hazel paused. Ash had been fighting all day. Zhey were facing down zheir mother, and not all the armour in the world could hide the cracks where zheir love for her still glinted. Zhey were gifting her with a vulnerability zhey were too exhausted and heartsick to hold at bay any longer.

Lady Cristati would only ever see weakness in it. She would take this gift and crumple it, as contemptuous as she had ever accused Ash of being about her gifts to zhem.

Hazel was sick with the horror of the choice Ash was facing now. He was trying to keep his face neutral, he was trying to bring himself to be zheir voice, to show his unwavering support the only way open to him. But his horror and his pity overwhelmed him. He couldn't look away from Ash. He could not make himself speak.

He had been quiet too long. Ash broke eye contact with Lady Cristati and looked at him. She followed zheir gaze. She must have seen everything Hazel was struggling to hide for Ash's sake, and it seemed to give her pause. For the first time, she wavered.

Almost to herself, she said, 'But neither of them had a chance to put the bomb there. I'll wager it.'

'You wager?' Hazel asked her. 'You're wagering the innocent lives of your people and the humanity of your own child.'

She gazed at him as she had gazed at Ash. She fancied herself able to see through the Mancer blankness to the true intentions of her youngest child, but she wouldn't see anything in Hazel beyond the distress writ large on his face.

Lady Cristati frowned. She gave a tiny shake of her head, looked back at Ash, and shook it once more.

Paolo spoke then, soft and hoarse.

'Mother, I set the bomb for Ash.' He walked to Ash, to face off against their mother by zheir side. 'I passed zhem the information about other strongholds, I helped zhem escape, and then I placed a Mancy device on the reservoir under instructions zhey left for me.'

For a moment, the only sound was the eerie wail of Izidore's violin voice. Then Ash set zheir hand on Izidore's throat and joined the song with zheir low hum. Zhey were looking at each other with apprehensive expressions. Ash reached into the folds of zheir clothes, and Hazel had one moment of nausea when he realised he didn't know if zhey'd had a chance to re-arm zhemself in the Cristati camp, or if zhey'd managed to grab another copperlit on the run up through the stronghold.

He stepped forward; no matter what, he would not let Ash fall back to any terminal plans, not against zhemself, and not, for the sake of zheir own sanity, against zheir mother.

When he moved, Albemarle started out of zheir to-and-fro twitching pattern as if awakening from a deep sleep. Zhey glanced at him, and the other Mancer guards, and Lady Fairhaven, and then reached a long arm out and set a finger on top of the mirror. Zhey opened zheir mouth to sing.

'Wait,' Lady Cristati cried.

She had both hands pressed hard to her stomach. She turned and looked west, toward her stronghold. The rooftop went silent as the Mancers stopped zheir song.

'Wait,' she said again. She briefly closed her eyes, then deliberately drew up into the dignity of the purple. 'What do you want?'

The answer was instant. ~Renounce me.

'Silverthorne, I can't protect you if you—'

~Renounce me.

Hazel repeated it, then added, 'That big sort of signing is a shout. Zhey are at the end of zheir patience, my lady.'

She sagged. 'I— I renounce my child—'

'Hold on, Adelma.' Lady Fairhaven bustled over to the Mancers grouped about the mirror, handing them the cloth her retainer had fetched for her and murmuring directions. 'I want an irreproachable witness for this.'

The Mancers tugged free the handkerchief and threaded the pink scrap of silk, a somewhat tattered ribbon, into place. They sang the mirror's song together. The reservoir shimmered away, replaced by a dark-haired and dark-skinned woman sitting at a table, looking startled. There were threads of silver in her hair and faint lines around her eyes. She was, suitably, very regal looking.

The murmur of voices behind the mirror's view could be heard. 'What?' said the woman. She raised a hand and the voices cut off.

'Good day, Adora, dear,' Lady Fairhaven said. 'So nice to see you. It's been such a long time.'

'Tashi!' the woman said. She adjusted her crown. 'How did you— I'm in the middle of a privy council meeting, Lady Fairhaven.'

'It's not a social call,' Lady Fairhaven said in her placid way. 'I formally request, as acknowledged castellan of Stronghold Fair Haven by the Sea and its atelier, the crown's witness for a statement of renunciation by your cousin, Your Majesty. It's rather important.'

The queen sighed and muttered, 'Lord, what's she done now?' The Mancers turned the mirror so she could see Lady Cristati. 'Well, cousin?'

Lady Cristati bowed her head. 'I renounce my child, Liege Ashlin Silverthorne Cristati,' she recited, mouth tight and small. 'I renounce all claim to guardianship. I renounce the same on the behalf of the Silverthorne paternity, which rights devolved to me upon agreement at birth. Zhey may no longer use the Cristati name. Zhey may no longer use the

Silverthorne name. Neither Cristati nor Silverthorne holds rights or responsibilities regarding…' She looked down. 'Ashlin Mancer.'

'Your Majesty, Haven demands the withdrawal of Cristati on grounds of flagrant covenant violation,' Lady Fairhaven said. 'Haven's allies will enforce.'

Queen Adora said, 'All is heard and agreed. The covenant will be enforced. The crown will act in Haven's favour should the violation not be repaired within the day.' She pointed a finger sternly at her cousin. 'Adelma, do not make Tashi have to interrupt me again for this nonsense.' Lady Cristati opened her mouth and she added, 'Don't think I can't guess why you've been hiding a Mancer all these years. You told me your third child *died*, cousin. I *grieved* for you.'

Lady Cristati closed her mouth and dropped into a very deep curtsey to her queen.

'That's better.' Queen Adora glanced back at Lady Fairhaven. 'Nice to see you again too, Tashi.'

Lady Fairhaven gave her a rather flirtatious smile as she waved her fingers in dismissal. Ash drew out the ribbon, and the mirror's surface clouded to blankness.

Ash ran the ribbon through zheir fingers, blankly watching as zheir mother, eyes burning, gathered up her people and began her retreat. She looked at Paolo, and he shook his head, shifting closer to Ash. He did look quite nervous, shooting glances both at his mother and at Lady Fairhaven, who merely smiled at him encouragingly.

Lady Cristati paused by Hazel. 'Zhey might walk away and never look back, is that it?'

'You made zhem strong. Take your consolation.' He did not think she deserved any, but he also thought she wouldn't take any.

Ash bumped against him, and he felt zhem slip zheir hand into his. He squeezed back. But zhey wriggled loose and tapped his hand; he glanced down and saw that zhey'd been trying to press zheir mother's handkerchief into his hand. Flushing, he took it. He held it out to Lady Cristati.

She stared at his hand, and then looked at her children. 'Paolo. Ashlin,' she said softly. 'Please, keep it. In case you want to call on me through the mirror.'

Since she refused to take it but Ash refused to take it back, Hazel was left holding it until Paolo edged over and collected it, pulling a cheerily gauche face at him to commiserate on the awkwardness of it all.

Slowly, clumsily, Lady Cristati signed, ~Ash.

Ash made a tiny negating gesture, a twitch of zheir head. Zhey put zheir hands behind zheir back.

'Don't push,' Hazel murmured.

Head proudly raised, Lady Cristati walked away down the stairs, her soldiers in her wake, Havens escorting them. After the rooftop door was judiciously closed behind the retreating party, Ash held zheir rigid pose for the count of ten.

Then zhey dropped, going to zheir knees in a boneless collapse, taking a gasping breath that rattled through the quietly relieved murmuring on the rooftop.

Hazel moved, but Izidore and Paolo were already there, falling onto zhem in a familial embrace.

'You did it, it's all right, you did it,' Paolo said into his sibling's hair, forgetting Ash couldn't hear it if zhey couldn't see it, or knowing zhey'd feel the words against zheir scalp and guess the meaning.

Ensconced on Ash's other side, Izidore said, 'The mountain celebrates the spring with the thaw,' and, ~You're safe, we're safe, you did it, Ash, you did it, we're safe now.

Ash huddled into their embrace. Hazel felt— not excluded as such, for he was sure that if he joined them, Ash would let him hug zhem too. He felt unnecessary.

'Albemarle.' Kito formally bowed to Haven's senior Mancer. 'My dearest, you were prepared to compromise your stance on weapons to save Haven.' She tapped her heart in lieu of touching zhem. 'That must have been so hard for you.'

'Save your congratulations. Izidore told me there was no bomb,' Albemarle said dully. 'Was there?'

'The cup runneth dry when the drunkard tips it up,' zhey said with a shrug.

Hazel waved for Ash's attention. '~D'you mean there was no bomb on the reservoir wall?'

Ash nodded. Zhey squeezed Paolo's shoulder before pulling loose from him and from Izidore, rising to face Hazel, ignoring the hand he automatically stretched out to help.

'~But you told me— You said you were going to obliterate Stronghold Cristati.'

Zhey flashed zheir small smile, with a thin sort of amusement. ~Hazel, you wear most of your feelings on your face. I was never going to fool my own mother with something as malicious as this. I needed you to fool her for me. I needed her to see you looking suitably horrified when I threatened Stronghold Cristati. So I couldn't tell you in advance that it was a bluff.

Hazel nodded. Part of him accepted this: Ash had been working to save Haven. But another part of him felt the new deception clang against the lingering anger and hurt of finding out Ash had deliberately targeted Haven, had deliberately targeted him, in the first place.

Outside the walls of Haven, Ash had coldly called him useful, and, lo, he had been useful. And how much of Ash's warm interaction with him, before and after that ice-cold moment, had been in aid of making sure he would be?

He suddenly noticed his head was still aching.

Ash's smile twisted, turned rueful. They bowed zheir head and drew zheir thumbnail across zheir heart, at a snail's pace. ~You wear your feelings on your face, zhey repeated. ~Hazel darling.

Zhey presented zhemself to Lady Fairhaven, offering her the queen's ribbon laid flat over both palms. Once she took it, zhey dipped zheir head. ~My deepest apologies for using Haven as I did. I will beg of you one night's rest. Then I will go.

'What?' Hazel said. He moved so that Ash could see his hands. ~You're free of your mother's guardianship. You can legally request sanctuary.

Ash shook zheir head. ~Say it, please.

~Ask for sanctuary.

The Mancer glanced about the rooftop. Holly was already limping about, checking on the other Mancer guards, checking on Albemarle, checking on Izidore, being the caregiver hardly anyone suspected he was.

Lord Valerian was at his side. 'You need to get off the knee, Holly, before you do yourself more damage.'

Holly waved him off like swatting a gnat. Ash took the opportunity to tug at Holly's sleeve and capture his scattered attention. ~Captain, tell Lady Fairhaven—

'No!' Hazel said. ~Ash, ask for sanctuary.

~I believe the message will convey itself, then.

And Ash marched off down the stairs.

~Thirty-Four~

THE SUBTERRANE WAS UNINHABITABLE. The smoke still hung thick, and the smell and stain of it coated every surface.

Kito, Nightingale and Titus oversaw finding temporary accommodations for the Mancers and their Mancer Guard, a convoluted task given militia and refugees also needing beds. Holly was consigned almost immediately to Valerian's apartment, which neither man complained of. The rest had to take the same guest hallway where Ash and Izidore had briefly been imprisoned. The mess the pet had left was thoroughly scrubbed away, and Hazel ensured the Mancers were at least not given the same rooms they'd been imprisoned in.

Notwithstanding the simple practicality of being unable to use the kitchen or the laundry or the baths, the atelier was the focus of the rehabilitation efforts. The clean-up started the same day, in concert with and around the grim task of laying the dead to rest, each according to their own people's practices, presided tirelessly over by Lady Fairhaven.

Every able person in Haven bent their attentions to the job: raking the still-smoking char and hot ashes well away from the moon gate and the ventilation intake and smothering the mess in sand; wiping down and beating and airing every piece of soft furnishing, made trickier by the continued intermittent rain squalls; removing the portable equipment from atelier and kitchen for soaking and scrubbing; scouring the furniture and walls and floors to get the soot and grit off; replacing what could not be salvaged, which was most of the little sitting area Hazel had made for Ash in the atelier antechamber, where a convolution of currents had concentrated the smoke and particulates. It took the rest of the battle day and all of the next day, dozens and dozens of people relentlessly working for the stronghold.

For most of that next day, Ash stayed closeted in zheir temporary quarters while the other two Mancers took over a corner of the dining hall, much to the great curiosity of the bustling undercroft staff. The Mancers worked on fixing Second Jerome's inefficient leg and Izidore's sundered pet, and started off some new project too, while learning each other's idiosyncrasies. Izidore, to no one's surprise, was the most flexible of the three Mancers—as long as zhey were indulged in the numbers of legs or tentacles zhey were allowed to install.

Hazel assumed Ash was sleeping off the worst of the previous day. In the afternoon, zhey finally emerged, looking unutterably exhausted, and even worse than zhey had the day before, because zheir face where Tassone had slammed zhem into the table had swollen and turned several sickly shades of black and purple. Hazel had to put his hands behind his back to not touch zhem.

Zhey were probably bruised and grazed from head to toe, under zheir clothes, and no doubt stiff from the unaccustomed exertions; even Hazel's thighs were tight from that frantic clamber up the Mancy locust's back, let alone the rest of the day. Sensing opportunity in zheir limp apathy, and the fact that zhey were finally unarmed, he inveigled zhem into an infirmary visit, zheir first since arriving.

Zhey had enough defiance left to insist that Paolo attend zhem rather than Miriam, which she only acquiesced to because she was so busy with the other injured Havens, including Holly and Valerian upstairs. She did take a moment to inspect Paolo's work—Ash's salved hands and face and the bandaged wrist and shoulder—and gave it a single grudging nod of approval before dragooning the marooned Cristati lord.

When she paused to ill-advisedly pick up her aural speculum despite Hazel's warning look, however, Ash turned on zheir heel and stalked off to the Mancers' makeshift worktables. Zhey went from there to the evening meal and back to zheir quarters while doing zheir best to not catch anyone's eye, especially not Hazel's.

Hazel knew the message in that. He'd been used, and Haven had been used, and Ash, it seemed, was done with both.

After his own short visit to the overworked Miriam to be cleared of concussion, he had resumed Mancer Guard duties, sore and scraped but at least on his feet. With three Mancers to guard, both Morano and Holly out, and proper recruitment taking its course, the others couldn't cope without him, even if he was still a little headachy.

Besides, without Holly, he was the only competent Trade user. He accompanied Ash to a meeting with Lady Fairhaven, Lord Valerian and Evelyn early on the second morning after the battle. The seamsters had replaced his small wardrobe of smoke-damaged clothes, and Paolo had handed his Mancer Guard coat back, cleaned. He was waiting on a bottle-green coat of his very own.

Ash walked beside Hazel, stiff and subdued and still wan-looking, dark smudges under zheir eyes. For all the hiding in zheir quarters, zhey weren't sleeping. Zhey kept zheir gaze down, zheir hands still, answering the summons like a person walking to their own grave.

As soon as they'd come into Lady Fairhaven's reception room and made a bow to the three authorities, zhey signed, ~I apologise. I was more tired than I thought. I will leave very soon.

Lady Fairhaven poured zhem a cup with her own hands, and pressed it into zheirs. Zhey sipped and put it down the moment zhey'd performed this small engrained politeness.

Evelyn cleared her throat. 'Ash, we're asking you to ask for sanctuary.'

Ash made the negatory fist.

Hazel said, 'I assume you don't need me to voice that.'

The hierarchy began to talk. They all said variations of the same thing, in tones of gentle persuasion, or firm request, or logical argument: Ash was safe here in Haven, there was no need to feel guilty, it was the literal function of a stronghold to protect its Mancers even if that meant some of its people died doing it, Queen Adora herself had written to explicitly express her appreciation that Ash had worked so diligently to turn zheir mother from her plans.

Hazel dutifully conveyed all of it. He could tell from Ash's stern face what the outcome would be: Ash thanked them for their concern and refused to ask for sanctuary, and refused again, and refused again, and then gave Hazel a look which said it was time to extract zhem.

'Very well,' Lady Fairhaven said; Hazel had no doubt she'd caught zheir imperious glance his way and recognised the plea behind it just as easily as he had. 'You are, of course, free to leave. Do you have an idea of where you will go? You will have to be careful which stronghold you approach, and even which route you take there, or you may end up in the same situation.'

Ash nodded. ~I am aware. I will take advice, should you be prepared to offer it.

'My word, will you?' Valerian said dryly.

Lady Fairhaven quelled him with a tap on the table. 'And is it Izidore's intention to stay with you?' she asked. 'I ask only because you make a strong team. A desirable team. It will affect which stronghold we recommend.'

~Izidore will stay here.

Hazel frowned and scissored his fingers in a loop, though he was sure he'd read it right.

Ash dutifully repeated zhemself, and then turned a little way toward him and added, ~Izidore and I are merely a Mancer partnership. We have no other ties. Zhey will stay here.

There was no point feeling relieved to hear Ash state baldly that it was not a love affair between zhem and Izidore. It had pretty much been a dice roll as to whether it was or not, given Mancers. It made no difference to Ash's feelings for him, or lack thereof.

Hazel stubbornly insisted, ~You have ties of friendship. Zhey will not be happy to be abandoned here by you.

~It is the best thing I can do for zhem.

Hazel couldn't help it; he signed, ~The best thing you can do for zhem is stay and be the friend zhey think you are.

Ash pressed zheir lips thin, hands locked together.

Hazel hesitated. ~Were zhey just useful, then, and that's all?

Like I was just useful and that's all?

The Mancer shot him a sharp look. Desperately, Hazel plunged onward. ~Cristati needed stopping and you stopped them. You asked me to tell you this again one day: you never need feel ashamed about doing what needed doing. But how you treat the people who helped you do it—

Eyes dark and mouth set, Ash pivoted away. Hazel looked at the others and shook his head. He didn't have the words for more, and Ash didn't want to hear from him anyway.

Evelyn said, 'Sorry, Hazel, but I have to check. Ash, if it is your current Mancer Guard that worries you—'

Ash jerked their fist up, though whether in rapid denial of the commander's concern or a strident refusal to discuss it, Hazel didn't know. All he knew was that Ash was avoiding him, even as they walked side by side back to the subterrane, which had been declared fit for reoccupation that morning. The kitchen was already back in full operation, much to the relief of a population that had been living off firepit camp cooking and cold siege reserves.

When he'd delivered zhem to the atelier door, he diffidently touched zheir wrist. '~Ash, when you go…'

~Yes?

'~Will you let me come with you? To escort you to your new strong-hold? Will you at least let me do that for you?'

Ash closed zheir eyes. Slowly, zhey signed, ~Because I am your Mancer.

'A-yah, you're my Mancer and if all you want from me is to be useful, then that is what I shall be, and there's no point answering you if your eyes are closed, so I'll shut the fuck up now,' Hazel said to the air over zheir head.

He nudged zhem, and zhey set zheir shoulders and raised zheir gaze to his. ~Hazel, I wish to give you a gift in your room.

Holly would have rolled out an obvious quip. But Ash was remarkably grim for someone giving either a literal gift or offering consolation sex in a euphemistic way. Zhey fetched the wrapped far-scry mirror from inside the atelier, where the other two were diligently settling back into the workspace, and silently held it out. He took its weight from zheir hands.

~I need to say something first.

'A-yah,' Hazel said, sighing.

He didn't think he was going to like this; he supposed Ash was going to say goodbye. Zhey'd finally run out of patience and were simply going to leave before Haven had a chance to find zhem a new stronghold. Zhey were not a prisoner here and no one in Haven was going to act like Cristati by stopping zhem from going. No one was going to risk making spiky Ashlin Mancer feel backed into a corner, either.

But Ash signed, ~It has been wonderful to feel protected by my Mancer Guard, rather than terrorised.

Wrongfooted, Hazel set the mirror at his feet. '~I imagine so.' He argued with himself before the *Ah, fuck it* won. '~So why avoid me?'

Why leave?

Ash took a breath, squeezed zheir body in a tight ripple of tension all over, shoulders hunched and fists tight, and then straightened again to face Hazel. ~It is an easy mistake to make, to misconstrue protection for love.

Hazel blinked. He said, '~Ah. A mistake.'

Given he'd started this conversation assuming Ash was looking to bid him fare-thee-well, he felt very much at sea. He'd expected an argument, perhaps. He hadn't expected to be openly and uncompromisingly chastened for loving zhem. He wasn't just at sea, he was in open waters in a tiny raft with Kisane setting a squall upon him. He wished they weren't having this conversation in the antechamber, where Mancer or Mancer guard might come past at any moment.

He could, at least, try to explain that he had not made the mistake Ash was accusing him of. If anyone knew when they were truly in love, it was Hazel.

But Ash had gone on, and Hazel forced himself to focus on the fluid grace of zheir dancing hands.

~I want to be honest with you, Hazel, of all people, after so signally failing to be. I'm trying hard to not make the mistake, so until I manage it, it's better if I avoid you. I don't wish for things to become awkward between us in our last days together.

Understanding dawned, in dismal harmony with a sickening twist of his heart. He reminded himself that he had been intended merely as a tool for Ash's plan. He reminded himself that Ash had gone to bed with him once and zhey zhemself had dismissed it as a selfish impulse: *you may have* this *and no more*. He had no right to expect anything to come of it. He certainly had no right to expect Ash to love him, or to even want to love him, after all zhey had been through. Zhey needed time, or someone else, or no one else, and, apparently, an entirely different stronghold.

And right this moment, zhey needed him to be professional enough to accept that zhey thought it would be a mistake to misinterpret zheir natural feelings of gratitude and trust toward him as being in love with him.

Fine. He could do that.

'~Fine,' he repeated aloud. '~Thank you for your honesty. I'm sure things will not be awkward at all.'

Thank fuck Ash couldn't hear sarcasm, because he didn't quite manage his tone thoroughly enough through that little speech, but his hands were as steady and sure as ever. He gave a brisk nod to cover anything Ash might want to try to read on his face, where he supposedly wore his fucking feelings so fucking openly.

Ash took on the same brisk attitude. ~Good. Thank you. Bring the mirror to your room.

Hazel led zhem down to his quarters, freshly washed from ceiling to floor and laid with new bedding. He himself had carefully wiped off the fronds of the little fern, and cleaned up his shrine, and set out the promised flowers. The blossoms were bright against the pale wood, still darkened from the scrubbing.

Ash glanced quickly at the bed and away. Hazel, following Ash's instructions, propped the mirror against the wall at the head of the bed, exactly where Ash had propped zhemself while Hazel's mouth had— and that was not a profitable path to let his thoughts wander down.

Ash unwrapped the mirror. Zheir hands were shaking, a very fine tremor, barely noticeable. Hazel, however, still noticed it, with doggedly detached interest. He'd not seen that before, and he'd seen Ash face down some frightening things with barely a flinch.

Zhey turned to him. ~Do you have something personal of your sister's? Like the hair ribbon? Or a letter you know for sure she wrote herself. Something she touched extensively.

Hazel had already moved to pull a metal box from under his bed. He was a-roil, stomach churning, because he had grasped what Ash's gift must be.

Indeed, once he'd handed over Maya's most recent letter, Ash carefully threaded it into the top coil. Izidore must have charged the mirror with Mancy already, for a few of Ash's touches along the nubs on the frame's edge made the mirror's surface go hazy, and then clear.

Hazel unbuckled his sword and got on his knees on the bed. In the mirror, he could see a dimly lit room, a recently stoked stove glowing in the corner, a large table dominating the space. Its surface was untidy with the detritus of life. A woman was pushing aside the paper and toys to set it with plates and cups. She had long, wild hair, tied back out of her face, and a spray of freckles across her warm brown skin.

Hazel silently watched her, content to do just that. She glanced up and paused as if in deep thought, but she appeared to be staring right at him.

'~Can she see me already?' he asked Ash without looking away.

His sister answered, ~I can see you.

Hazel said, 'Maya.'

~Hazel, Maya signed. ~Hazel.

She put her hands to her cheeks and started to noisily sob.

~Oh, no, baby, don't cry, Hazel signed.

He felt Ash's hand touch his hair, very gently, and he blindly reached out and caught zheir hand as zhey started to withdraw.

He looked away from Maya long enough to sign, ~Thank you. Ash, thank you so much for this.

Ash, eyes bright, smiled at him. Zhey kissed his hand before sketching a deep bow.

'~Are you going to Izidore?' he asked, conscious that he hadn't handed Ash over to another Mancer guard as protocol dictated.

Ash nodded, already turning from him, and Hazel himself had already turned back to Maya before zhey'd left the room.

Her family had come running when they heard her crying. It was much earlier there than here. They'd all just come upstairs from their bakery after getting the first loaves on. They were having breakfast at dawn, chocolate and croissants, and were in danger of spilling the lot in the excited chaos of his apparition.

All three of his nieces and nephews, two of the former, one of the latter, had to be introduced, and talk to their uncle in a mix of spoken and signed words—two of the three could hear but used Mutual interchangeably with Trade, endearingly with their mother's quirks and flourishes, so familiar and yet almost strange to him now after all his time with Ash. The oldest, a boy of around twelve, talked for fifteen minutes straight about a game he'd invented with the neighbour's children; while the middle child, a dark-haired girl with Hazel's eyes, talked over him with signs about all the interesting things she was learning at school.

The youngest girl was, unlike her voluble siblings, reserved and stand-offish. She had to be coaxed into exchanging words with her uncle, Maya shushing the other two to give her a fighting chance. She was more comfortable with Trade, and Hazel won a smile from her by teaching her some Haven slang. She taught him slang from Trifold in return and giggled wildly when he accidentally signed [horse] instead of [kitten], which was the name of the stuffed ragdoll she had lodged under one arm.

The husband had to be introduced. That was a good deal more awkward than meeting the children, but their stilted conversation soon relaxed into something more genuine. It eased Hazel's mind more than he could say to find that his sister's husband appeared to be a truly upright individual.

'~I've wanted to say for a very long time how sorry I am that I took her away before we could properly meet,' Damilola finally said.

~You did not take me away, Maya informed them both sternly. ~We decided together to go.

But once Damilola had ushered the children out of the room to give Hazel time alone with his sister, she signed, ~You're relieved. Did you really think I wouldn't marry a decent man after being raised by a decent man?

She paused, smiling at the expression he must be wearing, and then added, ~Hazel, I am sorry. Not that we came here, because it is a good life, but sorry we left like we did. Sorry I haven't come back to visit. Sorry I didn't encourage you to visit us more.

'~It's a long way and you're busy,' Hazel said simply. '~I had to let you go.'

~Yes. And I'm sorry, anyway. Maya wiped tears away. ~Shall we not waste too much time on the maudlin, Hazel darling?

It was odd feeling, to suddenly remember that it was Maya who had given him that sobriquet.

He glanced around, because his door had opened behind him. It was Izidore, who signed, ~Recharging the Mancy, and tiptoed, unnecessarily, across the floor to put zheir hand on the mirror. Zhey smiled absently at Maya through the Mancy window as zhey sang the mirror's song.

~Kisane's eyes, how many Mancers do you *have*? Maya asked, smiling, before looking alarmed. ~Albemarle?

'~Still here,' Hazel reassured her. '~It's, ah… We've had a busy time of it.'

Izidore snorted and slipped out of the room again. Maya made an encouraging gesture and listened round-eyed as Hazel told her the whole story, or as much of it as he could—she was, after all, always his little sister, and besides, he was still embarrassed about how easily Ash had seduced him.

When he was done, she signed, ~I'm glad you're safe. The grey-haired Mancer? That was Ash?

To his nod, she added, ~Striking. Smitten.

Of course she'd noticed what he'd skirted about. Hazel waved it away. '~Not what you think. That's another one I have to let go.'

She signed the Trade equivalent of a sceptical noise. ~Because zhey betrayed Haven?

Hazel glanced up indignantly and caught Maya's knowing look. '~Of course not. Because… Well, because zhey don't want me, Maya, and zhey don't want Haven.'

~Ah. It is what it is, right?

Hazel nodded, somewhat ruefully. It was, indeed, what it was.

They settled into the comfortable space of siblings, telling each other news, signing over each other, laughing and teasing as Maya told him stories of her silliest customers and asked after everyone she could remember.

'~Holly's in love with Lord Valerian,' Hazel told her. He thought of how smug Holly had been, when Hazel had been attracted to Ash and hadn't realised it yet. '~He hasn't worked that out, though. It's very funny.'

~Isn't Lord Valerian married to a woman?

'~Widowed and seduced by those legs.'

~Oh, those legs, those famous legs, Maya signed, then fanned herself dramatically, smiling that same old cheeky smile, his baby sister. ~You don't mind? I know you two…

Hazel shrugged. '~A long time ago, I would have been upset it wasn't me. But it was never going to be me, with Holly. We'll always love each other. There's lots of different ways people love each other.'

Izidore came in to sing the mirror song again. That must mark at least the second hour he'd been talking to Maya. When zhey'd gone again, Maya picked up, ~Speaking of love…

Hazel shook his head, adding a no both verbally and visually for good measure.

Maya looked up and past him, beyond the scope of the mirror. ~I have to get back to the bakery now. Hazel darling, I don't want to sound horrible and ungrateful, but I need to say this. Yes, you let me go, and I love that you did. But you let me go so easily that I maybe thought you were happy to let me go. That maybe you were relieved to let me go, so you didn't have to be a parent any longer?

'~Wrong word,' he said. '~Proud.' He thought of Ash. '~Sad, and proud.'

She touched her heart and went on. ~I love you, Hazel. And I saw the way that Mancer looked at you while you were looking at me. In the inimical words of your friend and mine, my *arse* zhey don't want you. Don't let this one go too easily. Don't be so busy fixing things for everyone else that you forget to fix things for yourself.

Hazel signed, ~I love you, too.

Maya refrained from rolling her eyes at his deflection, probably because she'd long outgrown some of the habits he remembered. ~Call again, soon. Tomorrow is not too soon. We still have lots to talk about. Including visits.

'~I think I'll have to share time on this thing with everyone else once word gets around they can find family with it, but I promise, as often as I can.'

She again signed, ~I love you, and he signed it back and pressed the knots on the side until one made her image fade away.

He sat smiling on the bed, hand over his heart. He hadn't realised how much of an ache he had been carrying because of Maya's absence, how much he had grown to tolerate it without being aware of having to tolerate it.

How stoic he had been about it all. If anyone else had come to him to tell him how much they missed their sibling, he'd have done his level best to help them, and yet when it came to himself, he'd accepted it with barely a murmur of distress.

His happiness was circling a different hearth as well. It had been on his mind that Ash was going to leave, like Maya had left, but stubbornly alone and friendless when zhey did not have to be. Every part of him wanted to go with zhem, except all those parts that were lodged in Haven—not just Holly, but Evelyn, Miriam, Kito, the rest of the Mancer Guard, the other deep friendships he held here.

But now Haven had the mirror, and the Mancers could surely make another, smaller one for him. He'd wouldn't really need to leave Haven behind when he talked Ash into letting him go with zhem, when zhey—

He stood up abruptly. The way Ash had touched his hair. The way zhey'd bowed. The way zheir gaze had gone opaque as zhey'd nodded when he'd asked if zhey were going to Izidore.

As Holly said, Ash was a shocking liar if zhey thought zhey were protecting Hazel.

'Shit, zhey've already left for the port.'

He flung open his door, prepared to run all the way if he had to.

~THIRTY-FIVE~

HOLLY IS HAVING A DAY OF doing as promised.

He promised to stay in bed until his knee was less swollen, and stay in bed he does, all the afternoon after their frenetic morning, all the next day, and part of this one, though he's bored out of his mind. It's Valerian's exceedingly comfortable bed, on the practical grounds that his quarters were the closest resting place involving the fewest stairs. Some people in the stronghold might even believe that.

Valerian, shoulder bandaged by an exasperated Miriam, ushered in visitor after visitor and entertained him with stories in between, after Holly made his aversion for long-winded books known. Between that and the endless cossetting—a warm damp flannel all over to wipe away the sweat and blood, warm compresses over the knee, tender care of his less severe cuts and bruises, fluffing and tucking of pillows, even his two favourite nimble-fingered laundry staffers brought up to re-do his braids—it was startlingly domestic in a way that Holly did not entirely dislike.

He's even been moved to reciprocate, circling carefully around some tales from his childhood, if only to embarrass Evelyn. He senses he'll get to the massacre eventually, and Valerian will listen in his serious way, and that will be one more step along this path they're on, which leads who knows where.

He hasn't ever been this consistently intimate with anyone except Hazel; in fact, Hazel, when he visited, looked between Holly and Valerian with an odd expression that Holly might have taken as jealousy if Hazel got jealous. His oldest friend went away looking infuriatingly amused.

One of Valerian's own visitors was Lorian, who also looked between his father and the former crush in his father's bed with a strange expression. Val took him off for a private, exceedingly long, chat, and did not comment on how it had gone, except Holly wasn't summarily thrown out of the apartment, so there's that.

Val has become delightfully creative in keeping Holly entertained during his imposed rest. It hasn't been overly restful at all, really, except that the man is stubbornly careful about not jostling Holly's leg, which constrains things without dampening them. Holly can safely vouch that Valerian and incompetent fumbling are not to be mentioned in the same breath ever again.

Now Holly's fulfilling his promise to write his name onto Valerian's broad thighs, biting and sucking marks across the man's expanse of pale skin while he writhes and moans and clutches at Holly's braids. Holly's only just started the first letter and he's not sure how much longer Val's going to hold out before he starts begging for Holly's mouth on adjacent real estate.

Holly's going to make him beg because Valerian has been terribly, unrelentingly sweet to him while he's been bedbound. Holly feels the need to reassert who's in control. Further, the lord came in despondent from a morning meeting where Ash was zheir prickly, stubborn, secretive self, so Holly also feels the need to cheer his lover up.

'Steady,' he murmurs against Val's skin, stroking the tips of his fingers up the crease between thigh and hip, letting the back of his hand brush against his iron-hard cock. It twitches, Val's hips twitch, he makes a needy sound, and Holly smiles. 'Steady, love, I haven't even finished the first stroke yet.'

Valerian, flat on his back, thighs spread, arm flung over his eyes, mutters to the ceiling, 'I'll give you the first fucking stroke,' and isn't that a delicious thought?

'A-yah,' Holly says. He sucks another mark into Val's thigh, licks the spot. 'I *am* looking forward to plundering your virgin arse, since you mention it.'

Valerian drops his arm and looks down at him.

'Only when you're ready,' Holly assures him. 'If you ever are.'

'I'm ready right now,' Valerian tells him softly. 'If it's not too hard on the knee.'

Holly nibbles his thigh and feels a quiver run right through him. 'Roll over.'

Valerian does. He nestles his face into the crook of his arm, passive, as if he's expecting Holly to get right down to it. And it's not as if Holly isn't greatly anticipating having all that breadth and strength straining in response under him, hearing the noises Valerian won't be able to smother. But not yet.

Holly smooths his hands over the man's broad arse, feeling the muscles there tensing and flexing under his touch. He bites, not gently, and Val jerks in surprise. Holly kisses the spot, soothing him, and kisses his way along until he reaches Val's crease, and there he spreads him and slides his tongue in. If Valerian was surprised when Holly bit him, he's shocked now, almost propelling out of Holly's hold.

'Steady,' Holly reminds him. 'All right, love?' He waits for the muffled assent before he nuzzles back in.

As Holly licks and probes with his tongue, Valerian gasps into his arm, short exhalations which are either Holly's name or cut-off exhortations to his people's Holy Mother, and either option pleases Holly well enough. Valerian's hips are rocking under his devoted ministrations; Holly slinks his hand under the man's body and takes a firm hold on his cock, letting him thrust into his tight grip in time to the thrusts of Holly's tongue into his hole.

Valerian reaches completion cursing and sounding like he means it, which is how Holly likes it. Holly flops languidly over his broad back and kisses under his ear. 'Good start? Flatter me outrageously at once.'

The lord makes a groaning sound of agreement, pleasingly helpless, then says with touching uncertainty, 'Are you going on?'

'Not today,' Holly says, adding, 'It is fairly fucking hard on the knees, and your shoulder too, Vee,' when Val draws breath to argue. He gives a little thrust of his hips against Val's lower back, bringing his insistent cock to his attention. 'Speaking of on the knees, though…'

Val puts Holly on his back with one excitingly assertive press of his hand. The lord slides down his body, heavy and intent. His hands are tight on Holly's hips and his mouth engulfs Holly's cock in wet warmth.

'Hmm, good boy,' Holly murmurs egregiously.

'You dick,' Valerian mumbles, and Holly, grinning, pushes his head back down and runs his fingers through the silly floppy hair as Valerian takes his cock, lavishing it with his mouth, making those wanton little noises of pleasure as he bobs and sucks and—

'Damn, I forgot,' Val says, abruptly sitting up. He abandons Holly and leaps out of bed. 'I'm supposed to be helping select the new Mancer Guard contingent for Izidore. I'm late.'

'Ah,' Holly says, looking down at his sadly bereft cock. 'Have you considered that a few more minutes here or there is not—'

Lord Valerian is scandalised. 'I've never been late for anything in my life!'

He flusters his way around the room, rapidly dressing and collecting himself and his bits and pieces from wanton disarray to lordly array. Finger-combing his hair and still muttering consternation, he bustles over to the bed, kisses Holly firmly on the mouth and says distractedly, 'Love you, behave yourself, see you after.'

He flurries out of the room without pause. Holly smiles at the ceiling. 'Love you,' he repeats fondly.

He knows that was a slip of the tongue, that Valerian, in his rush, tripped himself flat into domestic habits. He also knows the poor fucker is likely standing in the hallway outside roundly swearing at himself as his ears catch up with his mouth.

Indeed, when he slips on his coat, freshly cleaned of blood and mended, and steps outside, he finds Valerian resting his head against the whitewashed wall as if he'd just thonked his forehead into it. Possibly repeatedly.

'It's not that bad,' Holly tells him, drawing him in for a hug. 'I can't take seriously anything you say in the same breath as "behave yourself", after all.'

'That's how you want me to play, is it?' Valerian asks into the curve of his shoulder, rigid with tension in his arms. 'Pretend I didn't mean it? I know you warned me not to—'

'That was more in the way of warning you I wouldn't reciprocate.'

Holly pulls back, watching Valerian's face. He doesn't like the feeling of telling Val that, of watching the tiny bit of involuntary hope in the man's face extinguish. It feels wrong. He can feel himself frowning.

'I know it's just sex.' Val is striving valiantly for his usual cool demeanour, and just about getting there.

'Am I ever *just* anything, lover?' Holly counters.

He gives the only thing he can, his physical affection, and it's not a bad consolation prize as these things go. He leans into Valerian, kissing him with a good deal more intent than he should have, given the man is late and canonically doesn't want to be.

Holly still whispers, 'Come back to the room, Val.'

'I'm so late,' Valerian gets out between kisses, trying to edge out from between Holly and the wall.

'Don't cross me, Lord Vee,' Holly warns him, and then huskily murmurs an extra threat right into Val's ear. 'I will make you pay if you do not get your arse back into that bed and finish what you started.'

Despite his own efforts to wriggle away, Valerian's hands have delved beneath Holly's coat; it's all he's wearing and Val's taking full advantage. The lord's moaning, sagging back as Holly's lips and teeth and touch of stubble ravages his neck. Here's another round Holly has well and truly won, Val's zeal for duty melting like ice, melting like the man himself under his mouth.

Someone clears their throat. 'I believe the unspoken rule is not in the hallways, boys?'

'Holy Mother,' Valerian whispers, hands going into tense claws on Holly's back.

'I'm trying to get him out of the hallway, my lady,' Holly says to Lady Fairhaven, flashing his best smile. 'He won't go.'

'That is because he is late and he knows it,' she says briskly. She's at the door of her apartment, only just going downstairs herself—she's late, too, and Holly knows whose fault that is. 'Stop corrupting my most reliable vassal, Holly. Come along…' She clears her throat ostentatiously. '…Lord Vee.'

Val has turned a magnificent shade of embarrassment. Holly, grinning, pats him on the shoulder, says, 'This isn't the payback, Val,' and gives him a shove toward his lady.

'Nice legs,' Lady Fairhaven adds as he does his best to strut back to Val's room despite the still-swollen knee.

'Nice arse, too,' Holly sings, since he really is only wearing the Mancer Guard coat, and it's not quite long enough for any sort of true modesty.

He hears her give a peal of laughter and sniggers. He doesn't need to look back to know the face Lord Valerian will be wearing right now.

The purple have long gone by the time he's dressed and coming downstairs himself, not only because he'll start chewing off his own arm if he has to stare at the admittedly prettily decorated walls of Val's private apartment for one more second, but also because cheering up Valerian has now assumed a powerful importance in his mind, matched only by the need to make Hazel happy too.

He stops briefly at the great hall—the off-duty Mancer guards are with Evelyn to try out the candidates; Kito gets the pleasure of being the intimidating one today—before fetching up in the undercroft dining hall.

The Mancers, two of them, have spread across two tables. Holly pauses at that—Hazel assured him they're working well enough together, though Albemarle did wait for both Izidore and Ash to be present before giving a very long lecture about not even thinking about changing a single mote of the designs in zheir journals until zhey were dead and burnt, and even then, journals were a monument and—and, at that point Kito and Nightingale had intervened.

Since then, Haven's Mancers have been operating on a new schedule which, with minimal guidance from Evelyn, they negotiated together in a relatively collegial fashion. This is a scheduled break, away from the atelier to be sure it remains a break. But Izidore and Albemarle are sitting with their backs to each other at different tables like sulking siblings.

It's for the working room, he realises. Hazel reported that Albemarle salvaged an ashy scrap of the rare red fern from Ash's demolition; zhey must have been babying it along ever since. Its habitat by the moon gate was destroyed by the fire, so the stakes, and accordingly Albemarle's tension, has been high. Watched over by Nightingale, zhey are painstakingly potting it, a small bag of soil and gardening tools laid out on an oilcloth on zheir table. Zhey are concentrating on that as much as Holly has ever seen zhem concentrate on one of zheir designs.

Izidore, at the next table over, wears the same expression of intense concentration. Zhey are sorting zheir button collection, that Paolo stole from Stronghold Cristati for zhem.

'I couldn't bring all the cases, Izidore,' Ash's half-brother is earnestly explaining. 'It would have been a dead giveaway that I expected you to attempt an escape. I wrapped the fragile ones, though. Nothing broke.'

Izidore makes a low, grumbling noise and keeps laying out the buttons. Zhey've cut zheir hair short, and it's sprung into tight glossy ringlets, glints of bronze and copper amid the brown. Paolo grins over zheir bent head at Second Jerome, who is the on-duty Mancer guard at that table.

Paolo has been writing a letter, evidently. He picks up his pen. 'Where's Ash? I want to know if zhey'll let me send zheir love to Mother and Marco.' He chews on the end of the pen, which can be good for neither ink nor Mancy. 'Maybe zheir well wishes. Best regards? Maybe just normal regards.' He giggles and mimes writing, reciting in a deep and frowny voice, '"Ashlin sends frosty acknowledgement of your general continued existence".' He laughs again, face open and cheerful. 'I hope we reconcile but I really hope they don't visit.'

'How are you from the same family as the other Cristatis?' Second Jerome asks him in wonder.

'I take after my father,' Paolo says readily.

'And did your mother *murder* your father?'

'Well! Interesting story, that!'

Izidore finally surfaces out of zheir button-sorting trance enough to nudge him and smile. 'The fox pays regards to the lion.' ~Ash is gifting Hazel his sister with the far-scry mirror.

'That's nice,' Nightingale says from the other table, smiling wistfully.

It bloody isn't. It is clearly a gambit to keep Hazel and his puppy dog eyes out of the way while Ash removes zhemself from the stronghold.

'Quiet,' says Albemarle, slowly adjusting the tiny leaves of zheir successfully potted red fern. Holly assumes that means Albemarle agrees with him. 'Almost time to get back to work.'

A bell chimes near Izidore's hand. Zhey glance at it and fiddle with some Mancy mechanism. Zhey rise and speak with intense focus—zhey do not want to be mistaken. 'Don't touch anything. I must go add Mancy to the mirror. Do not touch any of these buttons, Paolo.'

That Izidore has been effectively also made absent by this supposed kindly gesture seals Holly's opinion of it. Staying quiet, he moves to the staffing quarters alcove by the south door. His knee is reminding him of its existence after the stairs, but he's otherwise moving better than two days ago, for now.

Back in Cristati, Ash would've almost certainly had zheir own compulsive pastime, and Holly is prepared to bet that it was obsessively plotting to escape. That would be a very hard habit to break.

Shortly after Izidore disappears down the subterrane stairs, Ash comes cautiously up. Zhey're wearing zheir old coat and shawl, and carrying a small bag. With a single glance at the Mancer tables, where Nightingale is helping Albemarle clean up and Second Jerome and Paolo are engrossed in chat and exactly no one is paying attention, the oblivious fuckers, zhey head for the exit.

Holly steps out to block zhem, and remembers, at zheir flinch, that Captain Tassone had rushed out of this very same alcove to smash zhem down onto a table. They were off to a bad start.

Ash lowers zheir hand—zhey instinctively shielded the puffy bruising on zheir face—and stiffly marches onward, looking as if zhey very much plan to walk right through him to get out the door. The spiky little fucker would probably kick him in the weak knee on the way past.

Holly extravagantly leans against the door, all long limbs and languor. '~The right noble and valorous Ashlin Mancer. Going for a stroll?'

~Get out of my way.

'~Seems to me that you've only learnt one way to solve your problems, and that's to run away.'

Ash looks at him unblinkingly. ~Also have some practice in stabbing my problems, captain.

'~You are a constant and endless delight,' Holly says gleefully. '~What is it that's making you run off and leave your Mancer partner and your brother and Hazel?'

~I promised Paolo nothing. I promised Hazel nothing. I promised Izidore only that I would get zhem away from Cristati. I have fulfilled that promise. We are too dangerous in our complementary talents to stay together.

'~Except in a stronghold that can protect you without exploiting you. A stronghold exactly like the one you're standing in. If you promised Izidore nothing more than a new stronghold, why are you sneaking away from zhem? And if you think you got away with promising Hazel nothing, my friend, you—'

~I cannot stay here. Not after the way I treated hi— them.

That comes in a wild burst of signing, and Ash turns [Hazel]—there are no pronouns in Trade, only in people's interpretations of it into Mutual—into [all][people] at the last second. Zhey are desperately trying to keep zheir expression under control, maintain the Mancer blankness, but Holly's hit the mark with that particular arrow.

Holly looks at the Mancer, tense and distressed, and he gentles his tone, because even though Ash can't hear it, it'll convey itself in his body language. '~Will you come with me, Ash? I want to show you something.'

Ash hesitates, watching Holly closely. Holly's unpleasant realisation when Tassone tried to recruit him flashes through his head, how vulnerable Mancers have been made by the very system meant to protect them.

The whole edifice of atelier and stronghold relies on a foundation of absolute trust. Ash is not looking at Holly in a particularly trusting way.

He shrugs and launches off with, '~I understand targeting Ari Hazlemere is manifestly different to falling in love with Hazel darling.'

He's not even halfway through his impromptu speech when Ash tries to dodge it, closing zheir eyes. Hazel tolerates that shit; Holly does not. He says, 'Nah,' and taps zheir shoulder, Albemarle-style—firm to the point of painful. When zhey open zheir eyes to give him a resentful look, he goes on.

'~I know you lump me in with the Cristati Mancer Guard. I'm not as nice as Hazel, granted, but I'm not them either. I'm not trying to trick you or punish you or trap you.'

It takes an irritatingly long time before Ash replies, ~I know.

'~And I also acknowledge that having someone like me as the Haven captain made it hard for you to resist being a secretive little shit.'

Ash informs him solemnly, ~Not to puncture your self-importance, captain, but I am perfectly capable of being a secretive little shit all on my own.

'~All right. And so now could you do me a favour and drop the "captain" bullshit?'

A tiny smile sneaks onto Ash's face. ~I will consider it. Captain.

Holly, laughing, signs [pejorative]; he can't even trot out a *my liege* in retaliation now Ash has been renounced. He steps away from the door, indicating that Ash is welcome to take the choice to walk out. But he again offers the first choice.

'~Come with me just for ten minutes. If you still want to leave after, I'll walk you to the port myself and don't you be giving me that pointed look at my knee, fuckster.'

The knee is still swollen, the skin purple and black, and despite Val's thrice-daily massages with salve, it is now throbbing a touch more than Holly cares to acknowledge. When Ash nods and follows him to the corkscrew stairs, he's moving stiffly enough that zhey even offer a hand, to which Holly gives a merry ~Fuck off.

He ushers zhem into the great hall, which is crowded with people. Some are earnestly talking to Lady Fairhaven or Evie or Val at a table set to one side of the room. Others are sparring with Kito, First Jerome and Titus or each other, all across the cleared floor.

When they replaced Schulze, they held the trials in the bailey, because there'd only been a handful of applicants, Titus the clear cream. But when word went out this time that the Mancers needed more guards, the response made it clear they'd need more room to assess the rush of candidates.

Ash doesn't understand the implication of the crowd. Zhey know as well as Holly does that there must be people in here who lost family or friends or both because of Cristati's attack. Zhey stop and give Holly a look like zhey think he has tricked zhem after all.

'~These people are here because they're vying to be in your Mancer Guard,' he tells zhem. '~Look. That's Shao's sister. She used to be Little Shao. Not anymore, obviously. She's here because she wants to help protect you.' He pokes Ash, who smacks his hand away, scowling. '~You're feeling guilty, right?'

Ash looks about the hall. Zhey turn zheir body so only Holly can see zhem sign, in very small gestures, the telling lift of zheir spread hand over zheir face. ~Ashamed. There's no point telling me I shouldn't be.

'~A-yah. You dragged Haven into the shit and people died. Your intentions were good, but people still died.'

Ash nods.

'~And forgiveness seems to be a somewhat alien concept to the Cristati.'

Ash shrugs and then nods again.

'~You've come from a people who, in their wisdom, linked love conditionally to behaviour. You behave well by their criteria, you're doled out approval. You behave poorly, you're— Well, I won't speak for your family but it's not an exaggeration to say your Mancer Guard hated you, is it?'

~It is not. Ash pauses, looking up at him, then goes on, ~I killed their captain, Holly. The Havens would hate me too if I killed you.

Holly puts his hand on his hips and scowls at the Mancer, not entirely playacting his outrage. Ash, with zheir naughty smile that reminds Holly exactly why Hazel unreasonably adores the little shit, adds [past signifier], turning 'if I killed you' into 'if I'd killed you', which only makes it slightly less offensive.

'~First of all—' Holly starts, poking Ash in the chest.

Ash shoves his finger away, still smiling, and Holy relaxes. He waves his hand over the dozens of applicants. '~It's not like that here, Ash. People can be angry about what happened to Haven, and angry and sad about losing loved ones, and they might blame you on their darkest nights before they remember it was Cristati's choices that brought them here. What they *don't* do, is hate you forever for it. We're a stronghold, and we all know what that means, and anyone who didn't before knows it now and can leave if they don't like it. And we're Fair Haven by the Sea, and we all know what that means, too.'

He leans closer, putting every inch of his well-hidden sincerity into his next words. '~You lived your whole life under a whip, Ash. You're not under the whip anymore. Stop putting yourself there.'

Ash clasps zheir hands together, silencing zhemself.

'~You think the people of Haven hate you, but zhey don't,' Holly spells out. 'Every one of these people is here because they want the honour of protecting Haven's Mancers. We know the price, and we want it anyway.'

~But what do these people really know of what I did?

'~They know you saved the whole east coast, they know the queen is grateful to you and to Haven, they're proud you chose us to help you.'

Ash is frowning fiercely. ~That is a fine smudging of the truth.

'~Nothing you're not used to, then.' Holly shrugs. '~It's a version of the truth that isn't actually false, now, is it? You did, in fact, choose us. You just didn't warn us you had.'

Shao, once Little Shao, ends her spar then, and comes to Ash. She makes a nervous little bob in front of zhem; Havens aren't used to the rules and regulations around formal obeisance.

She waves, another small and nervous gesture. 'I just want to say, I'm looking forward to working with you, if I'm selected.' She looks at Holly. '"Mancer Ashlin"?'

'Just call zhem Ash.'

'Ash,' she repeats, and reproduces zheir sign, too. 'I saw you fight the Mancy thing attacking the walls. Thank you for saving Haven. I feel… I feel like it will honour my sister's memory to serve you.'

Ash stares at her, retreating into stern Mancer blankness. Zhey shoot a fast and suspicious look at Holly, who signs, ~I promise I didn't set this up.

Holly is lying. He *absolutely* set this up. But he didn't feed Shao the words, and her sincerity shines.

Ash rallies and gifts Shao a quiet smile. ~Thank you. I look forward to working with you, too.

'~So gracious,' Holly says when she's plunged back into the trial with renewed vigour. '~Did they teach you that at little liegeling school?'

He gets an emphatic ~Fuck off.

'~Are you still planning to go cause chaos somewhere that can't cope with it, or are you truly going to be working with her? I should tell you, I'll probably be your captain.'

Ash doesn't look quite as appalled as he might have expected, but zhey do raise zheir expressive eyebrows in silent query. Holly explains, '~Kito should stay with Albemarle, and it's best if we put some distance between you and Hazel.'

He sees the flash of pain cross Ash's face, the same pain he saw Hazel wear when he'd come visiting and talked of Ash leaving. Zhey nod grimly and echo, ~For the best.

Holly refrains from saying, '~Oh, you *idiots*, sort yourselves out,' since he's given up all hope and is going to sort them out himself as soon as he's extracted Ash's promise to stay.

He contents himself with a mild, '~Professionally speaking, anyway. Apparently, I'm meant to have a policy.'

Ash sighs and looks at the ceiling and then looks at Holly. ~Take me to Lady Fairhaven.

'You should be in bed,' Valerian snaps at Holly as soon as they're close enough to where the hierarchy is interviewing applicants.

'Then put me there,' Holly advises him. He taps Ash.

Ash gives him a flat look but obligingly signs, ~Lady Fairhaven, I request sanctuary.

Lady Fairhaven lights up in a smile but she politely waits for Holly to finish voicing it before saying, 'Granted and thank goodness for that.' She presses Ash's hand across the table. 'We've been having a dreadful time finding somewhere safe enough for you. Albemarle ripped up our first list of potentials when we checked it with zhem and insisted only Haven will do. I thought you might take it into your head to depart before we could find a suitable place for you.'

She eyes Ash's coat as she says this. Holly adjusts the knot on zheir shawl and says, 'Ash would never do a thing like that.'

Ash bats his hand away, eyes narrowed. Just to annoy zhem further, Holly tells zhem, ~Fuck, you're cute.

~Do I really have to remind you what I did to my previous captains, Holly?

Holly laughs outright. He knows Ash would never bring that up if zhey actually intended to do him harm.

Well. Fingers crossed, anyway.

Evelyn says, 'I'm glad you told us before we finished here.' She's making notes, a list of names. 'We'll have to recruit a whole extra set of Mancer guards from this lot.'

'Evie baby, how are we going to pay for that? Do you know how much arse I had to lick for even the first increase in budget?'

He smirks at Lord Valerian, who makes a high-pitched noise and plants his face into the tabletop, groaning.

'Payback's a bitch, ain't it?' Holly says to him. 'Next time finish the job.'

'I would've warned you not to get involved with him if I'd realised you were foolish enough to attempt it,' Evelyn says, patting her patron comfortingly on the back even while exchanging an affectionately conspiratorial look with her sibling.

Lady Fairhaven says, 'I will add to the patronage funds, cousin, and in fact Lord Paolo has means independent of his mother, an inheritance from his father, and has expressed his wish to remain Ashlin's patron. No need to concern yourself.'

'Certainly, that was my concern,' Valerian says to the tabletop.

Ash bows and backs away. ~I am returning to the others, Holly.

'Give me a minute,' Holly said, eyeing off the sparring candidates. 'I'm going to see if any of these fuckers can get a hit on me. Kito shouldn't get all the fun.'

'Go back to bed, Holyoake,' Valerian says sharply. He's still blushing. 'I can see you limping.'

'Your Mancer is getting away,' Lady Fairhaven says.

Holly glances about and see that Ash has indeed set off alone. He dances back and gets in front of zhem. '~You can't go about unsupervised,' he says to zhem, and to Lady Fairhaven, '~Not my Mancer, Haven's Mancer.'

Ash is looking at him with growing indignation. Holly takes a stab at the source of zheir ire. '~Did I say unsupervised?' he says gaily. '~I meant unescorted, of course. Un-honour guarded.'

Ash demands, ~Why not your Mancer?

'~Are you offended? It's just tradition.'

He pauses. He's no longer quite so enslaved to tradition, especially not 'just' tradition. Tradition needs to change, everywhere. He doesn't know how yet, but Lady Fairhaven and Lord Valerian and Evelyn will help him sort that part out. He's not suited to long-term planning and influence like they are. It'll start with the academy, he suspects, his iron establishment which needs a little work to scrub off the rust. The queen will be sympathetic, given her intimate knowledge of her cousin's sins, and her influence will go a long way.

He lets it drop for now and explains, '~The academy doesn't like us calling you our Mancer. Stronghold's Mancer, always. Otherwise, it's a sign we're too attached. It's words. We get fairly fucking attached anyway.'

Ash stills, a hawk in the breathless moment before it stoops on its prey, before urgently signing, ~I have to go.

Zhey practically bolt from the great hall like zhey're off to stab a giant Mancy insect in the neck.

'Don't make me run,' Holly shouts after zhem, before sighing. 'Deaf, right.'

Titus has already waved to him and slipped out after the hurrying Mancer. He turns back to the panel of judges. 'Well, now, I *have* to join the spar. Hoi, Kito, we should lock the doors and set Izidore's pet in here, that'll sort 'em real fast.'

'For fuck's sake, go back to bed, Holly,' Lord Valerian says in exasperation.

'For fuck's sake, make me, love,' Holly says with a grin and accompanying wink that make Val blush again. Pink-cheeked and rumple-haired: adorable.

'Take him back to bed, Valerian,' Lady Fairhaven commands with smooth innocence. 'The last thing we need is him permanently injuring himself, is it? We're going to need the Holyoakes now every other stronghold knows the quality of our Mancers.'

Valerian looks uncertain, but he rises and offers Holly his arm. Holly looks at it scathingly, but then he shrugs and steps in and takes it because it gives him the excuse to snug his whole body up against the man and all the delicious muscle under his stolid exterior.

Outside the great hall, Holly nudges him. 'Let's stop by your office first.'

'Certainly, what— Oh. Oh, no, Holyoake, you're for bed. Bed *rest!*'

Holly's overcome with a wave of fond feeling for this quiet man hiding all his care behind his pragmatism and duty. He must be the only person in the entire crowded hall that hadn't realised Holly had finagled his dismissal so he could be thoroughly sexed up. Holly smiles; that means the man has no idea that a dozen or so men are sickly envious of him right now.

Then he frowns. Because he'd had a dozen options in the great hall, both previous and unexplored, and he'd cast over them with a Mancer Guard captain's eye, and it hadn't even occurred to him to fish for a different sort of entertainment to reel in later.

Holly turns the frown on Lord Valerian, who tsks and says sternly, 'I'm well aware you are owed. I'm not shirking, but I'm concerned you're not taking enough care—'

Holly stops thinking about it; his frown evaporates. 'Then will you take me to your office and put me flat on my back on your desk?'

'No!'

'"Who the fuck would ever say no?"' Holly parrots mockingly. Then he admits, 'I really cannot stand the same four walls anymore, Val. Can you help a fellow out, or not?'

'Yes, but not in a way that hurts you,' Valerian says stoutly. 'I anticipated this, actually.'

Holly says, 'Of course you did,' as Val takes his arm.

He helps Holly down the corkscrew stairs, supporting all of his lanky weight so the knee barely twinges, and out the south door where Ash was trying to sneak away a short time before. He sets Holly up on a stone bench by the fountain, making him sit sideways and stretch his knee out.

Then he puts a whole fistful of throwing knives in front of him.

'What are we—' Holly starts, before Valerian bends over something hidden behind the fountain and it whirs into life and scurries in zigs and zags across the courtyard: a many-legged Mancy creature, followed by several more. They are small and fast, and extrude bristling stalks sporting round ocular things on their ends.

'Targets,' Valerian says. He gestures at the throwing knives. 'I asked the Mancers to make them for you. It's a game.'

The creatures scuttle randomly; their stalks probe upward and retract randomly; their eye-like targets expand and contract randomly. Holly's too fixated on the whole impossible challenge of it all to wonder how Albemarle took the request for a commission; it is time to stop assuming Haven's senior Mancer can't cope.

He picks up his first knife. This is the best game he's ever seen, and he reckons he's got less than an hour to get good at it before Kito shows up and makes it a competition. He looks up and catches Valerian smiling at him with unalloyed pleasure; he realises he's smiling fiercely himself.

Holly drops the knife again, and when Val starts to say something, he waves both hands, shushing him. He's groping toward something here. He feels very known, and it's disconcerting, but not in a way he finds unpleasant.

'You. This. I've had plenty of regular lovers, in amongst the flings. I've never had one I thought I might want to—' He makes a grasping gesture as he tries to find the right word. '—devote myself to.'

Valerian's already nodding. 'We discussed this. I knew that already, you don't have to tell me again.'

Holly finally uncovers the shape of his epiphany and adds, 'Until you.'

It shuts Val up. Holly turns to face him directly and waits.

'That sounded sincere,' Valerian says eventually.

'I know, I'm quite impressed with myself.'

'Are you ever not impressed with yourself, Holyoake?' Valerian asks dryly, before taking a breath. 'Does that mean—'

Holly holds up a finger. 'Don't ask me to examine my own feelings, Val, it's not the direction in which my talents lie. I can't say further than that.

Do we have enough to be going on with for now?'

'That's… That's plenty, Holly.'

'Polite of you to say so,' Holly says. He knows he's offering a pittance to a man who's been brave enough to offer a damn sight more.

Valerian picks up one of the throwing knives and pushes it into Holly's hand. 'It's enough for me. I wouldn't say so if it wasn't true.'

He straddles the bench, his back to Holly, supporting him like a backrest.

'Nah,' Holly says. 'Cuddle, please.' When Valerian doesn't move, Holly says, 'Turn around and cuddle me, Lord Vee, I don't see what's difficult about this concept.'

The lord slowly turns about on the bench so that his chest is against Holly's back, his wide, muscular thighs settled on either side of Holly's legs, enclosing him in warmth. 'Like this, Hols?'

Holly rests his head back on Valerian's shoulder and lazily smiles at him. The poor man, he's besotted. 'Perfect, my love.'

After some time, Kito does come out, and the other Mancer guards, and some of the new recruits, and two-thirds of Haven's Mancers, and Evie and Lady Fairhaven, and undercroft staff, and upper retainers. They play with the Mancy targets until the sun gets low and the chill gets high. They light a bonfire, and someone breaks out the rice-wine and someone else starts piping and a third someone starts strumming. At some point, it becomes a party, and a celebration of life lost and lives that will go on in peace and hope.

Even though Holly still can't dance on his knee, it'd be perfect, if only Hazel and his spiky little fucker were here.

~THIRTY-SIX~

ASH WAS STANDING OUTSIDE HAZEL'S ROOM and looked like zhey had been for some time. Titus was with zhem, but now, as Hazel stopped dead in the doorway, she gave both Ash and Hazel a smile and trotted away.

He sagged against his door frame. He was so relieved he felt an unfamiliar sense of giddiness. But Ash was wearing zheir coat, zheir shawl twisted into a cowl about zheir neck, and carrying zheir bag. Zhey'd decided to do the brave thing and say a proper goodbye, then, that was all.

He faced zhem, forcing a smile. He restrained himself from a flood of Trade—I'm so glad you're still here, thank you for Maya, please talk to me, please ask for sanctuary, please stay, please stay, please stay—and merely signed, ~Good afternoon.

Zhey signed, ~I didn't want to interrupt, but I need to talk to you, please, Hazel.

'~I need to talk to you, too,' Hazel said. He indicated for Ash to come in, and as soon as he had the door shut behind zhem, blurted, '~Look, I know I made that cursed speech to your mother about letting you go, but— Ash, if you really must leave—'

Ash waved zheir hands and tapped zheir foot in the same attention-getting signal zhey used with Izidore. ~Me first, Hazel.

'~A-yah,' Hazel said, subsiding. 'Well, why not?'

~I've asked for sanctuary.

'Fucking *finally*,' Hazel burst out, and then winced.

~Indeed, Ash signed with a wry look.

'~Who talked you into it?'

~Holly, mostly.

Hazel made the two-fingered shake that meant [of course]. '~Should've dragged him out of Valerian's bed earlier.'

~He made it clear that what I thought was the right thing to do was very much not. He also pointed out something I hadn't realised. He said—

Ash paused there and looked at Hazel. He nodded encouragingly with a lift of the brows.

~I'm *nervous*, zhey snapped.

Hazel raised his hands placatingly. He was somewhat bewildered, given he was talking to the person who had brought two strongholds to their knees in quite the nerveless fashion. Surely whatever zhey had to say couldn't make zhem turn a single pretty silver hair.

'~It's just me,' he murmured.

Zhey waved him to silence. ~Hazel, I was under the impression that when you call me your Mancer, it's your way of reminding me that you're trained by the academy to protect me at any cost. That you're saying, in effect, that while your actions might *suggest* you've forgiven me, that's only because the training makes it look that way, and actually you—you still hate me for what I did to Haven. For what I did to you.

'~Never,' Hazel said. He touched his chest, hand over his heart. '~That's what you thought?' Zhey shrugged, then reluctantly nodded. '~Never. Just—*never.*'

Ash watched him intently. ~You forgive me?

'~I do not,' Hazel said, 'believe there is a single thing to forgive. When I say you did what you had to, I mean it.' He lost a little momentum. '~I can't speak for everyone in Haven, actually. You did kind of fuck us over. And I didn't appreciate you using Maya against me by proxy.'

Ash had gone very still, most likely because zhey realised in the same moment Hazel did that he had some unexpressed thoughts and unre-solved feelings built up, regarding the last few days.

With very small movements, zhey signed ~I understand. And I am sorry, for all of it, Hazel. I—

I'm not thrilled about it, he'd said, so blithely. *I won't forget.*

He made a broad gesture like swiping chalk marks off a slate. '~You did what you had to do, and it's done, and I don't need—none of us need—endless self-recrimination,' he said. '~Though… Next time you feel the need to do what you have to do, could you perhaps let me know so I can help you? I'll always help you, Ash.'

He won a tiny smile. Ash shifted zheir weight, hands raised but motionless, once again steeling zhemself to tell him something.

But Hazel was still thinking things through, step by step. '~So earlier, when you told me you refused to mistake feeling protected for being in love—'

~That isn't what I said.

'~You were actually reassuring me that you wouldn't mistake my dutiful behaviour for *me* being in love with *you*.'

Ash sighed, heavily, as zhey emphatically nodded and double-signed, ~Yes.

That was arse-backward, but he had to acknowledge the good intent. '~Fair.'

Zhey blankly repeated it back to him.

'~Yes,' he said. '~I will always do my best for you regardless of my personal feelings, because you're quite right about the training.' He shrugged. '~You are quite right to be careful about misconstruing that sort of thing.'

Ash looked down. ~I see. Yes. I see.

Hazel drew his thumb over his heart. '~But I interrupted. What were you saying?'

Ash paused yet again, this time for a very long time, watching his face. Zhey finally asked, ~Hazel, are you fucking with me?

'~No,' said Hazel, making [negatory] with one hand, [shocked] with the other, an ambidexterity that he lost control of the instant he noticed himself doing it.

Lowering his hands, he took a moment to review the conversation. Ash took a moment to let him, the vertical lines between zheir eyebrows pronounced.

'~Ah. I see where we've gone astray here. I didn't mean to imply that I'm *not*—'

Zhey threw zheir hands up and signed in one long ripple, ~Would you let me say my piece?

Hazel ran his hand through his hair. He was caught in the space between groaning and laughing. Of all the stupid—

'~Something you want to say to me, Ash love?'

~Apparently, people can be angry with someone, and not hate them. Apparently, they can be angry with them, and still…

For all zheir insistence, zhey stopped again, and looked at Hazel, pride and plea balanced in equal measure.

'~Love them,' Hazel couldn't help but finish for zhem.

Pressing zheir lips together, Ash slowly ventured a quote, capturing a highly familiar diffidence with zheir signs and expression.

~You do mean me, yes?

Hazel smiled, and saw the relief bloom like a snowdrop that zheir little sally had not been misplaced.

He said, '~I love you, Ash. Yes, I was angry with you for using me, and Haven, but I saw your side of it, and— I love you. I love everything about you, stubborn, secretive, spiky and all. I only didn't say it because I didn't think you wanted to hear it.'

Ash straightened and, looking particularly severe, signed, ~I love you, Hazel. You have— You have made a small and frightened person so much stronger. You gave me something to reach for, rather than just something to run away from.

Hazel looked at zhem, then, smiling helplessly, drinking in the beautiful stark lines of zheir face, his Mancer, his small and sudden storm.

Ash's tiny smile gradually appeared in return. ~Are you just going to stand there or are you going to kiss me?

'~Wonderful idea.'

He ran his fingers down Ash's face and tilted zheir chin up, and leaned in as zhey craned up. Their mouths met hungrily. Ash pressed against Hazel; without relinquishing zheir mouth, Hazel walked zhem backward until he had zhem hard against the wall. Since he knew zhey responded well to the feel of the tussle, he got his hands tight on zheir hips, pressing zhem back and up as zhey squirmed against him with mounting insistence.

Eventually zhey disentangled zhemself. ~Will you… Hazel, will you do that with your mouth?

Zhey didn't mean more kissing, or not on the mouth, anyway; by the time he'd realised what Ash was asking for, the Mancer was wearing zheir small smile again. ~Tell me if I'm imposing. I suppose you don't crave sex as such.

'~Likely not,' Hazel said equitably. '~I crave the feel of your skin, though. I crave the taste of you. I crave the quite loud noise you make when my mouth's on you—'

Ash rapped his chest with zheir knuckles, smile lighting up zheir whole face. ~You are definitely fucking with me now.

'~I want to be, but you're just standing there, so…'

This time he got a solid shove. ~Get on the bed. Get on the bed right now. No. No. Undress me first.

Hazel started stripping off zheir coat before zhey even finished the signs for that. The strap of zheir bag got tangled in zheir sleeves but he managed to peel both off in good time, and the shawl, and set to on the buttons on zheir vest. Ash closed zheir eyes and tipped zheir head back, exposing zheir smooth throat where a few scrapes from the collar remained. Hazel kissed those, and kissed down zheir torso as the buttons of the vest parted under his fingers.

He kissed zheir eyelids to get zheir attention. '~All the way?' He touched zheir undershirt.

Zhey nodded firmly. ~Naked. I want to be naked with you.

That provoked a small flurry of activity, though Hazel managed to slow down enough to make taking off zheir trousers and underclothes a series of long slow strokes of his hands and gentle brushes with his mouth. Zhey were whimpering by the time he'd laid zhem bare. Zhey indeed wore bruises and other marks all over from the day of the battle and he kissed each sign of injury as if he could wash it away for zhem. Zhey still had the bandage over zheir cut shoulder and he traced the edges of it carefully.

He took zheir hand, pressed his mouth to the tips of zheir fingers. 'I love you.' He said it again, against zheir wrist this time, over the tattoo. '~This is what it feels like on your skin when I say I love you,' he told zhem, before pressing his mouth against the side of zheir neck. 'I love you.'

Ash turned zheir face into his hair, hands pressed to his stomach under his shirt so zhey could sign in zheir turn against his skin, ~I love you.

He guided zhem to sit on the bed, and to lie back. After judiciously removing the mirror, he knelt before zhem, planting kisses on the three dragonflies at zheir hip. He looked up. Zhey were resting back on zheir elbows, watching him.

'~Pull my hair if you need me to stop.'

~I might…want to…pull your hair…when I need you…*not* to stop.

Hazel laughed. '~Tap my shoulder, then.'

Ash nodded. He pressed his mouth to the soft skin of zheir inner thighs, and pushed one of zheir legs over his shoulder to spread zhem before him. Ash's hands landed in his wild hair at the first touch of his tongue to zheir crux, and zhey did indeed take up fistfuls as zhey arched against his mouth. Cognisant of his close-trimmed beard against zheir bare skin, Hazel kept the pressure and rhythm of his mouth and tongue constant, and let Ash control how much zhey could take with zheir hold on his head and the cant and thrust of zheir hips against him.

It was not long before zhey were making zheir little bird noises, and he dropped a hand from his grip on zheir hips to his own trousers, but that was when Ash tapped him on the shoulder.

~No, zhey told him. ~Hands off yourself, your pleasure belongs to me this time.

Smiling, Hazel lost himself in the increasingly urgent flex and pulse of Ash under his mouth. He could feel that zhey were on the agonising cusp, zheir body tautly arched against him, both fighting against the threat of sensation suddenly becoming too intense to take, and fighting to push zhemself over the crest. He wanted to stop so he could tell zhem to melt into it, stop fighting either way, but he supposed if he denied zhem his mouth right now, zhey really might stab him. Zhey should probably just ride his tongue like last time, until zhey got used to so thoroughly giving zhemself over.

All at once, zhey went limp and he felt the throb on his tongue as zhey climaxed with one great cry and then a series of gasping wordless calls, hips stuttering as zhey chased the aftershocks.

Hazel wiped his beard and licked the taste of Ash off his lips. Zheir eyes were shut, and zhey were taking up most of the bottom half of the narrow bed in a sweetly languid sprawl. He was colluding, but he rather suspected that Ash's release, and the sleepless nights, and the very busy day in between, and all the weeks of secrets before that, had flattened his Mancer like a runaway cart.

He lifted Ash's hips and shuffled zhem up until zhey were fully on the bed, and crawled along the bed to squeeze in between zhem and the wall. He nestled zhem against him, head cupped against his chest. Zheir eyes fluttered half-open and zheir hands moved a little, but zhey didn't quite manage to achieve coherence. Zheir breathing evened out and deepened. Hazel watched zhem fall into sleep, smiling.

He lay with zhem for an unknown time, lost in pleasantly drowsy meanderings, one hand stroking zheir hair. He thought about kneeling before his shrine and thanking Kisane, for Ash, for Maya and her family, for Holly and all the rest, for Fair Haven by the Sea. He savoured the thought of Ash's agile hands on him. He wondered how Ash would want to go on, whether it would be a tap at his door every now and again or whether they'd end up knocking adjoining cell walls out to make an apartment near the atelier.

Albemarle would hate that. Hazel swallowed his laugh until he remembered the sound of it couldn't disturb Ash. Then he let himself laugh, holding zhem against his chest, letting his quiet joy shine.

Ash stirred and looked up at him. Zheir eyes looked glazed over, glittery. Zhey quite drunkenly signed, ~Love the feel of your voice.

Ah. Vibrations. '~Sorry,' he said. '~Sleep, love.'

Ash shook zheir head against his chest. Zhey rolled zheir hips, making Hazel hiss; his thoughts had repeatedly wandered to the anticipation of Ash touching him and he was still hard.

~You need your turn.

'~Ash, I need nothing you can't give.'

Ash abruptly sat up, fully awake and wearing zheir imperious look of offended pride to boot. It was mostly, Hazel thought, playful, but only mostly. ~I can give you anything, Hazel darling. Tell me what you want.

Hazel still hesitated—he wanted his Mancer to get more sleep and not feel obligated, and who knew how long it would take zhem, raised by Cristati, to sincerely believe that not everything had a price?

Ash, watching him intently, added, ~Your pleasure is my pleasure, yes? Don't deny me.

Hazel had to concede the point. '~Ah, well. Your hand, then, love.'

The Mancer looked surprised. ~Ask for anything you like. I'm not— I'm not averse, Hazel.

A ringing endorsement. '~Ash, I've been thinking about those quick hands of yours for weeks. I *am* asking for what I'd like.'

A look of shy delight dawned on Ash's face. Those quick hands of zheirs loosened his clothing, and zheir mouth kissed over his skin in the wake of the opening of buttons and laces. As zhey settled zheir weight over his thighs, his hands traced zheir geometry, the strong severe lines of zheir face, the curves and planes of zheir body. Zhey pressed kisses over his hairline, down along the scar. Zheir belly pressed against his bared cock and he felt his hips flex of their own accord against the pressure. Ash, smiling, took the hint and took him in hand. Zhey were watching his face, absorbed in reading his responsive pleasure to zheir firm, slow strokes.

There was nothing quite so intense as being the focus of a Mancer's rapt attention and he found the steady regard even more stimulating than the actual physicality of Ash's strong fingers wrapped around his cock, speeding up now, and zheir dexterous exploration of his tightening balls and arse with the agile fingers of zheir other hand. He gave himself over to it, locking his gaze onto Ash's until he could bear it no longer. Ash caught his cry in zheir mouth, leaning down for that hard kiss so that they were both splattered over their bellies with his spend.

After cleaning them up, Ash knelt on the bed, looking at him, face impassive, Mancer blank.

'~Do you need to go work on a project?' Hazel asked. '~I'd rather you slept again, but if you need Mancy, I'll escort you.'

Ash shook zheir head. Hazel therefore held open his arms, but zhey didn't move, just kept watching him.

'~Something bothering you, love?'

Ash looked offended, without an iota of playfulness behind it. Hazel watched zhem wrestle the indignation down. Shoulders stiff, zhey slowly admitted, ~My obsessive Mancer hobby was escape plans and I need to replace it with something soon or my next obsessive hobby will be you.

His first instinct was to reassure zhem, tell zhem he wouldn't mind that at all; he'd just had one of the most erotic experiences of his life because of the unblinking Mancer focus, after all, and he was a fixer of problems and a habitual accepter of other people's desires.

But being subject to that unwavering regard—the intense fixation it indicated—beyond the span of time devoted to lovemaking was not, all told, something to be stoically accepted. It was not a healthy ideal for either of them, especially, *especially*, given the breed of familial love Ash had been subject to.

Further, Ash had zhemself gone against Cristati indoctrination to both recognise zhey needed help with an incipient problem and to confess to it, and he would not reward zheir trust, zheir genuine effort to change zheir reflexively secretive ways, with a glib brush-off or platitudes.

Therefore he nodded solemnly. '~I understand. We'll come up with something else for you to collect and catalogue forthwith. I bet Albemarle has ideas. We'll ask zhem as soon as possible.'

He saw Ash's tension ebb; zhey looked almost astonished that it was that easy, which Hazel might have been mildly insulted at if he hadn't met zheir fucking mother. Again, he opened his arms, and zhey flopped down onto him with an endearing abandonment of zheir usual grace.

Zhey leaned zheir elbows on his bare chest to free zheir hands. ~I will not be able to talk for blushing now I know what you're thinking about when you're staring at my hands.

'~A-yah, and how am I supposed to say anything at all with you staring at my mouth with your own lovely wicked thoughts?'

~You can say "Take me to bed, Ash", and "I want to play you like a flute, Ash", and "Let me feed the hamster its treat, Ash".'

Hazel, laughing so that his signs wobbled everywhere, said, '~We are not calling it that, it's awful. This is the sign for oral sex.' He demonstrated the graphically self-explanatory sign. '~Practise that one as often as you want.'

Ash lazily signed, ~I'll practise.

Zhey gave no indication whatsoever as to whether zhey meant the sign or the act—until zheir mischievous smile made its appearance.

But zhey sobered quickly. ~Hazel, promise you won't let me impose on you. You insist on all the things I don't have to do. You don't have to do them, either.

Again, he felt the temptation to glib reassurance; again, he resisted it. '~I know. I won't.'

~And promise you'll never do anything for my own good.

Hazel nodded, though it took him a beat. His training suggested Mancer guards sometimes had to do things for the Mancer's own good. His training could go fuck itself, in some very specific regards.

Ash added, ~That also means I'd like you to fuck me all the way sometime and you mustn't say no on my behalf, only your own.

He could imagine it, then, Ash astride him, body arched as his cock filled zhem, zheir head tilted back, zheir lips parted, long line of zheir throat exposed, his fingers spread wide over zheir skin to span the distance between the bottom of zheir ribs and the top of zheir hips.

He swallowed, hard. '~Ah. If you happen to move from not averse to begging for it, I'll be delighted to assist.' After a moment, he delicately elaborated, '~And you can fuck me too, of course.'

He made the familiar two-fingered waggle again, which Ash could interpret howsoever zhey liked.

Ash propped zheir hands under zheir chin and stared at him without blinking for an extraordinarily long time before finally signing, ~We better go sort that new hobby out right now, Hazel darling. Right now.

'~All right, Ash love, let's go do that.'

They dressed and went upstairs, finding a party of sorts in progress in the central court beside the fountain, their friends by a bonfire and Holly snugged up on a bench with a slightly sheepish Lord Valerian.

'~And did we sort ourselves out?' Holly asked, looking between him and Ash with a rather smug smile.

'~Don't know, did we?' Hazel said, with his own pointed look between Holly and Lord Valerian.

Holly tugged on Hazel's shirt to pull him down for a kiss on the forehead. He looked past Hazel, to where Ash had become fixated on Mancy insects, like beetles, ambling about the bonfire.

Holly waved his hand to attract Ash's attention, then tugged on the hem of zheir vest when that proved inadequate, physically pulling zhem about so zhey could see his hands. Ash glared and Holly smirked.

He held up a throwing knife, and ticked its point illustratively in the air between Ash's chest and the Mancy beetles, which Hazel now recognised were moving targets.

'~Next time you feel obliged to throw a knife at your captain, you won't miss,' he told zhem.

Ash looked from the knife to the targets and back again. Hazel practically saw the new obsession lock into place.

Zhey took the knife from zheir captain, small smile glinting.

~Bonus Story~

'I think you'll find zhem a lot friendlier now…'

Oh, Hazel, you optimist. I think you'll *find everyone else knows Holly and Ash are going to give each other* endless *trouble.*

It's a lovely autumn day at Stronghold Fair Haven by the Sea, and the Mancers are arguing again.

They, and their respective on-duty Mancer guards, are out on the broad sward between the stronghold and the cliffs, testing their talos in the teeth of a stiffening breeze. Albemarle got wind of the existence of these mechanical sentinels and conceived an obsession with developing zheir own version to patrol the shore. Except Haven doesn't have a shore. It has a clifftop.

'What zhey think is coming up over the cliffs is a question,' Kito had said, but it is not a question that anyone asks of Albemarle. It's not like it will hurt to have a giant Mancy beast perambulating about the walls of Haven, once Izidore and Ash can persuade their colleague to allow the talos wider scope than an ocean view.

Albemarle designed its inner workings; Izidore was responsible for making it move, which means, of course, lots of legs. The thing resembles an armoured beetle.

Or it did, until it walked off the cliff a few moments before.

Ash, apparently, was responsible for steering. When the months-long project veered sideways, teetered back and forth on the edge of the cliff as if buffeted by the biting wind, and then turned again and marched deliberately into empty air, the other two Mancers directed their stares at zhem with admittedly accusatory eyes, and that was when the argument started.

Holly holds his distance and is narrow-eyed on Hazel and the less senior Mancer guards, silently insisting they hold off too. The Mancers aren't violent with each other, after all, no matter how emphatic Ash is getting with zheir hands.

Ash is getting *very* emphatic with zheir hands. Ash has been in a foul mood for some weeks now, and it is only worsening as time passes. Zhey've surpassed Albemarle as Haven's most difficult Mancer, even ignoring zheir determined effort to bring the entire stronghold down six months ago.

Adjusting the wrap around his braids against the whip of the coastal gusts, Holly strolls across the soft grass to Hazel, who has a hand in his wild hair and is frowning as he watches the Mancers' argument.

'Hazel darling,' he says, 'are you fulfilling your marital duties adequately?'

'Am I…' Hazel trails off, bemused but at least distracted from fretting.

'Or is there another reason your Mancer is wound up so tight lately?'

'I don't know,' Hazel says. 'Zhey won't talk about it.'

'That is because you coddle zhem and *let* zhem not talk about it.'

'May I point out that zheir Mancer Guard captain also does not know what zheir problem is because he also can't get zhem to talk about it?'

'No, you may *not* point that out, because zhey are astonishingly good at dodging being alone with me so I can discuss it with zhem privately. You're the one zhey feel safe to be alone with.'

'But not to talk about things zhey don't want to talk about, Holly.'

'I doubt there's any talking at all going on,' Holly says with a mock primness that makes Hazel smile. 'You're going to have to help me get the spiky little shit off by zhemself so I can find out what the issue is before zhey go for the jugulars of the other two.'

Hazel looks uneasy. 'I won't— I won't collude with you against Ash, Hols.'

And this, of course, is one of the very many difficulties of allowing a Mancer and a Mancer guard to indulge in a relationship beyond the professional. Lord Valerian, Holly's lover who torments him with annoyingly good points, has accurately and, indeed annoyingly, pointed these difficulties out, repeatedly.

This is guaranteed to make Holly unreasonable, but he is saved from snapping at his closest friend by the sudden appearance of Ash, who storms between them to shout, ~I will not have my Mancer guard colluding against me.

Hazel says, '~I was literally just refusing to—'

But Ash has not paused in zheir dramatic exit. Holly glances about to see that the other two Mancers are making zheir own dramatic exits, though Albemarle's is more in the way of zheir usual oblivious stomp toward the postern. Izidore, though, is looking surly as zhey follow behind with zheir arms crossed. Ash really has been a right fucker lately, if zhey could put that expression on zheir friend's face.

'You're with Izidore,' Holly reminds Hazel, who has taken a step after Ash.

Hazel pulls a face. 'Be nice.'

'You coddle zhem,' he says again.

'Zhey don't let zhemself be coddled, Holly. Please, be nice.'

Holly scoffs. He dismisses the other guards assigned to Ash to join the rest of the cavalcade back to the stronghold, and lopes after Ash, who has stalked off cliffward and is glowering at the horizon as if zhey wish zhey could set the ocean afire.

He has to tap zheir shoulder to catch zheir attention. Ash spins about, looking irritated to have been followed. Zhey look even more so when zhey realise who has done the following.

'~A-yah, Hazel won't come after you if you've made it clear—say, by shouting at him for colluding while he was in the middle of refusing to collude—that you don't want to discuss it,' Holly tells zhem. '~A great respecter of boundaries, is our Hazel darling.'

Ash gazes rather longingly after his lover, because they both know that Hazel might respect boundaries but Holly most certainly does not.

In the atelier, Holly has taken to flashing a copperlit on and off under Ash's engrossed nose to garner zheir attention, which Ash responds to about as well as Holly does to zheir own demand that he stop doing two things at once and watch zheir signs exclusively. Zhey stop talking if he's not watching, in point of fact, and thus he expects the same con-sideration now. He waves his hand in front of zheir face until zhey reluctantly meet his eye.

'~You might as well just tell me.'

~What?

'~Whatever's bothering you. Hazel's worried about you.'

Ash's face tightens. ~Nothing is bothering me.

Holly plays dirty. '~Is it Hazel? Are you finished with him and you don't know how to tell him?'

He gets a frown and both fists in the sideways clench that is [negatory]. Ash glances after Hazel again, anxious this time, and repeats the gesture with urgent firmness.

'~Izidore? Albemarle? Paolo? Those debates you have with Nightingale? The upcoming visit from your mother? I can play this game all day, Ashlin. Here's a guess. Are you plotting again?'

Here Ash pauses in giving quick, decisive negatory signs to Holly's suggestions and eyes his Mancer Guard captain blankly.

'~You're done waiting for Lady Fairhaven to engender change at the academy and conceived some notion of overthrowing it, and you're planning on dragging Haven into the shit again to get it done?'

~Of course not.

'~There's no "of course not" about it. You're keeping secrets and you're lying and the last time you did that—'

Holly perforce has to stop because Ash has put zheir hands over zheir face so zhey cannot lipread or watch his hands. It's a tactic Holly admires but does not allow to succeed.

He takes Ash's wrists and tugs zheir hands away. He raises his eyebrows eloquently.

'~What could the valorous Ashlin Mancer possibly be so afraid of here in safe little Fair Haven by the Sea?'

~You will send me away.

The rapid signing is the equivalent of a verbal blurt. Ash locks zheir hands together, face set in its sternest lines.

'~Oh, you catastrophiser!' Holly exclaims, though it's nothing he has a sign for, so he combines [disaster] and [hound] and trusts Ash to get the gist, which, based on zheir annoyed expression, zhey do.

He goes on. '~Hazel worships you. He'll let you go if you demand it and go with you if you allow it. But he'll never send you away and never let me or anyone else do it either.'

~Please. We both know you could dispose of me and tell Hazel any story you like and he'll swallow it.

This is both mildly insulting for the sweet and unassuming Hazel, and eminently true. '~Like he swallowed every lie *you* told him?'

Ash flashes an indignant glare, but zhey can't actually argue it with him, can zhey? Well. Zhey justifiably just about could, but zhey don't, because Hazel is right when he says zhey don't take coddling.

Putting his hands on his hips, Holly considers the Mancer. '~It's not working, is it?' he finally says. '~Dispose of you, the bones of my ancestors bless us all. You're never going to truly trust me. I'm too much like the Cristati guards.'

Ash looks down again, not agreeing but certainly denying nothing.

Holly flicks zheir shoulder to bring zheir attention back up. '~You could have said so at any time.'

He's striving for mockingly peeved because he's wounded, more than a little, notwithstanding he doesn't entirely trust Ash either. He suspects Ash of running a campaign, the prize of war being Hazel as zheir captain.

It's a game Holly is more than willing to play. '~But you can't have Hazel,' he says. '~And Kito is best with Albemarle. How do you feel about—'

~I don't want a new captain.

'~You don't trust me,' Holly repeats. '~I know you're not a whole-hearted supporter of the whole Mancer Guard establishment, but since you're stuck with it for now, you do need to trust your captain.'

~I trust you.

He cocks a hip and makes the eloquent [doubt] sign with some emphasis to convey his supreme scepticism.

Ash gives a silent huff. ~I trust you enough. My problem is not with any person.

Holly's patience, not a deep dish, is rapidly draining dry. '~Some situation is getting out of hand, then—'

He cuts himself off, because Ash is scowling at him again, and he realises that, before he jumped to interrupt, the Mancer was about to prove zhey trust him by telling him the truth. Which, after all, was the point of making a show of being upset about not being trusted.

~Back at Stronghold Cristati, I was forced to turn Izidore's projects into weapons.

Holly nods encouragingly, which just makes Ash glare at him even more; his encouragement probably reads along the lines of impatience. He does, after all, already know this.

~That means I was taking zheir projects and singing my own Mancy into them.

Another nod from Holly, now genuinely more impatient than encouraging.

Ash sighs. ~Holly, that means I was practising my own Mancy very regularly.

Enlightenment dawns. Holly gives a brisk single tap to his temple. '~And now you're not. You only get to help the other two. You don't get to use your own. You never get to, because Haven doesn't want weapons and Albemarle is actively against them. And it's winding you tight.'

Ash nods zheir fist and zheir head in forceful concert. ~I did not realise I was so dependent on it.

'~Were you planning on coming to me or Hazel for help?'

~I do not need help, Ash announces in high Cristati dudgeon, before sullenly adding, ~I am managing.

'~You're really not, you cranky fucker. Any day now Albemarle is going to refuse to work with you.'

~And then you will send me away.

'~And *before* then, I will take one of Izidore's little projects and bring it to you to sing your Mancy into it and that will take the edge off.'

Ash shakes zheir head. ~It will become a weapon.

'~At the risk of sounding like a dick…' Holly gives Ash a fond swat when zhey huff. '~Are you so sure your Mancy will still twist into making weapons? You must have been feeling very hostile toward your Mancer Guard at the time.'

~Feeling very hostile toward my Mancer guard right now, captain.

'~My point is,' Holly shouts, since Ash can't hear (though zhey have eyes and can see) that he's raised his voice and he has to get through this eminently frustrating conversation somehow. '~If you're happier, your Mancy must be happier. Fuck, sing it while you're riding Hazel's tongue, you couldn't be holding on to a single hostile thought.'

Ash looks horrified and waves both hands in a warding-off gesture before jerking out, ~Do not!

After a breath in which zhey glare and Holly laughs, zhey go on, ~My Mancy is what it is, no matter my mood. I make weapons. Albemarle hates weapons. I cannot do my own Mancy here.

'~What Albemarle doesn't know won't hurt zhem—'

~Have you learned nothing!

'Izidore will supply the projects, we'll bring them out here away from the stronghold, and you'll sing your Mancy—'

~What is it you do not understand? They will become weapons. They don't tend to go for me, but they'll find someone else to hurt.

'~And I will destroy them,' Holly manages to finish in the face of Ash's irritated signing. '~Come on, Ash. It's the only way. Stop being stubborn about it. You're only risking me, after all, and you can't care too much about that.'

He sees the impulse for refusal in every line of Ash's face before the Mancer finally admits sense and nods.

'~Good,' says Holly, smugly gracious in victory. '~Back out here, dawn tomorrow.'

Ash pulls an eloquent face.

'~I will *also* have to leave a warm body before cockcrow, and I'm not complaining, you ungracious fuck,' Holly points out. Actually, he will have to alter his plans, he thinks, swap shifts about and find time to catch Izidore in private. 'We'll make sure it works first, and then we'll handle telling Albemarle together, because I *do* learn, see?'

He slings his arm about Ash's shoulders, feeling the tension there and ignoring it. He begins to walk the Mancer back across the sward. The wind off the ocean is cold on their backs, which is probably the only reason Ash doesn't pull away from the friendly contact.

Ash eventually ventures, ~Does Hazel really think he could be my problem?

It is likely the thought has crossed Hazel's mind, and not merely once. Holly one-handedly nods his fist. He feels Ash's shoulders hunch under his arm, and frees the Mancer so he can say, '~Never mind. Go fuck him silly, that'll reassure him.'

Ash waves him off again with some vehemence, but, after a time of walking in an increasing tense silence in which Holly interestedly waits to see what's coming, zhey stutter out, ~I don't— He doesn't—

'~He does all the work,' Holly finishes for zhem. '~That man *lives* to give others pleasure. It's what make him such a wonderful f—' Here a hereto unsuspected sense of self-preservation or tact or both disinters itself. He smoothly switches his hand shape and motion. '~friend. Such a wonderful *friend*. I certainly wasn't going to finish that sentence any other way.'

Ash shakes zheir head. Again, it is a long time before zhey bring zhemself to sign; they're almost back at the postern before zhey finally say, ~I want to do better for him. I want to… I want to give him everything.

Holly repeats the [all] sign with some amusement. '~Oh, sure, but *I'm* the intense one.'

He is very familiar with what Hazel likes, or, more accurately, what it takes to make Hazel be wholeheartedly selfish in accepting what someone is very willing to give him, even if, especially if, that happens to be *everything*. But he doesn't think Ash is quite looking for a detailed instructional homily, as willing as he'd be to deliver it with diagrams.

Still, he removes the colourful silk wrap from his braids and dangles it in front of Ash for a scant moment before wrapping it illustratively about one wrist and then, with a deft twist, the other.

He holds his bound hands up to Ash, whose expression of mingled discomfit and fascination very much indicates that zhey have taken the hint.

He quickly unbinds himself—it's nothing he likes done to himself—to add, '~He says you don't let him coddle you. Prove it.'

Divested of both an *extremely* thoughtful Ash and his sword and coat, Holly swans into Lord Valerian's office without knocking. He dismisses the secretary with a peremptory thrust of a forefinger at the door. The bespectacled little man scuttles away with his Mancy pen in one hand and an armful of signed papers in the other.

'You work for me, you coward,' Val calls after him, but he sounds more resigned than annoyed. He leans back in his chair and gives Holly one of his slow onceovers, which he must know by now has an inflaming effect in direct proportion to the coolness of the appraisal. 'Yes, captain?'

Holly stalks behind the desk and plants his knees on the edges of the chair seat to simultaneously straddle and loom over the lord. Val makes an annoyed noise, and then a considerably more flattering noise as Holly bends to kiss him.

Fingers at his throat, mouth at his mouth, Holly murmurs, 'Can't stay over tonight, early morning. Best take advantage of me now.'

Dryly, Val says, 'I'll get right on that.'

'Oh, you're about to get right on it, lover,' Holly says, squirming closer as Val's hands close on his hips.

He elicits the half-exasperated, half-amused snort he's grown to anticipate from his bureaucratic paramour, and is smiling as he reinstates the kiss, a little demanding now, if he could ever be said to be only a little demanding; that very much depends on one's calibration, he suspects.

He's still smiling as his fingers work Val's buttons. He intends to see to Lord Val, and then bend him over the desk and see to him properly. The lord took Holly exactly that way a few times, fulfilling what appeared to be a longstanding fantasy, became quiet and contemplative, more so than usual, and then sheepishly asked for it the other way around. Holly does not quite understand this minor fetish, but he enjoys the helpless moans whenever he obliges him.

He's kissing and biting his way down Val's bared and lightly furry chest, on his way to getting on his knees, when the lord tugs at his braids and asks, very mildly, 'Who is he?'

'Who's that?' Holly asks, distracted.

'Who are you fucking tonight?'

Holly says, 'You?' in decidedly mystified tones, since he literally has his hand tight about Val's cock, before, enlightened, adopting his coyest, most languid manner and purring, 'You, my lord.'

'Later tonight,' Val coolly clarifies, refusing to be baited.

'No one,' Holly says. 'I have an early appointment; I've swapped my morning watch with Shao's this evening and then I'm getting some proper sleep so when Albemarle's blighted Mancy alarm device wakes me before dawn, I'll be functional.'

'Sleep. You?' Val laughs. It's rather hollow. He's not looking at Holly. 'Why not tell me the truth?'

Holly lets go of his tight handful and slides back off the chair and onto his feet. He's blindsided. 'I always do, Vee.'

'Then tell me you're tired of me and you're fucking someone else.'

Holly, if he'd had space to appreciate it, might have been amused that Val is accusing him along the same lines that he himself accused Ash, with respect to Hazel, while trying to rile zhem into admitting the cause of zheir ongoing foul temper.

Good tactic, he congratulates himself. *It works.* 'I would tell you if I were fucking about.'

'You would, if it were someone you didn't care about.' Val adjusts his clothes and leans back, face set and remote. 'It's Hazlemere, then, is it?'

It's Holly's turn to produce a hollow laugh. 'Have you considered that Ash would surely stab me if I tried to get between those two? I have Mancer work at dawn tomorrow, our plans have to change because of it. That is all.'

'Ashlin,' Valerian says, enlightened, and yet still not in the correct direction.

It's an outrageous implication, worthy of true laughter if Holly could have managed it. 'Zhey would *stab* me, Val!'

The lord does not respond, starts, in fact, to turn back to one of the collections of papers still on his desk. Holly feels the dismissal to his core; it's chilling.

Quietly, to the turned shoulder, he says, 'I told you I was devoted to you. Did you never believe it?'

Valerian silently straightens the piles on his desk. Finally, he admits, 'I never believed it would last.'

Holly pauses. He considers his next words, and what he will and won't tolerate, from Val compared to another lover.There is no reason, he decides, no reason *whatsoever* he should swallow jealousy, baseless or otherwise, from Lord Vee when he won't swallow it from any other man.

'Then we're done,' he says, and strides for the door.

It sounds like Val stands up in enough haste to scatter some paper off the desk, but Holly doesn't look around to that feathery sound, nor to the sharp call of his name.

He's already halfway out the door before Val, sounding alarmed, says, 'What does "done" mean? Done for now? Or…'

'If you can't trust me, there's no point to this.' He meant it when he expressed this sentiment to Ash earlier. He means it again now, but the wound is much deeper, more than he would have expected, if he had seen this looming at all.

His voice is flat when he says, 'We're finished.'

'Holly—'

'You knew it wouldn't last, Vee. Nice to be right?'

He only barely refrains from slamming the door behind him, and that is only because his sister Evelyn mocked it out of his sulky adolescent self. He's still fairly sulky in his aggrieved stalk back down to the undercroft, because she never did quite cure him of that.

At dawn, Holly slides into Hazel's new quarters, its size doubled from the usual small chamber by demolishing the walls between cells in the Mancer hallway. Izidore accepted the same renovation for zheir own sake, but Albemarle refused it—zheir walls are occupied—though zhey did take an extra room for more walls for zheir delicate rare ferns.

He's not pleased at being awake this early, even if his dutifully planned sleep hadn't been interrupted with self-righteous fuming. He almost threw Albemarle's Mancy alarm device across the room before remembering he and Ash have to give zhem the bad news about weapons; he therefore controlled himself from breaking one of zheir precious Mancy projects.

Holly's inclined to hold this whole bleak day against Ash personally, except Hazel is looking deeply contented there in his bed and it's difficult to remain irate at anyone who can put that look on his face.

Hazel's eyes open and, without otherwise moving, he sets a hand to his sword, which he has responsibly left in arms' reach, propped by the bedhead. His wrist, Holly notes, still has a length of silk tied about it. When he's woken up enough to recognise the intruder as Holly, he releases the hilt and sleepily smiles, thus endearing both himself and Ash to Holly even further.

Holly intended to collect Ash and go, but when Hazel shuffles further into the centre of the mattress and pats the space beside him, Holly willingly crawls in for a cuddle, as has been their years-long habit. This making of room is impressive, because the bed, though not as narrow as Hazel's old one, is already full of large guard and sprawled Mancer.

Holly catches hold of the trailing silk about Hazel's wrist, wrapping it about his own hand a few times so their arms are linked. 'Good night?' he asks, stroking Hazel's palm with his free hand.

'Hmm,' Hazel says agreeably. 'Yours not so much?'

'I'm not here for that. Ash has business with his Mancer Guard captain.'

Hazel glances down at Ash, zheir head tucked against his shoulder. 'Do you have to? This is the most zhey've slept for a while, Holly.'

'Coddling.'

'I miss this,' Hazel says, catching Holly's fingers. 'You can still come here like this, you know, when you need it.'

'Why does no one understand that Ash would *shank* me if I tried?' Holly says to the ceiling.

It's not as cheerful as he meant it to be. He turns his head abruptly into Hazel's shoulder, a mirror of the sleeping Mancer taking up most of the bed.

'Did you have a fight with Lord Vee?' Hazel asks, freeing his arm so he can slide it comfortingly around Holly's shoulders.

'Oh, that's all done with.'

'Is it?' He sounds surprised.

'You know me,' Holly says, wistfully.

'I do, love,' He nudges at Holly, shoulder to shoulder. '*Is* it done with, or did you perhaps have a minor disagreement and just need to wait till he remembers you're the best thing that's ever happened to him and comes grovelling?'

'I'm the third best thing, Hazel darling, he had a wife and still has a son. I'm just his midlife crisis.'

Hazel gives him a kiss on his forehead. 'I stand by it.'

There is really not much that can cheer up Holly more than blatant ego-stroking. It does work; more, it's getting late and the other Mancers will be up soon and notice Ash's absence at the breakfast table, if only to be relieved by it.

Holly darts a hand across Hazel's broad chest to poke Ash, who startles awake and then glowers at him where he's tucked just as securely on his side of Hazel as Ash is on zheirs.

Holly signs, ~Don't stab me.

~Get the fuck out of my bed, then.

~It's Hazel's bed, and he invited me.

Hazel interposes a firm, flat [stop] between them.

This, astonishingly, elicits an immediate and genuine-appearing apology from Ash. Holly, on the other hand, says, 'Zhey started it.'

'Holly, I will *let* zhem stab you, you fuckster.'

Holly rolls out of the bed, smiling. '~Get a move on, Mancer, I wasn't subject to the awful tune that Mancy alarm plays just to cuddle with your lover, as pleasant as we both find it.'

It takes some time before Ash, dressed in zheir long vest and an extra coat, joins Holly. Zhey're looking a little rumpled, and more than a little mollified: Hazel applied some of his own special brand of soothing in the interval, then.

Holly stops by the kitchen, and he and Ash share warm flat bread spread with sesame paste as they walk up into the dining hall and out the side door to the gardens, and then around to the postern.

Holly leads zhem most of the way to the cliff edge; he doesn't think the gate guards will try to spy, but the distance doesn't hurt, and if one of the Mancy creations turns into a particularly vicious weapon, having the option to sling it over the cliff also doesn't hurt.

The mist is clearing, the breeze is light, and the sun is rising on a glorious day. It isn't terrible.

From his coat pockets, he pulls the three Mancy projects Izidore handed over. '~Izidore seemed to think these are innocuous enough to not immediately endanger both of our lives.'

Holly expected Izidore, taken into confidence, to roll zheir eyes at Ash's dramatics and give over some projects that would fizzle into ineffective weapons upon application of Ash's Mancy. Instead, Izidore frowned and asked if he was sure he wanted to be the sole Mancer guard dealing with them.

Therefore, it finally occurs to him to ask, '~What should I expect here?'

Ash shakes zheir head, a tiny smile touching zheir face. ~Some people cannot be told. I warned you—

'~I'll handle it,' Holly says, tapping his sword. '~Just— what to expect?'

~Anything, Ash signs. ~It might lie there waiting to be triggered like the copperlits. That's good. But the copperlits are Albemarle's, and these are Izidore's. So it might leap from my hand for your throat with teeth bared. It might explode. One time, it produced a poison mist that choked me and my Mancer guards half to death, and the only reason that wasn't the weapon my mother wanted was because there was no way to set it off at our convenience instead of its own.

'~You are so much fun. Do it.'

Ash raises the first device, a large copper ball covered in overlapping plating and antennae. As with many Mancy projects, Holly has no idea what it is intended to be or do. Ash hums to it; Holly has a good ear and fancies he can hear the moment the tune twists from Izidore's to Ash's.

The thing cracks and expands rapidly, the plating ratcheting open. He's curious enough to wait to see what it's going to do, but Ash squeaks and smacks him across the arm, so he draws his sword and skewers it while it's in the middle of its transformation. It gives a shriek of agonised metal and goes dead.

Or dormant.

Holly goes to flick it off his blade and over the cliff, and Ash catches his wrist. ~We can use the parts. And…

'~And you and Izidore can see what it was going to do? Might help you control it better?'

Ash nods. ~One day, I would like to not have this talent, Holly.

Holly matches the Mancer's rueful smile and holds out the second project. It's a cube but with more sides, which shape Holly thinks has a name but he doesn't know it. As soon as Ash finishes singing to it, it bursts into white flame, bright enough that Holly sees it when he blinks and hot enough that the skin on his face tightens.

Ash waves him back. ~Let it burn out.

'~You know this sort?'

~The Mancy overwhelmed it before it could transform completely. It's the best result.

'~There must be some of Izidore's projects where you know exactly what you're going to get by now? Makes it safer.'

Ash makes a seesawing gesture with one nimble hand. Hazel loves those hands, thin-fingered and scarred. ~Izidore is a young Mancer.

'~I don't know what that means.'

~Good design. But not great design. Not like Albemarle. It would be much safer to use Albemarle's projects, if zhey could stomach it. Zhey are predictable and consistent.

This is fair. Albemarle likes zheir entire life to be predictable and consistent. That's most of the reason zhey find the other Mancers and the new Mancer guards annoying.

~Izidore is still learning that. Mancers spend their whole lives learning.

'~*People* spend their whole lives learning, love.'

The flames have died down now. Holly, given that he has just informed Ash that people can learn, checks with the Mancer before stamping out the last phosphoric flickers. He hands over the last Mancy project. Ash looks at it doubtfully, and when zhey hum into it, it crumbles.

~Broken.

Ash's straight brows set into zheir strongest frown and zhey glance about before crouching by the ball zhey transformed first. Zhey poke at its innards, holding zhemself tense, as if ready to leap away from it.

'~But the Mancy went somewhere?' Holly guesses, but Ash is too intent to catch the signing.

From behind zhem, over the cliff edge, he hears a scraping, soft under the whistle of the wind, and turns. He watches as the lost talos crawls up onto the headland.

The giant beetle-like Mancy creature seems larger than Holly remembers, and faster, and its legs are now more razor-sharp and flaily than legs strictly need to be.

'Yep, the Mancy went somewhere,' he says. He signs at Ash, the same name-sign over and over again as he engages in a cheery verbal escalation. 'Ash. Ashlin. Ashlin Mancer. The valorous Ashlin Mancer formerly of Stronghold Cristati.'

~What, what, what! Ash finally snaps at him.

He points. Ash turns. Zhey looks back at Holly, eyes widening in slow horror, and puts zheir head in zheir hands. Holly tugs zheir hands down, smiling.

'~I adore you,' he tells zhem. '~You make Hazel darling ridiculously happy and you give me such beautiful presents.'

~Stab it behind the—

'~No cheating!' Holly says joyously, twirling his sword and darting for the talos.

But Ash yanks on his coat. ~Albemarle and Izidore will not thank you for dismembering it. And Hazel will not thank me for letting you get dismembered.

'~Are you somehow under the mistaken impression I'm not as good as I say I am?'

Ash grimaces. ~Stab behind the right foreleg to slow it down, and the back of the neck will disable it.

Holly makes a rudely dismissive noise, the mouth movement of which he trusts Ash will interpret correctly, and bounces off into the fight.

He's back perhaps six minutes later. There's a slash in one arm of his coat, which did not make it through to his skin, and he's panting a little, but the talos has withdrawn its legs close to its body like a dead spider and fallen still. Holly dodged the stabbing front legs and rolled under the slicing rear legs and climbed along the round back to reach the neck, where stabbing didn't work, but slicing did.

Ash, after a moment of narrow-eyed poise, says, ~*Fine*. I did not believe you're as good as you say you are.

'~And now you do. This time next week? Better yet, an hour or two later.'

~I don't think we have to do it weekly. And I think we should tell Albemarle today.

'~Weekly,' Holly says, cheerfully ignoring the Mancer. 'And *I* think we should incorporate it into the Triple Mancer Guard spar.'

They leave the talos sitting dormant for the other Mancers to examine—Ash is going to tell Albemarle, and they'll manage that, because Albemarle is not nearly as poor at coping with change as everyone had assumed—and make their way back to the stronghold.

Near the postern, Ash signs, ~Thank you, Captain Holyoake.

'~Pleasure's all mine, Ashlin Mancer.'

The Mancer pulls Holly to a stop, making him face zhem. Face set in tight lines, zhey sign all in a flurry. ~You won't send me away?

Holly silently makes the negatory fist with both hands, then sets the fists to his heart, trying to make the promise as clear as he can.

~You don't hate me.

Holly raises an eyebrow. '~Do you care? Nightingale thinks your bricolage is borderline evil and that doesn't bother you at all.'

~You're Hazel's best friend. I care how you feel about me. Not…about what I do. About who I am.

'~I *adore* you,' Holly repeats, smiling at zhem. '~As you are.'

The Mancer, after a long moment, nods.

Holly snorts, since Ash is conspicuously not returning the sentiment. Nevertheless, he asks, '~If I hug you, will you stab me?'

Ash nods again, but zhey're wearing zheir tiny mischievous smile for the first time in some time and Holly is laughing as he hugs zhem anyway, feeling zheir tense stiffness soften against him.

The postern gate opens and Lord Valerian steps through, blinking in the bright blaze of early light beyond the stronghold walls.

Holly looks at him over Ash's head. The lord looks tired, cheeks flushed with the cold. Holly tightens his hold on Ash and plants a kiss on top of zheir grey-haired head for good measure.

Ash squirms loose. ~Coddling, zhey pronounce scathingly.

Holly makes a rude gesture to prefix his actual signs. '~This isn't the last altercation we'll have, love, and not even the worst altercation we'll have, and getting rid of you will never be my answer. I can handle you if you can handle me. Yes?'

Ash nods yet again, shoots Val one of zheir opaque looks, and vanishes into the stronghold.

Holly is meant to accompany zhem into the care of another Mancer guard. He pauses, though. He prides himself on staying on good terms with past lovers. There's no reason why he can't do so with this one, despite the irritated ant-crawling feeling the thought provokes.

He therefore signals for the guards to close the gate for now and raises his brows at Val in the ensuing seclusion.

Valerian's taking a moment to tug his coat tighter around him. 'I want to apologise,' he says eventually, still looking down.

'I can tell, from how enthusiastic you sound about doing so,' Holly says. 'Just spit it out, my lord, and we can all move on.'

Valerian has the unmitigated gall to roll his eyes but he sounds sincere as he goes on. 'I didn't mean to make you feel like I don't trust you,' he says. 'I do. I expect you to take other lovers, and I accept that. And I trust you will tell me when you plan to.'

Holly sets his hands on his hips impatiently. He is not sure what he wants to hear here. Well. He *wants* to hear a good deal more abject pleading. He's not sure what he *needs* to hear. Still, he doesn't argue the present tense, merely waits.

Val swallows. He sounds very stiff when he forces himself on. 'Yesterday was not truly about not believing you. It was about…' He gestures at himself. The frosty façade breaks as he shakily confesses, 'It was about not believing there's anything here to interest you, beyond the conquest.'

Holly is never immune to flattery, even of this sad paucity, and he melts whenever Val lets himself be so vulnerable for him. He steps closer, smiling. 'Conquest.'

Valerian's not a trained member of the purple for nothing. He straightens, pulling himself together. 'I think we both we know where we each stand, in that regard,' he says in his driest tones, watching Holly stalk him with studiedly cool appraisal.

'Tell me,' Holly says, hooking a thumb about Val's topmost coat button to draw them chest to chest. 'Lay it on thick, Vee. Make it outrageous.'

'Complete and total conquest,' Val says without hesitation, and Holly does so adore the helpless note he can't keep from creeping in. 'Of my body, of my mind, of my heart. Every waking thought, every impulse, every fibre of my being is yours—'

'Oh, that's good, keep going, lover,' Holly moans mockingly, but he's shoving Val against the wall of the stronghold as he says it and the poor deluded man can't add anything more for the kissing.

When Holly finally lets Val go, he's fairly sure he could make him do just about anything right here against the solid stronghold curtain wall under the wide blue sky. But he's also feeling kindly enough to let Val lead him back inside to somewhere more appropriately private.

He says, as they walk hand in hand along the upper hallway to Val's apartment, 'You do understand, don't you, Vee, that this so-called conquest was not a one-sided victory? Casualties were, ah, incurred on *both* sides.'

Val's smile is gratified, but he gives a shake of his head.

Holly turns to face him, making him stop. He ducks his head a little, so he can look the shorter man in the eye. 'The conquest, my love, is *mutual.*'

And it's a bloody good thing they're only steps from Val's bed, that's all.

~By the Author~

Thanks for reading. If you enjoyed this book, check out more titles and bonus material at wendypalmer.au.

The Domain trilogy
Wild Imperative
Cursed Girls
Lost Child

Mosaic Virus duology
Bastard's Grace
Six Feet of Ridiculous
Mosaic Garden: Stories from Aspermonde

Artisans
The Uses of Illicit Art
The Use of Myriad Arts

Standalones
Fair Haven
Domesticated Magic

6 3 7 1 1 5 0 1 *